VICIOUS INTENTIONS

PIPER STONE

Copyright © 2023 by Stormy Night Publications and Piper Stone

All rights reserved. No part of this book may be reproduced or transmitted in any form or by any means, electronic or mechanical, including photocopying, recording, or by any information storage and retrieval system, without permission in writing from the publisher.

Published by Stormy Night Publications and Design, LLC.
www.StormyNightPublications.com

Stone, Piper
Vicious Intentions

Cover Design by Korey Mae Johnson

This book is intended for *adults only*. Spanking and other sexual activities represented in this book are fantasies only, intended for adults.

PROLOGUE

It is said the Damned eat their prey, feasting on bodies and souls, taking what they believe belongs to them.

No limits.

No hesitation.

They have no moral code, no deference to humanity—only primal need.

And they are never satisfied.

Déjà vu: a feeling that one has seen or heard something before.

* * *

Cain

Storms.

The power and malevolence had always intrigued me. As if God was asserting his wrath on the Earth, prepared to destroy humanity. In my mind, humans deserved to die. So many were weak and devoid of understanding that at any moment their life could be destroyed. I wanted to be the hand of God, crushing those who dared oppose me.

My father had applauded the darkness festering inside, slapping me on the back more than once as pride filled his face. My mother had been different, determined to expunge the demons before they eradicated my soul. I wasn't certain why she cared. After all, I was the second born son of the Devil himself, the most powerful and feared mafia lord in the Midwest.

Darkness prevailed in our blood, the need for violence instilled at a young age. Yet, my mother remained faithful that her two sons wouldn't follow in our father's footsteps. Perhaps what she didn't know wouldn't hurt her.

A smile crossed my face as another bolt of lightning flashed bright neon across the sky, the tendrils of electric energy pulsing through me like rocket fuel. Soon I would be old enough to garner additional responsibilities. Not long after that, I'd rule over a unit of men capable of destruction. I'd become invincible, just like my older brother. Dayton would be handed the regime one day, but I'd be the man who carried out savage retaliation when needed. The thought was delicious.

My father was a brutal man and not only to those who defied him. He accepted nothing less than perfection from his sons, rarely acknowledging our existence unless we did something wrong. While I respected him as required, I'd also grown to hate him. The stench of his cigars. His patronizing attitude. His weakness for whores. I would be stronger, more resilient.

I would be a king.

As I stared at the glowing sky, I ignored the continuous pain. Allowing the bruises and marks to bother me was weak. I wasn't weak. I felt a presence and stiffened, only to remind myself that I was in my brother's house. I was safe. As safe as I could be with the demons plaguing me every night.

"Go to sleep," Dayton said softly. "You need rest."

I turned my head towards the bedroom door, scowling at the admonishment. My brother might be eight years older, but tonight was the first night he'd acted like I was required to play by his rules. Maybe that was because I was in his house, our parents refusing to leave me by myself while they traveled through Italy.

"Whatever," I told him, turning over in bed. I rarely slept. There was no need. I'd learned a long time ago what happened when I fell asleep. That's when the real monsters came out to play.

I could tell by the reflection of the storm in the window that he'd remained where he was,

"It's different here, Cain. You don't have to worry about Pops hurting you. As a matter of fact, he's never going to hurt you or Mama again. I promise you. I figured it out. This is your home now."

His words brought unwanted emotion.

And ugly memories.

"Don't you dare shed a tear, you worthless piece of human flesh. You are a Cross. You will act like a man."

"But, Papa."

Wham! "Don't you backtalk me."

How many times had my father used the same words after beating me for some infraction? At least his brutality had taught me resilience. Home. My stomach churned at the thought. "What does that mean?"

He walked closer, easing the blanket up to my shoulder. "Don't ask questions you don't want to learn the answers to."

Fine. Whatever.

When I said nothing, Dayton laughed cynically. "I do love you, brother."

"Love is for idiots who don't know the fury of life."

"Wow. What the hell did that man do to you? Families are about love. At least they're supposed to be."

"Go away, Dayton." Fury rushed through me when I heard my voice crack. I was twelve years old for God's sake. I was no longer a child.

He sighed but a few seconds later closed the door with a soft click.

I squeezed my eyes shut, balling my fists. Then I rolled over onto my pillow so he wouldn't hear me. No one could ever hear me. I couldn't cry. It was against the rules.

Damn it. No. No...

After a few seconds, I started to dry heave.

I pulled my knees close to my chest, trying to control my breathing.

Get control. Breathe. You are stronger than this.

Pain tore through me, but tonight it wasn't about the physical torture I was used to. The rush of adrenaline, the agony that filled my mind was about the life I wanted and would never have.

Finally, a few seconds later, I felt stronger. Maybe one day I'd find a way to escape. At least I had Dayton in my life. He did care about me.

Thump!

A single sound grabbed my attention. I twisted on the bed, listening carefully. It had to be a branch against the side of Dayton's house. After taking several deep breaths, I eased my head back to the pillow.

Then I heard it again.

Fear swept through me and I leapt off the bed, searching the nightstand for a weapon. Then I remembered Dayton had refused to allow me to have a gun in his house. I moved towards the door, opening it a crack and listening.

The muffled cry was filled with anguish. I rushed down the hallway towards Dayton's room, flinging open the door. As a single bolt of lightning lit up the room, I stared in horror, unable to process what I was seeing.

A man stood over my brother, a hatchet in his hand. A man stood over my brother, a hatchet in his hand. I saw the spark leave my brother's bloodied face as I lunged forward.

"No!"

The bastard issued a single backhand, knocking me across the room and against the hall. Dazed and confused, I struggled to get to my feet. The assassin turned and within seconds, he disappeared out the window.

"Dayton. Dayton!" I tumbled forward, dropping to the floor by the bed. Even in the darkness, I could see pools of blood, my brother's broken body lying in pieces.

While the asshole who'd taken my brother's life had been shrouded in darkness, I'd caught a glimpse of a single scar on the top of one hand, something I would never forget.

I rose to my feet, glaring out the window as almost every emotion was swept away with my brother's soul.

In its wake, a true monster had been born, a creature hellbent on revenge.

I would hunt down the person responsible. Then I would exact the kind of torture no man could tolerate.

And I would enjoy every brutal, bloody moment.

CHAPTER 1

Several years later
Cain

The taste of blood remained in my mouth. It had for years, the coppery stench lingering in my nostrils. I reminded myself often of the reason why.

My brother's blood had permanently stained my skin.

Why was I finding it more difficult to maintain a sharp focus, my need for revenge? Because of a woman, an innocent bird that I couldn't wait to trap, then keep inside a gilded cage.

Perhaps for a lifetime.

Obsession.

My father had said that anything that became necessary in someone's life was an obsession and should be condemned.

I'd laughed at his statement more than once, but as I stood watching the beautiful woman crossing the campus grounds, I realized my behavior, my need to possess her, had become my greatest weakness.

Sage Winters had no idea she had not one, but three monsters stalking her.

I'd wanted nothing more than to destroy her, exacting revenge for a heinous act from years before. She was easy prey, vulnerable, and unsuspecting. The fact that her father had allowed her out of her protected cage meant he'd grown arrogant. I'd planned for months on using his overconfidence that no one knew about his true identity against him.

A vision of the worst night of my life flashed through my mind. Sage would pay dearly for my brother's murder.

My father hadn't needed to order me to go hunting. I'd done so myself, beginning at the age of thirteen. But it had taken me seven additional years to track my prey, two more to perfect my vicious plan. The life I'd been born into was violent, death just a part of the scenario.

I was very good at exacting punishment, my methods more creative than any other member of my family. I would enjoy taking what was most precious to my brother's killer. My blood pumped wildly through my veins just thinking about the sweet release of retaliation.

The man known as the Iceman was an assassin, a hired gun for anyone who could afford his expertise. Little was known about the man who'd enshrouded himself in shadows, living another life as an upstanding citizen while using the darkness to hide his savage acts. However, I'd been provided with a gift years before, a single glimpse of a scar on his right hand, a burn from a mission that had almost taken his life.

In my years of planning revenge for the murder of my brother, I'd learned many things from my vicious father, including patience. I'd also been taught the best methods of seeking retaliation against our enemies were often the sweetest.

And the ones that would drive a stake through a man's heart.

His daughter would become the vessel for my vindication.

However, my original plans had changed since watching her, stalking her over the past months. Now I wanted everything, craving not only her blood but her body as well.

Little did Sage Winters know that soon she would belong to three powerful, ruthless, and unforgiving men.

After her father watched her final surrender, only then would I allow him the release of sweet death.

"She is spectacular," Hunter Augustine said from beside me. "I can't wait for my first taste." He was one of my two best friends, a man almost as evil and callous as I'd become. He could hide behind his wide grin and twinkling eyes, fooling everyone that he was a good guy, yet I knew his darkest secrets, his penchant for sadism. That was why we got along so well.

"One of many, I assure you." Grinning, I threw him a look before heading toward the dorm she shared with a girl already in the clutches of the Elite. Our group was generations old, children of some of the most powerful men and women in the country, many of whom worked on the wrong side of the law. Our power was unequaled, our true wealth undocumented. And it was widely known that graduates of the exclusive college would one day rule the world.

As if we weren't already doing so.

"Does her father have any idea she's being hunted?" Cristiano asked as flanked my side, his once heavy Latin accent all but erased from his deep immersion in the American lifestyle. As the eldest son of the Moreno Cartel out of South America, his future was laid out almost exactly as mine was. Soon, we would both lead powerful crime syndicates, taking over from our fathers. He was almost as brutal as I'd become, which was why I considered him one of the posse.

The three of us were tight. We'd performed various required acts of violence over our years of servitude to the system, including eliminating enemies determined to bring down our families.

Loyalty was the first rule. Secrecy the second. Obedience the third.

Anyone who broke even a single rule was banished.

Or worse.

All three of us had gone through an initiation period that only the strongest, most resilient people could survive. Now we ruled the estate where the members lived, our dominance more powerful than that of our ancestors. Even the administration had no control over us. However, the capture and control of sweet Sage would be our finest hour.

"If he doesn't, he's a fool. I've heard *The Iceman* is in the process of retiring." My answer was succinct. Maybe the fucker believed he could retire to Florida, spend his days basking in the sun.

"Where do you get your information?" Hunter inquired, his eagerness to enjoy the fruits of our labor well noted.

"You know I have my sources." I'd spent years tracking The Iceman's activities, learning everything I could about his actions, finally discovering his real identity that he'd gone to great lengths to hide. Xavier Winters had certainly aged significantly over the past few years, the birth of his only child a surprise to both him and his ageing wife. Most who knew him saw nothing but the pleasurable, kind man who owned a two-decade old Italian restaurant in Chicago as well as a food distribution firm servicing fifteen states. While many were aware of his extreme wealth, the fact that he didn't flaunt it by driving expensive vehicles or supplying his wife with jewels and furs had kept him mostly off the radar.

That was how he'd managed to stay alive, able to protect his wife and only child. If it hadn't been for the second slipup in his illustrious, decades-old career, I'd never have connected all the dots.

Killing him wasn't enough.

I wanted more. Much more.

"Yes, you do. It's time we moved forward with our plan." Cristiano was the quiet one, always observing. He was dangerous, more so than people gave him credit for.

"Patience, my dear friend. We're almost there."

"The party has been announced, our useful minions directed to attend, a few select guests invited to keep it interesting and full of activity." Hunter moved ahead of me, opening the massive door to the dorm.

The party was little more than a lure, allowing our first official meeting with Sage. The people he called our minions were some of the school's most beautiful female students, all vying to be chosen after graduation. Many hoped they would become a bride. Little did they know at best they'd become our whores.

The realization that there was only one woman for me had occurred the very first time I'd laid eyes on her. Sage likely didn't remember that she'd bumped into me on her first day at the school, giggling from nervousness and excitement. I'd spent two hours jerking off to the most intense fantasies about what I would do to her. Similar images flashed in front of my mind just walking into her dorm.

The beauty crawling towards me on her hands and knees. Around her neck she'd have a wide diamond-encrusted collar, her red lips open in anticipation of sucking my cock.

I'd also created vivid images in my mind of the beautiful strap marks that would cover her porcelain skin after I'd disciplined her for even the barest hint of an infraction.

But there was nothing like the torrid visions of fucking her from behind as she swung from a steel bar, her wrists wrapped in chains.

I was nothing less than a twisted fuck.

"Excellent," I managed, although in truth I could care less about the party. If it were up to me, we'd wait for her to return from class and take her. Both Hunter and Cristiano were more interested in tempting then tasting her. We'd stalked Sage for months, placing cameras inside her dorm room. I'd also watched her sleep, study, and shower, basking in the vision of her naked body, waiting for the day when I'd taste every inch of her.

The games were set to begin.

We entered the building, heading towards the stairs to the third floor. While there were students coming and going, no one dared question us or our intentions. They knew what would happen if they did.

The lock was easy to maneuver, and as soon as we stepped inside the suite, I took a deep breath. Her perfume lingered, the scent distinctly different than the girl she shared the three rooms with. I'd memorized every detail of Sage's room, touching everything. I pushed open her partially open bedroom door, entering her hallowed space. Everything about the room she'd occupied for almost two years was special. The bold color of violet on the walls, the thick comforter, and two sets of pillows. Even the art she'd selected, which was more erotic in nature than I would have imagined, told a story about her personality.

She was a born submissive.

I adored the fact that she was hiding her true nature under baggy clothes and thick glasses. However, I knew she was a little lioness in disguise. I also knew the secret she kept from everyone, including her parents. Such a naughty girl. Taming her would be delicious.

Hunter moved toward her bed, running his fingers across her pillow. Then he pulled it into his hands and against his face, inhaling deeply. The man was likely the sickest fuck of all of us, enjoying kinks that I had no interest in.

I moved towards her dresser while Cristiano remained in the outer room. As soon as I opened the top drawer, a smile crossed my face. For as prim and proper as Sage appeared on the outside, her true personality could be found underneath the holey jeans, sweatshirts, and ratty tennis shoes. The lingerie she wore was provocative. Unable to resist, I tugged a crimson thong into my fingers, rubbing the tips across the thin lace.

I'd taken photographs of her standing in front of the mirror in the bathroom wearing only a bra and panties. They always matched, and her choices had always made my mouth water. Soon, I'd rip my teeth through the material, tasting her for the first time.

And a couple of nights before, I'd stood over her while she'd been sleeping. I'd almost taken her then. I'd brought with me a gag and zip-ties, prepared to take her as my captive. Then she'd stirred, waking out of a deep sleep. I'd remained in the shadows as she'd sat up in bed, certain she'd seen me. But if she had, she would have reported me to the dorm resident.

Or maybe she hungered for my touch more than I knew.

Only after that had Hunter been able to convince me that having a party was the best move.

I shifted my hand across my aching cock, forced to adjust it given the hard crush of the zipper. The woman had no idea how close she'd come to becoming my prisoner.

I held her panties to my nose again, drinking in her essence. She was everything I wanted.

After pocketing the delicious piece, I left my calling card on her nightstand. A single blood-red rose petal. It was the second one I'd left in my many visits. I wanted her to discover she'd become my prey. But if she'd realized it up to this point, she hadn't expressed any alarm.

Or perhaps she enjoyed being the subject of dark, demented fantasies.

My heart continued to pound with adrenaline as it did every time I was anywhere near her. The anticipation was well worth the wait. After taking a deep breath, I let it out through my nose, another wave of anger rushing through my system. I'd waited ten long years. Everything had to be perfect. At this point, I'd allow my fury to fuel my desires and nothing more.

"Remove the equipment?" Hunter asked.

"Yeah. I don't want any complications."

"Understood."

As both Hunter and Cristiano snagged the cameras and audio recording equipment, I sat down on her bed. The main reason I enjoyed my visits so much wasn't about sniffing her clothes but about reading her journal.

Not only was she a talented author, but the fact she that penned her personal fantasies on paper ignited the beast inside, the creature becoming insatiable.

I pulled it from the drawer, tugging on the satin bookmark indicating where she'd left off. This time, her red pen was inside as if the book had been put away in a hurry. Almost as soon as I started reading, my cock pressed against my zipper painfully.

I felt the rush of wind as soon as he opened my window. I'd longed to see him again, hoping tonight would be the night. I didn't know his name, nor did I care to learn. This was our game, our playtime. It was filthy and dangerous, but that only added to the intense excitement. I needed to feel something, anything to mask the agony tearing through me every day.

I remained under the covers, turned on my side, the anticipation of his rough touch everything I longed for. As I'd done before, I pretended I was asleep, keeping my breathing even as I felt the weight on the bed change. My face was turned away, but I heard him searching through the duffle bag he always brought to our late-night adventures. Seconds later, he brushed his hand down my arm before dragging them behind me, quickly snapping the hard steel around both my wrists.

Moaning in appreciation, I took several sharp breaths, the excitement surging through me like white lightning.

"Good girl," he said in a gruff tone, the two words sending a thrill down my spine. He lowered his head, moving hair away from my face and neck before blowing his heated breath against my cheek. Every cell in my body tingled, and I struggled in my bindings just like he'd commanded me to do.

He continued his exploration, sliding the palm of his hand down my back, using his fingers to crawl the sheer nightie over my bottom.

"Did you shave for me, my good girl?"

"Yes, sir." His deep voice sent a rumble through me, and my stomach knotted from a hint of anxiety. I never knew what he would do. His needs became darker with every unexpected visit. Yet I craved his acts of savagery, the longing extending for hours after he'd left. The yearning to feel the marks he left crisscrossing my body was only increasing. I was wet with desire, my pussy throbbing, ready to beg him to whip me.

Then I'd beg him to fuck me.

He seemed to sense my hunger and grabbed the back of the nightgown. With a quick snap of his hand, he ripped it from my body. Then he jerked me up by my hair and onto my knees, wrapping one arm around my breasts as he nuzzled his head against my neck.

"Have you thought about me?" he growled as he twisted my nipple.

The pain was intense, but I knew better than to scream. Whispering my answers was a requirement, or the punishment would be much worse.

"Yes, sir."

He tweaked my other hardened bud before sliding the palm of his hand down my stomach, digging his fingers into my slicked folds. He toyed with my clit, flicking his thumb back and forth across the piercing he'd commanded me to get. Then he'd reminded me that he'd be the only man to suck it between his teeth.

I was so wet I could tell I'd soaked his fingers, my soft moans indicating the utter pleasure rolling through me. He continued rubbing, pushing me to a moment of climax.

"Ride my hand, little pet."

I bucked hard against him, fighting to feel more friction. He twisted his hand, thrusting his fingers into my tight channel. God, I wanted more. "Harder. Please."

He issued several hard cracks of his hand against my bottom, the pain instantly exhilarating. I was pushed into a beautiful moment of bliss, my tiny mews keeping him fully aroused. He smacked my buttock again, the sharp jar exactly what I needed. After several more, I was wetter than before, my mind a raging blur of need and want.

When he smacked my pussy with several fingers, then did it again, and again, I lurched forward. The agony was deliciously sweet, crackling electricity soaring through me.

"My good girl likes it brutal. Yes..." As he nipped my earlobe, he gave me what I needed, driving the heel of his hand into my mound. I gyrated my hips, dragging my tongue across my lips as I continued struggling, riding his hand like a bucking bronco.

"Oh, God. Oh..." As an orgasm tore through me, I bit down on my lower lip to keep from violating his rules.

"Yes, I am a god." His chuckle was dark, laced with hints of evil. I knew exactly what he was capable of, the brutality he thrived on.

And I wanted to feel it. All of it. I wanted to be his slave, to serve his every need.

He barely allowed me to finish before bending me over, pressing my face against the covers. Then he used his knee to drive my legs apart.

"Do you know how much I hunger to fuck your tight pussy, little pet?"

"Uh-huh." There was no doubt that I was the only woman who could provide what he craved.

Complete surrender.

I was frantic with need, wiggling my bound hands, taking gasping breaths as he freed his glorious cock. It was long and thick, and there was nothing like being fucked by him.

"My needy little pet. Aren't you? You're all mine, you little slut. Never forget that." He thrust the entire length of his cock inside, and I struggled to fill my lungs with air, doing everything I could to remain obedient. He wasn't gentle, plunging hard and fast.

"Yes... Sir... Uh. Uh. Uh. Uh."

My delicious stranger tangled his fingers in my hair, digging into my scalp as he pushed my face into the comforter. He fucked me long and brutally, stripping me of the last of my inhibitions. There was nothing I wouldn't do for him. Nothing.

When he pulled out, I gasped again, my whimpers that of a wanton girl in need. He raked his fingers down my spine before pressing the tip of his cock against my dark hole.

Then he thrust it all the way inside.

Fuck. My cock ached like a son of a bitch. Her stories were getting darker, more sadistic. It was apparent our perfect little pet liked it as rough as possible.

As I eased the journal into the drawer and stood, I was forced to adjust my shaft to relieve some pressure. Sage would be rewarded with exactly what she wanted. She would serve the three of us. She'd be well used.

Punished.

Tasted.

Fucked.

Branded.

The kinky girl would be forced to accept that her father had fucked with the wrong family.

Then she'd realize she belonged to the worst of the Damned.

The kind of monster nightmares were made of.

CHAPTER 2

Cain

"Bring the consort to me," I said in passing, refusing to move from my perch in front of the window, staring out at the manicured lawn.

The mansion where I resided along with the other members of the Elite was a perk of being in the top echelon of the school. It had taken blood, sweat, and violence to get me where I was today, a position I'd coveted. The sprawling campus was referred to as the City of Hope, coined by some ancient bastards who'd developed the facility in hopes the children of powerful, influential, and extremely wealthy families would become the future leaders of a society that continued to thrive on disparaging classes of people.

The school administrators turned a blind eye to the activities that had forged a union over three decades before.

Only the strongest survived.

And I was one of the strongest of them all, controlling almost every aspect of what occurred within the hallowed walls of the campus. I'd graduated top of my class as required by my father, obtaining a master's in business administration before being allowed to take the helm of my father's empire. I was eager to get on with my life, the four years spent inside the compound more like a prison, albeit one with significant perks.

My balls were still aching from the excellent read I'd had earlier in the day. I'd already masturbated once. As of the end of the night, I'd no longer force myself to abstain. Sage would be in our possession for the rest of her life.

"Are you certain you want to do this?" Hunter asked, a sly smirk on his face.

I turned, studying his expression. "Kelly is a part of our flock. We own every inch of her. She'll do anything required to become one of the chosen."

Chosen.

The term was informal, a name the girls had picked themselves, most of them giddy about the opportunity. They understood what was at stake. Wealth beyond their wildest dreams. They would become instant socialites, commanding whatever city they went to live in with their husband.

It was little more than a fancy way of calling them arranged marriages, just like my ancestors had entered into generations before. My mother didn't love my father and he had a number of whores. However, they had a mutual respect, and once married, the union could never end in divorce.

Only death.

Even my father had reminded me to choose wisely given the amount of power the woman had in the marriage.

However, if entering into a life of servitude was a goal, then the few women who were selected to serve our needs into the future had achieved success. They served a purpose, providing use of their bodies whenever commanded, offering other services as demanded. They did so willingly, all in hopes of marrying an Elite, living a life of luxury while producing heirs. Kelly was no exception, although I'd yet to fuck her. I wasn't interested in fulfilling carnal needs. I'd only had one thing on my mind.

Revenge.

But that had been until coming face-to-face with Sage.

"Are you suggesting Kelly's number will be selected tonight?" Cristiano threw out. He rarely spoke, yet when he did, those around him shuddered in fear.

"I'm not suggesting anything. We shall see how the night progresses, and if she's a good little girl." There was only one woman I was interested in, a lovely budding flower who had no idea three wolves waited in the darkness, prepared to strip away more than just her fake attempt at innocence.

I couldn't wait to introduce her to the very acts she'd written about since arriving at the City of Hope.

Hunter shook his head. "You can't get enough of the woman."

"Why should I need to?"

"Even I'll admit, after reading that passage today, I was hot and bothered."

Cristiano laughed at the two of us. "It will be much better in real life. Imagine strapping her luscious body to the bed spread eagled."

"Or keeping her in a cage," Hunter growled.

When I heard two sets of footsteps, I took a deep breath. Tonight would be the crowning glory of a plan that had festered in my mind since the day the unsuspecting daughter of my greatest enemy had stepped foot on the pristine college grounds.

The selection of at least a few of the consorts to be listed as the Chosen was merely a formality, fulfilling our sacred duties as outlined in the Book of Law, as it had been labeled.

I'd laughed the first time I'd seen them. I had no interest in rules.

"You asked to see me, sire?" Kelly asked.

I turned around, nodding to the fellow soldier who'd brought her into the great room. We called those just below the true reign of power 'soldiers', given all thirty of us living in the estate had been given our marching orders from our fathers to begin our rule of the world. Science. Politics. Media. Banking. Real estate. There wasn't a single division of wealth that we wouldn't represent, then control one day.

We were a mighty force indeed, this graduating class in particular.

As required, she was kneeling, her head bowed out of respect. Anything else would result in extreme punishment, although I enjoyed when the few women who dared defy us graced our presence. I was a sadist after all.

At this point, I wasn't in the mood to play games. I moved towards her, placing my hand on her head. We had rules of our own, perceptions that the three of us found ridiculous, but appearances were meant to be kept. We were examples to the rest of the grunts, legends to live up to.

"Congratulations, sweet bird. You've been anointed to handle a very special task for us." I stroked her hair absently while my cohorts looked on in amusement. Like me, they loathed the bullshit pomp and circumstance. I slipped my finger under her chin, lifting her head. Her eyes were glassy as the anticipation built.

"What can I do for you, sire? I will do anything."

Of course, she would. I preferred a woman who didn't give themselves so easily.

"Good girl. You're going to ensure that we have a very special guest at the party this evening."

Kelly narrowed her eyes in confusion. "Who, sire?"

"The lovely Sage Winters."

Her brow furrowed but for a few seconds, her lower lip quivering as if she were worried what we would do to Sage. "But she's not a member of the Chosen."

Her insolence couldn't be ignored. I slapped her face then fisted her hair. She was another one who enjoyed aspects of pain. I'd learned that early on. "You will do as I say. You're not to question my orders. Are we clear?"

While there was hurt in her eyes, it quickly faded, her lust returning. "Yes, sire. I'll ensure she's here tonight."

"Good girl," I mused, gently caressing the sting away. "Very good girl. I know she's become your friend, but you knew what was expected of you when I allowed you to share a suite with her. Yes? You also know your loyalty lies with every member of the Elite."

"Yes, sire."

I arranged almost everything inside the school, the administrators merely puppets. It had been imperative that Sage's head not be filled with vicious stories surrounding the Elite.

"Excellent."

"Would you like anything else from me?" She dragged her tongue across her lips. She was still a junior but had shown significant promise. There was no requirement for her to remain until graduation.

"You're a very good girl; however, I have other business to attend to prior to the party." I stroked the side of her face as a reward. "With obedience comes rewards. Now, rise and attend to your task."

She did as required, although I could see disappointment in her eyes. Perhaps she thought she'd be granted the gift of sucking our cocks. Not a chance. There was only one girl I hungered for.

After Kelly left the room, I turned toward the others, smug from the vile thoughts running through my mind.

"You're one sick bastard," Hunter said as he laughed.

"You have no idea."

"I gotta ask. You're certain her father is the one?" he continued.

"You've asked me that before, Hunter. Do you seriously doubt me?"

He lifted his eyebrows. The man knew how hot-headed I was.

However, there was no need to think about his question. I'd seen the top of her father's hand the day he'd dropped his daughter off, the scar something I'd never forget. My blood boiled with rage, my brother's death yet to be avenged even though my father had tried to find out who'd dared kill his firstborn son. "I'm positive. The girl will pay."

"So the plan is to fuck and feast tonight?" Cristiano asked.

"Absolutely. Sage will be well used during and after the party." My cock twitched, my balls tightening. "Then she'll be placed on an extremely short leash which will allow her to graduate. But only if she is very obedient."

"The house is ready for our arrival. I've taken the liberty of adding a few amenities such as a cage, just in case she needs a reminder of her place." The desire in Cristiano's eyes was about something else altogether.

I rubbed my jaw, contemplating what could come next. "And you say I'm a sick man."

"You are," both of my buddies said at the same time.

"And I make no excuses for being that way." I lifted my glass, waiting as the others did the same. I'd already made the decision we would claim her weeks before. It would be tricky given graduation, but I had no intentions of staying for the fucking ceremony. Our last exams were in three days. Then she'd become ours permanently.

"To the hunt," Hunter growled.

"Now, the capture." Cristiano added.

"Then we'll break her."

"Imagine the look on her father's face when he learns his baby has disappeared." Hunter smiled.

I had imagined. It had been all I'd been able to think about during my sleepless nights. While I hungered for the woman more than I had any other, there was only one end to the game I was playing.

Revenge.

Sage would pay for the sins of her father. She would be fucked, used, and punished.

Then when we grew tired of her, she would die in atonement for the murder of my brother.

CHAPTER 3

Sage

"I have exciting news!" As my dormmate burst into the room, I couldn't help but smile. The girl had a verve for life, which was something I aspired to. Kelly Cole had quickly become my best friend after I'd enrolled in the City of Hope's illustrious musical program less than two years before. God, I hated the name, but almost no one used Crandall University. Thank God at least it would be on my diploma.

My parents had finally agreed to allow me to attend a college far from home, the luxurious Kentucky setting both beautiful and serene. And far removed from the crowded streets of Chicago. While not my first or even my third choice in colleges, it had been my first taste of freedom, allowing me to enjoy the perks of being away from home.

They'd only agreed because of the exclusivity of the school, as it was designed for kids born to the rich and famous.

The environment was heavily protected, the grounds secure. I'd seen armed security guards constantly walking the property in search of unwanted intruders. There wasn't a kid on campus who didn't have a powerful family. I'd learned early on that money could buy anything.

Except for happiness.

I'd been lonely for almost all of my life. I'd had no siblings and no real friends until Kelly had bounded into my life. She'd taught me how to become more personable, dragging me from my protected shell, kicking and screaming. I was grateful for her friendship.

Once that had happened, I'd ventured out into the real world, pretending to be something I wasn't: a professional singer. It was my foray into perfecting my stage presence while not being forced to feel the competition from my peers at school. At first, I'd been terrified. Now, I relished in pretending I was Lola or Tina Marie or Sasha. I'd learned about myself while dressing in provocative clothes.

I craved the darkness.

The only other outlet I had was writing, and I dared not do it on my laptop for fear of someone else seeing it. My thoughts drifted to the latest story I was in the middle of writing. My sexual cravings had always been dark, but I'd yet to explore all the juicy things I'd researched. My fantasies had fueled my stories since arriving at college. However, if my mother saw them, she would die.

"Hello!" Kelly said, jerking me out of my almost trance-like state.

"Oops. Sorry. Meaning what? Or dare I ask?"

She waltzed closer, giving me a pouty look. "I managed to secure an invitation for you to the greatest party of the year."

I instantly tensed. I'd yet to attend a single party on campus. They were held frequently. Some were provided by the school administrators, but most catered by the elite groups that had formed long before I'd asked to enroll. The school had been around for at least four decades, the education top-notch, graduation ensuring a place in a doctoral program of choice. Considered a music prodigy, I was set to graduate in less than two weeks, only a single exam standing in my way of receiving a diploma. I'd combined two years into one since I'd arrived later than other kids. "I need to study."

"Oh, come on. You're brilliant and talented. You can take a Saturday night off."

She was right, and I really wasn't worried. I was a straight 'A' student with a 4.5 GPA.

While the City of Hope wasn't Julliard, there were a half dozen Broadway and opera stars and one rock star who'd graduated over the last ten years. I had high hopes of being the next discovery one day. At least a girl could dream.

"Besides," she added, pointing her index finger in my direction. "I know about your late-night forays into town."

"What?" I tossed one of the pillows from the couch in her direction. I'd done everything in my power to keep that a secret from everyone.

"Yup. You aren't the prim and proper shrinking flower everyone thinks you are."

"You're such a bitch!" I said playfully. Then we both giggled.

Singing offered peace of mind, a freedom that I'd never thought I'd achieve. I knew my behavior was risky. If discovered, my parents would force me to return home where I'd be followed on a daily basis by at least one brutal security man. My father had hired an entire army after the first threat made on his life. That had been when I was five or six. My mother had finally confided in me after I'd pushed so hard to be able to attend a regular high school. While it didn't make any sense given what my father did for a living, I knew anything was possible.

I couldn't stand the thought of returning to that life ever again.

"Which group?" I was almost afraid to ask. She had other friends given her popularity, but she never lorded it over me. I was a wallflower, preferring to remain alone with my music and writing. Thankfully, she'd never pushed me or made fun of me. When she hesitated, I groaned. "Don't tell me."

"Yes, girl. The Elite."

Bullies. The school was full of them. The Elite made some of the college bully romance novels I'd read look like kids playing in sandboxes. The boys believed themselves to be men and were rich and powerful, their families akin to gods in the corporate and organized crime worlds. They were the most entitled people in the world. I was certain of it.

I shuddered violently at the thought of people forced to spend time in the same room with them. Kelly's fascination with the boys who belonged to the club was ridiculous. Granted, the few boys I'd met were gorgeous, as if each one of them had sipped from the Adonis pool, but they were also rumored to be arrogant bastards.

I had a few in my regular classes. They insisted on being disruptive, and the professors always looked the other way. At least for the most part, none of them had ever paid me the time of day.

"Don't you mean the Damned?" Even with disdain in my voice, I dragged my tongue across my lips. Several were objects of my fantasies, but no one would ever learn that. Nope. It was my secret.

Such a bad girl.

Kelly rolled her eyes. "Oh, come on. That's just jealousy from other students who don't have what it takes to become a member. They're all smart, rich, powerful, and good-looking. Dreamy, if you ask me. I have my sights set on at least two of them."

Of course she did.

Jealousy wasn't the word I'd use. The boys who made it through the grueling initiations the older members forced them to endure became nothing more than bullies on steroids. They were some of the most entitled people I'd ever met in my life. I hated every one of them, although I had to admit more than one of them had appeared in my raunchy stories. If only they knew what the quiet girl could dream up in her imagination. "They wear all black, for God's sake. Doesn't that tell you something? I think they're Devil worshippers."

She rolled her eyes, flopping down on the couch beside me. "Don't be childish. It's a uniform of sorts."

Uh-huh. I'd seen them walking in groups through campus, taking up the entire sidewalk, forcing students to move aside or be shoved. They were typical bullies in every sense of the word. "Demonic creatures," I teased. "And I heard about their initiations. Brutal. I'm shocked a single boy ever considers joining their motley crew. Don't they drink the blood of animals or something?"

"Where do you get this stuff?"

I shrugged, taking a sip of my soda. "I hear things. I'm not the wallflower you think I am."

She smiled slyly. "So true. I assure you that they aren't demon spirits. But they do throw the most incredible, kickass parties on campus. It's the end of the year. Remember? You need to live a little."

She was right about living a little, something I'd never been allowed to do. I chewed on my lower lip as I thought about her offer. Students of the Elite lived in a massive estate on the outskirts of the property, the fifty acres sectioned off from the rest of the students. They even had their own stables that housed incredible horses. I'd always wanted to see inside, but not as one of their 'girls'. "What is this party?"

"Just a party. Come on. As I said, you need to live a little. It's going to be the event of the year," she taunted. "You're going to graduate and leave me. Please come with me?"

"Begging isn't going to help."

"What if I clean the room until the end of the year?"

"Oh, that's a lame gesture. Besides, I have nothing to wear." Which was true. I preferred jeans, sweatshirts, and tennis shoes, enjoying the comfort they provided. It also allowed me anonymity in a sea of wealth and power.

"I'll loan you a dress and heels. We *are* the same size." She pouted her lips again. I swear the girl could get anything she wanted.

I glared at her, knowing that when she put something in her mind, she refused to give up on it. "What are they doing at this party? Sacrificing a pig or something?"

"Girl, for God's sake. You really do need to get out more. It's just about music, hot men, and plenty of booze. We can flirt to our heart's desire."

"I don't drink."

"One glass of wine or champagne isn't going to kill you."

"They're not allowed to have alcohol at these parties."

"And you know rules don't apply to the Elite. They can do anything they want to do."

Her statement was true enough. The administrators always looked the other way since the facility was private. But that didn't make it right. From what I'd heard, the members were perverted as well as dangerous, some of the members sons of mafia leaders. "I don't know."

"Pretty please. I would really prefer to have you with me. You know, a friend?" She batted her long eyelashes, as if that technique would work on me.

"Fine. But only for an hour."

"Yay! Let me grab the dress I thought of. I can't wait to see you all dolled up."

I couldn't remember the last time I'd been dressed up.

As soon as she scurried off, I heard my phone and sighed, forced to race into my bedroom where I'd tossed my purse after getting back from class. I was certain it was my mother's regular three-day check-in. She'd remained nervous even after all this time. I turned on a light, then caught the call on the fourth ring.

"Hello, Mom," I said, without bothering to look at the screen.

"Baby girl. How is everything?" As usual, her voice was chipper. Connie Winters never allowed her guard to drop, even with her own daughter. She was everything I wasn't. Popular. The light in a room. The life of a party. Beautiful. Accomplished. I felt like the ugly duckling beside her.

"It's good, just like it was three days ago." I narrowed my eyes and walked closer to the nightstand, my breath catching. A red rose petal.

A cold shiver trickled down my spine. It was the second one I'd found in three weeks. I hadn't paid attention to the first, thinking I'd rubbed against a bush, but the way it had been placed directly in the center of the small table wasn't natural.

My mother jabbered on as I pulled it closer, taking a deep whiff. The scent was incredible, one of the sweetest fragrances I'd inhaled.

"You make it sound like you're upset that I check on my daughter."

I closed my eyes, positioning the petal exactly where I'd found it.

Then I turned around in a full circle, trying to process what she'd just said.

"Um... No, I'm not upset, but you can stop worrying about me now. I'll be home for the summer in less than two weeks." Sighing, I walked toward the window, looking out at the sprawling grounds of the campus. I could almost see the Elite's estate through the massive tree line.

"Both your father and I are coming for graduation."

I exhaled but the shivers continued. "That's good."

"Are you okay, baby? You sound strange."

"Uh... no. You know me, Mom. I worry about the finals."

Ice continued to prickle my skin. I scanned the room, noticing one of my drawers was open just a crack. I was anal retentive about organization, maybe slightly psychotic about how I left my things. I never left a drawer open. My legs felt like lead as I walked closer, tentative about opening it.

When I did, nothing jumped out at me, but I sensed someone had been in my room. In fact, I would swear it on a Bible. I closed my eyes briefly, certain two nights before someone had stood over me, watching me sleep. I'd jerked out of a dream to find my window open, which I hadn't remembered doing. The whole thing had left me with a creepy feeling.

She laughed, the sound practiced and perfect. "You need to stop worrying. You are my brilliant daughter."

"How's Dad?"

"Traveling as usual."

I sorted through the drawer, then realized my crimson panties were missing. Part of what my mother liked to call my neurosis was that I had to wear a matching panty and bra. The lacy bra remained exactly where I'd placed it, but the panties were missing. "I, um… I thought he was slowing down."

"Just a couple more trips and he'll stop traveling altogether."

Now raw fear tore through me. I'd had the feeling of being watched for as long as I could remember, but I'd forced myself to think otherwise. What if it was true? What if there were cameras placed in the suite? The thought wasn't farfetched. "That's good."

"Alright. I can tell you're in the middle of something. I can't wait to see you. What are your plans for the weekend?"

I could lie and say studying in my room, but maybe it was time my mother realized I was growing up and out of my parents' shadow. "I'm going to a party tonight." I moved into the bathroom, yanking open the hamper lid, tossing clothes right and left. My thong definitely wasn't there.

My heart raced and I spun around, looking for any obvious signs someone had been in the shared bathroom.

The glitch in her shocked sigh caught me off guard. "You don't want to do that."

"It's not off campus. Just a little get together with friends." Now, I was lying. I would never call members of the Damned my friends.

Her hesitation created a wave of tension. "Honey, you need to be careful."

"Mom. I'm twenty-one now, not a child any longer. Need I remind you that I've been a very good girl?" Now, I rolled my eyes. My parents were far too protective. I wasn't as breakable as they assumed I was.

"It's not you I'm worried about. There are some very bad people in this world."

Tell me something I hadn't already heard about a thousand times or more. "Mom. It's a party located in the most secure facility on earth. Nothing is going to happen. Okay?"

Another hesitation. It drove me nuts. "Just tell me you'll call me tomorrow. Okay?"

Exhaling, I returned to the main room, trying to control my breathing.

I wanted to be frustrated with her, but I was aware of the threats my parents had received over the years, although they'd surprised me given my father owned a food distribution firm and restaurant in Chicago. Yes, my parents were extremely wealthy, but why the threats? My dad was a down-to-earth guy. "I will. I promise."

Threats. Did the invasion of my privacy have something to do with my father? *Get a grip, Sage. Maybe they're folded in your jeans.*

"Okay, darling. Just remember your father and I worry about you."

"I know. I gotta go now. Love ya, Mom." I tossed my phone onto the sofa, chewing on my lower lip.

As Kelly returned with a dress in her hand, I shook my head. Maybe for one night it was okay to shove aside the shy girl who barely talked to anyone. I could consider the dress just another costume. The bashful girl wasn't the kind of woman I wanted to be.

The inner bad girl wanted to be the wild vixen I wrote about in my stories. But as much as I wanted to let go, the nagging remained.

"What do you think?" she asked as she shifted the gorgeous red dress back and forth like a prize.

"I think it's fabulous." My tone was flat.

"What's wrong?" she asked, her face falling.

I folded my arms. "I think someone has been in our suite more than once."

She opened then closed her mouth, her eyes wider than before. "Why would you think that?"

"There was a rose petal on my nightstand just like the one I found a few weeks ago. And a pair of my panties has gone missing."

I wasn't certain how she'd react, but when she smiled and rolled her eyes, I was surprised. "Oh, come on. Why would anyone come into a dorm room?"

That was the question. "Have you seen any evidence of cameras?"

"Of course not! Girl. I think you're just overstressed and I know you've been working yourself to death. You'll find your undies tomorrow. Now, can we go have a little fun?"

Maybe she was right. I'd slept maybe three hours a night for weeks.

"You're right. So, will you help me with my makeup and hair?"

Kelly beamed. "I would love to."

CHAPTER 4

*S*age

Storms.

Why did the flash of lightning add to the continued snippets of fear that kept me on edge?

The first rumble of thunder occurred as Kelly was driving through the gates of the Elite's estate, the guard giving us both a onceover. The ominous clouds building in the sky left me with knotted nerves in my stomach.

"Jesus. I hate thunderstorms," I said absently as I glared out the window.

"You're still jumpy. Wait until we get inside. The house is to die for."

"How many times have you been here?"

She shrugged. "A few."

That's what I thought. She didn't seem to take her college life seriously. Maybe the rumors were true and that this was the college of choice to find a wealthy husband.

Shut your mouth, Sage Winters. That's not nice.

I bit back a chuckle.

"I'm glad you wore your contacts," Kelly added, an obvious attempt to change the subject.

I felt naked without my glasses, used to hiding behind the thick frames. To most of the students, I was just a plain jane nerd behind ugly glasses and baggy clothes. "I decided to be someone else tonight."

My thoughts drifted to my filthy story once again, and I tingled inside. I had no idea why the thought of being dominated by a man thrilled me. I couldn't imagine it in real life. I guess that's what fantasies were made for.

"There you go. That's my bestie. This is going to be so much fun," she said as she was given the go ahead to drive onto the estate.

"The Elite are certainly cautious about who they allow in."

"They have every reason to be. They are the cream of the crop for our future."

Why did her words sound so practiced? As if she was spouting a required mantra.

"You look incredible," she added. "I'm certain you'll get more attention than I will."

Did I hear a hint of jealousy in her voice? She had nothing to worry about.

I'd never worn something so risqué, the material hugging every curve. When I'd stood in front of the mirror, I'd been shocked at the transformation. Kelly had worked magic, my usually unruly curls becoming sexy. I rarely wore anything but eyeliner and maybe some lip gloss. She'd added a sultry color to my eyelids, making them appear larger. I'd stood in the mirror, trying to recognize my own reflection. I felt beautiful for the first time in my life. Excitement and nerves remained at the surface, my mind spinning with possibilities for the night.

A car buzzed past us, heading to the exit, almost driving Kelly off the gravel road.

"Jesus. Asshole!" she yelled, and I laughed. She was a crazy driver herself.

The various vehicles parked in the single lot signified the incredible wealth of the students. Porsches. Hummers. Mercedes. Italian sports cars. There was at least two million dollars sitting in the secured space. Meanwhile, I'd insisted on driving a beautiful yet older Chevy Cruze, the compact car suiting my needs just fine.

She found a parking space on the grass, obviously disgusted at being forced to step out onto damp terrain. As soon as I started to open the door, she grabbed my arm.

"What's wrong?" I asked, surprised her breathing was labored.

"Look. Um. These guys are… well, they're not normal."

"What do you mean?" Now she decided to confess what I already knew? Was she purposely trying to scare me? "I thought you called them dreamy?"

The fact she refused to look me in the eye sent a single tremor of fear through my system.

"Oh, they are, but they're privileged." Kelly swallowed hard.

"I know that. So what? Are you trying to tell me they're dangerous? I already know that too."

"Yeah..." She raked her hand through her hair, and I was certain the dome light highlighted the fact that her arm was shaking. "So, anything goes at these parties. I mean anything."

"Drug use?" I had no idea what she was talking about.

"Some, but I've seen very little. Let's just say the men are... amorous."

Every word out of her mouth was stilted, but I had a feeling she knew what she was talking about. "Okay. I'm not a prude. I've seen people having sex before." Maybe the rumors of huge orgies were true. Why did my nipples become aroused at the thought?

"Yeah, but not like these guys. They are into some kinky shit."

"How kinky?" While I was surprised I'd asked the question, just doing so created warmth between my legs.

Just like my stories.

"They're sadists. All of them. They thrive on forcing women to submit to their sick needs, taking pleasure in inflicting pain. But they know how to bring you to the kinds of highs you'll never get another way."

My breath caught in my throat. "Do they do that to you?" I squirmed in my seat, trying to remind myself that writing stories was one thing, experiencing the darkness that I envisioned was something else altogether.

Her normally bubbly laugh was pained. "Let's just say I find them… irresistible. Be very glad your parents didn't drink the Elite Kool-Aid."

"What are you talking about?" Her parents were doting just like mine were, both highly respected doctors.

She threw me a look, the flash of lightning turning the dark night into an eerie setting, but it allowed me to see the fact that her lower lip was quivering. "I need to surrender to them no matter what they want me to do."

"Whoa. Hold on. That's crazy. Why?"

"Because my parents want me to be chosen."

I'd never heard her talk this way, even when I'd teased about the crap floating on campus about their lofty organization. "Chosen for what?"

"To hopefully marry one of the bastards one day. They want me to marry the President, but I know he doesn't like me. He wants someone else." She looked away, obviously angry some girl had caught this guy's attention.

I resisted laughing or worse. "Oh, for God's sake. That doesn't happen in this day and time," I finally chided.

"Don't kid yourself. The Elite have more power in this country than you understand. When you graduate, get the hell away from here. At least I'll live in the lap of luxury."

I didn't take her warning lightly. She was all over the place about the Elite and the crazy requirements. "Then why bring me here?"

"Because... because I need someone by my side tonight who I can trust. The other girls are bitches. They hate me because I'm well liked."

Sighing, I glanced at the window at the house. Why did the shadows suddenly seem malevolent? "Okay, I'm here. We're leaving together. Period. In and out. A drink or two, then we leave. Deal?"

Kelly finally turned her head in my direction. "Okay. Just be careful. If they lure you in, then you'll belong to them."

Saying I wasn't a prude was correct, yet I'd only had sex once and that hadn't been the best experience. However, that didn't mean I wasn't a red-blooded female with desires and fantasies. Very little bothered me.

Or so I hoped.

Besides, it was apparent everyone underestimated me. I had no intentions of surrendering to any man under any circumstances, no matter what appeared in my journal.

Then why are you quivering?

I wasn't entirely certain. My thoughts returned to my belief that someone had riffled through my things.

"And leave your phone here."

"Why?" I asked.

"Because I doubt you want your phone confiscated. They don't want any possibility of pictures being taken and seen on social media."

"Jesus Christ. What are they afraid of?"

"As I've told you, they're very private. They handle business that they don't want anyone to know about."

"They're fucking college students."

She rolled her eyes. "Don't be naïve, Sage. They are already millionaires from the various businesses they rule. Take the President of the club, Cain Cross. He's following in his father's footsteps and has been for a while."

Rule, not run. Her word usage was getting stranger. "Which is?"

Her nervousness was even more evident. "Mafia."

I'd heard kids of mafia families were enrolled in the school. It really hadn't bothered me until hearing the way she mentioned the single world. "So they really are dangerous."

"Oh, you bet. There are rumors they've handled business out of the house."

"Why are you just telling me this now?" I wanted to strangle her for the push and pull.

She took a deep breath. "I don't want you to get caught in the system."

"Don't worry about me. I have my entire life planned out. Why go to post-grad at all? Why not follow in daddy's footsteps and be done with it?"

"Because it's required. Come on. These parties are rare. That's one reason I asked you to come with me." She plastered a smile on her face, and I started questioning more than just my reason for being invited.

After tossing her purse in the back, she didn't wait for my response, exiting the vehicle in a hurry.

I thought about what she was saying, sliding my small clutch under the seat. The weirdness surrounding the Elite was becoming more disturbing. My thoughts drifted to my mother's phone call and the fact that someone had been in our suite. There was no way the events could be a coincidence.

As Kelly led us toward the front door, I noticed at least four security guards manning the front of the estate, two more burly guys at the door. For some reason, the sight of them bothered me more than it should. Were they hiding something I shouldn't be allowed to see? The stories about the Damned were the thing legends were made of. Debauchery and violence. I knew better than to believe fifty percent of what I'd heard. Still, my mother's words weighed on my mind. Yes, there were some very bad people in this world.

"Oh, you're going to be frisked," she said in passing.

"What for? Are they worried about weapons?"

"Hardly. They're all skilled marksmen. That's part of their training."

"Their training?" I stopped her on the sidewalk, more uncertain than ever if I wanted to go inside.

She cocked her head, the light from the lampposts allowing me to see her frustration. She'd gone from warning me to chastising me in the blink of an eye. "I shouldn't have mentioned anything, so don't ask about things you don't want to learn about. They're looking for anyone who's wired."

"What?"

"Privacy. Every ritual is secret. Even I don't know all that goes on behind closed doors."

I doubted I wanted to. "Fine. You owe me for this."

Kelly was allowed inside by face recognition only. I was forced to endure being patted down by a monster of a man with a surly attitude and rough hands. When he slipped his fingers under my dress, touching my panties, I shoved him as hard as possible, resisting driving my knee into his crotch. "Watch it, asshole."

"Tell your friend to keep her mouth shut," he snarled.

"She's a visitor." Kelly's voice was more timid than I was used to.

"I don't give a fuck if she's the freaking Queen of England, consort. She gets frisked."

Wow. The guy was a real asshole. "Just get it over with." I didn't add the nasty words to the end I really wanted to. His grin was lecherous as he moved to my chest, enjoying the hell out of fondling my breasts. I was nauseated, gritting my teeth to keep from saying something I'd regret.

"The rules for while you're inside," he snarled. "Stay in the party room, or you'll be expelled and you won't like how that happens. The rest of the house is off limits unless you're invited."

By the way he issued the statement, I had a feeling that wasn't going to happen.

However, I'd evidently passed the barbaric test, and our entrance was allowed.

"Jerk," I muttered.

"Shush," she whispered. "Just stay in the room and you'll be fine."

"What if I have to use the bathroom?"

"Jesus, girl. There's a suite of them adjoining the main ballroom. You're allowed to go there but nowhere else. And I mean it."

I was beginning to hate agreeing to come with her. What had originally sounded like fun seemed entirely different. Maybe I was wrong, but it seemed like she'd been summoned to the house, required to attend the party.

As soon as I walked inside the mansion, I was shocked by the opulence, especially for a house designed for college boys. From the Italian marble floor in the entrance foyer and the opulent chandelier hanging from the vaulted ceiling to the dozens of gorgeous red roses in a huge crystal vase on the glass table, the facility screamed extreme wealth. The curved staircase leading to all four additional floors was ornate, the iron work in the railings incredible.

I was used to seeing expensive things, but the entire setting reeked of power.

There were no escorts leading the way, but we followed several people, ending up in a great room that had to be at least fifteen hundred square feet. We'd passed through hallways adorned with exquisite works of art in vibrant colors, every piece a vivid vision of sexual acts. I found myself unable to take my eyes off them, my head spinning at the intricacy of how they'd been painted. There was no doubt in my mind that the artist had had live models as inspiration.

Whips.

Chains.

A cage with two naked women inside. The depictions were beautiful instead of being vulgar, but the egotism of the artist was evident by the bold strokes and thickness of paint. They were also a reflection of the misogynistic attitudes of the men who lived in the house. They obviously believed women were playthings and nothing more.

Swallowing, I allowed my gaze to linger for a little longer, memorizing the poses. What if someone had seen my journal and that was the reason I'd been invited? The thought was titillating, even though I knew I should turn around and walk out.

You can do this. Just enjoy it.

As if that was possible.

"The house is beautiful," I half whispered, fearful I'd draw attention to our arrival.

"You should see the bedroom suites. They are to die for." Kelly's off-the-cuff announcement didn't shock me more than any of her other behavior. She was a free spirit, which made what she'd said earlier more disturbing.

Every aspect of the ballroom was gothic in nature, the thick velvet drapes adorning dark woods and regal furniture. At least the music wasn't from the last century, the dark dance vibes pulsating in every muscle. I noticed a flash of lightning outside and shivered.

"Let's get a drink," Kelly suggested, leading me by the arm toward one of two massive bars in the room. I couldn't help but notice the bartender was gorgeous, his arm muscles pushing against the tight confines of his black shirt.

"I'll have a Coke," I told him, which forced Kelly to wrinkle her nose. She ordered a screwdriver and I sighed. It would seem I'd be the designated driver. I sensed her nervousness increasing, which kept me on edge. Still, a part of me was intrigued with why the Elite were given so much credit.

"Kelly, baby. There you are. And who is this luscious friend you brought with you tonight?"

The deep voice was intoxicating, the rumble his husky tone created shifting straight to my core. I glanced in her direction, noticing a split second of hesitation—or maybe it was raw fear—before she smiled.

"Cristiano. This is my bestie, Sage."

Cristiano. The name alone was something out of romance novels.

He took my hand into his, pulling my knuckles to his mouth. As soon as he pressed his voluptuous lips against my skin, a quiver drifted down my spine. To say he was stunning with his dark hair and sculpted muscles was an understatement, but it was his eyes that drew me in. They were luminous, a luscious emerald green tinged with gold flecks. I swallowed, trying to control my nerves.

"Quite possibly the most gorgeous woman in the room."

If Kelly was perturbed by his words, she didn't show it, turning toward a group of girls who'd approached. I could tell Cristiano thought I'd be bowled over by the compliment. I knew how guys worked. I wasn't immune to social media or the giggly girls in my various classes. They thought they'd find true love behind the walls of the City of Hope.

I knew better.

If anything, they'd find an unhappy marriage.

While stories involving the Elite were highly exaggerated, if what Kelly had said was true and that a few chosen women became trophy wives, then even the administrators were in on what was happening behind the steel gates. However, I wasn't lured into the fantasy that arranged marriages could work. They were barbaric to my mind. I still believed I'd find the perfect man, but only in the distant future after I became a star.

I pulled my hand away, giving him a polite nod. There was no sense in encouraging him. Nothing was going to happen tonight, especially nothing of a carnal nature. "Thank you, but it won't work."

"What won't?" he asked, genuinely curious, his eyes full of amusement.

"Seducing me. I'm not that kind of girl."

The flash of annoyance in his eyes couldn't be hidden, although he tried to mask it well.

Kelly suddenly interrupted, moving slightly in front of me. "Forgive my friend. She doesn't get out much."

"Well, little pet. You should explain the rules to your bestie."

Kelly's lips were tight, anger sparking in her eyes. Then it was gone.

He exuded power as well as darkness, enough that a little voice inside told me to run. While the hair stood up on the back of my neck, the fact that I remained attracted to him shoved away any hint of fear. There was nothing I hated more than men who lorded their prowess over women.

"She doesn't need to. I'm perfectly capable of taking care of myself. Don't worry. I'll be a good girl tonight. I'm just a visitor and nothing more." I pushed Kelly aside, realizing that whatever punishment she'd mentioned could be on the agenda for her if I didn't step in. I crowded his space, forced to tilt my head to look into his eyes. The flash in them occurred again, only this time I was able to look deeper into a black pit. As if the man had no soul.

We stood for a few seconds, neither one saying anything. His nostrils flared as he took a deep breath, purposely growling as if primal behavior would attract me.

Sadly, I was more aroused than I had been before, furious with my body for betraying me. I hated that his musky scent was intoxicating, prickles dancing on my naked arms.

"Be careful, delicate flower," he said softly as he rolled his knuckles down the side of my face. "Monsters come in all shapes and sizes."

I pulled my head away with an exaggerated move, irritated he thought his possessive bullshit would attract me. "Monsters I can handle, as well as little boys trying to prove themselves as men."

Chuckling, he gave me another salacious look before walking away. Only seconds later, I realized he was continuing to stare at me.

"What's his problem?" I knew the answer. He thought he was entitled. I was already uncomfortable.

She turned to face me, her expression more pensive than before. "What are you doing? You all but tossed gasoline onto a flame. He's already attracted to you."

"Oh, please. I bet his dick is the size of a peanut."

"You don't understand. This was a mistake. He's one of the three Elite members to stay away from at all costs."

"Why?"

The way she swallowed was a clear indication of how nervous she was. "Because he's bad news."

"Who are the others?" Why had she brought me here? She'd obviously been considered one of them for some time. I was beginning to feel completely uncomfortable, especially since Cristiano's eyes remained on me.

As she scanned the room, I sensed she was ensuring no one was paying attention. "Hunter and Cain."

"Like Cain and Abel?" Evidently, the president of the little club thought he had more power than he did.

Did my parents know about the school's reputation? They'd never said anything to me about the Elite. But my mother's strange reaction had been a red flag. Had they been pressured to send me here? Had I been the one to find the school?

No. I hadn't been. I'd nagged them for two years to allow me to take anything other than community classes. This had been my father's suggestion. My father had likely been a drill sergeant in a previous life. He'd barked orders after researching everything. There were far too many questions in my mind that I was worried I wouldn't like the answers to.

"Exactly like that. They rule the entire school. The other guys you see are fine, some of them very nice, but they won't interfere with whatever the three men want. Stay away from them."

"Why else did you bring me here, Kelly? Be honest with me. Did someone put you up to it?"

It was as if a light had sparked inside her head. Or as if she knew she was being watched.

"Don't be silly. I asked you because I wanted you to have some fun for a change. You can't allow three wicked boys to ruin the party. This is the place to be." Whatever the reason she was nervous before had faded away. "Let me introduce you to some other people. Okay?"

I allowed my gaze to lock onto Cristiano, noticing the smirk on his face.

A cold shiver drifted all the way down to my toes.

The moment she dragged me further into the crowd, I had a sense of being watched.

As if I'd been lured to the party for a specific reason.

Just like before.

As if I'd suddenly become prey to three big bad wolves.

CHAPTER 5

Cristiano

Fuck. My cock ached, pinched against the zipper of my trousers. Filthy visions tore through my mind. Soon, I would drive my shaft deep into Sage's tight pussy as she writhed underneath me.

I knew the objective, one that Cain had drilled into us for several months, but there was something about her that intrigued me. The three of us had shared women before, but a part of me wanted her all to myself. That shocked the hell out of me. I could have anyone I wanted in the world, but Sage had been the only one to spark something deep inside.

I'd barely paid any attention to the stories Cain had mentioned. Just reading a small passage from her journal had pushed me to the edge of need, so much so that sending her away wasn't an option. I couldn't wait to lock her inside a house where no one else could find her.

"Lucky bastard," Hunter said as he flanked my side.

"How so, brother?" As Sage disappeared into the crowd, I took a deep breath, filthy thoughts of what I would do to her lingering in my mind.

"You were the first to meet our new pet. I'm curious as to your thoughts."

In our world, women were considered commodities, even at our age. I knew the drill as well as any of the other members. Being an Elite was in our blood, our fathers anticipating we'd become stellar members of a pre-ordained, exclusive club with past graduates. I found it interesting my father had wanted me involved. Even more so that I'd been allowed to break the traditional mold of being welcomed since none of my ancestors had gone through the program. Program. What I meant was indoctrination.

I gave him a sideways glance, lifting the glass to my lips. "She's not as timid as we thought. In fact, there's an intelligence and vibrancy in her unlike any of the other girls. But she could be trouble." There hadn't been a single woman in the school who'd dared challenge me the way she had. My mind remained filled with images that some would consider heinous. I wanted her confined naked to a cage, only allowed free when she was to be used. That was my right. Somehow, I knew she wouldn't succumb easily. The joy would be in breaking her, stripping away her defenses.

"You finally figured that out? Her stories are a delicious indication."

"Not just her stories. I can tell there's a little lioness inside." My cock was pressing against my zipper, making walking uncomfortable.

"There isn't a woman we can't tame. A little fighter? That will make the evening more delightful."

Delightful wasn't the word. While deflowering the beautiful creature before destroying her had been Cain's suggestion, I hadn't planned on being so attracted to her. It was an honor bestowed by a fellow brother. Now, I wanted nothing more than to rip the dress from her voluptuous body, revealing the prize underneath. Defiling her would provide great contentment.

"She'll break," I told him.

"That's the plan. Would you like to wager a bet on how long it will take until she's screaming out our names after fucking her five times?" His laugh was often annoying, more so tonight.

"We need to get her alone first." A loud voice drew my attention and we both turned around. "Fuck. Look what the cat dragged in." There was nothing worse than when former members who'd been tossed out broke the rules by arriving at one of our parties.

"Theodore Watkins," Hunter hissed. "I thought the last time we escorted him out the front door, he knew better than to show his ugly face again."

"Some assholes never learn." The limp dick had refused to fuck one of the chosen in front of us, a requirement of the organization. The fact he hadn't been able to get it up proved him unworthy of holding the title of an Elite. That had been his first infraction, and for reasons that continued to piss me off, he'd been given a pass. Even after fucking up handling an enemy who'd caused us trouble for months, he'd been allowed to live, his only punishment being expelled. I knew all of the reasons, but it still pissed me off. "Why don't I handle escorting the bastard out this time?"

"Mmm... Be careful you don't break him. You know his daddy will attempt to make our lives a living hell."

I glanced at my friend, unable to keep a grin off my face. "If the worthless bastard tries, I'll have my pops intervene." My father was truly a sick bastard. If I made a single phone call, William Watkins' severed head would be delivered by special courier to Theodore's dorm room. As leader of a South American Cartel, my pops could care less about American laws or those believing they had influence over everyone else.

Hunter chuckled, shaking his head. He had no idea what my father was capable of. Fortunately, I was turning out to be a carbon copy of the brutal man. "Now, that is something I'd like to see."

"Why don't you check on our lovely prize for the evening while I handle Theo?"

"I think I'll do that. My cock is itching for action."

"Careful. Cain wants to fuck her first."

"Cain. Always the man in charge. Whatever. That doesn't mean I can't snack on her sweet pussy."

"Good point." I tapped my fist on his arm before slamming my drink on one of the tables and heading into the crowd. The fact Theodore had whined to the school administrators about his expulsion from the Elite kept a bad taste in my mouth. The fact that he'd fucked up an assignment had almost tarnished our savage reputation. It was past time he realized fucking with one of the Elite hadn't been in his best interests. Even being considered for the coveted position was an honor; most kids in the worthless school would die for a chance to join the illustrious organization.

Not Theodore.

Pompous dick.

I had to remind myself that not everyone could tolerate being a member. The requirements were not for the faint of heart. Theodore had faltered, showing his true colors. Even worse, it had been in front of the entire house, other members chanting that we should kill the bastard for failing us. While Cain had prevented us from doing so, it had been with prudence in mind. We didn't need the hassle months before graduation, especially since the fucker's uncle was in the FBI. Yet the cockroach wanted more. Maybe I'd handle the situation once and for all.

My way.

Theo was obviously out to prove himself. His father had been an Elite member and had expected his son to do the same. Unfortunately, the jerk didn't have the killer drive in him. However, he could make our lives a living hell with the influence he had within other areas of the school.

My approach was stealthy, in complete silence. He was conversing with three of the chosen women, our entertainment for the evening. They seemed enamored, which pissed me off even more. I waited, standing behind him, listening to him bragging about being accepted to Harvard law school, his future mapped out.

Finally, one of the girls noticed my casual stance, smart enough to know looks could be deceiving. Gina was devoted to the house, likely gathering information to expound on later. I'd remind Cain to make certain she was selected as one of the final candidates.

"Sorry, Theodore. We need to freshen up," Gina said, immediately guiding the other two girls away.

"What the fuck?" he huffed under his breath.

"It would seem you're lost, Theodore," I said quietly. There was no reason to ruin such a lively party.

He turned around, a smug look on his face. It was apparent the manner in which he'd been expelled hadn't stuck. "What do you want, Chicano?"

"I'm surprised at the level of your slur given your supposed intelligence."

His grin was meant to irritate me. Either the kid had a death wish or enjoyed pain. I smelled whiskey, his slightly slurred words indicating he'd already had one too many. Maybe booze had made him stupid. What annoyed me more than anything was that I couldn't kill him. He knew it as well, which was what made him so fucking bold.

"Well, I call it like I see it."

"Since there is a party going on, I'm going to be polite and ask you to get the fuck out."

He took a sip of his bourbon, acting as if by consuming the same liquor his father guzzled, he'd become a man. "You don't own me anymore than you rule this house."

I inched closer, keeping a smile on my face. "It's a shame the blood running through your veins is tainted."

My comment struck him as odd, his eyes narrowing. "What the fuck are you talking about?"

While I ordinarily wouldn't be in a rush to provide an answer, I had better things to do with my time. "Let's just say that art never lies." I had proof his father had knocked up another girl, someone underage who'd given birth to another son. I'd been taught early on to track down every dirty little secret of my enemies. Theo was no exception.

"Don't play games with me, pusshead. I'm in no mood."

When he dared attempt to take another sip of his drink, I ripped the glass from his hand, tossing it against the wall.

A few of the girls in the room squealed then returned to flirting as they normally did. No one gave a shit what went on inside the estate.

With a single exception. The delicate innocent flower. Sage stood apart from the group, studying me intently. If I didn't know better, I'd say there was admiration as well as lust in the warm glow of her blue eyes. Then she smiled, her attitude obviously shifting to admonishment. My cock only ached that much more.

"What the fuck?" Theodore snarled.

While I was momentarily distracted by the girl's beauty, he managed to drive both hands against my chest, almost pitching me to the floor. That broke the near trance-like state I'd been in. I lunged toward him, issuing a brutal punch to his gut, then wrapping my hand around his throat.

Cain immediately approached, giving me the nod to deal with the asshole outside the party room. I heard him encouraging the party to continue as I dragged Theodore into a more private section of the estate, tossing him inside one of the rooms. I had to admit, I was curious as to whether the innocent flower would follow, unable to resist finding dirt on the Elite. Maybe. Maybe not. However, my main objective was to issue a harsh warning.

This wasn't about holding a conversation any longer. The fucker had not only invaded private space where he didn't belong, he'd insulted a member of the Elite. With a single brutal punch, a crunching sound indicated I'd broken his nose.

He cried out in pain as his body slumped against the wall. I'd give him credit. With barely a shake of his head, he threw himself in my direction, snarling like some fucking animal as he tried to wrap his hands around my throat. I issued an undercut to his throat, knocking the wind out of him. Then I let loose, punching him several times. After his knees buckled and he dropped to the floor, I stood over him, fisting his hair and jerking him up by several inches.

"This will be the last warning you get, Theo. Stay the fuck away from the house. You're not a member of the Elite. You're too much of a pussy to be one." When he said nothing, just glaring at me with tears in his eyes, I spit on him then backed away. "You're disgusting. You were never man enough to handle the required responsibilities. Get out. If I see your face again anywhere near this estate, I won't hesitate to slice off your dick and shove it into your mouth. That will be the beginning."

He had the good sense to remain silent until I was in the doorway.

"Be careful, Cristiano. Those boys you think so highly of will betray you just like you betrayed me."

I laughed, not bothering to acknowledge his statement. Although I knew what he said was the truth. As close as I was to Cain and Hunter, I could never turn my back on them.

Taking long strides from the room, I grabbed the first Elite member I saw. "Jonas. Escort the bastard out of the building."

"Yes, sir."

God help the fucker if he showed his face again.

* * *

The fact I'd left Theodore alive jerked at the evil man inside of me. I wasn't accustomed to controlling my brutality under any circumstance. I headed away from the party and into a room reserved for Elite members only. Hunter and Cain were inside, studying me intently the moment I walked in.

"Is it done?" Hunter asked.

"If you mean tossing him out, yeah. I would have preferred to drive my knife into his gut instead. I had Jonas escort him out."

"Jonas has become a godsend," Cain said, chuckling under his breath.

"Yeah, he has his sights set on being president next year." Hunter grinned. "He's fucked up like the rest of us. He'll make an outstanding prez."

"You know why we need to be careful, but only for the time being," Cain said harshly. He wasn't usually the voice of reason. I certainly didn't approve of towing the line for anyone, especially a shithead like Theodore.

A sharp knock irritated all three of us. When Jonas stuck his head into the door, he had an evil grin on his face. "He's out the door."

Cain exhaled. "Any trouble?"

Jonas shrugged. "Gave me some lip but I'm used to that. He's thinks he's invincible cause of daddy."

I glanced at Hunter, who clenched his fists. "Yeah, I should have handled the issue before."

Cain waved his hand. "He'll get his at the right time."

I'd known Cain long enough to know he kept his promises. The man was a sick fuck.

"Something else?" I barked when Jonas didn't leave.

"There was a mighty sexy chick listening in on our conversation. Never seen her before. New girl?"

"Red dress?" While my tone sounded demanding, I already knew the answer. She was a very bad little girl after all. My balls tightened at the thought.

Jonas rolled his hands down in front of him as if he was stroking a beautiful woman. "One I wanted to rip off with my teeth."

Cain turned his head, glancing at Hunter and then to me. The glint in his eyes shifted as desire roared into his system. "She's just visiting."

"You want me to send her on her way?"

"Don't worry about it, Jonas. Just watch her until we're finished with our discussion."

"Will do."

After Jonas left, I couldn't help but laugh. "I would call the beautiful Sage more than a handful. I had a feeling she would try and figure out why and how we hold so much power."

"Clever, but she could become a serious issue." Cain rubbed his jaw as he paced the room. "Still, we can handle Sage given our plan to keep her. But it would seem our buddy Theo is determined to make things difficult for us."

"What are you thinking?" Hunter asked, the gleam in his eye telling. He was eager to dissect the man as much as I was, sending his body back to daddy in several plastic bags.

"We wait until graduation. Then no one can touch us." Cain was right in that once freed from the institution, we would be above the law, controlling anyone we chose.

I nodded. While I had no patience, it was necessary. Two weeks wouldn't change anything. "What about the girl? What are the illustrious plans for tonight, given she's not quite the vulnerable girl we suspected?"

"Did you talk to her?" Cain asked Hunter.

"She disappeared right after Cristiano escorted our unwanted guest out of the party room." Hunter grinned. "At least now we know what she was doing."

Cain snorted. "Yes. She certainly has balls for an innocent little thing. I wonder if her pussy tastes as sweet as she pretends to be? I also wonder how eager she is to enjoy the darkness she describes so eloquently."

"My guess is that she has no clue," Hunter offered.

"I told you she was a fighter. I think she needs a lesson in understanding that she's a guest in our abode," I said before glancing at both men. "But depending on what she heard, we may not be able to let her go as planned, even on a tight leash."

"Mmm... agreed." Cain chuckled. "We'll know by the way she reacts after we enjoy spending time with her."

"I know what you said before, but how are we going to explain her disappearance to her parents if that becomes necessary?" I was curious as to his answer. Cain believed himself to be omnipotent in all things. Perhaps we all did.

"Once we're finished with her, the good little girl will do anything and everything we command her to do. I have confidence in our abilities." He smiled. "We'll provide her with exactly what she's been craving. Remember, she wants to be called a good girl."

"I do love the man's attitude," Hunter chortled.

"You mean his sadistic ways." I grinned.

"And she likes being called little pet."

"Mmm..." Hunter murmured.

My balls were tight as drums, images of forcing her to kneel in front of me wearing nothing but a collar a beautiful vision to behold.

"Perhaps we'll start with punishment before pleasure," Hunter suggested. "That will provide an excellent introduction into our world."

Punishment. Given our brutal tastes in providing needed discipline to either a wayward candidate or the women who were required to surrender to us, I had a feeling we'd learn just how much of a fighter the lovely Sage could be. "Yes. I think that's exactly what needs to happen. Find her, Hunter, and bring her to our playroom."

Cain grinned. "And I thought you weren't interested."

"I'm interested. In fact, I honestly do believe keeping her in a collar and on a leash for the duration of her stay in City of Hope is required."

"Cristiano, select a single implement for tonight. Choose wisely. The thought isn't to terrify her just yet." Cain narrowed his eyes, the sick bastard inside of him eager to provide more than a simple lesson.

"I have just the instrument in mind. Pain and pleasure it is." I chuckled under my breath.

Hunter laughed. "Then so be it. I'll return shortly. Then we can begin."

CHAPTER 6

Sage

Oh my God. Everything I'd heard about the Damned was correct. They were absolute psychopaths who thought they could control everyone around them. I was shaking and wasn't certain if it was from fear or anger. Why would Kelly's parents want her to have anything to do with this insanity? Why would they dare push her into marrying one of the assholes?

I took several deep breaths, trying to collect my sanity.

Visions of Theo's bloodied face remained in the forefront of my mind.

I'd watched as Cristiano had dragged the poor guy from the party room, shoving him into another. Then I'd followed, hiding in the shadows and listening from only a few feet away. No one had paid any attention to my departure, or so I'd hoped, although I could certainly sense there were eyes everywhere. Waiting. Watching.

I'd shifted into a darkened room as he'd stormed by, holding my breath for fear of being caught. Several rumbles of thunder had added to a heightened level of fear, but they'd been unable to mask the brutal thuds indicating the poor kid whisked from the ballroom was getting beaten. Who the hell did these assholes think they were?

Then I'd remained where I was, still trying to catch my breath and calm my nerves. The man who'd been used as a punching bag had limped from the other room, gasping for air. Another man appeared out of the shadows, leaning against the wall with his arms crossed. What I'd overheard had horrified me.

"Don't worry, Jonas. I'm leaving," the poor guy had said as he'd continued gasping for breath. His lip had been split in two locations, and there was no doubt he'd have two black eyes in a few hours—let alone that his nose would need reconstructive surgery.

Jonas had chuckled, the sound sending an icy chill through my veins. *"You fucked with the wrong people, Theodore. You're lucky you're still alive."*

"Fuck you, buddy. You can't touch me, and everyone in this house knows it."

"Don't fool yourself. You knew the rules. You broke them. Kill without question. Follow orders. Don't tell."

Kill without question. I'd had imagined I'd heard the words. I'd been shocked I hadn't screamed, merely shrinking further into the darkness of the room, praying to God another member of the Elite wouldn't grab me in the process.

"I did what was asked of me."

"You left a witness."

My mind could barely process what I'd heard. A witness. What was the group really doing? Mafia. I'd been a fool to think the brutal life wouldn't bleed into their activities. They were trained killers.

"You asshole. I wasn't sent to kill his wife. That's sick."

I managed to dart a quick look into the hallway, almost losing my footing. Jonas had jerked his head up, issuing a primal growl as he glared toward the room I'd hidden inside of. The scar on the side of his face had been almost as terrifying as the moment.

"No. Witnesses." Jonas had snapped. *"Go before I kill you myself."*

As they both passed, Theodore had slapped his hand on the wall, leaving a bloody handprint. It was obvious he'd done so on purpose. I was sick to my stomach. How could this be allowed to happen? How could Kelly be a part of this charade? There was no way my best friend could know what was happening. None.

Still shaking after another two or three minutes had passed, I'd finally eased from my hiding place. I'd decided at that moment that I would force Kelly to leave even if I had to drag her out of the building. I thought about telling my father or going to the authorities, but what good would it do? While I'd purposely tried to ignore the gossip mill threading through the campus, it was obvious that the Elite owned more than just the people working for and around the campus. They owned a good portion of Lexington, Kentucky as well, including the police.

Now taking quick steps and constantly glancing over my shoulder, I returned to the main room, realizing several new people had arrived. As I milled through the crowd, the feeling of being watched continued. Even the girls were scrutinizing me, their hate-filled gazes a clear indication I was an outsider.

In fact, I had a feeling I was the only person invited to the party that wasn't a member of their private group. My journal continued to plague my mind. I had no desire to become a member, and I planned on convincing Kelly she'd be a fool to accept what her parents believed was good for her. I ignored the harsh glares, thankful that Cristiano hadn't returned to the room. However, suddenly I had the creepy-crawlies, my skin tingling. While everyone was dancing and drinking, there didn't seem to be a student in the room who wasn't watching my every action.

I jumped from the sound of thunder, my yelp attracting even more attention.

Rain was pouring down outside, bolts of lightning flashing through the massive floor to ceiling windows. Still no sign of Kelly.

"Where are you?" I asked under my breath, noticing Jonas from the corner of my eye. My skin crawled again, unable to lose the feeling that he'd somehow known I was hiding. Oh, God. This was so bad. He wore a smile that could only be described as manic, the look in his eyes crazed. I gave him a once over on purpose, controlling my breathing.

The crowd was suddenly suffocating. I wasn't used to them. Most of my classes were small in comparison to others, the majority of students studying business and marketing. My heart drifted into my throat, a light fog forming around my eyes. I needed air but refused to leave without her. Damn it. I'd only been gone for two minutes.

After searching the entire ballroom, I thought I noticed her bright blonde hair from a distance, although I couldn't confirm given the distance. Relief flooded me, and I quickly followed. She was heading through another doorway, glancing over her shoulder at least once. Was there fear in her eyes? And who was the man leading her? I pushed my way through the guests, wrapping my fingers around the lever just before the door closed. Without thinking, I ventured into the hallway.

When the door shut, I heard a soft click and realized the area was private, no one getting in without a code. What was she doing here? Was this where all the incidents of debauchery took place or where they killed their victims?

My thoughts drifted to what she'd told me earlier—that the members of the Elite were sadists. Was she being punished for the fact that I'd mouthed off to one of the Elite? I knew enough about the practice of BDSM to understand that even though it was supposed to be consensual, there were those who enjoyed inflicting pain for the art of doing so.

There were a few people up ahead of me, all moving toward something. I could feel it. I tried not to call attention to myself, hanging back as I trailed behind them. The design of the hallway reminded me of catacombs leading into a cave, and I could swear we were going underground given the slight slope of the floor. If I was correct, that meant there was likely no other way out than the one I'd entered.

I was fooling myself by continuing to say I could handle the situation. Terror ripped through me, but I refused to allow anything to happen to Kelly. She'd do the same for me.

Strange murmurs from a distance kept my attention rapt, although those walking ahead of me remained quiet. I could swear there was reverence as well as purpose in their steps. I hung back as one by one they began to disappear through an oversized doorway. What little light illuminated the corridor was limited, almost as if the room was glowing. The closer I came, the more I realized the lights were flickering. Candles.

I darted my head into the doorway, realizing I was correct, although the candles were flameless instead of being real. That didn't change the fact the glow only made whatever was going on seem erotic in nature. While I could barely understand what I was seeing, I was certain Kelly was being led up to the stage.

No. No! This was crazy.

Only after rising onto my tiptoes did I realize the girl I'd followed wasn't Kelly after all. Before I had a chance to venture any further inside, I felt a savage pull and was jerked back into the hallway.

Thick fingers wrapped around my throat, and I was pushed against the wall. I immediately slammed my fists against a hard body, fighting with everything I had. "Get off me."

"I heard you were a little fighter." The stranger tightened his hold, his fingers digging into my skin.

I wanted to respond, but my heart was in my throat. He had a vengeful look on his face, his strong jaw clenched tightly. I involuntarily dragged my tongue across my dry lips, and he snickered.

"You're in a restricted area, little pet."

Little pet.

I was thrown by the use of the two words, and my body's immediate reaction, my nipples taut.

While I didn't recognize the man's deep voice, the husky tone was unsettling. The dim lighting made his features appear ominous. The stranger was very tall, at least six foot five, dwarfing me easily. He was broad shouldered with huge arms, the muscles bulging against his suit jacket. His scent reminded me of a forest just after a rainstorm, fresh and inviting. Yet I sensed danger infused with his use of power.

I continued to fight him even as it felt as if the breath was being sucked from my body.

Nothing could hide his gorgeous, carved physique. His jaw was chiseled, his lips meant for kissing. I blinked several times, fighting the ridiculous urge to see what his mouth tasted like.

"And you're a very bad girl."

His seductive tone was tainted with a hint of implied danger. It was also a clear indication Jonas had seen me.

"Don't touch me."

He laughed. "I take what I want. That's a privilege afforded to members of the house."

His lips were dangerously close to mine, his heated breath cascading across my face.

"Let. Me. Go." My voice was raspy, my throat closing.

"Mmm... Is that what you really want, Sage?"

Oh, God. He knew my name.

"No," I squeaked.

"Aren't you intrigued by what's happening in the bowels of this building?" He laughed softly, daring to brush his lips across mine. "Do you want to see hot, sweaty bodies fucking, or would you prefer to participate in a kinky orgy? Maybe you'd enjoy remaining a voyeur. Huh? Maybe you'd like to feel the lash of a whip or be chained naked for the entire party to see. Do you crave humiliation? Would you enjoy if I force you onto all fours, collared and leashed?"

When I didn't say anything, he gently stroked his finger down the side of my face.

"You're a psychopath," I hissed. *Oh, great. Entice him even more.*

"We're just men who appreciate a beautiful woman. And you are exquisite."

The deep rumble of his voice sent a wave of vibrations through me. Why didn't his words make me sick? I squeezed my eyes shut, trying to turn my head, but he wouldn't allow it.

"I will enjoy having you as a little pet."

Pet? The man was absolutely out of his mind. *Or he knows about your stories.* "Fuck. You." I needed to get the hell out of here.

"We'll get to that. I promise you. Every hole will be used appropriately, leaving you wet and sore."

Rage tore through me and I jerked my arm back and cracked it across his face. He didn't react, other than the fire in his eyes burning brighter.

Then he yanked my arms over my head, easily wrapping one massive hand around both wrists. He took a few seconds, allowing his heated gaze to fall, enjoying the fact that he was tormenting me.

"You shouldn't have done that, but I do like a girl with spirit. It makes breaking them much tastier."

Breaking me. I'd been lured to the party on purpose. I was certain of it. Why? Was Kelly in on it? If so, why warn me?

"What do want from me?"

"Mmm... your total compliance. Eventually, your complete surrender."

"A cold day in hell will occur first." My mouth was dry, my throat starting to close. This entire thing had been nothing but a setup. But for what purpose?

His laugh was throaty, insinuating raw danger as well as primal needs.

Why were my nipples aching, straining against the soft material of my dress?

"That can be arranged, but not before you're well used."

I was sick to my stomach, but more so because something stirred deep in my core, a red-hot moment of arousal that embarrassed me. "Who the fuck do you think you are?"

"Hunter. And I live up to my name. Are you my little prey, beautiful Sage? I think you are." He captured my mouth, and I did what I could to push him away. My actions were worthless. When he tried to shove his tongue past my lips, I managed to keep him from doing so, still wiggling in his hold. Then he pressed his thumb under my chin, the move forcing my mouth to open. He thrust his tongue inside, the kiss rough and passionate.

My heart thudded against my chest, raw and filthy images floating through my mind.

This was just like what I'd written. Oh, God. This was nothing but a game.

The taste of him was sweeter than I'd anticipated. I'd thought someone so vile would taste of acid and bark. Instead, the hint of peppermint and bourbon infused my senses along with his lingering scent of sandalwood and spices, a toxic combination. I was lightheaded, more from the continued pressure he was using. When I realized that I'd arched my back and my fists were clenching his shirt in my fingers, I was mortified.

How could I feel anything other than repulsion for this bastard of a man?

He dominated my tongue, acting as if I belonged to him. Then he slipped his hand under my dress as he used his knee to force my legs open further. I wanted to be repulsed by the touch of a stranger's hand, but I wasn't. Another series of electrified sensations shot through me. For the first time in my life, someone was touching me intimately, and it felt so good, igniting the darkness inside.

The kiss became more passionate, his tongue sweeping back and forth aggressively. He rolled the tip of his finger across the front of my thong, and I moaned into his mouth. A part of me was sick inside, but the dazzling vibrations humming through my body accepted his forceful gesture. How could I feel so electric inside when everything about the man was something I abhorred? I arched my back, struggling with the emotions even as electric jolts jetted through every cell.

He toyed with me, sliding his finger up and down the thin lace, obviously able to tell my panties were soaked. When he jerked my thong to the side, easing his hand underneath, another wave of lust curtailed any rational thoughts. The moment he touched my clit, flicking the tip of his finger back and forth, I felt my knees buckling. No. This couldn't happen. I wasn't this kind of girl, and especially not with a man who made my skin crawl.

He wasn't taking no for an answer, teasing then pinching my clit until my entire body was on fire, the need unstoppable.

I started to fight him even as he thrust his fingers inside, pumping several times. Every cell in my body was suddenly ablaze, my pulse skipping. No. No. Even though I'd longed to have someone in my life, it wasn't about this.

Or him, no matter if he was a perfect god.

Yet I couldn't get free from his hold as the man collected my moans in his mouth and rubbed his thumb around my clit, pumping hard and fast into my pussy. Stars floated in front of my eyes, the wildfire spinning out of control.

He broke the kiss, a low growl rumbling from his chest. "That's it, little pet." He was goading me into a climax, and I couldn't seem to stop the madness.

My body betrayed me completely as tingles erupted into white-hot pinging stabs of heat.

"Oh. Oh… I can't. I just…"

"Sshhh… This is a gift, good girl. Take it. It's only the beginning."

His voice was melodic, luring me into a nightmare that I couldn't evacuate from. But even worse, I wasn't certain I wanted to. I lolled my head, unable to stop the freight train. An orgasm tore through me, and I bit back a scream, aware that several people had walked past, watching my humiliation occur. I'd lost myself completely to the rapture, bucking against his hand just like I'd envisioned myself doing.

He never blinked, the edges of his lips curling.

"What a very good girl indeed."

His praise was surprisingly appealing, tiny prickles dancing across my skin as a warm flush swept up from my throat.

When he finally backed away, I was breathless, my heart thudding against my chest. My eyes were hazy, but I watched as he slipped his fingers into his mouth, the slurping sound exaggerated but strangely arousing.

"I was right. Very sweet."

"You're... terrible."

"Yes, I am. Be careful, little fawn. There are beasts crawling in these hallways. I wouldn't want to see you get eaten."

Suddenly, I found my resolve and maybe a little of my lost mind.

"Are you out of your mind? Who the hell do you think you are?" While I tried to push away from him, he had me crowded against the wall, one leg casually pressed against mine. He wrapped his hand around my throat for a second time, and I felt a hitch in my chest, panic rising to the surface. Once again, I refused to provide him with a second of satisfaction that he'd unnerved me, glaring in his eyes with utter defiance. Everything about him screamed control and power, the corded muscles in his neck straining.

"I'm one of the hosts for the evening. It would seem you've been a naughty guest, snooping where you don't belong. The things you could see might make you go blind."

There was no doubt Jonas had seen my face. Another trickle of fear pounded my system, but I refused to let Hunter see how scared I was. At this point, the objective was to get the hell out of here in one piece. "I was looking for my friend. Maybe you're right in that one of your Neanderthal assholes plans on eating her."

He laughed, finally releasing his hold on my neck. I took a deep breath, mesmerized by what appeared to be a luminescent glow in his eyes. However, the look on his face was pure evil.

"Nah, darlin'. Kelly already belongs to us. She knows we can do anything we want. We own her."

Jesus. The sense of entitlement was worse than I was used to, even at a school where the kids wore an attitude like an allowance given their stature in life. "You can't own a person, or did you skip out on your history lessons? You certainly don't appear that intelligent." I knew I was pressing my luck, but maybe if I ruffled his feathers, he'd leave me alone since I refused to be one of his groupies.

The look of amusement on his face faded. "I suggest you watch your mouth."

"Why? I can do and say anything I want since I'm a free woman."

He pulled away a few feet, and I took that as the single chance I'd get to run. I didn't make it more than three feet before he snagged my arm, yanking me toward him with my back against his chest. As he ground his hips, pressing his throbbing cock into my bottom, I hissed, doing what I could to elbow him.

"I've been patient so far, sweet Sage, but a man can only handle so much. I suggest you learn your place."

CHAPTER 7

Sage

This was getting serious, more so than I understood.

What unnerved me the most about Hunter was how aloof he was, as if manhandling a stranger was just a typical day in his world. The traitorous sparks continued to swarm my core, the electrified heat unwanted yet impossible to ignore.

Hunter continued glaring at me with an impassive, lecherous desire. He truly believed I was his for the taking.

"My place? Let me go, or I'll have you arrested." I realized my threat meant nothing to him. When he laughed, the sound reverberating in my ears, I shivered uncontrollably.

"You have a lot to learn, but your training starts now." He kept me in his clutches, my struggles meaning nothing as he led me down a different hallway to a set of stairs. There was no way I was getting out of his hold. When he jerked me into the stairwell, he pushed me against the wall, gripping my chin. "And baby, as of right now, you belong to us."

Us.

Who was he talking about—the entire house, or the particular group of men Kelly had warned me about too late? I glared him in the eye, doing everything I could to keep from showing any fear. The bastard didn't deserve a single emotion other than rage. "I don't think you have any idea who my family is." While Hunter was extraordinarily gorgeous, there was a detachment in his eyes that kept a cold shiver flowing through every inch of my body.

As if he had no conscience.

"I assure you that we know everything there is to know about you, including the adorable mole just under your left breast."

"What did you say?" Had the bastard been watching me? Oh, my God. The rose petal. I almost choked on the realization that I'd been one hundred percent right.

"You look particularly delicious in your pink nightie, and I do so love the flamingo shower curtain you girls selected. Girlie and innocent. Is that what you are, little pet?"

Now I couldn't stop shaking. He and his disgusting friends had stalked me. They'd gone through my things. They'd had cameras installed. Oh, God. Nothing had been sacred. I chewed on my inner cheek to keep from making a single sound, a feat I was certain I couldn't maintain. Why did I have a horrible feeling Kelly had allowed them inside? No. I refused to believe that about my friend. We'd talked about boys and our future and how many kids we wanted to have, lamenting over our controlling parents. She wouldn't do that to me. That meant the three Elite members she'd warned me about were more dangerous than I'd thought. The question remained. What did they want from me? A plan so extravagant couldn't be just about sex.

While I was paralyzed with horror at a reality that seemed far removed from anything that could possibly occur, he laughed.

The sound was dark, angry, and very seductive. When he lowered his head, his lips only centimeters away, I bit down on the lower one until I tasted blood. Hunter didn't react right away. Then he jerked his head back, issuing a low, throaty growl.

"Bad little pet. You're going to pay for that." He wiped his thumb through the drops of blood, shoving it into his mouth and acting as if he was sipping nectar from the gods. "As far as the fucker who spawned you. I assure you, princess, that he can't save you. We are far more powerful than daddy dearest."

A prickle of heat mixed with the increasing fury. There it was. The reason for the charade. The hatred of my father was evident. But why? He didn't run in the same circles. He was a good man who had happened to make a fortune. The vile determination in Hunter's voice kept my stomach in knots. Challenging him would mean nothing.

After laughing again, he pulled me up the stairs with enough force that I tripped several times. By the time he got to a door on the fourth floor, I was in a panic, fighting him with everything I had.

He was too strong for me and pushed me into a room without much trouble.

"Our lioness had arrived at our lair," Hunter chortled.

Two other men were inside, one of them Cristiano. Hunter released his hold, shoving me further into the room, then standing in front of the door.

The third man that I'd seen but hadn't talked to studied me intently, his eyes full of the same hunger I'd seen in the other two. They were also just as hypnotizing, drawing me into a level of darkness that yanked at the already lit fire in my core. I would never understand nor forgive myself for my body's reaction. However, whatever they had in mind had nothing to do with passion. Their determination was all about power and complete control.

And revenge.

I felt it in my bones.

He had a sharpness about him that made it feel as if a cold arctic blast had shot through the room. He looked at me as anyone would when regarding a possible purchase.

To him, I was nothing but something to be owned.

"Well. Well. The little lioness bites," the third guy said after glancing at Hunter's lip, his deep voice resonating in vibrating jabs.

"Yeah, I do. You should see what I can do with my fists," I responded, backing as far away from them as possible. I'd spouted the words without thinking. Now, my heart was in my throat, a crushing boulder threatening to suffocate me.

When the three of them laughed, I shivered visibly. The third guy swaggered closer until he was only a few inches away. "My name is Cain Cross, Sage. I've been waiting for a very long time to make your acquaintance."

"I wish I could say I'd paid any attention to you at all. You're just not noteworthy." Of course, I'd seen him before, all three of them. They were impossible to miss as they strolled through the campus together, shoving aside anyone who'd dared get in their way. But something nagged at the back of my mind. Then I remembered. I'd literally run into Cain on my first day. He'd been helpful, including managing to find my dorm room. As his dark eyes assessed me, I realized his assistance had been nothing but a ploy.

"Is that really the truth, lovely Sage? I've noticed how you watch us cross the campus. I've seen the clear look of lust in your eyes."

He wasn't wrong, all three men being the things my darkest fantasies were made of. "Then you need to get your eyes checked."

The three of them laughed is if watching a comedian on stage.

"I decided this is the perfect moment for the three of us to claim you." Cain was obviously in control.

"You mean, you've been stalking me."

The corners of his lips turned up, and he raked his heated gaze down to my toes. He was just as gorgeous as the other two, sophisticated in a way most twenty-two-year-old boys couldn't be. He appeared older, the dark, curly hair thick, the stubble crossing his angular jaw adding to a sense of danger and seduction. As if sensing I was attracted to him, the moment he eased his lingering look upward, he stopped on my breasts, dragging his tongue across his sensual lips.

"We do anything we want to those we own."

God, the arrogance was disgusting.

"As I told your buddy, you can't own a human. You're not just an asshole but a fool if you think you'll get away with keeping me for any length of time. My father will see to it that this house and every member of the Elite is expelled. And I'll be there when they toss your asses outside the pearly little gates."

Cain obviously didn't like my smile or my sense of humor. He grabbed my arm, twisting it around my back as he pulled me against his heated body. "That can't happen if you're locked inside a cage, but I'm getting ahead of myself. First, you're going to be punished for your egregious actions. Going where you don't belong inside this house will only provide you with answers you won't like. But afterwards, if you're a good girl, we'll teach you what rapturous pleasure is all about."

"You're out of your mind." When he dragged me onto my toes, fisting the back of my hair, I reacted without thinking, spitting in his face. "Let. Go. Of. Me."

Cain closed his eyes, his nostrils flaring. He kept his fingers tangled in my hair, freeing my arm as he wiped the glob of saliva from his face. When he opened his eyelids, the deep gray I'd seen before drifted into obsidian black, the snarl he wore cold and calculated. I expected him to backhand me or worse. What I didn't expect was the smile crossing his face.

"I like this girl very much. More than I should. I think all three of us will enjoy playing with our new pet tremendously."

Pet? The three of them? He was serious. I glanced toward the door, and Hunter shook his head. I could swear they were able to read my mind. The scenario was almost exactly like one I'd written about three months before. The tightness in my throat increased from the knowledge they'd been watching me for some time.

Cain lifted his eyebrow, his low-slung growl rumbling in my chest. "What's wrong, princess? Are you afraid every single fantasy you have will come true?" All three laughed, Cristiano dragging his tongue across his bottom lip. The revulsion continued racing through every muscle, but the sick desire I had was winning the battle.

"Yeah? Well, I don't like you," I told him before driving my fists into his chest, my voice nothing but an ugly whisper.

"You witnessed something that was only allowed to be seen and heard by Elite members. And you disobeyed the rules. You were told to remain in the party room. Were you not?" Hunter asked the question casually as he removed his jacket, walking closer.

As he unfastened the long sleeves of his crisp white shirt, I couldn't seem to take my eyes off him. He was even more muscular than I'd originally thought, and as he rolled the material over his forearms, I was struck by the magnificence of his chiseled angles, veins throbbing on both sides.

"You mean witnessing Cristiano almost beating a man nearly to death for no real reason?" I snapped.

"At least she freely admits it," Cristiano said as he took long strides across the room and almost out of my sight. "I assure you that Theodore deserved much worse. He is a true pervert."

And they didn't think they were?

"Yes, you're right. That means perhaps we'll go easier on you, our little pet, if you repent of your sins." Cain rubbed his hand on his trousers, then jerked me closer. Everything about the man was possessive. But there was something else I couldn't put my finger on, the kind of obsession that could make a man go mad.

"Repent of my sins? What does that mean?" I blurted out, hating the sound of the weakness in my voice.

"That means I'm giving you a choice," he answered, then threw a look toward Hunter.

"What?"

Hunter grinned, desire emblazing his eyes. I could tell the three of them had a close relationship, which created a storm of butterflies inside. A sick vision of being taken by all three of them popped into my mind. "Let me think," he continued as he tapped a finger across his lip. "Ah, yes. You can either accept our punishment, or your little friend Kelly will receive it tenfold, and you'll be required to watch. It's entirely up to you."

Every word out of his mouth, his superior attitude, and the way he acted as if he already owned me should have repulsed the intelligent girl inside, but I was far too excited to be angry. Or concerned. This was everything I'd wanted but had denied myself. Still, I refused to give in.

"What kind of punishment?" The three men were serious. Maybe the best thing to do was cooperate for now.

Are you still trying to fool yourself?

My inner voice was chiding, more so than I could handle.

Somehow, I'd find a way to tear down their organization. Even as I promised myself I wasn't an active participant, my skin burning with desire from their controlling touches, I couldn't seem to stop trembling, my resolve starting to crumble.

The fight inside of me continued, the woman I wanted to be versus the one I'd been forced to accept.

Cain's intense words was some crazy cue for Cristiano to turn around. In his hand was a leather strap, but not like a belt. It was thinner. I sucked in my breath as he cracked it through the air, moaning as the action made a crackling, whooshing sound.

"You're going to beat me with a whip?" I was mortified, but suddenly, my panties were damp. I was crazy for wanting something so... brutal. Kinky. I had no thoughts to adequately describe what I was thinking.

"We might be savages, beautiful Sage, but it would be too much of a pity to mar your gorgeous skin. A simple spanking tonight will suffice. However…" Cain allowed the comment to linger. "I assure you that we won't be as gentle with Kelly should you decline."

"You're a fucking bastard."

All three men obviously thought my words were meant as a compliment, beaming from ear to ear.

"Actually, we are very reasonable men," Hunter added.

"You expect me to believe that?"

"You have a choice," Cain continued. "That's only fair. What will it be, our disobedient pet?"

I had no other choice if I wanted to get out of here. "As long as Kelly and I can leave afterwards, then spank me. I don't care. But you won't touch Kelly. You won't hurt her."

"Hmm… Should we trust her?" Cristiano asked the others as he moved closer, still cracking the strap as if trying to terrify me.

"Why not? She's a very nice girl, and we know where she lives. And we have cameras keeping an eye on her every move. Here's the thing, Sage. As of tonight, we own you. That means you'll come to us when we call, and you will do as we say, or the deal you just made is off. Is that understood?"

Cain was enjoying every moment of this. If they thought for one minute I'd surrender to them under any circumstances, then he and the rest of them were out of their minds. I'd call my parents, then move us to a hotel until the end of the semester.

"Fine. Agreed." When I threw out my arm for a handshake, Cain lifted his eyebrows. It was a move he hadn't expected.

He took a deep breath, the anger I'd seen in him fading slightly. Then he shook my hand, even more surprised my handshake was solid, more like a man's. An instant shot of electricity tore through both of us, the current red-hot. Suddenly, my mouth was dry, my pulse racing.

Hunter broke the odd connection by yanking out a chair. "I get to go first." He patted his lap, and I instantly felt like a bad girl. There was no reason, nor did it make any sense. I turned my head, biting my lower lip. The way the thin material of his trousers stretched across his massive thighs was pronounced, but not nearly as much as the cloth over the thick cock between his legs.

He caught my lingering gaze and smiled. Then he beckoned with a single finger, patting his lap a second time. "Come here, little girl."

Shame tore through me that I'd even agreed to this ridiculous moment. The only justification for losing my mind was that I knew they had some kind of spell over Kelly. They would follow through with their promise if I ignored the deal I'd just made.

I moved closer, realizing both Cain and Cristiano were not so patiently awaiting their turns. The way Cristiano was snapping the strap against his hand had a strange effect on me, my mind foggy as it tried to block out the sound. But the anticipation was exhilarating instead of terrifying.

Hunter pulled me across his lap, yanking my dress up to my waist.

"What are you doing?" I immediately struggled in his hold, almost slipping off his lap. My action pushed his throbbing cock against my stomach, and I gasped.

He jerked me against his chest, holding me in place as he ripped down my panties. He had his arm wrapped around my waist, and when he issued a single hard crack against my bottom, I threw my hand back. Snagging it immediately, he pushed my arm down, digging his fingers into my skin.

"You're going to remain a fighter. Aren't you?" There was amusement in his voice instead of anger, the man obviously toying with me. When he brought his hand down several additional times, I sucked in my breath, trying to keep from tearing up.

"Yes!" I hissed, holding the anger deep inside of me. I kicked out my legs, which only added to the friction. My stomach remained in knots, but a crazy sense of desire formed in every cell. Panting, I tried to block out what I was thinking, but with every crack of his hand, both the pain and the wetness between my legs prevented me from doing so.

Hunter issued six in rapid succession, moving from one side to the other. Then he had the audacity to caress my skin, issuing a husky growl. "I think our little pet is wet. What do you boys think?"

No. No. No. I was horrified that my resolve had shattered so quickly.

Cain moved closer, crouching down, his grin practically evil. He rubbed his fingers across my face, then rolled the tips down my back, ever so slowly moving down the crack of my ass. When he eased his hand between my legs, I sucked in my breath. He was just trying to get a reaction.

I promised myself that wasn't going to happen, yet when he slipped a single finger past my swollen folds, the scent of my desire wafted to my nose. Another moment of mortification tingled every muscle, embarrassment staining my skin. The fact he shouldn't be touching me made it filthy and sinful, awakening the woman inside.

"Yes, she's very wet." Cain practically purred his answer, pumping several times. My body reacted involuntarily, shifting back and forth against Hunter's thick cock. "And tight. So very tight. Don't worry, little pet. We will enjoy shackling you just like you so desperately crave. All in due time."

"You don't own me."

"That's where you're wrong. You have three masters now. Make no mistake that when we take you, and that will happen, you will learn what pleasure is. When you come the first time, you'll beg for more, exhausted and overwhelmed with raw ecstasy. And I assure you that it will be the beginning of a beautiful affair. Every hole will be well used, but you'll crave more, begging the men who own you to continue making you weak."

"No," I managed, but the pleasure he was providing was already luring me into a place of surrender.

"Yes, little pet. After we've broken you down, we'll put you together piece by piece. Then we'll start all over again. As of right now, this very moment, you belong to us."

His words sent another wave of heat straight to my core.

He added another finger or two, thrusting harder and faster. I was lightheaded, bucking against his hand, the build-up of fire in my belly unlike anything I'd ever experienced. I wasn't a virgin, but Cain was touching me more intimately than the single man I'd been with had done. As if he knew my body better than I did.

A single whimper escaped my mouth, and I did what I could to bite it back, fighting the desire that burned brightly inside. I did everything I could to keep from releasing, but as a climax roared into my system, Cain seemed pleased with my reaction, the look on his face even more carnal than before.

"Oh…" When the single whimpered word left my lips, he closed his eyes in satisfaction.

Seconds later, he pulled out, staring at his glistening finger before shoving it into his mouth. The sounds he made were exaggerated as well as disgusting.

"Yes, she tastes like peach nectar. I think it's time she's handed off to Cristiano." He stood, wrapping his hand around my arm and guiding me to my feet. As he brushed his hand down my side, he took a deep breath and held it. Then he ripped off my panties with a single snap of his wrist, pulling my thong to his mouth and nose.

I was swaying, my heart aching from the fact that I'd enjoyed the moment of pleasure.

"You will be delicious to break, little pet. More so than I thought. The three of us will enjoy taking our time with you." He didn't wait for any response, pulling me away by several steps then tossing me over the edge of the round table in the room. He pressed his hand against the small of my back, holding me in place as Cristiano walked closer. "Continue being a good girl for us. Will you?"

Was he seriously asking that question?

Cristiano moved behind me, yanking my dress up even further. "I'd grip the other side of the table if I were you."

I reluctantly slid my arms across the table, wrapping my finger around the edge and digging my fingernails into the wood. Then I took several deep breaths as he teased me by sliding the belt down my back to my leg. He took his time rolling it to my thigh then shifting to my other leg, pulling the tip back to my bottom.

The first crack came without warning, the sound as the strap hit my skin shocking. Then I felt a tingle of discomfort. Then another strike was issued. Then another. As pain washed through me, I gasped, uncertain I could withstand the two men taking turns.

He remained silent as he yanked my legs further apart. I had no doubt he was able to see my glistening pussy lips. I cringed deep inside, keeping my eyes closed as he issued four more, one coming right after the other. I heard myself crying out, terrified to admit to myself how the anguish pulled another wave of longing. My mind was still foggy, unable to process that I'd agreed to this.

His sigh was exaggerated, and he rolled his finger from one side of my bottom to the other. The heat from the spanking pulsed, my pussy throbbing. He brought his hand down again. And again. Now the anguish was blinding. I jerked up from the table, gasping for air.

"Relax, little pet. You're doing well." The husky tone of his voice was even more ominous than Cain's, thrilling in an entirely different way. "There's more to come." He chuckled darkly, then cracked out six more, two hitting my upper thighs.

I kicked out, shifting back and forth. When I opened my eyes, I noticed Cain was standing in wait, his eyes narrowed as he remained unblinking. I stared at him, knowing he was the one behind this. But his purpose was so dark and demented that another slice of terror skittered through my system.

As his expression of hunger increased, he finally motioned to Cristiano that his time was up.

Cristiano growled his response, then leaned over, planting his hands on either side of me. When he nuzzled against my ear, his heated breath seared my skin.

"Just wait, beautiful one. Just wait."

Cain snapped the implement from Cristiano's hand, taking his time walking toward me, the sound of his boots hitting the floor jarring.

"Such a bad girl. Aren't you?" The words were almost accusatory.

I remained quiet, thinking it better not to poke the beast any longer. He also wasted no time in bringing the thin strap down, only his strike was more brutal. The agony was instantaneous, sucking all the air from my lungs.

Give him no satisfaction. The mantra continued to tear through my mind.

He chuckled softly and issued three more. Then he pressed the full weight of his body against mine. The fact that he remained silent added to my apprehension.

The man was full of possessive need. I could feel it straining deep within him. After cracking the strap four more times, he tossed it away, his laugh dark and demanding. As he pressed his full body weight against me, for a few seconds I couldn't breathe. He shifted his cock back and forth across my bruised bottom, and I trembled from the heat of his breath.

From his scent.

And from his increasing hunger.

"Do you know what's going to happen now, little pet?"

I managed to grab a few very short breaths, the self-loathing continuing as the scent of my longing permeated the air around us. "No."

He pressed his lips against the nape of my neck, rolling his lips toward my ear, his whisper harsh. "Now we fuck you in every hole, filling you with our cocks. After that, we'll start over again. Would you like that, bad girl? Do you hunger for three men to fulfill your dark, sinful fantasies?"

I wanted to say no, to scream it out to anyone who would hear. But if I did so, I'd be lying, especially to myself.

So, I answered with the ugly truth that would likely haunt me for the rest of my life.

"Yes…"

CHAPTER 8

Cristiano

Her admittance was all the three of us needed. Sage was breathless, the blush of red on her bottom the perfect color. As she mewed, I glanced at Hunter, who seemed hypnotized by the entire situation.

We'd waited so long for this moment that our needs were little more than animalistic.

Lust.

It was all consuming for the three of us. The fact that I'd shared two different women with Cain and Hunter during the years showed a pattern, but neither event had awakened the darkness inside. Somehow, Sage had managed to do that as well as invoke the demon living inside of me. I was the big bad wolf, and my little lamb had no understanding of the filthy things I wanted to do to her.

The thought of sharing her for the long term didn't seem as insane as it once had. We'd even talked about combining our businesses, forming a powerhouse corporation that could never be bested. Maybe that was exactly what would happen after graduation. I'd heard Chicago was a cool place to live. My cock twitched, throbbing to the point of pain from just thinking about the possibility for a future together.

Did I really think she'd go for it, or that her parents wouldn't interfere? If her father was the assassin, then he'd put bullets in our heads the first opportunity he had. I wanted to laugh at myself given capturing her had initially been about revenge. Now, I was thinking about sharing my life with her. Jesus. I was suddenly thinking like Cain, which was ridiculous.

I'd watched in near silence as Cain had taken control over stalking her, watching her as if she was a little bird trying to flee her cage. I would swear she knew we'd been voyeurs, her provocative dances in front of open blinds as close to portraying sexual acts as I'd ever seen. I'd hungered for her to the point of masturbating almost every night, keeping an image of her face in the forefront of my mind. Now, I couldn't wait to have her plump lips wrapped around my thick cock.

Cain gathered her into his arms, immediately yanking her dress over her head as he helped her to a standing position. Then he cupped her breasts, pinching her nipples between his fingers. While she struggled in his hold at first, within seconds she was rubbing her palms down his thighs.

My cock had been completely aroused for too long, my hunger reaching levels I'd yet to experience. All because of a beautiful girl who'd gotten on the radar of a monster. Who was I to judge Cain? I'd participated in the beheadings of my father's enemies during a trip home for Christmas.

It was the way of my life as well as Cain's, and Hunter's wasn't much different given the notorious reputation of his father. But to think that Cain was dead-set on keeping Sage permanently meant we were entering another realm of power that would change everything, including our futures.

However, I was also smart enough to realize that Cain was fucking nuts. He'd likely toss her aside after getting his fill. In my eyes, she was far too special to spoil. She hadn't known I'd been in the audience at every performance she'd participated in, including the few off campus, something her professors had no clue about, and if I had to guess, something her parents would freak out over.

She'd always disguised herself, appearing the heady rocker when singing her heart out. Red hair. Blonde hair. Hell, she'd gone through a phase of wearing a neon pink wig. None of her disguises had ever fooled me. I'd been there, sitting in a seat for as long as she performed, protecting her against the evils of the world.

Blood had stained my skin from beating a stupid drunk asshole who'd hassled her three nights before. He'd threatened to call the police. In turn, I'd made certain he knew that if I needed to have a 'talk' with him a second time, he'd lose more than just one of his fingers. I'd do it all over again to keep her protected.

As Cain yanked her head back by her hair, crushing his mouth over hers, I ripped off my jacket, tossing it aside. Then I curled my fingers around the back of my shirt, yanking it over my head to the floor. By the time I approached, her nipples were rock hard, the scent of her desire forcing me to lick my lips.

I rubbed my hands around her waist, crawling them to her thighs.

Cain pulled away, winking as he glanced at me. "She's all yours, brother. At least for a few minutes."

I spun her around, enjoying her expression as I fisted her hair. "You are beautiful."

Sage placed her hand on my chest, allowing her heated gaze to fall slowly to my belt buckle as she chewed on her lower lip. When she brushed the tips of her fingers down to my belt buckle, I sucked in my breath. A part of me wanted this to last all night long, but I had a feeling my body wouldn't cooperate.

When she lifted her chin, I wrapped my hand around the back of her neck, pulling her onto her toes.

"You will never break me," she said, yet the twinkle in her eye indicated she was intrigued by the possibility.

"We shall see, little lamb. Won't we?"

She jerked at my belt, managing to unfasten the buckle. Then I pushed her down to her knees, taking a deep breath as she rolled the material over my hips.

"You don't waste any time," Hunter said as he approached.

"No, brother. We've wasted far too much time as it is."

He growled as he crouched down, easing the hair from her face. "I can't wait to slide my cock deep inside your pussy." I watched as he raked his fingers down her back, his expression darkening.

When she wrapped her hand around the base of my cock, I couldn't hold back an intense moan. "Suck me, little lamb. I want to see your lips surrounding my cockhead."

Sage pumped the bottom of my shaft, twisting her hand until she created friction. Giving me a salacious look, she slid her other hand between my legs, teasing my balls. She rolled them between her fingers, squeezing until the pressure caused another growl to escape my throat.

"Be careful taunting me," I said under my breath.

"Why?"

Her question made me laugh. When she finally wrapped her voluptuous lips around my cockhead, I grabbed the top of her head. It was difficult not to ram my shaft deep inside her hot little mouth. I was able to maintain control as she used her strong jaw muscles to suck, yet my body started to shake almost immediately. "Fuck."

"That hot?" Hunter mused.

"You have no idea."

"She's a little firecracker." He rose to his feet, unfastening his belt. As soon as he freed his cock, she eased her hand to the base, pumping as she'd done to mine.

I tangled my fingers in her hair, closing my eyes as the pleasure increased. I didn't want to shoot off my load too early. I'd prefer to do so in her tight pussy. The thought brought a smile to my face.

As soon as Hunter groaned, I opened my eyes. She was giving him a hand job, one with a magical purpose in mind. I had to wonder just how innocent our little lamb truly was. Perhaps the erotic stories she wrote had been from experience. Or maybe she was a quick study. Whatever the case, I was in seventh heaven.

"That's it, beautiful girl. Suck me."

Sage pulled back, blowing across my cockhead. Then she tugged against my hold, pouting her lips until I gave her some freedom. She licked across Hunter's slit before taking his cockhead into her mouth. He immediately threw his head back, issuing a harsh bellow.

I heard Cain chuckling from the other side of the room where he stood as if emperor and director of the seduction. I rolled my hand down the taut muscles of my stomach, stroking the base as she took Hunter's cock down an inch at a time. While it was more than fair to allow him to enjoy her wet lips, my needs were selfish. There'd be no way I could hold off for long.

After grabbing a handful of her hair, I tugged her back, my gaze hazy as I stared into hers. A man could find his soul in the sapphire depths of her eyes.

If there was a chance one could be found. I'd accepted a long time ago that I'd grow into a man with no conscience just like my father. It was strange that after the limited time she'd spent in my clutches, I wanted to become a better man. Maybe the fucking bourbon was spiked.

I allowed her to drag her sweet tongue down the underside of my cock, tempting me into becoming more brutal when she popped one of my balls into her hot mouth.

"Fuck, woman. Careful." As if my suggestion was going to be heeded. She'd shed her inhibitions, accepting her fate in the hands of three savage men. I admired her spunk and tenacity, but that only made me want to break her even more.

As soon as she pulled the tip of my dick into her mouth, I impaled her throat, unable to keep my extreme hunger at bay. She had one hand wrapped around Hunter's cock, still twisting, the friction driving him nuts, but she placed her other hand on my thigh. The way she dug her fingernails into my skin was strangely appealing.

I rolled onto the balls of my feet, fucking her mouth as if I was a dying man. It had been so long since I'd been with a woman and this was... shit, I could come easily. My mind was a freaking, blurry mess from the buildup of stripping her of her innocence.

"That's it," I managed, barely able to focus. The strangled sounds she made were beautiful music, the only kind I wanted to hear. I'd already lost my precum to a slice of her tongue raking across my cockhead. My balls were aching, and I wanted to fill her mouth with my seed, requiring her to clean off every drop.

"My turn," Hunter growled, ripping her from my arms. I didn't fight him, needing to cool down. The scent of her pussy was far too attractive. Later, I'd come in her throat.

I backed away, fighting to keep from stumbling as I adjusted my trousers. Then I grabbed a glass, filling it in with Blackjack. "She's fucking incredible."

"Yeah, she is." Cain's gaze hadn't left her since I'd forced her onto her knees, forever watching like a hawk. He'd already removed his clothes and was now idly stroking his cock with enough pressure I could tell he was in pain. He was truly a twisted fuck, but that's why we got along so well. Hunter was the Yin to our dark Yang, keeping us centered when we often preferred going off the rails. "She's going to be a powerful addition to our lives."

"So, we'll get a big house in the outskirts of Chicago, defy the normal traditions?" I was mostly teasing, but as soon as I issued the suggestion, it was as if a light had gone off in his mind.

"That's exactly what we're going to do. She'll marry us. We'll raise a fucking passel of kids and rule the goddamn world. If anyone wants to fuck with us, they'll realize they made a huge mistake."

While I laughed, I could tell the man was serious. "We'll keep her in chains, tied to a huge bed."

He snorted, his eyes no longer focusing. "Something like that."

Nothing Cain said any longer shocked me. While I'd hungered for her almost as much, I hadn't imagined us together forever in the vision of my future. I wasn't certain any woman could handle my sadism or the heritage I'd grown up with.

"And how do you propose to keep her father from tracking us like dogs?" I pounded back a portion of my drink, curious as to his answer.

"That's simple," he said as he shrugged. "We kill the bastard. But first things first. We need to fuck her. Then we'll go hunting. In case you haven't experienced it. There's nothing like live, human prey."

CHAPTER 9

Sage

Sucking cock wasn't on my list of accomplishments, but as soon as I'd held Cristiano's thick shaft in my hand, all the fantasies that had chased every dream exploded in my mind. The taste of him was salty yet sweet, much like Hunter had been. I was shocked how large both men were, even more so that they were able to fit into my mouth.

I hadn't anticipated wanting this, even if I'd secretly admired them from afar.

"Baby. You are just off the chain," Hunter murmured as he ran his fingers through my hair. His legs were shaking, every muscle in his body stiffening almost from the beginning. The musky scent of his testosterone filled my senses, creating a series of tingles that matched the ache felt in my butt cheeks.

The spanking had been harsh yet erotic, pushing me to the edge of reason and sanity. For the first time in my life, it had felt as if I was flying free from the tethers of my life. And dear God, I wanted more.

Hunter fisted my hair at the scalp, holding me in place. "Open your mouth, little pet. You're going to take every inch."

I did as he commanded, swirling my tongue around his shaft as he gently pushed several inches inside. As soon as I began to suck, his breathing changed, more labored than before. They were all beautiful men, but there was something softer about Hunter. Maybe because he didn't come from cold-blooded killers like Cain and Cristiano. He was someone I almost believed I could trust, even if he would stop at nothing to take what he wanted.

After squeezing his balls, I hungrily engulfed another two inches. But that wasn't enough. He shoved my head down until my lower lip was resting on his testicles. I gagged but did what I could to relax my throat even as my eyes watered. His pants fell to the floor, and I wrapped my arm around his hips, pressing my hand against his rock-hard ass.

Goddamn the man was built, every muscle carved to perfection. As he started to pump, taking over control as Cristiano had, I continued to stroke the base. The moment and experience kept me lightheaded, my mind still trying to process everything that had happened. The thought of being their captive was insanely enticing.

I sensed Cain's return. I could also smell his need, as if seeing me with the other two had been too much for him to tolerate. Hunter laughed, pushing my shoulders then lifting my chin with a single finger. "That's just the beginning, baby. I'm going to take your tight little asshole."

"You might have to fight me for it," Cristiano growled.

"She's mine to claim first." Cain's voice had a deep vibrato, the husky sound adding to the anticipation.

Hunter tugged me to my feet, and when I glanced at Cain as he approached, I pressed my hand over my mouth. He was even more enticing naked, the deep 'V' leading from his abdomen making me shiver. A flicker of gold drew my attention to his thick cock, the piercing something I'd heard about but never seen before. Kelly had mentioned that it added to the sensations, able to cause a powerful orgasm. I wouldn't know.

He had an indescribable look on his face, immediately jerking me off my feet, forcing my legs around his sculpted hips. Then he strode toward the wall, shoving me against the hard surface with just enough force that I moaned.

"They got to experience your wet mouth, but I get to fuck your tight pussy first, sweet pet." He pushed me further up the wall, and I struggled to hold on, digging my fingers into his shoulders.

"Don't worry, baby. You're not going anywhere." He hoisted me up even further until my legs were wrapped around his shoulders.

"What are you doing?" I had no clue how I'd managed to speak at all.

"I'm a hungry man who needs to be fed. And you're the sweetest thing around." He wrapped his lip around my clit, immediately pulling the tender tissue between his lips.

"Oh. My. God." I was thrown into a complete moment of rapture, stunned from the number of electric shocks coursing through me like white lightning. Every sound he made was like an animal in heat, and within seconds, my hardened bud was tender from the roughness of his actions.

But I could care less, the pleasure unlike anything I'd imagined. I lifted one arm over my head, slapping my hand against the wall, tangling the fingers of my other in his thick hair. Saying I was lightheaded didn't cut it. I was lost in a sea of pleasure that I hadn't known existed. "Oh. Oh. Oh."

He finally released my clit, dragging his tongue up and down the length of my slickened folds. I tossed my head back and forth the second he darted his tongue into my tight channel. Then I heard myself laughing, then moaning, my toes curling from the intensity of his actions.

Panting, I noticed both Cristiano and Hunter had finally removed their clothes, not so patiently waiting for their turn by the stern expressions on their faces.

I was allowed to bask in their ruggedness until my vision became too fuzzy from the rapture.

"Mmmm... So sweet. Nectar of the gods," Cain murmured, then buried his head in my wetness. He was an expert at what he was doing, bringing me close, then pulling back.

I laughed nervously, my heart thudding against my chest. My toes were curled as the first hint of a climax tickled my senses. It was incredible someone could bring me to this point with his mouth alone. I clenched my eyes shut, bucking hard against his hold.

Cain growled and dug his fingers into my hips. "Come for me, little pet. Don't make me tell you twice."

The deep rumble of his voice and heated breath against my wetness was all that was needed. He sucked on my clit once again, and I erupted in a powerful orgasm. No vibrator could do what this man was doing to me, pushing every button, driving the rest of my inhibitions aside.

"Yes. Yes! Oh, yes!" My cries were bedraggled and there was no sense in opening my eyes. There was no chance I could focus on anything.

Yet I heard the other two hungry men and their labored breathing. It wouldn't be long until they returned to take possession. Wasn't this every girl's fantasy? Three men?

I bit back another cry, fighting to keep my mind intact as another orgasm swept through me. This time, my scream was little more than strangled syllables, the ecstasy so intense.

Seconds later, Cain kissed and licked the inside of one thigh, then the other before easing me down by a few inches. But he wasn't about to let me get away, thrusting the entire length of his cock deep inside. When he shifted, I could feel his piercing rubbing against my pussy walls. The intensity was incredible, tiny prickles of heat jetting through me like rocket fire.

My muscles stretched, a flash of pain because of his huge girth quickly turning into such intense pleasure that I couldn't make a single sound. I felt a smile cross my face as I trembled in his hold. He pulled all the way out, driving into me again, shoving me against the wall.

"So tight, my pet. So fucking tight. I'm going to stretch you. Fuck you. Fill you. Isn't that what you want?"

"Yes."

"Mmm... I thought so. All those times you masturbated in the shower, were you thinking of us?"

I wanted to be incensed, disgusted that I'd been right about the cameras, but his filthy words only enticed me more. "Maybe." I was breathless with my answer, my skin both crawling and tingling at the same time. The array of emotions was killing me as much as his tempting words thrilled the hungry girl inside. I was torn between driving my fingers into his stunning eyes and clinging to his massive shoulders as he fucked me like a bad little girl.

"Maybe? I guess I'll need to convince you." He lowered his head, nipping my lower lip as he pulled out, plunging into me again. His breath was scattered, hot as Hades as he blew across my face. It only added to the wildfire threatening to consume me.

Even through the thick walls, I could hear thunder rumbling all around us, another flash of lightning catching my breath. I closed my eyes, allowing the fantasy to take over. When I sensed movement, I held my breath, Cain pulling me away from the wall. Another set of hands brushed down my back, caressing my skin as a lover would do.

But these men and this experience wasn't about romance but sheer fucking, taking a possession so others would know to keep their hands off. I wasn't certain I minded. Was this what being one of the chosen was about? For a fleeting second, I considered it until I felt fingers sliding down the crack of my ass. They were wet, slickened with something.

Moaning, I opened my eyes, stretching to see Hunter was right behind me. His eyes danced like flames licking at crackling logs, the wry smile on his face more seductive than before.

"Your ass is mine," he growled, then pressed a single finger inside my dark hole.

I was thrown by the shame of being invaded this way, the heat climbing from my core, exploding into my extremities. My arms and legs tingled, my pulse racing, I was terrified and aroused, the combination damning.

"That's it, little pet. You're going to feel so full," Cain whispered as he lowered his head, licking the shell of my ear.

A single crack to my aching bottom pushed a series of moans from my throat. That was the moment Hunter added a second finger, stretching them open as he began to pump into my asshole.

"Even tighter," he murmured. "Maybe we'll have you wear a plug all day and all night. Yes. I think that's what we need to do."

"I'll order several," Cristiano said from a few feet away. His laugh was dark and dangerous, a promise of things to come. While Cain was pure evil, his lack of humanity evident in everything he did, I sensed Cristiano was the most sadistic of the three, thriving on providing pain well before pleasure.

I craved it. God help me but I did.

Cain continued to thrust into me slow and easy while Hunter drove a third finger inside, his actions becoming rougher. I could tell by his hitched breath that he was losing his patience, hungering to be inside of me.

I tensed the moment he pressed the tip of his cock against my dark entrance.

"Shush, little one. I'm make it nice and easy the first time." Hunter's soft, seductive words put me in a slight trance, so that when he pushed a couple of inches inside, I didn't scream, merely shuddering audibly.

"That's it. Such a good girl, aren't you? She can take it. We know she likes it rough," Cain said in a gruff voice.

Of all the endearing names they called me, good girl was more thrilling than it should be. The haze forming around our heated bodies intensified, a thick fog that was impenetrable. I had my arms over Cain's shoulders, tugging on his dark curls as Hunter drove another two inches inside. Pain shot through me, my ass aching. Then Cain picked up his rhythm, rolling onto the balls of his feet and changing the angle.

"Oh…" Cristiano was not to be denied, cupping one breast, kneading until it ached. "You're mine next, sunshine."

The piercing found a perfect sensitive spot, and I was tossed into rapture, barely realizing Hunter had driven the remainder of his cock deep inside. As they developed a rhythm, Cristiano pinched and twisted my nipple, adding to the delicious anguish. Our combined sounds of growls and moans filled the space, the rumbles of continuous thunder adding to the sultry atmosphere.

As they started to fuck me brutally, I was completely relaxed, barely hanging onto Cain. I turned my head, licking my lips so Cristiano could see.

He inched closer, capturing my mouth as he continued tormenting my aching bud. I adored the taste of him, the sweet hint of bourbon infused with something tangy. I could have kissed the man for hours, but I sensed he wanted more.

The electricity was building to a precipice, the dazzling vibrations stealing my breath. I blinked several times, trying to eliminate the building haze surrounding my vision, suddenly clawing Cain's shoulders.

"That's it, little pet. Come with me. Come while I fill your womb with my seed." Cain's words were so deep and dark that I had to strain in order to hear him. I had no way to hold back. I squeezed my pussy muscles around Cain's throbbing shaft, and seconds later, there was nothing I could do to stop a powerful orgasm from driving straight to the heart of me.

"Oh. Oh. Oh!"

"Fuck!" Cain roared, fucking me like a crazed animal as my body continued to float to pure ecstasy. He threw his head back, panting several times as his body spasmed.

My climax left me exhausted and unable to think clearly. Hunter continued to hold me, plunging slow and easy as I struggled to control my breathing.

"My turn," Cristiano demanded, pushing Cain aside, then forcing my legs around his hips. "No pretense, baby. I take what I want." He wrapped one hand around the base of his cock, rubbing the tip up and down my slickened pussy, then plunged every inch inside.

My muscles immediately reacted as they'd done with Cain's, clamping around the delicious thick bulge, pulling it in as deeply as possible. His eyes were almost unrecognizable when he lifted his head, taking shallow breaths as he studied me. Then he smiled, and I thought the entire world was going to burn down.

"Okay, little lamb," Hunter said breathlessly as he shoved hair away from the back of my neck. "We're going to make you feel even better."

As both men began developing a rhythm of their own, as if playing a priceless instrument, I was thrown by how much the entire situation intrigued me. Did they really believe I would belong to all three of them? Did they see this as long term?

Revenge.

Remember, it's all about revenge.

My inner voice was right, but what if what we shared could be more? I refused to allow worries about something I had no control over to ruin the moment. I lolled my head against Cristiano's shoulder as both men fucked me. I'd never felt so full in my entire life. I dragged my tongue across my parched lips, then around Cristiano's mouth. He allowed me to tease his tongue, as I swept mine back and forth across his.

When Hunter eased his arms around me, cupping both breasts, I knew I'd died and gone to heaven. There could be nothing more explosive and wonderful than having three men pleasure me at the same time. Nothing.

"Such a bad girl," Hunter whispered. "Taming you will be delicious."

Taming me. Crazy visions rushed into the back of my mind, the kind that could very well turn into a naughty story. "Yes."

"At least she admits it," Cristiano said casually before crushing his mouth over mine. Together the three of us developed a rhythm that could rival anything. I could sense Cain was watching, always observing.

And he didn't necessarily like what he saw.

As the delicious moments continued, I raked my nails down Cristiano's back. I could tell both men were losing control at the same time. I bucked against their hold which seemed to surprise them, their actions becoming even more brutal. Together, we were shot into a moment of euphoria.

"Fuck. I can't hold it," Hunter snarled.

"Then don't, brother. Come for us, baby girl." Cristiano's voice opened another wicked well of darkness.

As I stared into his eyes, I followed his command, the three of us climaxing at the same time.

This wasn't just heaven. This was the beginning of the descent into Hell.

They held onto me for a couple minutes, both nuzzling against my neck. I wanted to believe they cared about me, but I knew better. This was the beginning of a nightmare, even if my heart didn't want to believe it.

As my senses slowly started to return, I pushed my hands against Cristiano with enough force that he lifted his head, his eyes searching mine.

"We're just getting started, sweetheart." Now his words seemed like more of a threat.

They eased me down, allowing me to walk away, and I immediately jerked my dress from the floor, covering myself as I tried to slide into it. I was shaking all over, stunned by the revelation of what had just happened. Another wave of anger and hate tore through me, but remnants of pure pleasure remained.

I hated myself because of it.

Cain studied me with the intensity of a lion. "He's right, our little pet. The night is still young."

"I need to leave," I told him defiantly, remorse kicking in.

He started to swagger close to me. Then there was a sudden knock on the door and he snarled.

"You guys better get downstairs," a voice said seconds later.

"What the hell?" Hunter asked, immediately grabbing his trousers while I forced my stiff muscles to help me slide the dress over my shoulders.

Another wave of humiliation set in, my throat tightening.

"There's a fire." It was obvious by the man's deep, shaking voice that it was a serious situation.

"Shit," Cristiano huffed.

Cain hissed as he grabbed his clothes, struggling into them. "You will stay right here, little pet. We'll return."

The three men grumbled as they quickly dressed, Cristiano giving me a longing look.

I held my breath as the three of them walked out the door.

And locked it.

I folded my arms, waiting for a few seconds before taking long strides towards it. After jiggling the handle, I closed my eyes. Then I started to pace the floor, moving towards the windows. While I didn't see a fire, I did see several people outside, some running back and forth. What in the hell had occurred?

A cold shiver replaced the fiery heat, my mind still trying to process what had happened between us.

Seconds later, I heard the jingle of the lock and sucked in my breath. When I turned around, I wasn't expecting the person who walked in through the door,

Theodore.

I backed away, darting my eyes towards the door.

"Come. I can get you out of here, but you need to hurry," he encouraged.

"I'm not leaving without Kelly."

"She asked me to find you. Come on before they get back. You saw what they can do."

I hesitated, uncertain I could trust anyone at this point, including myself.

"Come on. I only bought us a few minutes."

"Okay." As I headed for the door, he darted a look over his shoulder.

As soon as I was close, he grabbed my arm. Then he raised his other arm and a flash of something caught my eye.

A syringe.

Just as I was about to scream, he brought down his arm. I felt the prick of a needle.

Then…

CHAPTER 10

Hunter

I'd had several 'what the fuck' moments since becoming the cream of the Elite echelon, including the first time I'd killed a man in cold blood because it was required. After that, killing had become easy, a part of the requirements of living the opulent life of one of the Damned. I'd laughed the first time I'd heard other students whisper our name as I'd passed, said as if they'd been issuing a curse.

The truth was, the members of the Elite were untouchable, more so since Cain had taken charge of the house. Cristiano and I knew he'd tracked the former Elite President to his parents' vacation house in Maine, shooting him between the eyes like he would a deer. That was the beginning of our rise to power. It was pointless for administrators to waste their time attempting to crate the animals. They were simply looking forward to the day of our graduation.

While Cristiano was a scary fuck, his hot temper getting him into bloody situations, I was known as the charmer, someone who could easily get under a person's skin, destroying them before they had a chance to blink. Then there was Cain, a man born evil. He enjoyed the act of torture more than anyone else I'd ever known.

However, I hadn't honestly believed he'd go through with the plan he'd concocted a year and a half ago regarding Sage. He'd been so hell bent on plotting her demise that I was shocked he'd managed to accomplish anything else. This entire night was a 'what the fuck' moment that would remain at the top of the list for a long time.

Not that I hadn't enjoyed the art of seduction with the beautiful woman. She'd stirred something inside of me that I'd thought no longer existed. A single taste of her would never be enough. I ached with need, longing to drive my cock into her tight pussy. What concerned me was his obvious obsession with her. I had no qualms admitting I wanted to capture and keep her, but I had a feeling Cain would go too far just like he did with everything else.

If her father really was the assassin called The Iceman, then the man wouldn't take a backseat to the fact that his daughter was missing. As far as I was concerned, taking the word of a traumatized twelve-year-old hellbent on revenge, which was the age he'd been when his brother had been murdered, wasn't intelligent. However, challenging Cain had its own issues.

Now we were standing in the middle of a freaking rainstorm since some fucker had set one of the outbuildings on fire just to piss us off. I had a feeling I knew who'd done so to prove a point.

Theodore.

He'd been an issue since the beginning, believing he'd become president of the house because his father had been. Not a chance in hell, the weak piece of shit.

"Fuck. Fuck!" Cain hissed. "You know it's that fuckhead."

Cristiano stood with his arms crossed as other members of the house used fire extinguishers to augment the slowing rainstorm.

"Find the fucker!" Cain yelled. As with every order one of the three of us doled out, four of the other members jogged into the night in search of Theo. My guess was that he'd hung around to watch the circus.

"We can't be sure it's him," I suggested, but there was no other logical choice. But at this point, if there weren't limits placed on Cain, he'd go off the deep end.

He shot me a hateful look. "You know better, dude. I'm going to hunt that bastard down and handle him the right way. He's going to bleed."

He'd raised his voice to the point that the folks remaining outside glanced in our direction, including a few of the girls huddling under the front porch. While our reputation as bastards, monsters, and killers went far beyond the pristine iron gates of the college, up to this point there'd been no evidence left of a single crime. And I certainly hadn't spent four long years in the establishment to have it yanked out from under me two weeks prior to being freed.

I got in his face, struggling to get his attention. "You need to keep your mouth shut. That asshole isn't going anywhere. Maybe keep your voice down so no one knows what the hell is going on."

"And why don't you shut your trap," he retorted, getting all the way in my face.

While most of the time I could tolerate his bullshit, tonight wasn't one of them. I shoved my hands against him, shaking my head.

He grinned but didn't hesitate, issuing a hard punch, then another.

"Jesus Christ," Cristiano snarled. "Why don't the two of you knock it off."

I rubbed my jaw, noticing Kelly had joined the group of girls. It was easy to tell she was searching for her friend. "Yeah, fine. He's fuckin' long gone by now. Let's get back to our night."

Exhaling, Cain stood to his full height. Then he issued a hard jab to my gut. That was it. I was finished with dealing with his crap. I lunged my body toward him, bending over and catching him in the chest, the force pitching us both to the ground and into the mud.

"Fight! Fight! Fight!" several of the other members cheered.

Both Cain and I issued several savage punches. This had more to do about Sage than it did anything else. He wanted her all to himself, and that wasn't going to happen.

No one tried to stop us. They knew better than to get in the middle.

After issuing several additional jabs, I struggled to my feet. The man was fucking deranged as far as I was concerned. Cain remained where he was as I paced the area.

"You're an asshole. You know that"?" he asked as he hoisted himself to his feet.

"You both are," Cristiano finally piped in.

Before I had a chance to launch into Cain again, the three other members returned.

"What did you find, Franco?" I asked.

He walked closer, eyeing the girls then turning his back. "Theo's car is still here."

"Fuck," I snarled, unhappy I'd been right. "The fucker wanted a distraction. That's what the fire was all about."

"That means he's still in the estate." Cristiano took long strides closer.

"Sage. He'll do what he can to use her against us," Cain hissed. "The party's over. Get everyone out of here!"

At least he had one decent idea. "Go around the backside to the playroom," I instructed Cristiano.

"He can still get into the room," he explained. "The locks weren't changed."

A stupid move on our part and one I had a feeling would cost us.

"Exactly." I trailed behind Cain as we entered the house, both of us bounding up the master stairs to the fourth floor. We didn't need to go to the end of the hallway to discover the door was open. I jogged there anyway, checking the room quickly. "Not here."

While it was possible that she'd managed to get out of the room, my bets were on Theo's interference. Whatever he had planned for her was meant to embarrass us or worse.

We couldn't allow that to happen.

"We need to fucking find him!" Cain roared, his rage reaching a new level.

"Spread out. Room by room!" I bellowed when I saw Cristiano.

"Whatever happens, Theo doesn't leave alive."

Cristiano and I glanced at each other as Cain kicked open one of the doors. Then he lifted his fist in solidarity.

We did the same.

I might not like his tactics or his all-consuming anger, but when a member breached the rules, we came together as a force. When outsiders threatened our wellbeing, we reacted without remorse.

No hesitation.

No regret.

And no conscience.

We were a brotherhood. We'd made an oath to protect the house, the traditions, and other members. As well as the women who served our needs.

No matter what efforts were necessary to do so or the consequences.

Theodore Watkins would pay the price.

* * *

Sage

Run. Run. *Run.*

That's all I could think about. But I couldn't break free of Theo's hold. I was woozy and dizzy as hell, but I'd fought him hard enough that he'd dropped the syringe before issuing the full dose. Still, he had one hand over my mouth, his other arm pressed against my throat. Even as I struggled, jamming my heel into his foot, nothing stopped him. He dragged me to the other end of the house and down another set of stairs, laughing softly as if taking me from the three men who'd captured me was any worse.

When he jerked us both to a stop, dropping his hand to reach for a doorknob, I let out a horrific scream. But I knew deep inside the sound would never be heard over the thumping music. I wasn't even certain I'd made a noise.

He shoved me inside, slamming then locking the door.

The force he'd used pitched me back against a washing machine, the brutal impact knocking the wind out of me. I'd lost one shoe, my dress already torn from where he'd grabbed me. My vision was still foggy, images blurry. I blinked several times, fighting the drug with everything I had.

"Get... away from me!" I hissed, scanning the room for anything I could use as a weapon.

He grinned lasciviously as he raked his hand through his hair, swaggering towards me, then allowing his gaze to slowly fall to my breasts. "Don't worry. It'll wear off in time. Those assholes think they can take everything without consequences. So strong. So entitled. Well, I found their single weakness. That's you. I've watched them for months stalking you, as if they thought they were so clever. Do you know why they did?"

"Uh-uh," I said. My mouth was like sandpaper. Even worse, his words echoed.

"It seems your daddy is a very bad man. Did you know that?"

What the hell was he talking about? I tried to say something and almost tripped.

"Careful, little girl. You didn't know, did you?" Theo laughed.

What was he talking about? "No."

"Oh, yes. Your daddy is an assassin for some terrible men."

An assassin? No, I wasn't hearing him right. "Na... no. He owns a restaurant."

"I feel sorry for you. That's why Cain hates you so much. Your daddy killed his brother."

This was some kind of sick game. I shook my head, gulping for air. "Let me go."

"That's not going to happen. You're very valuable. Imagine the fun we're going to have using their desire against them."

"What the… hell are you talking about?" I inched away from him, trying to calculate how long it would take me to get to the door. *Don't trip. Run. Run!*

"You. You're the only thing that's mattered to them for the past four years. They act as if they own the world, but you brought them to their knees. Did you know that? Do you know how special that makes you? I guess you must taste pretty sweet, huh?" He licked his lips, making a sucking sound.

Disgust tore through me that was entirely different than before. "I don't belong here. I'm not one of you."

"The fact you're in the house means you are one of them now. I can smell them on you. They've already marked you with their scents. That doesn't matter."

Jesus Christ. What kind of a sick game was everyone playing? These boys were barbarians. When he licked his lips again, rubbing his hand across his crotch, my blood turned to ice.

I could read his thoughts. He believed that if he raped me, then their little pet would be spoiled. There was no way I was going to allow that to happen. I shifted another few inches, watching every move he made. God, why couldn't I think clearly? Was it possible my father was an assassin? No. It was crazy.

"Come here, little girl. We're going to have so much fun together."

When he took another step closer, I realized there would be no better time to try and get the hell away from him. I threw myself at the door, managing to get it open, screaming at the top of my lungs.

Theo slammed his hand against the door, immediately backhanding me. As I tumbled to the floor, he jumped on top of me, tearing at my clothes. I continued yelling, fighting him with everything I had, but the drug still had its claws in me. He managed to shred the bodice of my dress, squeezing my breast.

"Such a little bitch, aren't you? I can tell you like it rough. Trust me, baby. That's what you're going to get."

He positioned himself between my legs, yanking the material up to my thigh on one side.

I punched him in the face.

"You're going to pay for that."

"No. No!"

Wham!

The cracking sound reverberated in the room, the rush of air and the deep growls echoing in my ears. Suddenly, the weight of him was jerked off, his body flying through the air and driven against the wall. Rolling over, I fought to get to my feet, blinking several times to focus. I clutched the torn bodice against my chest, gasping for air as tears streamed down my face.

Cain, Hunter, and Cristiano had found me.

As they continued to punch Theo, I backed toward the door, shaking like a leaf. Shaky, I backed even further, wincing with every brutal punch. I could see blood from the savagery inflicted on the man and a part of me knew Theo deserved it.

Theo continued to fight back.

Then a glint caught my eye, something shiny and metallic.

A knife.

They were going to kill him.

Oh, God. Oh, God. Oh, God.

That's the moment I turned and fled, racing down the three sets of stairs, bouncing from one side to the other. My vision was still foggy, but I refused to stop, frantically searching for Kelly.

"Sage. Wait!"

I heard one of them calling my name, the sounds of their footsteps pushing me to escape. I found the front door, throwing it open, racing out into the rain in my bare feet. My name echoed in the night as I fled, struggling to find my way in the dark. I heard more than one set of footsteps.

The rain continued to call, the darkness overwhelming. I almost slipped several times but kept going. Images floated in my mind, faces of ugliness. Blood. It was crazy. I had to get away.

Seconds later, bright lights formed a glow in the trees surrounding me, the roar of an engine getting close. I turned around as a car veered over the hill.

They were going too fast.

Too fast...

"No!"

CHAPTER 11

Ten years later
Hunter

As I strode through the lobby of the resort and casino, I shook my head. I had to give it to the man, he'd made a fortune over the years. Not that Cain Cross hadn't been born with a silver spoon in his mouth. Well, the truth was that so had I, yet I had a feeling I'd worked harder to achieve billionaire status than he had.

Especially since a good portion of the Cross family wealth had been made through unscrupulous methods. Although I was a man who had crossed the line more than once or twice. Chuckling, I headed into the lounge, immediately finding a seat at the bar.

"Whatdya have?" the bartender asked within seconds.

"Macallan double cask single malt."

"A man of impeccable tastes. Chuck, I'll have the same. This is my very good friend, Hunter Augustine. Take good care of him and whatever he wants is on the house."

"Yes, sir, Mr. Cross."

Grinning, I turned my head then stuck out my arm for a shake. "Cain Cross, as I live and breathe."

"Who did you expect to find?" His eyes twinkled as he accepted the gesture, pumping my hand as if in recognition of the number of years it had been since we'd seen each other. "This is my empire. What do you think? I should add, one of many."

"Now you run several empires. Still arrogant as fuck."

"You know it. Well-deserved, I might add."

"That remains to be seen." I'd seen pictures, the eligible bachelor appearing in several glossy magazines with one gorgeous woman after another adorning his arm like prized poodles.

He laughed, and as soon as Chuck placed our rocks glasses on the napkins, he lifted his drink for a toast. "It's been too long, my friend."

"Yeah, it really has." I'd almost resisted calling him after making plans on traveling to Chicago on business. The last thing I wanted was to rehash old memories. I'd moved on with my life. But as had happened before, I wouldn't be allowed to get away without talking to him and maybe Cristiano as well.

"What has it been, six years?"

"About that." I took a sip of my drink and scanned the bar. "Ten years of freedom from the City of Hope." Shit. Now, I was the one who'd mentioned the place where the Damned had fucked up several lives. The entire system had crumbled after we'd left, the myopic society that had once held the world in the palm of their hand collapsing. Maybe it was better for all involved, although I doubted the three of us would ever be invited to a reunion.

Cain hunkered over the bar. "It wasn't all bad."

"Speak for yourself." After the incident, I'd taken my last exam and left without bothering to share in the graduation celebrations. I'd planned on never seeing a soul again, including my two buddies, but it seemed fate continued to find the need to remind us of the tragedy. We'd gotten together every couple of years, the first under less than pleasant circumstances.

"What brings you to Chicago?"

"Business for one. Elite business for another."

"Elite business?" He turned so he could face me. "What happened?"

I took a deep breath, glancing at the crowded space before answering. "I think The Iceman is still alive."

His eyes opened wide. "What makes you say that?"

"Because I was attacked last week in my office. The asshole almost succeeded in putting a bullet in my brain."

"Don't take offense, but you're no poster child for good will. What makes you think it was him instead of one of your other enemies?"

I held up my arm, wiggling my fingers. "Scar on his right hand. More like a burn but strangely ornate like a symbol. Right?"

Cain took a deep breath. "Yeah. Exactly like that. I heard it was from a botched assignment. I'm curious. Did you get a good look at him?"

"No. He knocked out the power before coming inside. The only reason I managed to see his hand was because I almost broke it while smashing it into the window. The moonlight gave me a split-second look."

"You let him get away?" He smirked.

"Let's just say I wasn't expecting an assassin at my private office for which no one knows the address. I didn't have my weapon on me at the time."

"Now you'll learn never to go anywhere without it. It's funny how the Iceman has a way of finding whatever information he wants. The guy has to be in his sixties minimum by now. Plus, there hasn't been a sighting or report on him for…"

"Eight years," I answered for him. So the idea was farfetched. That didn't make it impossible. "Since the last time an attempted assassination was made." Cain had been lucky to survive, the bullet centimeters from shattering his heart. He'd spent three weeks in the hospital while Cristiano and I had attempted to track the assassin down to no avail. He was like a ghost.

Two years later, Cristiano had been involved in an attempted assassination that couldn't be confirmed as the work of the notorious man.

He rolled his eyes. "Don't remind me. Why now, after all these years?"

"No clue. Maybe the anniversary of the death of his daughter." The ten years since Sage had been hit by one of the Elite members driving like a maniac had recently played fresh in my mind. I'd never been able to get the horrific visions of her broken and bleeding body out of my mind. Fuck. I'd held her as blood had oozed past her lips, terror in her eyes as she'd gripped me with one hand until the ambulance had arrived. Just before she'd been taken away, she'd pressed her fingers against my face.

There were times when I looked into the mirror and could swear her bloody fingerprints had permanently stained my skin.

"I'd forgotten about that." He took a gulp of his drink.

He hadn't forgotten. None of us had. I could tell by the shadow crossing his face he had the same nightmares that Cristiano and I had. Sage had hung on for a week in the hospital after falling into a coma, but there'd been no brain activity, her parents finally pulling the plug. It had nearly gutted all three of us, although Cain had never admitted it.

"Ten years is a long time to suffer and grieve," I offered.

"Maybe so. Perhaps he's simply preparing to finish his list before he dies."

List. The member who'd been behind the wheel had had been killed only six months after graduating, his lifeless body found thirty feet in front of his penthouse. While his death had been ruled a suicide, the three of us had known better. We'd expected The Iceman to continue his bloody path of revenge then, but the man had waited for eighteen months before attempting a hit on Cain.

Then Cristiano.

Now, this. While I'd looked over my shoulder for five years, I'd stopped doing so a couple years before. Cain was right. I had enough enemies who could have been responsible for making the hit, and I wouldn't have suspected otherwise unless I'd seen the man's hand.

"Maybe you're right." I rubbed my jaw, the memories kicking my ass all over again.

"Incidentally, I had a call from a Kentucky detective asking questions about Theo."

Snorting, I narrowed my eyes. We'd never be free of the nightmare. And we shouldn't be. "After this many years?" Hearing Theodore's name always left a bad taste in my mouth. After the asshole had been stupid enough to try and rape Sage just to prove his worthiness, the three of us had handled him in the only acceptable manner. That didn't mean his justifiable death didn't weigh heavily on our minds.

Or maybe I was the only one of the three of us with a conscience.

William Watkins had done everything to pin a murder on the entire house when there'd been no body to find, no evidence of any kind as to what had occurred inside the third-floor laundry room.

"New to the job. Assigned a cold case," Cain chortled. Ice remained in the man's veins.

"And it's getting colder."

"I wanted you to know in case the asshole tracked you down. I've already warned Cristiano." He gave me a look that was a clear reminder of my requirement to keep the code of silence until the day I died. There was no need to challenge him. All three of us knew the score and what we could lose.

"Noted. You and I know there's nothing to find."

He'd handled the disposal of the body, and I hadn't asked questions then, nor did I plan to now.

As far as I was concerned, the kid was dead and buried where he belonged.

No one attacked a woman in my world and lived.

Cain took a deep breath. "Look, I have some business to attend to I can't get out of. I'll return, and we can continue discussing this. Incidentally, I convinced Cristiano to fly in." He grinned as he waited to see my reaction.

"All the way from South America?"

"You obviously don't keep up with the news, do ya?"

"I have a fifty-billion-dollar company to run." It was a slight to the man standing in front of me. While we'd remained friends, our respective businesses had kept us from getting together more often.

He lifted his glass again. "You always were in competition with me. Including with women."

"Women? All three of us had our pick if we wanted." We'd been taught to believe we could have anything and anyone we wanted. While I'd enjoyed the years of feeling as if I was a king, I'd learned that anything worth keeping was also worth working for. I wasn't certain Cain had managed to claw his way out of the vacuum his father had imprisoned him in.

"I'm talking about one woman in particular." He lifted his arm and index finger to reiterate the point.

Neither one of us needed to mention her name. In allowing her to become an obsession, we'd all built some aspect of our lives around her. Her death had driven all three of us into dark, icy conditions and had yet to release its brutal hold.

"Very funny," I said, although none of it was funny in the least. If I didn't change the subject, we'd become mired in the quicksand as we'd once been. "At least I don't burn down buildings to inflate my ego and my bank account."

"Once an asshole, always an asshole." He tossed back the rest of his scotch, issuing a slight growl. "How's the suite?"

"The penthouse? Almost better than my estate. Almost."

"Only the best for my buddy." He stepped away from the bar then turned back. "By the way. In case you get bored, check out the entertainment in the auditorium. I'm impressed my Entertainment Manager was able to come through with the booking."

"Hmm... I'm certain whoever you have headlining is a stunning female."

"Why, yes, she is. And no, I'm not fucking her if that's what you're thinking."

I threw up my arms, chuckling under my breath. "Does that mean you're waiting for the right woman?"

He thought about my question, his expression becoming haunted. "Maybe I am. We're not getting any younger, you know."

"Who knows. Maybe we'll find the right woman to share the rest of our lives with us."

"You still think about that?"

"From time to time."

We'd talked about sharing a single woman for the rest of our lives in a jovial discussion over a bottle of liquor. Even then I'd known it was a pipedream created by monstrous men with god complexes. Yet we'd been serious about Sage.

As he rubbed his jaw, he got a faraway look in his eyes. "It could have worked you know."

"With Sage?"

"Yeah. She was everything I'd ever wanted and more."

A quiet tension settled between us. "You were in love with her."

Cain nodded several times, taking a swig of his drink before answering. "Yeah, I was. It's funny how no one else has mattered."

I almost felt sorry for my friend. He'd lost his way after his brother's murder. Now, he was nothing but a shell of a man going through the paces.

Maybe all three of us were.

"You need to let the past go."

As he lifted his head, the shimmer in his eyes surprised me. "Have you been able to do that?"

I wasn't surprised I had no answer. Or maybe I was terrified that if I admitted my feelings, I'd break the slight tether I still had to the beautiful girl with the stunning eyes.

"That's what I thought." He walked away and I was surprised. Maybe he was softening in his old age.

"Chuck. Let me have another one."

"Yes, sir, Mr. Augustine."

As I watched Cain leave, another pang of guilt and remorse settled into my system. The three of us were fucked up men living an emotionless life.

And as had occurred several times before, I wondered what would have happened had fate not torn the four of us apart.

* * *

"I don't give a shit what your problems are, Bart. We had a deal, and you're going to uphold every clause in the fucking contract." As I paced the floor of the hotel corridor, I was surprised how angry I'd become. I'd been working on a deal with the man's firm for almost six months, the connection and contract we'd entered allowing for additional distribution of my family's products into several countries. The fact that he was attempting to yank back on the deal at the twelfth hour was infuriating.

And unacceptable.

"You don't own me or my company, Hunter. We can do what we want. Besides, I heard you were dirty. Read all about it."

Fuck me. He was attempting to go down that road? There were just as many articles praising my corporation as attempting to undermine it. However, whatever he'd read had him on edge.

Bart had no idea what kind of wrath I could bring down on his firm, including destroying his reputation. There was very little I wouldn't do to ensure the contract went through as planned.

Including violence.

For years, I'd thought of myself as a different animal than either Cain or Cristiano, but my methods of procuring business had taken a much darker side. I owned the unions in Philly, had control over several politicians, and had enough power to alter every financial institution, real estate development firm, and manufacturing corporation in the city and beyond.

People were terrified of what I could do, and I'd earned myself a savage reputation that far exceeded the control my father had held during his prime. In turn, I'd increased the family's wealth by billions of dollars.

I'd been forced to face the fact I was no different than my two friends, my mannerisms and that of very trusted enforcers within my organization akin to how the mafia handled their business activities. What I'd also learned was that with every success, every dollar added to my bank account, I'd become even more of a cold, vile man.

Did that mean I wasn't happy?

The jury was out on that one. The old adage was true that money couldn't buy happiness.

I took a deep breath before answering. "I'm going to say this to you once. Fuck with me and face the consequences."

"You don't scare me, Augustine. If you dare try and interfere, I'll ruin you."

It would seem I'd been too soft on the man. That would change. "Let the games begin." I ended the call, hoping he'd begin looking over his shoulder, worrying about what I could and would do.

I'd crush the man and his corporation like a bug.

Then I'd take over his entire operation. Perhaps coming to Chicago had been inspirational.

I shoved my phone into my jacket, running my fingers through my hair as the lilting sound of a song finally drew me out of my enraged fog. I was drawn to the woman's beautiful voice instantly, the husky tone as she belted out a powerful rock song unlike anything I'd ever heard.

I hadn't planned on taking Cain up on his recommendation, music never soothing the savage beast, yet the song and the singer drew me in. I found myself opening the door to the packed auditorium, the neon lights swirling around the stage suggesting a raunchy, entertaining set.

While the expansive room was huge, the atmosphere was meant to seem quaint and cozy. The tablecloths were crimson, and on each table was a single candle, the flickering light unable to take away from the lightshow on stage. I was lucky to find an empty table near the back. As I took my seat, my eyes never left the entertainment.

The singer was dressed provocatively in tight leather pants, a shimmering crimson top and thigh high boots, her long blonde curls shifting back and forth across her shoulders as she moved from one side of the stage to the other. The energy in the room was electric, the guests mesmerized by her stage presence. Even from my vantage point, which was far removed from the platform, I was able to admire her beauty.

She had a voice that tingled every muscle, the thumping beat of the drums as she powered out a song mimicking the thudding of my heartbeat. When the song ended, she threw back her arms and the crowd went wild, the standing ovation well-deserved.

I remained in my seat, ordering a drink from the lovely waitress as soon as she approached. Perhaps the set was over, which would be a shame. When the lights dimmed until only twinkling lights crisscrossed the front of the stage, I leaned forward.

The singer eased a stool from behind the curtains, taking her place with only a microphone in her hand. I wasn't expecting the soft strains of an acoustic guitar as her only accompaniment. She lowered her head, holding the microphone in both hands. When she began to sing, I was floored at the change in her voice. After a few seconds, I had no idea what words she was singing, only concentrating on how emotional the performance had become.

Somewhere in the back of my mind, I knew she was singing a song from decades before, *The Rose* was a signature piece for another entertainer. But the way the girl handled the various octaves reminded me of what an angel from heaven would sound like.

As the song concluded, my drink was presented. In the quiet before the storm of applause, I drew the waitress closer. "What is her name?"

"Rose."

"How perfect."

"You don't know who she is?" the girl asked. When I said nothing, she seemed flustered. "Only the most famous singer out today. You should look up her band Halo on Tiktok or Instagram. However, at least in my opinion, she's what makes the band special, and we're lucky to have her."

I pulled out a business card, handing it to the girl. "I'd like to arrange a short meeting with her. I assure you that Mr. Cross would approve."

She glanced at the card, her body stiffening. "Oh, my gosh, Mr. Augustine. You should have told me who you were."

"Why?"

"We were all instructed to provide you with a perfect stay in our resort. I could have found you a seat up front."

I laughed. Cain had certainly wanted to make an impression. "It's fine. Just see what you can do about arranging a meeting."

"Yes, sir. I'm certain she'll be eager to meet you."

As the girl scampered away, I returned my attention to the beautiful woman on stage taking her bows. My cock had stirred for the first time in as long as I could remember. The fact that Rose had managed to entice me in such a short period of time was something I couldn't ignore. I sipped on my drink, yanking my phone from my pocket. While I used social media every day, I wasn't the kind of man to peruse either Instagram or TikTok for anything other than business.

I typed in her name and was shocked at how many followers she had. As I scrolled through the pictures and videos, my balls tightened. The woman was exquisite in every way, sultry and dazzling. My breath was caught in my throat, which was even more unusual.

Why did this girl have such an effect on me?

The entire band had left the stage, the lights lifting in the auditorium. It was obvious by the fact people were beginning to leave the room that the show was over. I drummed my fingers on the table, hoping that Rose would take a chance meeting a stranger.

The waitress returned a few minutes later, a smile on her face. "She's agreed to meet with you in her dressing room. I'll show you the way."

I left my drink, trailing behind the girl to a door on the opposite side of the auditorium. It led to a private hallway, several of the band members roaming the corridor along with reporters and other people offered the privilege of being backstage.

She rapped on a door that had no name attached, giving me a hard onceover after she did. I had to wonder what Cain had told his employees.

"Come in." The voice was just as sultry as I'd heard on stage.

The waitress opened the door, allowing me in, then closing it behind me. Suddenly, I was alone with a superstar. I didn't see her at first. Then she eased from behind a panel where she'd changed clothes. Now, she wore jeans and a simple blouse, appearing even more inviting than before.

I wasn't the kind of man to be awestruck by anyone, but I found it difficult to say the right words. She stared at me, her eyes opening wide, almost as if she was trying to figure out where she knew me from. I'd remember a gorgeous creature like her. She was tall, yet I dwarfed her voluptuous body. She wasn't skin and bones like so many rock stars, her curves meant for a man's hands.

My hands.

I could tell the attraction was instantaneous between us, a smile finally curling on her lips.

"Mr. Augustine," she half-whispered.

"Thank you for seeing me, and please call me Hunter. I'll feel old otherwise."

"A man who tracks his prey. To what do I owe the honor?" she asked, still studying me with cautious eyes, remaining where she was. I could sense her apprehension, and rightfully so. I was a bad man who was curious if I could convince her into being seduced.

The thought crossing my mind was as surprising as the fact that I'd asked to meet her in the first place. I could have any woman I wanted. I'd been photographed with some of the most beautiful women in the world on my arm for various functions. However, almost all had been for show and little else. I had several female friends who acted the part of my love interest when requested. For some of them, the nod of being on my arm had allowed them to climb the social ladder.

Uncomplicated suited my needs as well as theirs. Perhaps I was as arrogant as I'd been called on more than one occasion, but I'd had my share of women vying to marry into wealth and power. I wanted no part of an arranged marriage as had been proposed to both Cain and Cristiano by their families.

Maybe somewhere under my black heart, I believed in the sanctity of love.

"Yes, I capture and keep the prey I hunger for. I won't lie to you, Rose. I enjoyed the portion of the concert I was lucky enough to see, and I prefer being around beautiful women."

Her laugh was natural, filling the air with a light that electrified every molecule in my body. She seemed to notice the growing bulge between my legs, but there was no embarrassment on her face. The fact that she dragged her long tongue across her plush, bottom lip meant she approved of the stranger standing in front of her.

"It's delightful to meet a man who doesn't dare shower me with useless compliments or try and pretend he's the best thing since sliced bread. But I've never met a hunter I couldn't outrun."

The banter was just as enticing as the woman. When she pursed her lips on purpose, brushing her fingers lightly down her chest, she knew exactly what she was doing. It was the same kind of action I'd seen on stage, enticing every male in the auditorium to fantasize.

I breathed in her perfume, the cords on the side of my neck immediately tightening. The scent was exotic yet light, citrus and jasmine infused with a dash of vanilla. I'd never analyzed a woman's choice of cologne before. I had to wonder why I was doing so now. "I don't mince words, Rose. I'm not that kind of man."

She folded her arms and walked closer, cocking her head as she locked eyes with mine. "I'm curious as to what kind of man you are?"

Her challenge brought out the beast in me, a hunger that had the chance of being difficult to suppress. However, I had a feeling she wasn't a one-night stand kind of girl. "The kind that takes what he wants."

"I'm not for sale."

"I never said you were."

"Oh," she mused. "You're the dominating type, someone who refuses to take no for an answer."

I took two steps closer, the ache in my cock increasing. A wry smile twisted across her pursed lips, and I sensed she wasn't the kind of woman to back down from any challenge. That made me desire her that much more. "I am many things."

"Mmm... I can tell you are. Rich. Arrogant. Dominating. Unethical."

The last word surprised me. "Now, how would you know I was unethical by talking with me for a few minutes?" When I took another step, I was certain she'd back away, only inches between us.

"I have an innate knowledge of these things. You own a powerful business, and you got there by toying with gray areas." She inched even closer, and I found it almost impossible to keep my hands to myself.

"I rarely toy with anything, including my women."

"Then what do you do with them?" Her voice had dropped to a sensual, low pitch that vibrated against my skin. She tilted her head, her chest rising and falling from her ragged breathing.

"Provide endless nights of unbridled passion."

When she gently, cautiously placed her hand on my chest, I almost lost all control. If I had my way, I'd toss her against her makeup table and fuck her relentlessly.

The loud, single knock on her door brought a husky growl to my lips.

She sighed as she looked past my arm, irritation in her intense blue eyes. "Yes?"

The door opened and whoever her visitor was, he had heavy footsteps. "Rose, darling. It's time for your interview."

"I need a couple minutes, Brett."

I turned slightly, enough to catch the disdain on the overweight man's face. He obviously didn't like the fact that she had a visitor.

"We're talking *People* magazine for God's sake. You can't keep them waiting. And what are you wearing? That's dreadful."

My hackles were raised. The man as asshole as far as I was concerned.

She frowned, then winked at me. "They'll take me as I am or nothing at all. I'll be right there."

"Fine. It's your career." Brett walked out, slamming the door.

She chuckled. "I apologize for my manager. He hasn't been out from under his rock for long."

"I don't want to keep you from what you need to do." I backed away, gathering a whiff of my explosive testosterone.

"Perhaps we'll meet again."

"Yes. Perhaps." After heading toward the door, I gave her another look, one that should highlight exactly what I had planned for the lovely jewel.

Soon, she would be writhing underneath me as she screamed out my name.

CHAPTER 12

Cain

There were several requirements of the people I did business with, much like I demanded from my employees.

Loyalty without question.

Making appointments on time.

Respect.

Following the hierarchy.

No abuse of women and children under any circumstances.

They were aspects my father had drilled into me over the years. While I had no morals or conscience per say, after what had happened to Sage, I'd doubled down on standing behind the rules that been a part of our family for generations.

A single breach meant punishment, no matter who the person was.

As I headed to my private business suite located on the top floor of the entertainment wing, I buttoned my jacket. It had been a few weeks since I'd thought of Sage, a welcome relief after the years I'd spent privately grieving. I should have celebrated her death given that's what I'd originally wanted, but as soon as I'm heard she'd been taken off the machines keeping her alive, I'd gone on a violent rampage.

She'd belonged to the three Kings of the City of Hope. We'd claimed her. The fact that someone had dared touch her in an inappropriate manner had allowed the savage killer in me to see the light of day.

Now, with the detective breathing down my neck and the fact both my old buddies had arrived or would shortly, I had a feeling I'd have several sleepless nights.

I moved through the crowded lobby, remembering the press conference that had been approved through my office. Fortunately, the reporters were headed out. I doubted my illustrious guests appreciated the interruption or the possible inclusion in a rag paper or internet site. For my clientele consisting of dignitaries, politicians, actors, musicians, and corporate moguls, their loyalty in selecting my resort was rewarded with very unique perks, including entrance in what people frequently called my world of debauchery.

On one side, a kink club catered to and allowed kinky activities without reprehension. On the other, the private casino hosted games of blackjack and poker where the stakes were limitless and creative, including the use of beautiful women as a decadent surprise for select winners. I had three more hotels modeled after this one, all four alone making me a very rich man, the facilities laundering almost one hundred percent of the money my corporation was worth.

I considered reporters the scourge of the earth, every one of them out for their fifteen minutes of fame, no matter the damage to the person they were interviewing.

I watched the exit of the cockroaches and sighed, something catching my eye. I'd yet to meet the entertainer of the hour, a woman who had come with her own entourage and the reason for the onslaught of reporters. But I'd been curious enough to download several of her songs to Spotify. Her voice was that of an angel, melodic and limitless.

After noticing she was having a terse discussion with someone, I pushed my way through the crowd to get closer. By the time I'd passed through the large group, the man she was with had his hand around her arm, jerking her towards a corridor. It was obvious to see she was furious with him, her face contorted with anger.

I pushed through the rest of the people in my way, snarling at his treatment of her. Where the hell was her security detail?

When she yanked her arm away and he acted as if he was going to slap her face, I intervened without question. He didn't see me coming and when I snapped my fingers around his wrist, pitching him against the wall, he almost crumbled to the floor. Then the bastard was stupid enough to launch himself off the wall, lunging towards me.

With a crack to his gut, then another to his jaw, he was flipped up and backward, crashing against the door to one of the men's rooms, where he stayed, which was in his best interest. I took a deep breath, the ache in my fist barely providing what I needed to calm the desire for bloodshed. It came and went, but tonight I was in the mood to break bones.

"What the hell do you think you're doing?"

The demanding tone in her voice instantly caused a reaction, my cock stiffening. I did so love a woman with spunk, unafraid of opening her mouth. I turned slightly, inhaling Rose's perfume as I studied her attire, the look entirely different than the many changes of clothing she'd worn while on stage.

"Removing a leach."

"That's my manager you just beat the shit out of. I'll have you know I can take care of myself."

While the aggravation regarding my actions remained in her voice, I couldn't help but notice she wasn't attempting to discover his condition. There was a fire in her eyes that drew me in, as if there was no one else in close proximity.

I certainly didn't want there to be. "You have no idea what men are capable of."

She laughed, her tone haughty. "Oh, I think I do. Men are conceited pieces of shit who truly believe they can lord that fact they have a dick between their legs over women." Huffing, she raked her fingers through her tussled hair, the look adding to her sexy kitty-kat exterior. I'd seen the faces of several of the male reporters. They were just as aroused as I'd become.

"So jaded at such a young age." Her words amused me.

"I have my reasons. What in the hell am I supposed to do about Brett?"

"Fire him," I told her casually as I headed in her direction.

Her eyes flashed with venom and ice, a dangerously sensual combination. "I would if my record company hadn't hired him."

"Ah, yes. You sold your soul when you were young and for nothing but a chance at stardom."

"I'm sorry. Is there a reason I should bother talking to you other than your arrogance and determination to ruin my evening?"

The fire buried deep within her core was explosive. Visions of stripping off her clothes, fucking her against the wall powered into my mind. I couldn't remember the last time a single woman had challenged me so openly. Most were terrified of what I would do. It was also obvious she had no clue who I was.

I backed her against the wall, planting my hands on either side of her. I was several inches taller, outweighed her by well over a hundred pounds, yet she wasn't intimidated. She was aroused, her nipples clearly accentuated through the thin material of her silk blouse.

"The only reason that's necessary. Hunger."

"I beg your pardon?" She pushed herself as tightly against the wall as possible, but the way her breath hitched meant she remained completely aroused.

"You heard me, little pet."

She narrowed her eyes, glancing away. I couldn't tell if she was offended by my words of endearment or furious. Not that I cared. She wasn't a delicate flower by any means, which excited me, more so at the thought of taming her.

Breaking her.

I exhaled, allowing the heated breath to cascade across her jaw. Her lips quivered, her eyelids half open. I lowered my head while she tilted hers, our lips almost touching. There was a sense of longing that awakened the man inside, allowing me to feel something for the first time in years. However, even a single taste was dangerous.

I backed away, doing what I could to curtail my hunger. The last thing I needed was to get involved with the princess of rock. There were far too many stragglers of business that needed my constant attention. That included having additional guards stationed at both the resort and my estate given the assassination attempt Hunter had dealt with.

I refused to be caught with my pants down the way my buddy had. If The Iceman wanted to make another attempt, it would be the last one he made.

"I do hope you can regroup a part of your evening, beautiful Rose. Until we meet again." As I walked away, a woman was rushing towards Rose, concern on her aging face. I'd sensed she'd stiffened when she realized who I'd been talking with.

Now I had the lust for violence. If I couldn't satisfy my body's hungers, I would satiate my mind's.

The poor asshole who'd dared put his pregnant wife in the hospital would beg to die tonight.

* * *

Rose

I had to be in some bubble-like fantasy. Two of the hottest looking men in the country were sharing the same space. I brushed my fingers across my lips, wishing I'd taken a leap of faith and kissed him. Then there was the hunk from before, his desire evident by the delicious, huge cock between his muscular thighs.

Whew. I needed to curtail my filthy thoughts. I'd made the mistake of hooking up once with a guy I didn't know on tour. It was my biggest regret and had almost turned into a public relations nightmare. Never again.

But a girl could dream.

I'd taken out my anger and years of frustration about Brett and his 'handling' of me on a stranger. Granted, the gorgeous hunk of a man had an attitude that I was surprised fit in the building, but he didn't deserve the venom that had splattered from my mouth. Maybe I was tired, needing a vacation as I'd been told at least once by everyone I knew.

I couldn't relax yet. There were far too many award ceremonies, and a few stops on our tour in Europe. After that, I'd take a solid two months off and be by myself.

Alone.

The thought left me feeling cold and achy inside.

Jillian bustled towards me, her face beet red. The woman needed to take a break every now and then herself. As my assistant, makeup guru, and wardrobe challenger, she'd become a godsend. However, she never left me alone for very long.

Shaking my head, I snorted as I looked at Brett still passed out on the carpet. I'd been shocked at the stranger's reaction, although I had to admit that I was enthralled he'd use such Herculean methods to save me. That wasn't something I was used to.

"Are you completely out of your mind?" Jillian's assault with words left nothing to the imagination.

"That depends on who you ask. What's wrong?"

"That man you were talking to. He's a… He's the…"

"He's one of the hottest men you've ever seen before. You're right, but there's more than one predator crawling the halls of this posh hotel."

She narrowed her eyes, doing what she could to process my cavalier behavior. "Predator is the correct word."

Brett finally groaned and rolled over.

Maybe I should check on his wellbeing. Nope. The man had become more of an ass over the last two years, including demanding a significant raise. What I'd told the gorgeous stranger hadn't been a lie. I'd love to toss his ass out the door. "Are we really going to play games tonight, because I'm ready for a glass of wine and a hot bubble bath."

"Stay away from that man."

"If you mean Brett, gladly." I slipped my practiced prima donna smile into place, and I could tell she wanted to wring my neck. "If you mean the man I was talking with, then I'll be happy to ease your fears. I have no idea who he is. However, he did come to my rescue when Brett was being an asshole." I made certain the last word was said with a boost in decibels since Brett was fighting his way to a standing position.

Jillian threw him a look, then motioned us further away from him. As we walked through the lobby, I noticed she was scanning the perimeter. "You really don't know who your mystery hero is?"

"Not a clue."

"His name is Cain Cross. He's considered the most ruthless, brutal mafia leader in the country. This is his resort and casino. He rules Chicago."

I took a deep breath. No wonder my father had tried to advise me to keep Chicago and the four-week residence off my calendar. But it hadn't been entirely up to me, other members of the band weighing in on the lucrative decision. My opinion wouldn't have won even if I'd known the man's identity.

Or cared. "Okay."

"Did he threaten you?"

"I already told you—no. Why are you so concerned?" I knew she was from Chicago, while I'd grown up in Southern California where my parents still resided.

"Because he's the kind of man that once he sets his sights on you, he believes you belong to him."

"Jilly. You know me better than that. I could care less about dominating men who think I'm going to fall at their feet. He's just a man." Albeit a gorgeous man. My mama hadn't raised a stupid girl. I knew how to handle myself with big, bad men who believed themselves to be wolves in sophisticated, expensive attire.

She relaxed visibly but shook her head. "Just stay away from him. The only reason I didn't raise a stink about you guys accepting this gig was so you could have some time to yourself to regroup and refresh."

"Meaning I need to stop making irrational decisions. Right?" The word wasn't the one she'd used. While she was only fifteen years older, she'd acted like my surrogate mother since coming to work for me. I was a grown woman, intelligent enough to know that at thirty-one, acting like the persona I'd become over the last seven years had gotten old.

And it had almost gotten me into trouble a few times. While I wasn't thinking about retiring anytime soon, I knew I was due for a long break and possibly a change in direction. If I even breathed a word of it to the other band members, they'd have me hogtied and whipped. We were far too successful to consider anything crazy.

She squeezed my arm. "I just want what's best for you. That's all."

"I know, and I appreciate that." I chewed on my lower lip, unable to keep my thoughts off both men. How many times had I fantasized about a threesome or foursome? I almost laughed at the ridiculous thought. There certainly couldn't be a third equally stunning man roaming the halls of the hotel.

"What's best for me is a glass of wine in my suite all by myself. I have tomorrow off, and I plan on getting a little sun and perhaps taking a nice, long swim."

Her smile was forced. "You do that, honey. You earned it."

"Why don't you do the same, mommy dearest?" We both laughed, and she wagged her finger at me before walking off. I waited a couple seconds, then strode towards the bank of elevators leading to the residential wing, lurid thoughts forming sexy visions in my mind. Thankfully I had the cold, steel box to myself. After pressing the button to the top floor, I closed my eyes, allowing the desire that had sparked within me to rush to the surface.

"Come here, little pet. On your knees." Cain's voice was disturbing and raw, the low growl in his throat possessive.

I slowly dropped to my knees and onto all fours, tossing my hair back and forth before crawling towards the two men who owned me. As soon as I was close, every inch of my skin became covered in goosebumps, a deep longing keeping my core on fire.

"That's it, baby girl. Come to your daddies." Hunter's voice was just as powerful, enticing me in a way I hadn't expected. My throat was tight, my pussy so wet my inner thighs were covered with my juices. In his hand was a tawse, the six tails of leather keeping me tingling all over.

As soon as I was close, Cain lifted my chin with a single finger, peering down at me with unbridled lust in his eyes. "My good girl," he whispered, then brushed his hand through my hair. "But also very naughty." He wrapped his long fingers around my throat, squeezing. Then Hunter gently brought the strap down on my buttocks, brushing it back and forth. I shuddered audibly, keeping my eyes locked on Cain as required.

"Yes, she requires intense discipline," Hunter said in his gravelly voice. Without hesitation, he brought the tawse down with more force, cracking the tails against my backside.

I was on fire almost instantly, my core already ignited.

"Don't worry, little pet. If you're very good, you'll be provided with all the ecstasy you desire."

Exhaling, I dragged myself out of the vision. It seemed so real, as if I could reach out and touch them. I hadn't indulged in a fantasy so spectacular in several months.

As soon as the elevator doors opened, I took long strides towards my suite, fighting to get the card into the slot. All of a sudden, I wanted to write down my lurid thoughts. I was used to writing songs, had dozens of them in reserve that I planned to record, but this was different.

This was much more personal.

Once inside, I flew into the bathroom, stripping off my clothes and struggling into the thick terry cloth robe. Then I headed for the kitchenette, yanking a wine glass from the cabinet and filling it with merlot. After taking a sip, I realized the only paper I had with me had been prepared for musical notes, not a story.

What the hell? I'd put the thick pad to good use anyway.

I yanked a pad from the credenza where I'd placed some of my things, taking it and the wine into my bedroom. With the light on, I flopped on the bed. After another sip of merlot, I placed the glass on the nightstand.

Then I began to write furiously, my pussy aching after only a few minutes. Perhaps I'd meet up with Hunter, exploring something naughty. My thoughts drifted to Cain, my nipples aching. I slipped my hand under the robe, rubbing then twisting my nipple. What was so wrong with having a sexy fling with a bad boy or two?

I eased back on the pillow, rolling my other hand down the robe, sliding the two sides apart. As I rolled my palm around my bare mound, I envisioned both men together. Desire roared through me, and I flicked my finger across my clit, biting my lower lip to keep from making a single sound. The moment I closed my eyes again, a flash of an image shot across my mind's eye. It was different, certainly not as deliciously filthy as the earlier one.

For some reason, the swarm of butterflies I'd experienced earlier turned into a raging group of biting fire ants. I jerked up, my body shaking.

Why did I have a terrible feeling that Jillian's warning was one I should listen to?

And that she knew more than she was telling me?

The ugliness of danger was stronger than it had ever been before, as if I should know them from some point in my life.

Hissing, I grabbed my wine. Several years of my life were missing, an accident. My parents had told me nothing about the circumstances, but for some crazy reason, I knew it was important that I remember them.

But why?

CHAPTER 13

Cain

Soon...

The single word texted from a burner phone that had likely been tossed had changed my mood entirely.

To say I was wired would be a serious understatement.

If the implied threat was meant to send me cowering into a corner, it had provided the opposite effect.

I was ungodly enraged. Anything could set me off, and something had.

After dealing with the prick who had Rose's life in the palm of his hand, I was hungry for blood. I considered myself to be a tolerant man most of the time. However, when I got to a certain point, people knew to stay out of my way. Even looking at me sideways could be grounds for termination or worse.

"You're on edge. Again." The words were said as I strolled into the outer room, my righthand man waiting for me. Brock Carter was the only person in my employ, and one of three in the world who could get away with tossing out basic insults.

He had his arms folded but threw his hand out, his palm pressing against my chest to stop me from barreling into the room where the jerk who'd almost killed his wife was being held.

"Don't do this, Brock." My snarl was laced with venom. At this point, there were two methods of soothing the anger and settling the darkness furrowing inside like a rancid infection. Unfortunately, brutal sex was off the table. I wasn't in the mood to pretend I gave a damn about a woman long enough to get my rocks off.

The second was just as enjoyable, albeit messy. I wanted to peel away every inch of skin from the bastard who'd dared attack a woman. I'd done it before, but this time it would be personal.

Exhaling, he didn't budge. He simply shook his head. "I wouldn't be doing the job you hired me to do if I allowed you inside that room right now. You'll kill him and that jerk still needs to provide for his family. He's all they have."

"Who gives a fuck?" I backed away, taking a deep breath and holding it.

"Well, unless you plan on saddling yourself with paying for a wife and three kids for the rest of your life, then I suggest you take a beat and calm the fuck down."

Exhaling, I glared at him but finally nodded. He was right, as he usually was. "Fine. I'll take a minute."

"Good. Now, what the fuck happened to make you crazy?"

Crazy wasn't the word for it. It was as if I'd been dragged into the past, the nightmare of what had occurred all those years ago coming dangerously close to the surface. If Theodore's father was dead set on bringing us down, then we'd have no recourse but to end the chapter. What bothered me was that there would be additional questions, especially since he'd likely talked to the detective who'd bothered me.

Fuck. This situation was getting out of hand already. I knew better than to allow any loose ends to remain, but both Hunter and Cristiano had convinced me to back away. Why was it all coming crashing down now?

"Be careful when your past comes back to haunt you," I told him.

"The shit from the Elite?"

I'd kept many dark secrets in my life. It was a necessity in my line of work. The fact that I'd trusted him enough to mention the power we held during those four years over a bottle of bourbon hadn't been in my best interest. I'd even considered ending his life because of what he'd learned, but the man was far too valuable. He'd saved my butt on more than one occasion.

"Yeah."

"Well, if you need me to handle anything, I'll be happy to take care of it."

"You're a twisted fuck, just like I am. It may come down to that. I'll let you know." I took another deep breath, then brushed my hands down my jacket, unbuttoning it at the same time. "Let's get this over with."

"You sure you don't want me to deal with Barrett?"

I managed to grin, which was usually the sign I wouldn't become a total psychopath. "I think the lesson needs to come from me, or he'll consider doing it again."

He nodded. "Good point."

As he opened the door, my thoughts briefly drifted to Rose, a smile crossing my face. As an image of her lovely face slipped into the forefront of my mind, I was pleasantly surprised how calm I'd suddenly become. Perhaps she was a good luck charm of sorts. I made a mental note to insist she have dinner with me.

One taste could be all I needed. Or maybe not.

Several lascivious thoughts lingered as I walked into the soundproof room. I'd known the moment I was taking over the casino that I'd need to spend an exorbitant amount of time handling the renovation and subsequent operation of the expansive resort. That meant I needed a secure area to handle different, more brutal aspects of my business. Including doling out punishment as necessary.

With a separate entrance, a secure gated parking lot with eight-foot concrete walls, the location allowed for maximum privacy when handling disposals as necessary.

The existence of the 'special' facility was widely known in the ranks of my employees as well as listed as an ugly rumor with my enemies. Which of course I'd started. I'd learned early on that an unsaid threat was just as powerful as one issued in person. Plus, it fed the sadistic man inside of me.

I enjoyed seeing them sweat.

Which was exactly what Barrett was doing. People who knew him called him the Bruiser because of his use of his fists. In this case, his misuse.

By the glint of fear in his eyes, the room had worked his magic.

He'd been snatched up just getting off from work by Brock and another Capo, Marty, with two other soldiers remaining in the back of the room in case things got messy. Barrett had been a damn good dealer in the casino since the opening, but the stories of his abuse to his once beautiful wife had finally crossed a line.

The boys had roughed him up pretty good, leaving me enough real estate if I wanted to create an entirely new face for him. I would ordinarily enjoy carving his wife's name onto one cheek, the word 'abuser' on the other, but given my sudden good mood because of Rose, I might use another tactic. It depended on his actions and level of remorse.

I grabbed a chair, twisting it the opposite way and sitting down in front of him, crossing my arms across the stiff back.

Barrett seemed surprised at my actions, flinching.

I glanced around the room at the various instruments and tools I'd acquired with nothing but punishment in mind. Inside these walls, I could carve a man into filet if needed.

"I don't need to tell you how badly you fucked up, Barrett."

"I did nothing."

His insistence irritated me. "So, you enjoy beating your wife on a regular basis?" As I lifted my head, glaring into his eyes, I could tell he wasn't clueless as to what I was talking about. That gave him one bad boy point. I rated the men who sat in this chair. If they stayed under three, they were given a decent warning. Four or five, things started to get messy. Anything a seven or above and they'd shit themselves before begging for death.

Something else I enjoyed was betting on the number I'd ultimately give them. My guess was a six, just below the threshold where I'd be required by my rules to provide for his family for the duration of their lives.

"Fuck you," he spit out. "She's my wife. I can do anything I want with her."

Mistake and bad boy points two and three. "You have children to think about, including the one inside her belly."

"Bitch. I don't think it's mine."

I pulled back, glancing at Brock, who shook his head. It was apparent that Barrett was a clueless Neanderthal. We were up to five points. It wasn't looking good for the heartless prick.

"Let me ask you a question. Do you love your wife?"

He hesitated but only because he hadn't anticipated the question. "Yeah."

Certainly not a romantic dude. "Then it's your responsibility to treat her like a queen. I assure you that that child growing inside is yours. A boy, if I seem to recall. A legacy that you will treat with love and respect just like you will with your wife. Do you understand what I'm saying?"

I always made it a point to know what I was talking about. For all the wrong reasons, his wife still adored him and would never stray.

"Like I said before," he threw out through clenched teeth, his words slightly slurred from the beating he'd taken, "she's my wife."

And just like that he found himself on level six. It was almost like playing Russian Roulette. Perhaps that would have been more effective. "I can tell my requirements aren't getting through to you, Barrett, and that's a shame. I'm going to have my men ensure that they get through to you in just a few moments." I stood, taking my time to return the chair to its original position. Then I casually pulled my weapon from my jacket, studying it in front of him before shoving the barrel under his chin.

He finally had the fear of God flash in front of his eyes.

"Let me be very clear, Barrett. You will never raise a hand to your wife or any of your children ever again. I do mean ever. I don't care if she comes to her senses and fucks every man in this resort, or if your kids grow up to hate you, which they should, you will not touch them. If you do, what happens after I leave this room will be considered child's play compared to what will happen in the future. Because I'll be the one providing your punishment, which will take days since I enjoy inflicting pain. I think you know people refer to me as a twisted psychopath. Yes?"

He swallowed, his eyes coming close to bulging. Then he nodded once.

"Excellent." I started to turn away, grinning given Brock's surprised expression. He wasn't used to seeing me in such a good mood. I rubbed my jaw, looking at Barrett again. "Oh, and when you recover, which could take some time, you will buy your wife flowers once a week. Don't always purchase roses. Make them special, her favorite color. Got it?"

"Yes, sir." Suddenly, he grinned as if he had something on me. I waited, narrowing my eyes. "By the way. People know about that night."

"That night?" I froze, instantly on edge. "What night are you talking about?" I tipped my head enough to see his eyes. He thought he carried some big, bad secret with him, one worth money or a get-out-of-jail-free card.

"Does the term the Elite mean anything to you?"

"From four of the best years of my life. What's it to you?"

"People know what you did."

"People?" I laughed. "I did a lot of things, Barrett. Care to expound?"

He glanced towards Brock then back to me. "No, sir. I was just agreeing that you were a psycho."

Why did I have the feeling there was more to his warning?

I slipped the weapon into my jacket, happy with the outcome at this point. Brock followed me to the door, laughing softly under his breath.

"I don't know what liquor you had, but consider it your drink of choice," he said.

"Not liquor, my friend. Something better. A beautiful woman who might get me out of my dry spell."

"Well, then. She must be something special." Brock guided me out the door. "What did the dirtbag mean by dishing your alma mater?"

"I'm not certain. See if you can get it out of him."

"No problem. What treatment do you want?"

"I think the use of the Louisville Slugger will work."

"Top or bottom?"

I threw Barrett one last glance. "Let's go bottom. As you reminded me. He does need to provide for his family, so he needs his arms and hands. However, there's nothing in the rules against our dealers sitting. Permanently."

"You got it, boss. You're still the sickest fuck I know."

"I'll take that as a compliment, Brock. One last thing. Have one of the men drop off an envelope of cash and a bouquet of flowers to his house. His wife will need a little help for the time being."

The sound of his laughter followed me as I left the room. As soon as I did, another grin slipped across my face.

Maybe I'd invite Rose to my suite instead. I could only imagine what kind of mood I'd be in after spending an entire night with her.

It would be good for employee morale.

CHAPTER 14

Rose

Run. Run. Run!

I couldn't race fast enough through the forest. They were following me. I knew it. I could feel it in my bones, the monsters on my heels. My breath skipped, my heart aching from the exertion as I tore through the blackness into the trees. When I tripped over a log, I fell hands and face first into briars. Pain tore through me, but it was nothing like the horrible sense of being hunted like a wild animal.

"Oh, little pet. Come out. Come out wherever you are."

I jerked up, my mouth open in a silent scream. The entire space in front of me was nothing but a warm glow of golden rays, adding to the wooziness and my foggy mind. I took a few deep breaths, utilizing the exercises I'd learned to control my stage fright and clenched my eyes closed. When I opened them again, I was able to make out furniture inside a room. The suite at the resort. Exhaling, I scanned the room, then laughed to myself. It had just been a nightmare.

As I thought about the images that had forged a place in my mind, I realized they were similar to ones I'd had a long time ago. In the nightmare, I was always running through a forest, being chased by unseen monsters. The dreams had never completed in any satisfying conclusion. I doubted they ever would, visions meant to torment my shattered mind.

I threw back the covers, realizing I'd fallen asleep in my robe. Then I noticed torn off pieces of paper from the music pad I'd used to write the story notes. There were dozens of them. What the hell?

As I picked them up one by one, I was shocked, a trickle of fear skating down my spine. The words on the pages were definitely my handwriting. There were two dozen or more pages of them. Each one numbered as a reminder of which came first. Then they'd been tossed across the bed almost as a blanket.

Jesus Christ.

I only remembered writing the first page and nothing more.

What was wrong with me?

I hesitantly eased onto two feet, reaching out then yanking my hand back twice before I managed to gather all the pieces of paper. Why I was taking the time to sort them in order was beyond me, but after I did, I took a few minutes to read from one sheet to another.

The story was good. No, not just good. The damn thing was brilliantly written, beautiful in its sexual content. By the time I stopped reading, I was wet and hot, my sore nipples scraping against the robe.

Bam. Bam!

"Oh!" A gasp flew from my mouth as the sound reverberated in the room. What the hell? "Stupid girl. Someone's at the door." It was almost noon for God's sake. Normal people were up, soaking in the summer sun instead of expressing their fantasies enshrouded in darkness.

I took the papers with me into the other room, placing them on the coffee table. I was shocked I hadn't moved to my laptop. I'd only intended on using the creative side of me for a release after the two shows the day before. It was as if I'd been possessed to finish the story.

After pulling the robe tightly around me, I opened the door a crack.

"Ms. Sadler? I have a delivery for you."

The bellman had been the one who helped me with my things when I'd checked in. "I didn't order anything."

"It would seem you have a secret admirer."

I opened the door all the way, shocked to see at least three dozen of the most gorgeous roses I'd ever seen in my life. The color combination was a spray of orange, lemon, and crimson. "Oh, my goodness. Those are gorgeous." I allowed him inside, trying to remember where I'd left my purse.

"Where would you like them?"

"The coffee table is fine. Let me get you a tip."

"Not necessary. The sender was very generous."

"Now, you have me curious."

He placed them where I asked, then turned around, pinching his forefinger and thumb together, pretending he was zipping his lips.

"Hmmm… Thank you, Johnny. You are wonderful."

"That's the best type of tip a man like me could receive." He backed away, offering a bright smile.

I waited until after he'd left to walk towards the bouquet, running my hands across several of the barely opened buds. The softness of lush velveteen tickled the tips of my fingers. Then I bent down, gathering a deep whiff of their incredible scent. Amazing. How long had it been since anyone had given me flowers? Even my shithead of a manager had never done that. Oh, yes. My father had brought me a dozen red roses to my first couple of shows, trying to brighten my night after the sparse crowd had barely clapped. He'd been my rock and encouragement.

I noticed a card and bit my lip, uncertain why I hoped the beautiful treat was from either one of the gorgeous men I'd met. I tugged the small note from the envelope, feeling slightly giddy when I read the words.

. . .

Good morning, sunshine.

Come meet me by the cascade pool at noon for a little bubbly.

If you dare...

Hunter

Why did his words thrill me so much? I was crazy to meet with a complete stranger who'd insisted on meeting me then sending me the most gorgeous flowers in the world. Or was I?

I glanced at the clock and squealed. I had ten minutes to prepare. This was one of those 'why not' moments I planned on killing.

I managed to put myself together, grabbing a sexy yet comfortable dress and sandals and heading out with a couple minutes to spare. The cascade pool was on the other end of the sprawling resort, and by the time I made it outside, I was five minutes late. There were already dozens of people enjoying the cloudless day and light breeze, music pumping from invisible speakers.

The vibe was tropical, with palm trees and tiki bars, umbrellas in a dazzling array of colors. I moved through towards the open-air restaurant, forced to don my sunglasses. When I didn't see him after my first tour, disappointment squelched my excitement.

Then I noticed several tables on a raised platform, the area roped off with no customers.

Except for a single man.

Even from the distance, I was still taken aback by the man's incredible prowess and utter control as he gazed into the waterfall below. It was as if he was looking at his kingdom. I moved slowly towards the stairs, realizing I was holding my breath. He noticed me just before I reached the bottom step, immediately standing. As I walked up, I was able to take a better look at the man I'd fantasized about.

He was at least six foot four, his shaggy dark hair covering the color of his short-sleeve Henley. Wearing casual, lightweight trousers and sunglasses, he reminded me of a movie star from a couple decades before, the Miami Vice vibes creating a pool of knots in my stomach.

As soon as I was close to the single table prepared for diners, he popped open a bottle of champagne, his expertise in doing so notable. By the time I got to the table, two crystal stems had been poured, a strawberry from the gorgeous display of fruit swimming inside.

Then he placed his hand on his chest, shaking his head slowly.

"What's wrong?" I asked, the coyness in my voice surprising.

"You are a vision in the morning, just as I knew you'd be."

"Thank you for the lovely flowers."

"I thought the ray of sunshine that I experienced last night should be gifted to the woman who brought so much joy to a lonely man." His grin was lopsided, highlighting the dimple in his chin. With the two-day stubble aligning his chiseled jaw, I was swept into another naughty fantasy of being with a bad boy.

Shame on me.

"And here I thought you weren't the kind of man to use come-on lines."

His laugh was deep, rumbling through my stomach. "I assure you it wasn't a come-on. You'll know the moment when I claim what I want."

As he pulled out the chair, encouraging me to sit, he brushed his fingers across my bare shoulder, and I was thrown by the intensity of my reaction. It wasn't just electrifying. It was as if a volcano had erupted, spewing hot ashes a hundred miles away. My breath was stolen, the same lightheaded feeling I'd experienced the night before muddling my senses.

He inhaled sharply, continuing his exploration, turning my arm over as he trailed his finger down to my wrist. When he traced the scar, a scowl crossed his face.

"It's not what it looks like," I told him.

"Meaning?" He lifted a single eyebrow, and the look belonged on the cover of a men's fashion magazine.

"I didn't try and kill myself. I'm much stronger than that."

"That's not what I was thinking, sweet Rose."

"Then what were you thinking?"

"That whoever hurt you should be punished. Now that I've claimed you, no harm will come your way."

The words were satisfying and adorable in a Neanderthal kind of way, but his possessive tendencies forced my heart to go pitter-patter.

"It was an accident I don't even remember. And I feel it necessary to warn you, Mr. Augustine. I'm not easily claimed by anyone under any circumstances. I've never been, and I don't plan on it anytime soon."

He sat down, pulling his chair closer to mine, then easing his arm against the back. When he wrapped his hand around the flute, I noticed a massive black onyx ring on his middle finger. There was a crest of some kind with a red ruby positioned in the center. I could swear there were two swords but didn't want to make it apparent I was staring. He lifted the glass, cocking his head.

"To a fascinating and beautiful woman."

I pressed my crystal rim to his, the man able to hold my gaze for longer than necessary. Heat rushed from my neck to my jaw as he lowered his eyes, his nostrils flaring. He wasn't just unwrapping the package underneath. He was peeling it away slowly, tasting me as he prepared to consume me whole.

"To a dominating man who believes he has a right to obtain every possession that might satiate his desires."

Grinning, he gulped almost half the glass. Everything about him was sexy, including the way his Adam's apple bobbed up and down as he swallowed. "You overestimate my power."

"I don't think so. What do you do, Mr. Augustine?"

"I think we're way past formalities, Ms. Sadler. Don't you think?"

"Meaning what?"

When he leaned in, his masculine, musky scent was immediately intoxicating. Who needed expensive champagne to feel raw euphoria?

"Meaning, budding Rose, there's no need to dance around our attraction. Now is there?"

In the sunlight, his deep chocolate eyes had become almost luminescent. If he thought I was so enthralled I'd soak up his charm like a dried-out sponge, he was sorely wrong. I took control of the situation, running the tip of my nail around his full lips, slowly removing my sunglasses. Then I leaned in so close our lips were almost touching. "Our attraction might be carnal, desire brimming the surface, but unless there's something honorable under the handsome, polished exterior, then I will never be interested."

His breathing was labored, his eyes becoming hooded. I refused to lean away, daring him to make the first move.

I wasn't prepared for the treachery of my body when he rolled a single finger down the side of my face and under my chin. Tingles prickled every nerve, my breath skipping more than a beat or two. When he wrapped his fingers around my cheek, keeping his thumb positioned under my chin, I finally stiffened.

"As far as your question. I own a textile manufacturing firm in Philly."

"Did business bring you into town?"

He sighed. "Yes, the circumstances not what I'd hoped. It would seem a contract could possibly go south, which doesn't bode well for my personality."

"I'm certain you'll strong-arm them into doing what you want."

"Yes, I plan on it."

"A take charge kind of man."

There was something deliciously dark about his grin. "I am in every aspect of my business and personal life."

"Does that mean you'd control me?" I could tell my question enticed him.

His nostrils flared as he took a deep whiff. "Let's just say I might make you my little pet."

"Ride my hand, little pet."

The words filtered into my mind followed by a strange vision. A red dress. A night of passion. Then... pain. Where in the world had that come from? I looked away, trying to remember the various details of the dream. Were they the same?

"Are you alright?" he asked, able to bring me out of the moment.

"Absolutely. However, I don't think I'd made a good pet. I'm too unpredictable."

"There isn't a woman I can't tame."

"Hhhmmm… Which means you've owned pets before. I might like to hear the fascinating story of just how you managed to tame them."

"Not for long. What you find underneath could scare you. My methods have been called… sadistic."

"I don't scare easily." The use of the last word brought an array of naughty images into my mind. Being tied to a bed, masked, and gagged. Waiting for my master to arrive. Being spanked like a bad little girl, marks covering my buttocks and thighs. Wow. I was stretching my imagination more than ever before. I felt heat rising on my neck and shuddered.

"Mmm… I do so love a woman who can handle the darkness." His voice had dipped dangerously low, becoming more enticing than before.

"I can handle almost anything. But it's my decision as to whether I'll allow it or not."

His deep, very low growl rumbled through every inch of my body. "Yes, little pet. I'll keep that in mind, but I have a feeling with the right training, you could become a very good girl. Do you think you'd enjoy spending some time with an arrogant, dominating man?"

"That's it. You're such a good girl."

The voice in my head refused to go away. Suddenly, my pussy was throbbing, my panties damp. With the few men I'd dated in my life, none had ever attempted to take control of the limited relationship. Not once. I chewed on my bottom lip, thinking about his overt question.

"It depends on what you have in mind."

"Let's just say I'll provide you with the kind of enjoyment that you've likely never experienced before." He took his time pressing his knuckle back and forth across my pursed lips. While I didn't know him, I found the move one of the most sensual I'd felt in a long time.

"That does sound… fascinating."

"I assure you I don't bite, although I do very bad things to naughty girls."

"Whips, chains, and ball gags?"

His eyes opened wide and he gripped my chin between his thumb and forefinger. At that point, I was certain he could gather a whiff of my desire. Instead of being embarrassed, I was so aroused, I couldn't think clearly.

"Yes, and many other depraved acts. However, a spanking is always necessary to help a woman fully understanding her requirement to surrender."

Just the way he lowered his voice was enticing. Maybe I was crazy, but this was the kind of risk that could bring a sweet reward. "Then I guess it's a good thing I'm a very good girl."

"That remains to be seen. If you aren't, I have no issue taking you over my lap, spanking your bottom until its crimson."

Dear God, as my pussy muscles clenched and released, I had a terrible feeling I might climax right there.

He captured my mouth, holding our lips together in quiet reverence. Then his grip tightened, pulling me even closer as the moment of passion developed an intense urgency. I pressed my hand against his chest, and the moment my index finger found his heated skin, the tip was seared. Electricity spiraled between us to the point of being out of control. As his tongue dominated mine, sweeping back and forth as if in a desperate need to taste, I swooned from his powerful touch.

That never happened to me.

Unable to stop myself, a moan rushed up from my core, Hunter capturing it and issuing a growl in response. I was lost in the moment, stars floating in front of my eyes. I raked my fingernails up and down, my panties soaked from the desire roaring through me. Everything was a beautiful blur, and letting go with the stunning stranger felt perfect.

He pulled me from the chair and onto his lap, keeping his firm hold. I wrapped my arms around his neck, and when he jerked me closer, the feel of his hard cock pressing into me electrified every muscle.

But with all deliriously delicious things, the powerful moment shared came to an abrupt end when someone invaded our space, clearing his throat.

Hunter didn't react for a few seconds, choosing to continue tasting me, or perhaps he was laying claim. When he did pull back, it wasn't before he nipped my lower lip. The slight shot of pain was a strangely addictive reward, my nipples aching more than before.

"I see you waste no time."

The deep male voice was easily recognizable. Now I had a name to add to the chiseled face.

Cain Cross.

As I glanced up towards the sound, his gaze held mine, and I was certain I heard rumbles of thunder in the distance announcing his presence.

Hunter rose to his feet, easing me to my chair, then folding his arms as a grin popped across his face. "You made it, buddy."

I sat back down, immediately reaching for my champagne glass. I couldn't get the phrase 'little pet' out of my mind, and it was the strangest thing, along with writing the story I had the night before.

Cain wasn't alone, the man standing beside him utter perfection in tight black jeans and a casual white shirt, the sleeves rolled up exposing bronzed skin and colorful tattoos. The material was so thin, the light breeze continuously exposed his carved abdomen. Broad shoulders accompanied a long, muscular torso, thighs that I could barely surround three quarters with both hands.

He threw his hand out, Hunter eagerly shaking it. When Hunter pulled him in for a bear hug, that was a clear indication the three men were close.

"You know I wouldn't miss our little get togethers for the world," the stranger teased, then tossed me a quick look. "I heard about your near... accident. I think the three of us should talk and compare notes."

The way he chose his words so carefully indicated he was doing his best to hide something from me. Why did it sound ominous?

Hunter nodded, shifting his gaze back and forth between the two men. "I don't think the challenge I faced was by accident or coincidence."

"Agreed," Cain said under his breath, his piercing eyes locked onto mine. I'd never felt so uncomfortable in my life, the man so dominating my chest tightened.

"Any indication our friend is moving?" Hunter asked as he absently ran his fingers through several strands of hair.

"Not that I've been able to detect. However, I do have some information both of you need to hear." The stranger's voice deepened, the man just as careful with his words as Hunter had been.

Cain was furious, but not with what his friend had said. "We should have handled the situation before."

"Maybe so. Time to let it go, gentlemen. Remember, I'm enjoying a lovely Sunday morning." Hunter turned his head, grinning at me.

"Ah, yes. The beautiful woman. I must admit I'm envious," the stranger murmured, his tone sending a series of sparking bolts into every muscle in my body.

When the stranger removed his dark shades and directed his attention to me, an involuntary gasp left my throat, which amused the new god-like creature and annoyed the hell out of Cain. His eyes were green like the warmest waters of the Aegean Sea. It wasn't possible that three perfect creations were standing inches apart.

Suddenly, I was overwhelmed with pheromones, longing to lick every inch of what appeared to be eight pack abs.

Jesus. A little sexual banter, a heated exchange, an even hotter kiss, and I was in the throes of committing every dark sin.

I lifted my head, locking my gaze with Cain's. The look of possession I'd seen before had almost been crowded out by the reflection of jealousy in his cold, dark gray eyes. The look was so... obsessively enraged that I had difficulty pulling away.

Until the stranger spoke.

"Rose Sadler from Halo. How in the hell did you get so lucky to have her grace your dilapidated hotel? She's far too fabulous to accept your paltry rates." He grinned and that shattered the insane spell, all three men laughing. It was obvious they were friends, and I'd noticed they were wearing identical rings. Besides, I doubted a man like Cain would allow anyone to disrespect him that way.

"I assure you that she came with a price," Cain said through gritted teeth.

Why did I suddenly have the feeling the price was my complete surrender to three, gorgeous rogues?

And why didn't that bother me in the least?

"Rose, this is Cristiano Moreno," Cain said, studying my reaction carefully. "And it would seem you've met my other good friend, Hunter."

"We were just getting to know each other more personally," Hunter mused, then gripped my shoulder. What was it with men who thought they needed to advise every other male within seeing or hearing range that the woman he wanted to fuck was off limits? Should I be annoyed or flattered?

For a few seconds, my thoughts drifted to the story I'd mysteriously written in the middle of the night, and for once, I wondered if I might be able to pry myself out of my conservative shell. What was the worst that could happen by having a wicked, filthy tryst with three god-like creatures?

Then I remembered something my mother had told me more than once.

"Nothing good happens from an incident of wanton sin."

Maybe my mama was wrong. Or maybe I was tired of living in the shadows while my alternate personality took the lead on stage and in every aspect of my life.

I'd become an excellent observer over the years, something I'd learned as a performer. I could weed out the stalkers and other freaks with uncanny accuracy. However, with the three men who'd suddenly appeared in my life, I wasn't able to grasp their true personalities versus their practiced, perfect facades and obvious long-term connection.

However, what I did know left me wondering if I was losing my mind.

All three were fantastically gorgeous.

All three radiated a dark intensity that had absorbed almost every female's attention for as far as I could see. Whether eighteen or eighty, every chick was planning on my slow demise.

All three exuded the kind of brutal danger that should have me running far away.

The worst realization of all was that a teensy, tiny part of me wanted nothing more than to be sandwiched between all three.

Because that was exactly where I belonged.

CHAPTER 15

Cain

Goddamn it, I wanted her. Not just for a quick passionate tryst or even for the duration of her time spent in my resort, but because I'd been unable to sleep during the few hours I'd had to myself.

Visions of her face and her imagined naked body had continued to plague my mind until I'd finally given up, going to the gym for two hours straight.

My good mood would ordinarily be driven into the toilet at this point except that the perpetrator of the egregious afront was one of my two best friends. However, seeing Hunter with Rose had driven a shot of jealousy into my system, which was a feeling I hadn't experienced in years.

Hmmm... since seeing Theodore with his filthy hands on Sage. While the few women I'd dated had been beautiful by any man's standards, none of them had provoked the green-eyed monster into rearing from his lair.

This was entirely unexpected.

Rose tilted her head, using her hand to keep the glare from the sun out of her eyes. She studied me as if uncertain she wanted to give me the time of day after our exchange the night before. Fortunately, the dazzling light couldn't hide the dark craving or the look of desire she had. Unless I was wrong, she felt that way about all three of us.

"My," she said in a strong voice. "The three of you look as if you're ready to take down a heavyweight champion."

Hunter grinned, and I was certain Cristiano had plans on ravaging her body at some point soon. I certainly couldn't blame him.

"We've been known to handle certain issues together." I was curious as to what her response would be.

"I've heard you're a dangerous man, Mr. Cross. In fact, I was warned about you."

"I'm certain you were. They were right to do so." I heard the hint of amusement in my voice.

She shifted her gaze slowly to Cristiano. "And you? Should I be leery if I run into you in a darkened hallway?"

Cristiano crouched down next to her, taking her hand into his. When he rubbed her knuckles across his lips, she took an audible breath. "Yes, you should be very afraid. I regularly hunt beautiful women, taking them back to my castle where I perform filthy, sinful acts."

"You should know very little either bothers or terrifies me, especially after the things I've seen while touring the world."

Her answer brought a smile to Cristiano's face, which was rare. "A woman after my own heart."

"Be careful, brother. She sees right through entitled bullshit," Hunter said, half laughing.

Rose turned her full attention to Hunter, the spark in her eyes what I wanted to see. "I already know you have sharp teeth."

I was tossed back in time to our plans with Sage, the desire to keep her stronger than any of us had wanted to admit. While a percentage of women might enjoy the thought of having a foursome for only one night, there were very few women who would likely enjoy more than a couple of days.

Especially if they weren't in charge, which she would never be.

How long had it been since I'd allowed my mind to go off the deep end? It was impractical to think she could be mine for anything other than a single taste.

Or was it?

"Yes, I do. We'll be right back," Hunter told her, the smug look on his face forcing a smile. He'd sensed the level of irritation seeing the two of them together had created. He knew my mood swings better than Cristiano, something I doubted he'd ever let me forget. I'd been a very bad boy during my time at the City of Hope.

"There's a good chance I won't be here," Rose retorted, giving the three of us a playful but heated glare.

He bent over, placing his hands on either side of the armrests of her chair. "Then I guess I'll need to live up to my name, but I wouldn't just use my sharp teeth in order to catch you."

While it was only brief, the flash of mischief in her eyes shifted to an unrecognizable emotion that I couldn't read. After blinking twice, she obviously shook off whatever had troubled her, pushing his chest gently. "You boys obviously don't know what I'm made of. Perhaps it's time for you to find out."

Cristiano issued a low, husky growl, which further amused her. Her laugh was spectacular, just throaty enough to make a man weak in his knees.

And in my case, my cock hard as a rock.

Hunter added his own growl as he returned to his full height, lifting his eyebrows as he tossed me a look. When one side of his mouth quirked, I knew exactly what he was thinking.

That she could be another conquest. It had been his way of making a suggestion back in our arrogant-as-fuck days.

We headed towards the bar located on the second floor. I'd been curious as to why a special request had been made to block off the most prestigious area for outside dining. Now,

I knew why. Hunter had paid a pretty penny to ensure his request was filled.

"I'm sorry to hear about your father, Cris," Hunter said first.

Cristiano laughed. "Don't be, my friend. I killed him with my bare hands. It was time for him to die."

I watched as Hunter's face became clouded, which meant the man had changed significantly. He'd once enjoyed the chase and the kill as much as I did. Or maybe he simply didn't have it in him to commit patricide.

"We all have our crosses to bear." Hunter's answer amused the hell out of me, but Cristiano seemed to reflect on the words.

We'd all changed significantly over the years, no longer the eager kids who were certain they could conquer anything tossed in front of them. While I was no shrink, I'd venture a guess that loneliness had taken a toll. When on top of any industry, trusting anyone enough to allow them into our world was dangerous.

A quiet tension settled between us, the three of us occupying the moment of silence by staring at our lovely companion.

"God. The woman is a tease. It's obvious why she sells millions of CDs, sold out concerts everywhere." Cristiano shook his head.

"She certainly doesn't mince words," I told them. My cock was still aching, the desire for her keeping a wave of electricity coursing through me.

"You were right about Rose, Cain. Her performance last night was spectacular," Hunter said as he started the conversation.

"Do you mean before or after you took her to bed?" Perhaps I was more irritated than I thought.

"Here we go. Why is it that every time we get together, you two fight like fucking brothers?" Cristiano asked.

"Because we are brothers," I snapped. "She is beautiful, and she's a challenging woman."

"She is, but well worth getting to know."

Cristiano sighed. "Those days are over. Besides, we have business to discuss."

"He's right, but I didn't mean to jump on you, Hunter. She doesn't belong to me. This crap with the rise of The Iceman from the dead and good ole Theodore's father igniting his lynch mob again has obviously gotten under my skin. We need to figure out what the hell is going on. If The Iceman has returned to active status, then he's just getting started."

"You were almost killed?" Cristiano asked as he nodded toward Hunter.

"Yeah. I don't have any doubts it was The Iceman."

"By my calculations, that would make him somewhere around seventy-five years old," Cristiano offered as he glanced back and forth between us.

"How do you know this?"

"The stories about him go back at least fifty years. Hell, my father swears he met him a long time ago. And I'm not kidding." He leaned against the bar, shoving his hands into his pockets. "I don't know about you, but I can't see a seventy-year-old scaling walls and jumping from building to building."

"Have a little ageism, why don't you?" Hunter teased.

"Be real. You know the business we're all in is brutal on the body as well as the soul. Besides, if the assassin had wanted you dead, you'd be dead."

I took a deep breath. Cristiano's claim was fairly accurate. If what Hunter told me about the circumstances was true, then by all rights he should be nothing but ashes in a box, the assassin's bullet hitting its mark. "How do you account for the fact that Hunter's assassin had the same scar on his hand?" Maybe I was trying to make sense of what had occurred.

"You just think it's the same one. You were twelve, for fuck's sake," Hunter said. "Not to berate you, but there was a violent storm going on, and it was dark."

"There are some things people can't forget, even at twelve." I turned my head towards him, almost wanting to be furious, but I understood why he wasn't convinced. Meanwhile, I'd built my adult life around the certainty that The Iceman had been responsible. What if there was someone else pretending to be the man?

No, I had enough crosses to bear to worry about that.

"Look, I'm not suggesting anything, and I'm not saying it's impossible. I'm just reminding all three of us that what went on in college stays there. Plus, if you are right that Sage's father was The Iceman, after her death, he went into a freefall for a few years, finally falling off the radar. Last he and his wife were seen, they were living in Fiji. Plus, not a single other soul made the connection that Xavier Winters was The Iceman. Not one."

"You know I'm right!" I realized my voice had carried, Rose turning her head in our direction.

"Keep your damn voice down," Hunter hissed.

"All I'm saying, Cain, is that I find it hard to believe, because it's been ten years if he's reenergized his earlier career." Cristiano wasn't easily shaken, but I could sense he was being more tentative than usual.

"I understand what you're saying. We'll need to be cautious. Keep the security tight around you. However, you know I don't buy it when things look too easy or if they appear to be a coincidence. That being said. We could have another problem," I said as I shoved my hands into my pockets, purposely watching the beautiful woman enjoying the bright sun.

"Spill it," Hunter demanded.

"I had to deal with an unruly employee last night. In his quest for salvation, he tossed out that people knew about what happened years ago. When pressed, he said several employees received a cryptic email less than a week ago." I hated to admit it and had spent part of the night working with the computer technicians and the two hackers I'd recently hired to try and locate the source.

"Is that the truth?" Now, Cristiano seemed interested.

"Yeah, twenty-two emails were sent, five going into spam, two going to employees who no longer work at the resort. It appears the emails were sent from a bogus Gmail, the IP address somewhere in Brazil, China, the Soviet Union. You get the drill."

"A hack job for certain," Cristiano agreed. "Why? To make you look bad? I doubt your employees give a shit. They know what you really do for a living."

Chuckling, I scratched my jaw. "They do. I have a feeling whoever sent it knew at least one of them would mention it to me."

"Interesting scare tactic."

Hunter took a deep breath, half laughing before asking a question. "Do I want to know what these emails said?"

"Simple and to the point. 'Ten years ago, three men of the Elite including Cain Cross murdered a bright rising star. Her soul has yet to be freed.' Poetic."

The two men sucked in their breaths. "Someone is playing a game," Cristiano said. "We need to find out who."

Hunter took a deep breath. "Did either one of you get a strange text last night?"

I couldn't help laughing. "One word. Soon?"

When Hunter nodded, Cristiano exhaled. "Yeah, I tried calling the number. Not in service."

"Yeah, well, don't bother. Burner phone. No doubt," I told them.

"Meaning you've gotten more than one text." Hunter lifted his eyebrows.

"Yes, I have." I scanned the restaurant, almost laughing when I saw Rose's personal assistant watching her from a distance. The woman certainly didn't like me very much. As if I cared.

"Well, ain't this peachy," Cristiano growled. "I think we're being set up. Why Chicago, Hunter? New business?"

Hunter's expression went from confusion to disgust. "Yeah. Bart Coplan is supposed to sell his textile firm, but he's having seller's remorse."

I rubbed my jaw. "Strong company with tremendous profits. Why try and sell?"

"Why does the name Coplan sound familiar?" Cristiano asked.

"You're right, it does," I said in passing.

"He's legit," Hunter insisted. "But the change in his attitude was unexpected, forcing me to come to Chicago."

Too many things were out of place, leaving a trail of bloody breadcrumbs. I glanced at Cristiano.

"You mentioned earlier that we needed to talk. What other joyful information did you bring us?" Whatever game was being played was already taxing.

He nodded, obviously mulling over everything that was going on. "William Watkins is determined to ruin us one way or another. An article came out in the Times in New York. Somehow, he either convinced or bought off a reporter to tell his story regarding the Elite. It's a doozy. I took the liberty of printing a copy of the article for you. While he's careful not to commit himself to a libel suit by mentioning us specifically, he paints an ugly picture of the university and the Elite."

After he handed us a copy, I scanned it briefly. Then I balled the two sheets of paper into my fist. "The motherfucker needs to pay." Why would he attempt to do this now? It didn't make a lot of sense.

"Maybe that's why the contract I came here to finalize has a chance of going south," Hunter hissed. "It would seem to me a plan is in motion to destroy us one way or another."

We can't allow that to happen, gentlemen," Cristiano said as he looked from one to the other.

"At least it's the university a-holes who'll be forced to deal with this. I bet their attorneys will have this article retracted within a week, maybe sooner." Hunter folded it neatly, shoving it into his jacket pocket.

"That's not the point, and you know it. However, if anyone asks us questions, then we'll deal with it. Until then, we watch and wait to see who rears their ugly heads. And I assure you that they will." Still, I was furious to the point additional security was in the process of being installed on every computer and communications system.

If the fucker wanted to play hardball, then so be it.

"Go enjoy your day," I told Hunter, although the jealous beast wasn't too far under the surface.

He suddenly had the same look cross his face that he'd expressed before. "There's no reason we can't enjoy her together."

Cristiano snorted. "Are you suggesting we could share a woman for real?"

"Are you dating anyone?" he asked. "Are you, Cain?"

I shrugged.

Cristiano slowly turned his head towards Rose. "I've been busy with building the business."

"Why do I have a feeling you're going to say the same thing, Cain?"

This time I lifted my eyebrow. "We live in different parts of the country, gentlemen. Unless she's interested in a few nights of passion only, I'm not certain what our attraction could matter." We barely knew the girl, but she had certainly sparked all our interests.

"It could be fascinating to see if it could work out. She does travel more than we do." Cristiano chuckled. "But we can't be serious. We're grown men who need to eventually settle down."

"Who said anything about settling down?" Hunter threw in. "As mentioned, the girl is tough. What makes you think she'd want anything other than a casual fling?"

"Notice our boy here is certain he's going to get her between the sheets. Talk about over confidence," Cristiano said, laughing.

Cristiano had lightened up in the years that had followed our graduation. It was good to see the banter between us was the same. "Let's face it, gentlemen. One night destroyed a huge part of us. Whether we want to admit it or not."

Hunter shook his head.

When neither one of them said anything, I thought about the suggestion. "But we could see what happens for old times' sake. Rose has the night off. I know the perfect place where we can spend some quality time while engaging in pure sin. Are the two of you game?"

"I thought you'd never ask," Hunter answered.

I folded my arms and walked closer by a few feet. She seemed to be eyeing us carefully. When she removed her sunglasses, giving all three of us a onceover, I decided to take matters into my hands.

"All kidding aside. What would you think about keeping her?"

Hunter flanked my side. "Are you being serious?"

"I am."

"As a pet?" Cristiano asked.

"Perhaps. Perhaps more." I mulled over the idea. Suddenly, a risky scenario slipped into the back of my mind. I wanted the crap with both The Iceman and Theo's dad to be finished with once and for all. There was one way to ensure that happened.

To use a lure.

"And the logistics?" Hunter asked.

I tipped my head towards Hunter. "We're three of the most powerful and wealthiest men in the world. I think we can handle logistics when they arise."

He laughed. "You're right, my friend. And I must admit, even though I've spent only a little time around her, she would be incredible to own."

"There's another reason," Cristiano said as he studied my expression. "Isn't there?

The deep breath I took didn't fill my lungs. I had an ache inside for the woman and the thought of putting her in harm's way was damning, yet it might be the single time we could effectively work together to eliminate our enemy. If things worked out, then we'd own a beautiful pet. "The obvious objective of both The Iceman, if he still exists or handed his legacy to someone else, as well as that of William Watkins is to either destroy or kill all three of us."

Hunter got in my face. "You want to use her as bait. You son of a bitch."

"Not bait exactly."

"Then what the fuck do you call it?"

I shifted my gaze towards him first, then to Cristiano. "She won't be of interest to either one of them. Only the three of us will be."

"And what if something happens when she's with us?" Hunter asked through gritted teeth.

"It won't because we won't allow it to."

Cristiano laughed, the sound bitter. "Same old Cain. He thinks he can control the world."

"Do you really want to spend your life wondering when or if you're going to be shot at or arrested?"

Hunter dropped his head, cursing under his breath.

"I hear what you're saying, Cain, but that beautiful woman doesn't deserve to be used." Cristiano was adamant. "I thought you were interested in Rose, not in the fact she's simply someone we can share. That's no longer acceptable. I want to spend time with someone I care about, not just want to fuck. I'm ready to share my life with a special lady. Maybe have a few kids. The three of us talked about sharing someone for a long damn time. And you know? The idea was ridiculous to me at first. Then the more I thought about it, the better I liked it. But I will not use her. No fucking way."

"Ditto," Hunter snarled.

There was no denying what I'd wanted. I glanced in her direction, overwhelmed with the kind of desire that would never leave. I'd experienced it once in my life and lost it. I wouldn't do it again. "I care about very few people. You both know that. Women matter little in my life, or at least they haven't up to this point. Like you, Cristiano, I long for more than just a night or a weekend of fucking. It was fun while we were younger. It's not fun any longer, just... it simply satisfies a physical need. I want her. Rose. The woman. The beautiful talent with a laugh that can light up a room. I want her body and soul, but yes, I want her damn love as well."

The two men were silent for a few seconds. Then Hunter moved in front of me once again. "Maybe you do have a heart after all, Cain. If you really feel that way, then fine, we will enjoy getting to know her, hoping for more. But you will fucking promise me that you'll do everything in your power to keep her safe. If anything happens to her, I'll fucking kill you myself."

I knew in my blackened heart that I would do anything to protect her, no matter the circumstances or the cost.

"Then so be it. We begin the process. Within a few days, the lovely Rose Sadler will belong to us."

CHAPTER 16

Rose

"Imagine what else we're going to do to you, little pet? In the end, we're going to fuck every hole, taking you over and over again."

I could hear Cain's voice in the back of my mind, the promise sounding more like a warning during the middle of passion. While it should be unnerving as hell given the dream I'd had, my skin continued to tingle from the thought.

Déjà vu.

I wasn't certain why I had that feeling other than it had struck me the moment the three men were standing together. As if we'd been together before. But with one being from New York, another from Philadelphia and Cain from Chicago, I couldn't imagine where I could have possibly been in the same place at the same time with them.

Maybe I'd gotten the feeling from the intense sexual prowess they exuded, but it remained unnerving.

Even some of the words they'd used had presented a thick fog over my mind, leaving an eerie feeling that I'd yet to shake.

Little pet. I stared at myself, thinking about what that would mean. I was no prude. I'd seen enough movies, had read countless romance novels about BDSM and submissive women. I'd convinced myself I couldn't stand the thought, but now, I wasn't so certain given my reaction to being pulled into a man's lap.

Like I was a little girl.

Whew, it was suddenly very hot in the bathroom. I spritzed some perfume, then grabbed my purse, uncertain why I was so nervous.

Maybe because it wasn't every day that a girl was asked out by three gorgeous men. At the same time. I laughed softly and returned my attention to the mirror, making faces at my reflection. I'd enjoyed a delightful lunch with them, although Cain was called away on business only minutes after sitting down at the table. What had shocked me was the intensity of the three men as well as the obvious camaraderie.

That alone had instantly made me comfortable around them. I found them more than just pleasant to be around, their banter keeping me laughing almost the entire time. It was funny that they were so different in their actions and demeanor, yet they were also very close, even able to finish each other's sentences.

However, there was an electric charge humming through all three men that exuded danger, as if I were their prey. It was something else I couldn't push aside. I knew who and what they were. Perhaps that was the only reason for feeling that way.

The fact that they'd been college buddies and had remained friends wasn't that unusual, but their strong connection was. Or maybe I didn't know what I was talking about. Being in Julliard hadn't necessarily given me a true representation of the life of a college student, especially since I'd only attended for one year. That was okay. I'd met all the right people, and here I was today, a mega star.

It was strange, though. As I'd waited for them while they'd had a business discussion, and I'd observed their actions to try and learn more about them. There was no denying their closeness or the fact that they were attracted to me. However, their conversation had taken a darker turn. At one point, I'd been certain they were going to start fighting. The strangest thing of all was that I was certain they were arguing about me.

As to whether they wanted to share or whether they had to fight amongst themselves for a date with me? A girl could dream that she was the object of affection for three hunky, powerful men.

I rolled my eyes and took another look before spinning around, checking the time on my phone. I wasn't entirely certain where we were going or who would pick me up, but I'd been told to be ready at seven sharp.

While both Hunter and Cristiano had told me what they did for a living, I gathered a sense that both men were dangerous as well. It was the way they carried themselves, and the fact that I'd caught a glimpse of the weapon Cristiano carried. He'd also scanned the restaurant and bar several times. Maybe the dead giveaway had been the beefy looking man standing only fifteen feet from the table on the bottom deck.

What I hadn't told them was that during their lengthy discussion, I'd searched the internet on my phone. The information I'd found had been enough to skyrocket my pulse and should have been the reason I walked away from the table before they returned. Two were from mafia families, although Cain's family had disguised their operations, his parents living in the lap of luxury in the Hamptons alongside senators and 'A' list actors. Their businesses were mostly legit, though it had been easy to sort through the glossy magazine spreads and realize that their underground businesses had made their fortune.

Cristiano's family either didn't have that luxury or had never wanted to. In South America, they were gods, ruling almost everything. The fact that his father had been recently murdered had allowed for his rise to power.

Hunter was the anomaly. His father had built a textile empire that had limited competition. However, he'd taken the massive corporation to a darker side, using blackmail on a regular basis. Or so said the single article I'd been able to scan prior to their return to the table. It had been written recently, including on a university they'd all attended. I'd tagged it as a favorite to return to at a later time.

Everything I'd learned had given me the chills, although strangely enough, I'd been excited the entire time I'd spent with them after their return. I'd felt alive, free of the obnoxious tether to being a good girl I'd had my entire life. I had no idea what to expect for the night, but I was looking forward to it, nonetheless.

When I heard my cellphone ring, I groaned. I was a grown woman living on my own and had been for years, yet my mother had told me more than once that she required a once-a-week check-in like I was still in high school. I adored my parents, but it was getting ridiculous.

"Hello, Mom. Yes, I'm doing great, Mom. Of course, I've been eating, Mom." I couldn't help but laugh when she snorted.

"Is that any way to talk to your loving mother?"

"It depends. How are you and Dad?"

"If the man will ever stop finding excuses to go back to work, I'd be just fine."

"I thought he was retired for good."

She sighed. The poor woman had been dealing with daddy going out of town with limited notice for years. Granted, she lived in a gorgeous estate in San Diego, but I knew how much she wanted to travel.

"You know your father. He likes to have his hands in the middle of everything. That's just the way he is."

"Oh, yes. Your daddy is an assassin for some terrible men."

What the hell? I glanced from one side of the room to the other. A man's voice. Oh, God. I was absolutely losing my mind or needed some additional sleep.

"Rose, are you there?"

"Uh, yeah, mom. I'm right here." I rubbed my arm, a cold chill lingering.

My father almost never talked about his work, but I knew he had wealthy clients all over the world who refused to accept his retirement.

"Anyway? I just wanted to see how everything was going there."

"Fine, Mom. Just like it was the first day I got here. The resort is gorgeous, my suite bigger than my place in LA. I met the owner. He's... fascinating." I thought about Jillian's comments from the night before and cringed. I had no intentions of telling her that I was going on a date with the man and his friends. I returned to the living room, walking towards the beautiful roses.

Then my eyes settled on a single petal that had fallen. When I picked it up, a jarring memory rushed into the forefront of my mind.

"I think someone has been inside our suite."

It was my voice even though it echoed. But who had I been talking to? What suite?

"Mmm... well, it sounds like you're being treated very well. Just like you should be. I still worry though. I wish you hadn't gone there."

"Why? You've never once told me why." I brought the petal to my nose, closing my eyes as I inhaled the lovely scent. Why were goosebumps popping down both arms?

"The city is dangerous. You know that."

Danger. Danger. Danger.

"Mama. I've toured in New York," I told her then walked toward the window, studying the gorgeous scenery below. The atrium was gorgeous, the greenery adding a special touch to the hotel.

"I know, but Chicago is different."

"Okay. Whatever you say. I'll take your word for it. Anyway, I have a date tonight." Why did I tell her that?

"With the owner?" Now her voice sounded hopeful.

"Yes." A little white lie never hurt anyone.

"What's his name?"

My mother had likely never paid any attention to mafioso families. She'd lived a sheltered life with my father. I doubted they even understood the true meaning of the word crime. "Cain Cross. He's very handsome."

When I heard a knock on the door, my heart pitter-pattered. I took long strides, returning to the bathroom to grab my things.

"What did you say?" she asked. It almost sounded like her voice was shaking.

"Mom. I gotta go. He's here."

"Baby girl. Wait. You can't."

"I can't what?" I could tell she was flustered. I headed for the door, uncertain why she was acting this way. "Mama. What? Date the boss?"

"Yes. Yes, that's it."

"Is there something you're not telling me?" I heard the demanding tone in my voice and admonished myself for trying with my mother. She and my father had been strange for the past few years, never talking much about the past. I'd stopped asking after I'd moved out. "What secrets are you keeping from me, Mother?"

The tension was strange. Suddenly, my heart was beating erratically.

"We should talk. Your father and I think it's time. Maybe we should have told you before."

"Time? What are you talking about?" The second knock on the door was more insistent. "I need to go."

"Please. Don't go out with him. I beg you."

"Mama, you don't need to worry because he wasn't the one who hired me. Love and kisses. I need to go." I ended the call before things got stupid. Even for her, trying to dictate who I dated was unusual.

The fear in her voice had been palpable.

My mother had never been very good at confiding in me, even when I'd asked questions about a memory loss that troubled me today. The doctors had told me that one day the missing months would return, but I wasn't certain I believed them any longer.

Or maybe I didn't want to remember what I'd endured during the accident, the one everyone refused to expound on the details. Why had my mother chosen now?

And why had she been so nervous about my trip to Chicago? My thoughts drifted to the single article I'd just read, making a mental note to do some additional checking tomorrow. For now, I'd enjoy my evening.

I pressed my hands down my dress, then opened the door. Cristiano was leaning against the alcove wall, his legs crossed and his hands shoved into his pockets. He was dressed in all black, the luxurious material of his long sleeve shirt unbuttoned to the midway point on his chest. I noticed a dazzling display of ink I hadn't seen before, the intricate scrolling art drifting up to his neck. His trousers were also obsidian in color, accentuating his long, muscular legs. He wore a dark expression as his eyes traveled down to my high heels.

"You look radiant," he said in a half whisper. This time as he spoke, I was certain I detected a hint of his Latin accent. The tone was sensual, enticing, and I was just as drawn to him as I had been the others.

"I must admit, you don't look too bad yourself."

His face lit up, the smile crossing his face an unexpected surprise. "Not too bad. I think I like that. Are you ready to go?"

"Where are we going exactly?"

"Now if I told you that, then it wouldn't be a surprise. Would it?"

He stood back as I walked out the door, immediately pressing his hand against the small of my back, guiding me towards the elevators. There was an entirely different energy about him, a level of sexual dominance that ebbed and flowed beneath his gorgeous exterior. He was also possessive, which I realized I appreciated.

As we waited for the elevator, he crowded my space, taking a deep breath. I hadn't noticed the two-day stubble before, but it added character to his strong jaw.

"Tell me more about yourself, Rose. What do you do if you're not singing your little heart out?"

I almost retorted with a question about what he did when he wasn't hunting down and killing his enemies. He was the most brutal of the three men, his kills in South America legendary, people on several continents terrified of him.

"You already know the basics. Halo takes up the majority of my time, which means I have few hobbies. At this point in my career, I spend a lot of time on the road with my band."

"Does that make you happy?"

"Why shouldn't it?"

He seemed thoughtful about his response. "Because often what we allow ourselves to be dragged into isn't what we would have chosen for ourselves."

I wasn't certain if anyone had asked if I was happy before. "That makes me think you're the unhappy one."

Cristiano laughed. "How could I be unhappy? I'm a wealthy, powerful man with all the toys money can buy."

There was a haunting sound in his voice. He wasn't happy at all.

"Well, being a musician is what I've wanted since I could remember. Not singing would kill me."

"I'm curious. What else would you do if you weren't singing?"

"Honestly, I have no idea. What do you do?" In my internet search, I'd come to the conclusion that all three men were as respected as they were feared. If I was a smart girl, I would have backed out from the date. I'd been far too intrigued to do so.

"I'm going to venture a guess that you've already determined that." As the elevator pinged, the corners of his mouth turned up, his eyes piercing mine.

"You would be right."

"Good girl." He guided me into the empty elevator, pressing the button, then backing me against the wall. "Are you a very good girl, Rose? Or would you consider yourself naughty?"

"That depends on the situation."

"An honest answer." He pressed both hands on the cold steel, lowering his head. "You are aware that for every infraction there are consequences?"

"Isn't that the code we live by, or do you refuse to follow any man's rules?"

"You are a very feisty woman. I can tell I'm going to thoroughly enjoy tonight's festivities."

Why did I have a feeling he was choosing his words carefully?

I tilted my chin, daring him in a sense to kiss me, which was what I'd wanted to do since meeting him earlier in the day.

He exhaled and the elongated breath was full of fire. Then he didn't just kiss me. He devoured my mouth, a dying man desperate for his last taste. As he swept his tongue past my lips, he crushed his body against mine, his hard, throbbing cock pushing into my stomach. I was instantly lightheaded, no other sound capable of cutting through the rapid thudding of my heart.

I pressed my hands against his chest, clawing my fingers into his shirt as if holding on for dear life. He rolled one hand down my side, the brush of his fingers electrifying. I pushed hard, breaking the moment of passion long enough to take a deep breath. He chuckled in a deep throated vibration as he rolled his hand down my thigh, gathering the material of my dress into his fingers.

"I'm going to fuck you," he whispered in an unrecognizable voice. "But before that, I'm going to feast on your sweet pussy." His words were merely a statement of things to come. There would be no saying no to any of the three men.

Not that I wanted to.

He returned to the kiss, dominating my tongue as he slipped his fingers under the thin elastic of my thong. The moment he thrust a single long digit past my swollen folds, I rose onto my tiptoes, daring to slide my hand down his chest, flicking a single finger back and forth across his thick bulge.

I had no doubt the moment of pure sin wouldn't have stopped if the loud ping of the elevator reaching its destination hadn't interfered. He broke the kiss, laughing softly, taking his sweet time to ease his hand from under my dress. When he did, he cocked his head and rolled the tip of his slickened finger across my lips.

"You truly are a very bad girl. You will surrender to everything I command." With that, he took my hand in his, dragging me from the elevator and onto the main lobby floor. I sensed various guests watching us as we strode through the sublimely decorated area.

"Rose!" The single syllable was like a battle cry.

Within seconds, I felt a crush of people, at least two hundred of them surrounding us. I noticed the van of a local station parked outside the entrance doors. While there wasn't a chance in hell they'd arrived at the hotel on the off chance I'd be leaving the building, the reporters certainly didn't mind taking the opportunity to add to their fifteen minutes of fame.

"That's Rose," someone said.

"She's beautiful," a deep voice said from another direction. Almost instantly, Cristiano growled, shifting his hand to the small of my back.

When a little girl jumped in front of me, we almost collided. I burst into laughter and was aware that at least a dozen photographs were being taken.

Without hesitation, I crouched down. "Well, what's your name?"

"My name's Rose too," she chirped. The little girl was adorable, her bright red hair and freckles just about the cutest thing I'd seen in a while.

"Well, Rose. Would you like an autograph?"

"Pu-lease."

"I'm sorry," a breathless woman said as she approached. "I couldn't catch her. She just had to see you. You're her favorite star in the whole world."

"The whole wide world!" the little girl repeated, stretching her arms out wide.

"Well, in that case. We must get a picture together. Yes, mama?"

"Oh, God. You've just made her year. Hold on. I have some paper too if you don't mind an autograph."

As the mother got everything together, I glanced at Cristiano. His expression reminded me of a guard dog, his eyes almost pitch black from the glint of the last rays of sunlight, his brow furrowed and his jaw hard as a rock. He constantly scanned the area, and I honestly wondered if he was more worried about someone coming after him or after me.

For some reason, several colds shivers jetted down my spine.

"Here we are," the mother said, and I grabbed up the little girl, squeezing her tight. When I finished giving her an autograph and a kiss, I could tell there were other people who wanted to have their pictures taken with me. Cristiano was having none of it.

"Get out of the way!" he barked, grabbing me by the arm and dragging me towards the entrance.

"Hold on. Those are my fans. I have a job to do."

He ignored me and I resisted struggling because I knew it would make the front page of some shitty ragtag online magazine.

"They want more than that."

As we hit the wall of glass doors, I noticed a huge Suburban in black, the windows tinted so no one could see inside. I shouldn't have been surprised, but I was. The driver immediately climbed out and opened the door, ushering us inside. The guy could only be described as a brute, at least six foot four, weighing over two hundred and fifty pounds of muscle.

And I had no doubt he had a weapon tucked into a holster under his jacket.

Photographers and fans came from everywhere. I'd been an idiot to think I could go out on a date without being seen. If Cristiano was recognized or the vehicle which likely belonged to Cain, the morning news should be juicy. Was that what they were trying to do? If so, why?

"Our little pet arrives," Cain's deep voice rumbled in the stylized back of the SUV. His gaze was predatory with a hint of annoyance for the length of time it had taken us. The intensity lingered, the scent of testosterone thick.

"Our little star," Hunter teased.

"I can't ignore my fans." I eased against the plush leather seat, suddenly feeling as if I'd stepped into a lion's den, the three beasts inside famished.

The interior had been altered significantly, now resembling the posh environment of a Limo. I wasn't surprised that there was a bar, a bottle of champagne already on ice. Jazz music was playing from unseen speakers. And the other two men sat dressed in similar attire—trousers and an open shirt. While Hunter had chosen white, accenting his rich chocolate eyes, Cain had selected cobalt blue, the color dazzling with his long, dark curly hair.

"The photograph with the little girl will be in all the major papers tomorrow," Cristiano mused.

Why did I have the distinct feeling his statement wasn't said out of admiration or making polite conversation about their dinner guest? Both Hunter and Cain smiled, glancing from one to the other as if this was nothing but a game.

"Our popular, beautiful pet," Cain said as he poured a glass of champagne, leaning over and handing it to me. The immediate jolt of current created a rippling effect, my heart racing and butterflies tickling my stomach. He allowed the touch to linger, drinking in my essence before letting go. "However, from now on, you will follow the rules that we've established."

"Rules?" I continued to quiver, the touch far too enigmatic. "What if I don't follow them?"

Hunter shifted towards me and slid his hand along the outside of my leg, resting his palm on my thigh. "Then, our beautiful little lamb. You will be punished."

Cristiano smiled as he locked eyes with mine. "Yes, sweet Rose. As of now, you have three masters because you belong to us."

As I lifted the glass of champagne for a sip or a gulp, a strange set of sensations surrounded me, fog drifting before my periphery of vision. Then as it cleared, a strong vision replaced reality, one so vivid that I couldn't tell if it was a fantasy or a memory.

"That's where you're wrong. You have three masters now. Make no mistake that when we take you, and that will happen, you will learn what pleasure is. When you come the first time, you'll beg for more, exhausted and overwhelmed with raw ecstasy. And I assure you that it will be the beginning of a beautiful affair. Every hole will be well used, but you'll crave more, begging the man who owns you to continue making you weak."

"No," I managed, but the pleasure he was providing was already luring me into a place of surrender.

"Yes, little pet. After we've broken you down, we'll put you together piece by piece. Then we'll start all over again. As of right now, this very moment, you belong to us."

When it faded, I lifted my head, studying the three men who'd laid claim as if I was always meant to belong to them.

And for the first time in my life, I was terrified.

Or was it the first time?

Something was off. I had to find out what.

And more importantly, why.

CHAPTER 17

Cristiano

"Do you believe in love at first sight?" Rose asked, as if the question was weighing heavily on our minds.

It wasn't.

Men like the three of us, creatures who'd been aptly called the Damned had no capacity for love. It was a foreign notion presented in a gift wrapped package by authors and musicians, filmmakers and move stars, who grit their teeth in front of the public eye while loathing the person they were in a relationship with.

"I believe in the lure of attraction," Hunter answered, always the man of reason, the one voted most likely to be able to fake a normal life.

"Hypnotic sex appeal, dangerous and provocative," I added.

Her expression held an air of amusement. "Pheromones refusing to be denied, a burning need that can never be satisfied? Almost like the taking of a man's life, watching as the light is vanquished from his eyes. Yes?"

Her stark wording brought a smile to my face, a twitch to my cock. It would seem our little pet had spent some time finding out who we were. I couldn't blame her. In fact, I was surprised she didn't have an army of security watching her every move. She was enticed by the aspect of danger, her desire swirling in a wave of uncertainty. I'd never known someone to be so turned on by the thought of three dangerous men. That made me want her that much more.

"Are you certain you want to go down the rabbit hole?" I asked, deepening my voice.

She licked her lips, not out of fear but out of a dark need to feast on sin that had festered inside of her for years. It was quite possible that the vulnerable woman was as insatiable as we were.

Cain lifted his glass in a toast. "I do believe our little prey has ripped off our masks, which is no small feat."

"And what have I found?" she cajoled, taunting us with her knowledge.

"If I told you monsters, would you run when given the chance?" I leaned closer, running my finger from one side of her jaw to the other.

She slowly turned her head in my direction, the look in her eyes almost as predatory as the one I knew I had for her. "No."

I wasn't certain what she was attempting to do, but I reveled in her ability to allow her inhibitions to fade away. As an electric wave pulsed through the back of the SUV, I longed to pin her to the seat, releasing the pent-up anguish of my self-proposed hell, refusing to give into my carnal needs. Now, I wanted nothing more than to cut her panties to shreds, unleashing the feral side of me.

"So be it. Be careful what you ask for around us, sweet Rose. The secrets that lie beneath the sophisticated façade could ultimately mean your demise," Cain told her in his cold, stark manner. Only he could turn a night of passion into foreplay for manipulation.

"Are you trying to scare or warn me?" she continued, her voice little more than a raspy purr. The woman knew exactly what she was doing to each one of us, using her feminine wiles as a mastered craft. But with her, it wasn't merely an attempt to get what she wanted. Her reactions to us were as uncontrollable as ours were to her.

The ultimate prey.

"Both," Cain muttered.

"Then duly noted." She gifted us with a laugh before settling back into the seat, sipping on her champagne like the queen she should be. "But that's what I want."

Jesus. The hard press of my trousers against my cock was becoming unmanageable.

I shifted in my seat, the three Damned studying each other from our respective corners. Who would be the first to claim her? That's what we were thinking. Blood roared through my head as my pulse increased, the rush of adrenaline fueling a fire I'd put out a long time ago. Now I feared Pandora's Box had been opened, the hinges snapped from the lid, which meant the insatiable man inside, the one labeled a savage killer, would never be locked away again.

As she gave each one of us a hated look, I could swear she was more of a manipulator than I'd originally believed. There was a crazed need building, an intense and raw sense of understanding that very few couples achieve. We were defying the odds, and I barely knew anything about her.

Sexual tension was yanking at my resolve, tearing away every possibility of self-control.

The saying 'one kiss wasn't enough' continuously flowed through my mind as Cain's driver left the resort area bound for the suburbs of Glenco. I wouldn't have expected Cain to live in any other location.

As the glistening tall buildings made of steel passed, a strange dreary series of clouds formed in the distant sky, an ominous foreboding forming in the back of my mind. I sipped the smooth scotch my buddy had offered, musing over the fact that no one would ever consider me a romantic. I didn't date women, I fucked them just to satisfy my needs. Or when spilling blood had begun to bore me. I'd turned into my father's son, brutal and unforgiving, and during the last ten years, the Cartel lifestyle had suited me.

However, now that my father was dead, I had significantly more responsibility on my shoulders. The weight of being the Cartel leader while trying to bring my father's corporation into the next century had taken a toll. I was tired of coming home to an empty house or waking up with a girl whose name I couldn't remember.

I couldn't take my eyes off Rose's face. The fact that she was mesmerizing didn't amaze me. What did was how down to earth she was, refusing to fall into the diva mode like so many superstars I'd met.

While I'd never seen her in concert, I had two of her CDs in my collection, the dramatic difference of her heavy metal songs compared to the subdued ballads leaving me with a haunted feeling. Her music suited my usually dark moods. To date, I'd found no other musician who could take away the ugly, burning need for violence affixing itself to my soul, a leech draining my life's blood.

I'd seen the look of admonishment in Hunter's eyes at the news about my father. I felt no guilt, only partially because I'd freed my mother from a life of abuse and disrespect. Far too many bones had been broken by his hands. Finding him choking her had been the last straw.

What I'd also learned was that the demon plaguing him, driving him to his contorted view of humanity, had been greed. The ugly beast had twisted his blackened soul into a disfigured creature. He'd attempted to make me believe that every human had been born in the womb of violence, his lifestyle just following the example set.

Maybe I'd had far too much of his poisoned Kool-Aid, his death the antidote, but I'd been struggling with needing more for months. Five minutes spent with this sensual creature and everything about my world was about to change.

It was ironic as fuck.

I'd found myself ravenous with the kind of hunger that could drive a man to madness in trying to satisfy his needs.

That was almost as unusual as the intense connection between the four of us. I'd never believed in the concept that there was only one person for another. If that were the case, the world wouldn't be so overpopulated. What I did believe was that if one was lucky enough to find what great scholars and other idiots called their 'soulmate', they could rule the world. For all my riches, billions that I could never spend in a lifetime, estates in four countries and the most expensive sports cars in the world, I'd only been happy once in my life.

But as with all evil men, happiness wasn't allowed.

However, I'd allowed myself a single ounce of something that had never been in my vocabulary.

Hope.

It was quite possible Rose had come into the lives of three savages for one reason.

A single offer of salvation. If so, I for one wouldn't be stupid enough not to grab onto it as a lifeline. In learning to be more philosophical over the last few years, I'd come to realize that I'd made myself devoid of emotion to survive the vast displays of human pain, but it had taken a significant toll. The darkness that had once provided comfort now prodded me with the red-hot end of a fireplace poker on a regular basis. A reminder that I'd spend all eternity in Hell.

Not one kiss, nor a single taste would be enough to endure the damnation I deserved.

I shared in Hunter's concerns that the game we were playing would have dire consequences. I had one regret in my life, something that if I had an opportunity to change, I would jump at it. I'd abandon everything and everyone I knew, donating every penny of my wealth to resurrect Sage from the dead.

Remorse doesn't look good on you asshole.

Maybe not, but history wouldn't repeat itself.

With my eyes remaining locked on her shimmering face, I gulped the remainder of my drink, jamming it into the holder. "Come here."

Rose knew instantly I was talking to her, a slight flush painting her lovely cheeks. The hint of embarrassment caused my balls to tighten. I decided to give her one more opportunity before I took matters into my hands. "I said, little pet. Come. Here."

She purposely ignored me, staring at the window as if she'd find answers to some puzzle I'd seen forming in her eyes.

God, I wanted this woman, my cock swelling.

When she didn't comply, I grabbed her arm, easily tossing her over my lap.

"What are you doing?" she squealed, immediately struggling to break free of my hold.

"You were told you are to obey the rules, yet you ignore them."

"You didn't tell me the rules."

Hunter chuckled. "They're quite simple. You do anything we ask you to do."

"And since you failed to do so, a punishment is required." Tonight, my sadistic needs wouldn't be satisfied. That wasn't the point of our evening. Part of what the Damned had hoped to accomplish had already been achieved. I'd orchestrated a crowd in the lobby, fans eager to catch a single glimpse of a rockstar. I'd even been so evil as to call a local news station, who'd eagerly accepted the opportunity to grab some vivid footage of the massive star.

To say anything else was icing on the already sweet cake was blasphemy. I planned on enjoying every moment of making certain she knew that her world had also just shifted to the dark side. There was a good chance she already knew it given the obvious distress tearing at her mind. She was churning in a dark abyss of emotions, most of which I couldn't read.

I jerked up her dazzling emerald green dress, revealing a matching lacy thong. She looked entirely different than her larger-than-life persona on stage. Leather pants. Clunky boots. Shimmering crop tops. This was the woman I could fall in love with.

Laughter threatened to give my thoughts away, but I shoved them back into the ugly vortex of my demented mind. Instead, I rolled the silky thong over her buttocks, taking my time to shift them to her knees.

"This isn't fair," she said, although there was limited conviction in her voice.

"'We must always remember that it is when passions are most inflamed that fairness is most in jeopardy,'" Hunter said quietly as he sipped his drink. When I lifted my brow, he grinned. "Susan Collins. One of my favorite quotes. In other words, our little lamb, there is no such thing as fairness in the face of serving three masters."

I parted her legs, pressing down on her back with one hand as I brought my other to her bottom. Within seconds, the scent of her desire wafted into the confined space. I issued three swats without blinking an eye, the twisted man inside of me striving to break free. She was far too delicate, an innocent woman in a sea of sharks. Hurting her permanently would serve no purpose.

Creating an addictive need for domination would, perhaps even one to pain.

As she squirmed in my lap, throwing her hand back more than once, I glanced from Cain to Hunter. They both had voracious appetites, eager to sink their razor-sharp teeth into her skin, sucking out enough of her essence to feed their own. We were truly sick individuals, which was what made our friendship unique.

The light glisten on her skin was a clear indication of her arousal, her need to submit even if she wasn't entirely certain why. She shuddered in my hold when I caressed her skin, adoring the deepening blush as well as savoring the heat on the tips of my fingers. If I had my way, they'd be seared from the deep lashes crisscrossing her perfect porcelain skin.

"Does this feel good, Rose?" I asked, the dusky whisper barely audible.

"Of course not."

I adored her defiance.

I brought my hand down again. And again. This time I made certain not only did the sound create a wave of anxiety, but the pain would quickly turn into a rush of anguish. I repeated my actions, aware that neither man had taken their eyes off me. Even the driver found it difficult not to keep his gaze glued to the rearview mirror.

She would endure bouts of humiliation during her time spent with us. My mouth watered in anticipation. The thought was a powerful aphrodisiac. "I'll ask you again. Does this turn you on?"

Rose moaned in a subtle way, yet to me it was as amplified as her rapid heartbeat. I felt it in my throat as well as the heated sensations of her desire between her long legs.

"Never." Her tone of voice had changed, almost lilted like her laugh that I could listen to for hours.

"Your body betrays you, little pet." I eased my finger between her legs, rubbing it up and down, taunting her to deny she was wet, glistening with her juices.

Her single whimper managed to be amplified given the stark quiet in the SUV, the bulletproofing also eradicating most sounds of traffic. In addition, neither one of my buddies had been this quiet before. There was a moment of reverence that seemed to take all three of us aback, as if the footprint of the harem we were developing had been set in concrete.

I thrust my finger into her tight channel, immediately rewarded with a series of husky moans. Inhaling, I held the scent of her perfume and her desire in my nostrils as I returned to the spanking, smacking one side of her bottom then the other with precision. She beat her small fists against the leather seat, still undulating her hips. The friction was about to drive me insane.

I'd yet to ask how long until we arrived at Cain's McMansion, but I honestly didn't care. The need for her was creating a fissure in my sanity. At this point, I needed blissful release, or I wasn't certain I could be responsible for my actions. I plunged several fingers deep into her pussy, savoring the sound made from driving into her with brutal thrusts.

Rose now rocked on my lap, bucking against my hand. Control wasn't a strong virtue, but I pulled out, cracking my palm against her bottom six more times, a reminder that she would never be allowed to take a single moment of control.

Cain's chest rose and fell, his breathing labored. I'd seen the same look in his eyes once before. The moment we'd tasted sweet perfection on our tongues and in our hands, one so satisfying that everything else would be bitter in comparison.

But the greatest high had been turned into a devastating low, a crushing blow not one of us had ever recovered from.

I was almost frantic in my need, sliding my finger under the elastic of her thong and with a single snap of my wrist, alleviating a problem. Then I pulled her into my lap, forcing her to straddle me.

My pulse sped up with lust, a kind so dark and demanding that for a few seconds, I was pulled into the strangling images of my past. "What do you want, little pet?"

"Fuck me. Just fuck me."

CHAPTER 18

Rose

I no longer recognized myself.

I wasn't entirely certain I wanted to.

Telling the three predators to fuck me was the most out of control I'd been for years, maybe my entire life. I'd craved their touch, ignoring the signs of danger the entire day. I'd thought of nothing else, weaving a powerful moment that we would share into another story. At least it was one I hadn't dared to write down. I'd shoved the mystery piece into my suitcase, embarrassed by what I'd written, but not enough that I hadn't read it in its entirely twice.

I'd been impressed with myself.

As I shifted in my seat, a feeling of discomfort sent a thrill through me.

The spanking had been just the appetizer, an act that had almost pushed me into a raging climax. To think that three men had that much control over me was crazy, but even so, it also allowed the feeling of freedom to continue.

"Pull off your dress," Cristiano demanded.

An immediate and very intense heat bloomed in my core from the darkness woven in the simple command. I quickly glanced at the front of the SUV. There was no partition like those installed in limos, the rearview mirror positioned for the driver to be able to see what was happening. Should it bother me? Yes, but I'd never felt so eager in my life. I tugged the silk over my head, tossing it aside.

The intensity of his gaze pulled at every deep emotion, igniting a fire that would burn brightly for some time to come. My core throbbed to the point that I squeezed my thighs against his, gasping for air. He wrapped his hand around the back of my throat, pulled my head down until he was able to capture my mouth.

As he'd done in the elevator, he became ravenous, his mouth devouring mine. The sense of silence was deafening, the hard thudding of my heart now echoing in my ears. We were already insatiable, but there was a different vibration as the two men looked on, waiting their turn. I knew predators had little patience.

Cristiano dug his fingers into my skin, the hold completely possessive. As he sucked on my tongue, I was stripped of the lingering inhibitions, the need to have one then the other inside of me as intoxicating as their combined musky scents.

He broke the moment of intimacy, yanking me to my knees and spreading me wide open with his hands. I was forced to wrap my arms around his head as he buried his face in my pussy. I threw my head back, his actions managing to steal the air from my lungs. The ache deepened, my pussy clenching and releasing. As a string of vivid lights flashed across my eyes, I couldn't stop panting.

The way he was devouring me was frantic, every sound he made guttural. Within seconds, I was crashing, the wave of pleasure a crescendo of want and need that had kept my vibrator busy. This was so much better.

"Oh..." I struggled to keep my eyes open, the rapture ebbing and flowing like a tidal wave. I'd never experienced such a powerful orgasm, but I wanted more. Panting, I struggled to reach his belt buckle, determined I wouldn't stop even if he commanded me to do so.

Three masters.

Three men who wanted what only I could give them.

The thought was gloriously enrapturing. I fought with the zipper, finally freeing his cock. I wasted no time, pumping the base like a crazed animal in search of her first meal in a month. His labored breathing was a clear indication that my desire to touch and explore wouldn't be allowed for long.

He glanced into my eyes, and I heard Cain growling from behind.

"Hurry up, brother," he said. "Or I'll steal her from you."

I tossed my head over one shoulder, licking my lips at the sight of Cain's hand wrapped around his thick shaft. He was huge, long, and thick. I shuddered from the sight, concentrating on the piercing he had.

A jolt of electricity soared through me, a single image flashing into my mind. I'd never been with a man who'd had a piercing. Yet...

"You can try," Cristiano answered, cutting through the third moment of déjà vu. He rolled his hands down my sides, giving me a commanding look. "Slide my cock inside you."

When I played with him, rubbing the tip up and down my wet pussy, he cracked his hand on my ass. The sound forced a whimper from my lips, and I immediately sensed we were being watched by the way the SUV drifted across the road. I did as he demanded and as soon as the tip was inside, he pulled me down with such power that I issued a sharp yelp, the brutal impact forcing me to quiver.

My muscles stretched to accommodate him, the slice of pain given how tight I was quickly becoming a dancing array of dazzling sensations. I half laughed as I struggled to breathe, wrapping my fingers around his hair. The image remained, boring into the back of my mind.

What the hell was wrong with me?

I hadn't realized I'd looked away until Cristiano grasped my jaw with his fingers, tugging my head until I looked into his eyes.

"Ride me."

His voice was deep and throaty, and the desperate need returned, all thoughts of anything else fading away. There was no ignoring his plea. I undulated my hips, riding him until vibrations danced down the backs of my legs. God, how I wanted his naked body pressed against mine, but my fingers fumbled as I tried to unbutton his shirt, the pleasure becoming sheer bliss.

I dug my fingers through his buttonholes, closing my eyes as the touch sent another round of current into me. He fisted my hair at the scalp, holding me close as I bucked even harder, wanting nothing more than for him to slam all the way into me. The thought was sinful and raw, making the moment feel like something dirty was happening between us.

I sensed Hunter getting closer. When I felt the touch of his fingers on my naked back, I let off a series of moans. He caressed me as a lover would before wrapping his hand around my jaw. "Suck my fingers, little lamb."

His term of endearment pushed me to another edge, yet Cristiano was in control, one hand now positioned on my hip, guiding the rhythm. I opened my mouth wide, allowing Hunter to thrust his fingers inside. It was almost more intimate than being fucked by the gorgeous man.

"Such a good girl," Hunter whispered, then nuzzled into my neck, not only blowing hot air across my skin but also nipping my earlobe. The wash of instant pain added to the crazed enjoyment.

I sucked and licked his fingers even as his plunges became rougher, so much so that I felt my gag reflex kicking in.

"That's it," Cristiano muttered. "Soon you'll have a thick cock inside your tight mouth." He lifted his hips, taking more control. His cock continued to throb. I was so close to coming. I could feel it.

As soon as Hunter removed his fingers, Cristiano pulled me closer until my back arched. I had no understanding of what he was doing at first.

Until Hunter wiggled a finger into my dark hole.

Another powerful orgasm swept through me, my core erupting.

My moan was bedraggled, barely recognizable. I no longer cared if the man up front witnessed everything that was happening between us. This was a pure slice of heaven that I hoped would be repeated. "More," I managed, the sound demanding.

"Don't worry, baby girl," Cristiano breathed against me, his voice hitching and indicating he was closer. "There's gonna be much more." His thrusts became wild, unrestrained as he drove himself closer to releasing.

Hunter continued finger-fucking my ass as I rode Cristiano with everything I had, the blissful moment becoming something I'd remember for a long time. As soon as Cristiano's body started to shake, I squeezed my pussy muscles. He erupted deep inside, his strangled roar one of satisfaction.

I wasn't allowed to bask in the moment for long, Hunter pulling me away, taking the seat next to Cristiano, then pulling me down onto his lap. I was now able to stare at Cain, studying his hard, cold eyes as they pierced mine. There was a darkness in the intensity, a need that was entirely different than the others.

He never blinked, only allowing his gaze to roam across my naked body. Then he lifted his eyes towards the front. "Keep driving. We're not finished yet."

"Yes, sir."

I shuddered at the rawness in his voice, then dragged my tongue across my lips as I concentrated on the glisten of precum covering his sensitive slit. He chuckled, then beckoned with a single finger.

Hunter eased me into the floor, my torso fitting perfectly between the two sets of seats.

Cain wasted no time, wrapping his fingers around my long curls, jerking my head up so I was forced to look into his eyes. Then he fought to drag his pants down further on his massive thighs. I noticed a powerful tattoo on his right thigh, a dragon with a deep red eye that seemed as if it was staring at me.

His cock was a creation of beauty, so perfect with the veins on either side pumping with blood, the tip a dark purple. He grinned, seeing what had to be an expression of awe. I'd never sucked a man who had a piercing, and as the excitement built, he issued a ragged growl. "Suck me, baby. Don't stop until I tell you it's okay."

He pushed my head down until I was able to drink in the musky scent of his testosterone. There was something especially dirty about being on all fours inside an SUV made for a mafia man, a vehicle to keep him safe and alive. And the thought of sucking his cock made my mouth water. I licked around his cockhead, taking my time to savor the flavor.

He settled further into the leather seat, keeping his fingers tangled in my hair. Every breath he took was labored; his jaw clenched as he stared at me.

The man was in total control of himself, as if he would lose everything if he weren't. It was a strange feeling, yet one I knew to be true. I rolled my hand under his cock, fingering his balls. They were already swollen, yet tight. When I squeezed the sac, a look of satisfaction popped onto his face.

I raked one nail up and down the side of his shaft, swirling the tip around his cockhead. When another bead of precum trickled past his slit, I was greedy, dragging my tongue through it. He laughed as if the small amount was just the tip of the iceberg. The feeling of Cristiano's cum dripping down the insides of my thighs was scintillating, adding to the moment of raw pleasure.

Seconds later, Hunter squeezed behind me, planting one foot on the carpeted flooring, immediately tapping his cock against my aching bottom.

"My turn, little lamb," he whispered, then bent over, licking and nipping my shoulder. "And I have a feeling you like it rough."

Cain allowed me to answer, stroking my hair briefly as he peered down at me.

"Yes." I was shocked at the ease of my quick reply, wanting to hate myself for admitting what I'd only allowed in fantasies.

"Good girl," Hunter praised, and I shivered to my core. Even the sound of his voice added to the rush of excitement. How had the three men seen through the carefully crafted armor I'd kept around me for as long as I could remember?

It had been a useful tool in my line of work, keeping the nasty comments from people in the industry who tried to break me down as well as the temptations in a distant space. Maybe that's why I'd never turned to drugs or alcohol as a crutch.

And why I'd craved wild, passionate sex.

The thought revealed a lot about me.

Cain pushed my head down once again, opening his legs ever wider. "Take my cock into your hot mouth."

I engulfed his cockhead, swirling my tongue back and forth. More than anything, I wanted to please him. The thought heightened the taste, tangy yet sweet.

Hunter rubbed his cock up and down the length of my pussy. When he finally pushed the tip against my swollen, wet folds, I almost stopped sucking.

The light taps of Cain's fingers against my cheek brought a muffled moan.

I resumed my task, relaxing my throat muscles as I took more of him into my mouth. I would never claim to be an expert cock sucker. I'd had limited experience, partially because I'd never been interested. But this was different, the taste of him igniting another fire deep inside. The dull roar as the tires rolled over the road was somehow comforting, a stark reminder that what we were doing was sinful.

At least that's what I'd always been told. I mentally laughed at myself. I was thirty-one years old, and I'd kept tight reins on every aspect of my life. Maybe this was me sowing my wild oats, something I wasn't certain I'd done before.

Hunter continued caressing my skin as he guided the tip of his cock to my entrance. I stiffened, the anticipation keeping the fire burning deep within. The moment he thrust the entire length of his cock inside, Cain lifted his pelvis, shoving his shaft into my mouth, the tip hitting the back of my throat.

The momentary gag reflex was replaced with the desire to suck him. I wrapped my lips around his thickness, getting used to the way he throbbed inside my mouth as Hunter powered into me. His strokes were long and even, driving into the very core of my being. He was just as thick and hard, my muscles still aching from the delicious fucking Cristiano had given me.

I was crazed with desire, barely able to think clearly as I pulled my mouth off Cain's cock, something he allowed me to do. I could sense he was watching me closely, just like I knew Cristiano was. All three men were possessive, so much so that they'd each lay claim in their own way.

The music was still soothing, but the sound of the men's heavy breathing was the only thing I paid any attention to. It was already stifling in the vehicle, only it had nothing to do with the air temperature. I dragged my tongue down the underside of Cain's cock, teasing his testicles by flicking my tongue from one to the other.

Cain growled in appreciation although I sensed a subtle warning.

Hunter continued to stroke my back as his actions became more aggressive, driving his cock with enough force that I was pitched against Cain. I licked up to his cockhead, taking it into my mouth again.

Now the two men took over, Hunter's fingers digging into my hips, Cain's two hands on either side of my head. I pushed mine against the edge of the seat, trying to keep my eyes locked on the most dangerous man of the three. The various emotions crossing Cain's face were almost unreadable, but his eyes were shimmering as if there was so much going on inside his massive brain.

Plans for what they would do with me.

I allowed the sheer pleasure of what was happening to keep me on a beautiful edge, the sound of Hunter's rough fucking filtering into my ears. The sensations were incredible, more so than I would have thought possible. I was pulled closer and closer to a moment of nirvana, my entire body trembling as another powerful orgasm threatened to consume me.

"Perfect," Cain muttered. "Your mouth is perfect."

"Her pussy is hot and tight," Hunter added.

"Don't worry, brother. I plan on experiencing it very soon. Yes, I will, little pet. You belong to us now."

Why did Cain's words thrill me so much?

I continued sucking, swirling my tongue back and forth, wrapping one hand around the base. As soon as I twisted my fingers, creating a wave of friction, Cain arched his back, fighting losing all control.

Hunter smacked my bottom several times, then slowed down his rhythm, bringing me close, then backing off. I was almost exasperated, moaning over the thick invasion, pushing hard against him.

His laugh was deep and raspy, the sound sending a jolt of electricity through every muscle and tendon. Cain lifted his pelvis off the seat, powering into me savagely. Hunter mirrored his rhythm, finally bringing me to the point of release.

Another series of stars floated in front of my eyes as a climax rushed into my system. I bucked hard against the two men fucking me, my body shaking uncontrollably. The single orgasm wasn't enough, Hunter pushing me harder. The pulsing of his cock kept me so aroused, I was lightheaded.

He reached under me, cupping my breasts, kneading them. I closed my eyes, barely able to control my mouth and tongue. When Hunter pinched both nipples between his thumbs and forefingers, I let out a ragged scream around Cain's cock.

Cain issued a series of low growls, lifting my head with my hair then thrusting in short jabs into my mouth. Blinking rapidly, I was in a state of awe as both men fucked me like wild beasts. Hunter twisted my hardened buds to the point I issued a single, bedraggled scream.

Then I sensed both men were ready to erupt. I rolled my hand up and down Cain's shaft while I squeezed my pussy muscles. Then, as if they'd coordinated their efforts, both men released.

When I was a little girl, I often pretended I was Cinderella, hoping that one day I'd find my Prince Charming. For a few crazy, off-the-wall seconds, a fleeting thought entered my mind that I hadn't just found one, but three.

Then an icy grip wrapped bony fingers around my throat, pulling me into the darkness that I'd experienced far too many times. As if what we'd shared was the beginning of something cataclysmic.

And in the end, there's be nothing left but tragedy.

CHAPTER 19

Five days later

Rose

"What a very good girl indeed."

I snapped my head up, my pulse racing. I could swear the voice was right behind me. I scanned the room in the mirror, seeing no one. I hadn't experienced a single flashback in days. Why now? The note. It had to be because of the note I held in my shaking hands.

"You're... terrible."

"Yes, I am. Be careful, little fawn. There are beasts crawling in these hallways. I wouldn't want to see you get eaten."

I bit my lower lip to keep from making a single sound. My voice. Who was I calling terrible? A dull ache formed behind my eyes, and I closed them for a few seconds. Then the pull from what I'd discovered earlier dragged a trickle of fear down my spine. I took a deep breath, holding it as I peered at the crudely written statement, the warning threatening to shatter the beautiful world I was attempting to create.

You don't know who you're sleeping with. They are murderers.

Swallowing, I wanted to crumple the fucking piece of paper and throw it in the trash. Instead, I read it for a fifth time. I'd walked into my dressing room to find it taped to the mirror so I wouldn't miss it. Whoever was determined to ruin my life had a twisted sense of humor, writing the words using a quill pen dipped in red ink, allowing for the author to be creative in his or her lettering. The words appeared as if they were written in blood.

Exhaling, I looked away, uncertain what to think or do. It was the second note I'd received, the first only telling me to be careful. I assumed they meant being cautious about Cain, Hunter, and Cristiano. I was no fool. They were dangerous men, but with me they were entirely different. I'd become the light to their darkness. I was certain of it.

I'd also grilled them on who they were, even laughing with them as they'd talked about the article I'd found, sharing with me stories about their enemies. Nothing crazy had happened, the three men handling business while weaving time spent with me both as a foursome and singularly.

Everything had been like a blissful whirlwind, the time more enjoyable than any other I could remember in my life. We'd lounged in the sun, and Cain had even taken me on a tour of Chicago. We'd eaten at two incredible restaurants, both times returning to his estate. The four of us. Maybe I should have spent more time asking questions than pretending I was living every girl's fantasy.

Or maybe someone was trying to derail our happiness. They were some of the most eligible bachelors in the country. And I was a rockstar. Laughing, I attempted to push the anxiety aside.

I closed my eyes, trying to conjure up the dreams from days before. Little pet. The two words seemed to spark the memories and dreams. But were they false memories as the doctor had mentioned was possible? I wasn't certain what they were any longer. What I did know was that for the first time, I felt like I belonged to someone and had something special.

Damn anyone who tried to take it from me.

I reminded myself that bits and pieces of what had occurred around the mysterious accident could come to me. The doctor had said the memories could return like clips from a movie, which was exactly what was happening. He'd also said they could be skewed or completely wrong. He'd suggested I keep notes, and that at some point, my mind would be ready to accept the truth.

I'd done it for a little while, then stopped. Recently, I'd started again, given the tenacity of the nightmares. What I didn't want to happen was for my psychosis to interrupt either the residency or the joyous time spent with my gorgeous hunks.

My three men also always managed to catch at least a part of my show. I tingled just thinking about them, my entire body sore from the hours of making love.

As well as the numerous spankings I'd received. I twisted on my seat, biting my lower lip to keep from moaning. The afternoon spanking had been a doozy, and while I hated to admit it, justified. I'd purposely gotten away from one of Cain's bodyguards so I could do a little shopping on my own. I wouldn't be able to sit comfortably for a couple days given my bottom was covered in strap marks.

Now, my pussy quivered from the tongue lashing I'd received afterwards, my legs spread wide open and Cain's face buried in my wetness. "Stop it, girl." I fanned my face and returned my gaze to the note.

Another canvas of color floated in front of my eyes, but a light prevented me from seeing who was holding my arm. This time the vision was even more vivid, although the details were still foggy.

"Na...no. He owns a restaurant." I was insistent, but to whom?

"I feel sorry for you. That's why Cain hates you so much. Your daddy killed his brother."

I could tell I was terrified. I was also groggy. Like I'd been drugged. *"Let me go."* My voice didn't even sound like my own.

"That's not going to happen. You're very valuable. Imagine the fun we're going to have using their desire against them."

Oh, God. I recognized the angry male voice. No. It couldn't be one of them. Not my men. No. It wasn't possible.

"Girl. Calm down." At least saying the words out loud dragged me from the vision. My father couldn't kill anyone. Cain's brother? I didn't even know he had a brother.

What I did know was that it was time to grill my parents. I'd been pushing it off because I didn't want to know if there was some ugly secret from my past. Now, I doubted I could avoid it any longer.

A chill remained, but the moment I entertained the sweet thoughts of having all my holes filled with their fabulous thick cocks, I was warmed up. Was it possible someone could fall in love with three powerful men? How would that work? The thoughts added prickly heat as well as desire. Love wasn't on the table. I knew better than to think that.

The hard knock brought a smile to my face. I quickly shoved the note into my drawer. "Come in."

I knew Jillian was behind the huge bouquet of flowers, but it was difficult to see anything from the number of roses creatively placed in the crystal vase. "More flowers."

I couldn't help but giggle, which didn't suit my personality at all. However, in the five days since I'd spent a magical night with three of the most gorgeous men in the universe, everything had changed. My attitude. My outlook. Even thoughts on my future, although I'd kept those little pinpricks of information to myself for the time being.

"They're incredible. I didn't know roses existed in bright orange."

She sat the vase down close to the other two that had arrived only moments before, shaking her head as she stared at the massive array. "Honey, you can get them in any color of the rainbow, including black. They're dyed. And if those boys give you black flowers, run far and fast."

I rolled my eyes and finished powdering my nose. "Don't be so melodramatic."

"Who's being melodramatic?" She came up behind me, staring at our combined reflection in the mirror of my dressing table. "It's just that they are obsessed, and I don't like that."

"Because they give me flowers?"

"Not just once, but every night you perform. They follow you around or have one or more of their guards trapse behind you like lapdogs. Cain has taken to having every person who comes to your show checked for everything from weapons to God knows what. Now that's fine and dandy, but it tells me that they know you're in danger because of who you are."

"They're just a little possessive."

"I don't like it."

I swung around on my chair. "Jillian. You've alluded to the fact that Cain is a bad guy. Now, you're telling me all of them are. What exactly aren't you telling me?"

The look on her face changed. She twisted her mouth, sucking on her lower lip. "All I know is that your parents won't be happy that you're spending time with one of them, let alone three. It's all a sick game."

"That's it." I stood, folding my arms. "What in the hell is going on? Did my parents hire you? Did they send you my way to watch out for me?" My voice had risen several decibels, the tone terser than I'd ever used with her. At this point, I was finished with playing anyone's games, including my parents.

She backed away, her face turning red. "I...I..."

"Talk. Now!"

Several emotions crossed her face, bearing down on her. "I can't."

"You can't, or you won't?"

"You don't understand. I've grown so fond of you. More than I thought."

I laughed bitterly. "You're exactly right. I don't understand in the least why everyone needs to get in my business. I'm a big girl and can take care of myself. Talk."

"They swore me to secrecy."

"Who? My parents?"

All Jillian could do was nod.

Fuck this. Now, I was angry. I took a deep breath, raking my hand through my hair. "Are they paying you to watch out for me?"

"Oh, honey. I love being with you."

A headache formed behind my eyes. "Get out."

"What?"

"You heard me."

"You don't mean that."

No. Yes. Maybe. At this point, I wasn't certain of anything. "Who else is on my parents' payroll?"

"No one else that I know of. They're protective of you. Nothing more."

Protective wasn't the word.

"Fine," I hissed between clenched teeth. "Do you tell them all my dirty little secrets? Do you mention every date I've been on or how many times you suspect I've had sex?"

"No! Of course not. I never tell your father anything about your personal life. They just want to make certain you're safe."

Uh-huh. They knew I wouldn't tolerate a permanent bodyguard. I shook my head. "Very clever. Leave me alone for a few days, Jillian. I need to figure out what I'm going to do." And what terrible secret lingered in the shadows.

"I didn't mean to deceive you, Rose. Please know that I've enjoyed these last few years getting to know you. You're like the daughter I never had."

There was nothing left to say at this point, or if I did, the words wouldn't be considered very nice. "Just go. Now."

Jillian had been the rock I'd been able to lean on, hearing me cry over issues, calming me down when I'd wanted to strangle one or all of the other band members. She'd helped me choose outfits and purchase sparkly dresses. She'd remembered my birthday every year.

An ache had already formed in my heart, and as I watched her walk out the door, I was determined to get to the bottom of the great mystery. Tonight.

I turned to face the mirror, the lights surrounding the mirror suddenly seeming garish. I leaned in, studying my face. "Who are you?"

Another knock meant it was just about time for me to get on stage. Tonight, singing felt like a chore, the noose hanging around my neck.

When the door opened, the person walking inside wasn't who I'd expected.

"Hello, beautiful."

My Hunter. Mine. I almost laughed at the thought. "Hi ya, hunky man." I pushed away from the table as he approached. When he wrapped his arms around me, I took a deep inhale of his aftershave. All three men had an entirely different scent. Hunter's was woodsy with fresh rain in the spring, a testament to his name.

"How is my beautiful little lamb tonight?"

Lamb.

Little lamb. *Little lamb.*

I repeated the words several times in my mind, and a strange series of sensations tickled their way through my system. It wasn't unlike the cute phrases they used for me, but it struck me differently tonight.

"I'm good."

"I can tell something's wrong. You can't lie to me," Hunter said in his low, husky, and very sensual voice. He nuzzled into my neck, his hot breath tingling more than just my skin.

"I'm fine. I just had a little argument with my assistant. Nothing I can't handle."

"Lying to me isn't in your best interest."

When he swatted my bottom playfully, I issued a slight purr.

Hunter nipped my earlobe and crawled his hand down my skirt, tugging on the hem until he was able to get his fingers underneath. The moment he slipped several past the elastic and lace of my thong, a moan escaped my lips.

"Is my baby wet?"

"You're so bad," I whispered and leaned my head against his chest, spreading my legs as wide as the tight confines of the skirt would allow. He flicked his finger back and forth across my clit, and I was certain I'd melt into him. His touch was different, his needs more intense than I'd originally realized. And the man had a kinky streak that shocked me.

"Tonight, I'll shackle you to the bed blindfolded. Then you'll wait until we're ready to return. You won't know which one of us is touching you. Tasting you. Or will you?"

"I'll know."

"Hmmm… We're going to mark you, spank you, tease you. But you won't be allowed to come until we give you permission. Do you understand?"

"Yes, sir." My knees were ready to buckle, desire swimming through me. He had a way of bringing me close with just the sound of his voice.

"You have three masters now."

"How will that work? A big house together, a huge, king size bed?"

"Absolutely, but when you're a bad girl, you'll sleep in a cage."

A thrill jetted through me. Then another flash, another face. Cain's face.

"That's where you're wrong. You have three masters now. Make no mistake that when we take you, and that will happen, you will learn what pleasures us. When you come the first time, you'll beg for more, exhausted and overwhelmed with raw ecstasy. And I assure you that it will be the beginning of a beautiful affair. Every hole will be well used, but you'll crave more, begging the man who owns you to continue making you weak."

When had he issued the statement? I knew it had been Cain. I'd recognize his voice anywhere. But when? How had I known them before? There was only one possible way.

The college they'd attended, but it was far removed from the one I'd gone to. How was it possible that we'd met, and why didn't they recognize me?

My mind was fracturing. I was losing control of reality. Fear and uncertainty grabbed at every part of me, enough that I was paralyzed.

"Are you certain you're okay?" His tone held concern.

"I am when you're here."

Then Hunter pulled me even closer, pushing his thick cock into my bottom. "Such a tease my beautiful, little pet."

His words were enough to push me to an orgasm, but when he drove all four fingers inside, my core was ready to explode.

"I can't wait, baby girl, to fuck you tonight." He kept one arm wrapped around my waist as he tormented me, swirling his thumb around my swollen nub.

I clung to his thigh, digging my fingers into his trousers. The man knew how to make me feel euphoric in seconds. "Mmm... May I come?"

Hunter chuckled, the sound reverberating in my ears. "Yes, you can, little pet."

My body had betrayed me over and over again around the three gods of men, and tonight was no different. As an orgasm swept through me, electric vibrations shot through every cell and muscle, leaving me trembling all over. He continued pumping his fingers, flexing them open and curling the tips, already knowing exactly the spot to keep me soaring.

"You will come for us, little pet, only when we allow you to."

I opened my eyes, staring in the mirror. Hunter hadn't just spoken the words. They were in my mind, but... it was his voice. Just like I'd heard Cain's before. Panting, as I started to come down from the high, my body stiffened.

"What's wrong?"

As I pulled away from his hold, he slipped his fingers into his mouth. Everything I thought I knew was wrong. I was certain of it. I folded my arms, the icy chill coursing through me burning.

"Rose. What is it? You're white as a ghost."

I lifted my head, uncertain what to say. "Are you going to be at the show?"

The concerned look remained on his face. He gripped both of my arms, and I shuddered, certain what I was experiencing was a memory.

"That's one reason I stopped by. We have some business to handle, so we won't be at the show. However, we'll return by the time your last set is complete."

"We, meaning the three of you?" Three different families. Three different businesses. One connection.

Crandall University.

"Yes, just something we're considering doing together. Some business. I'm going to ask you again. Are you certain that you're okay? Did anything happen?" He continued to brush his fingers up and down my arm.

"I'm perfectly fine, and why would anything happen?" I pulled away, sensing he was concerned about something himself. What were they hiding from me? I wasn't fine at all. In fact, I was certain that whatever my parents had hidden from me revolved around a university I'd never been to.

The pieces of the puzzle were starting to collide.

"We'll see you later. Knock 'em dead, baby." Hunter returned his fingers to his mouth, licking whatever taste lingered on his heated skin.

Before he walked out the door, he turned his head, studying me intently.

There was no doubt I'd met him before, that I'd been with him before.

And with the others.

I could also feel their combined touch searing my skin, echoes of their whispers tormenting the fog wrapped around my memory. But it was being peeled away minute by minute that I remained with them. My head was pounding, my blood pressure skyrocketing. I could feel it, as if at any moment my head would explode. I'd never felt such pain before in...

Pain.

Yes, I had. Very slowly I lowered my head, glancing at the scar on the inside of my wrist. As I pressed my fingers across the indentation, a ghostly sensation of agony almost made me double over.

Knife. Blood,

"Kill the fucker," Cain roared.

"I'll do it," Cristiano snarled.

All I could think about was getting away from them. No. No!

"No, Sage. Come back here. Don't run," Hunter pleaded.

As happened every time, the vision faded before I was provided with answers. But the sensations remained.

Panic. Terror.

I couldn't stop shaking, the vision as if it had just occurred. This time, I was able to capture and store it in the back of my mind, as well as the feelings I'd had. Run. I'd convinced myself to run far away from them. But why? Who had they intended on killing? They were chasing me. A dark forest. Rain. And blood. I clenched my eyes closed, trying to clear my mind and control my breathing. Slowly, another memory slipped into the darkest part of my mind.

"Where the fuck are they?" the male voice yelled. "She needs help. Now!"

Sirens. Lots of sirens.

"They're coming! I hear them."

"Not fast enough. Stay with us, baby. Stay with us." His voice, pleading.

Blood. So much blood covering his face. So much...

"No. No. No!"

I pushed myself against the wall, dropping my head into my hands. As had happened before, the vision lingered long enough for me to capture three faces. Three faces I knew, their dark clothes covered in blood.

Cain. Hunter. Cristiano.

The three men who'd already altered my life, shattering my innocence several years ago. And the ones determined to do it again. Only this time permanently.

I'd lost control before, but that wasn't going to happen now. I would learn the truth.

Yes… I would expose the ugliness behind the secret.

Then there would be hell to pay.

CHAPTER 20

Hunter

The slight buzz indicated a new text.

I'd already had my terse phone call for the evening with Bart. He'd undoubtedly waited until after seven in the evening to call, hoping to get my voicemail. He'd gotten a taste of my wrath instead. And it was just the beginning. I was finished playing games with anyone. I'd invested a significant amount of time as well as money in the discovery phase initiating a purchase.

I refused to lose several hundred thousand dollars because of a twisted fuck trying to orchestrate a failed deal. While Bart Coplan would learn very quickly what happened to assholes who crossed me, William-fucking-Watkins was next on my list.

As I headed towards the elevators, I yanked out my phone. What I read sent a shot of adrenaline straight to my veins.

I know what you did.

Oh, please. If the fucker really thought his threat was going to unnerve me, then the idiot needed to get over himself.

As I stepped inside the elevator, I allowed my thoughts to return to Rose. She'd acted strangely, as if she'd seen a ghost. She'd mentioned she'd had trouble sleeping but had said little else besides her dreams had been plaguing her. I leaned my head against the wall, thinking about the haunted look in her eyes. We'd spent some of the most enjoyable days I'd had in several years together.

Hell, I'd spent time online searching for the perfect home for all four of us to share. I'd found several that could work. The requirement for the right selection? A huge bedroom suite and an area that could be turned into a playroom for adults. I was one sick pup, my needs spiraling out of control. Tonight, she'd be introduced to the lifestyle we preferred, one that she hungered for as well.

If all went well, the three of us had discussed collaring her soon. I laughed, closing my eyes and envisioning her in nothing but heels and a collar. She'd also have a matching leash.

The ping of the elevator drew me out of my moment of revelry. Before I could bask in the beauty of her naked body, there was business to take care of.

I stepped out into the corridor, yanking my phone into my fingers. While I figured the asshole who'd sent the text had already tossed the burner phone, my anger was elevated given Bart's bullshit. Before I walked into Cain's suite, I texted the son of a bitch back.

I will hunt you down. Then the fun will really begin.

Laughing, I shoved the keycard into the lock, opening the door then shoving the phone into my pocket. Both Cristiano and Cain were already inside. In the last few days, we'd established a communication room—or maybe I should have called it a war room—in order to put the pieces of the puzzle together. Tonight, the three of us were headed to deal with Bart. I had a feeling given his earlier call that he'd been either hired to provide a ruse or told in no uncertain terms he wouldn't sell to me.

"There he is," Cristiano said, barely glancing at me.

"How's our girl?" Cain piped in.

I wasn't entirely certain how to answer the question. "Anxious."

Cain lifted his head. "How so?"

"Has she said anything to you guys about the dreams she's been having?" It was obvious from the expression on Cain's face that he had no clue what I was talking about.

Cristiano sighed. "Reoccurring nightmares from when she was a child. Why?"

"I don't know. She stared at me as if she didn't know me."

"She's not a stupid girl, Hunter. She googled us. You know she did. That's why she asks so many questions."

"The recent Times article is connected to our names." I made the statement more in passing. "We should talk to her about it."

"Agreed," Cristiano said casually, although I knew he was just as concerned about her as I was. However, I couldn't read Cain's expression.

"Did you get a text?" I asked, immediately nodding to Brock, who knew all about our time spent in purgatory at the university. While Cain might still have fond memories, I loathed having my name and the schools on the same piece of linen paper. Maybe that's why I'd only framed my master's degree from Yale.

"The words were like a rip-off of a stupid horror movie from the nineties?" Cain asked sardonically.

"Yeah, that one."

"It would seem our mysterious poker player is getting bolder," Cristiano said.

I nodded. "I want to know how he got our private numbers."

Cain snorted. "You know that anything can be discovered for a price."

"True enough. Let's hope Bart has something concrete to offer us."

Cain rubbed his eyes. "Well, I have a piece of news you'll find interesting. Watkins isn't behind leaking the information about the Elite and the various functions we held."

"Then who is?" Maybe we were idiots to assume anything about the situation.

"An unknown source that had detailed information, including pictures. Although those weren't used. I pushed the guy, but it was obvious he really didn't know who'd sent him the information."

"That means it could be Watkins," I mused.

Cain shrugged. "Not his style. He has no problem accusing us out in the open."

"Pictures?" I asked, surprised as hell that Cain wasn't angry.

He nodded. "Yeah. In reading over the article, I found it interesting that what happened at the end was barely mentioned. Even Sage's accident was glossed over."

"Wait a minute. Are you thinking that whoever is doing this is holding the last card, waiting for the perfect moment to use against us?" I thought about what could possibly link us to Theodore's death.

"I do. I also think the person or persons responsible are anticipating we'll make a wrong move."

I tilted my head. "Which is why we need to be careful how we handle Mr. Coplan." The perpetrator was setting a trap, allowing us to finish our demise.

"Christ," Cristiano huffed. "Why bother talking to him at all if we need to go easy on him?"

I rubbed my jaw and grinned. "Because there are several ways of getting information out of people without killing them."

Cain burst into laughter. "And I thought you'd gotten soft in your old age."

"Who's getting old? You?"

Brock chuckled from behind us. "Yeah, he is."

Cain shot him a nasty look. "I don't think so." He threw back the rest of his drink. "It's time to take control of our little party."

I heard a buzz and smiled as I pulled the phone into my hand. "Well. Well."

"What did you do?"

"I threw out a bone and texted the number just to see if I could get a response. It would seem our dog is very hungry." I held out my phone for my buddies to read.

Game on, fucker. Come get it.

"Then let's go," Cain said with a growl in his voice. "Brock. Don't let the lovely Ms. Sadler out of your sight. I have a feeling this is going to get dicey." His eyes were practically glowing with the same bloodlust I'd seen before.

"You got it, boss."

* * *

There was more than one way to skin a cat. That was my father's favorite expression. As a kid, I'd believed he was a man who never played in the gray, until I'd walked into his office unannounced and uncertain of what I was seeing.

I'd been sure my father would get angry with me, but he'd welcomed the interruption. A man I didn't know and never saw again was tied to one of my father's office chairs. I'd often wondered why he'd purchased very plain looking hardback chairs with arms for his guests or employees to sit in.

That was the day I learned the reason, and the memory remained fresh in my mind as if I were twelve years old all over again.

I'd been gifted a tutoring session, including the ceremonial torture of someone I'd learned later was a friend he'd once trusted. He'd even considered the man like a brother. The man had betrayed him with someone who owned a rival corporation.

I sat behind Bart's massive desk, having retrieved a very similar chair that my father had used to provide a lesson in one of the outer offices. A bogus call had been made to Bart's house indicating an issue that an employee had needed help with.

Bart had bought it.

Unfortunately, it had taken more time than I'd originally wanted.

Now, he sat tied to what looked like a very uncomfortable chair, beads of sweat sliding down both sides of his face.

There was nothing like the stench of garlic oozing from a man's pores. I drummed my fingers on his desk with one hand, rolling the implement I'd brought with me to use in the other.

Both Cristiano and Cain remained leaning against the wall. Cain was eager to see me work. Cristiano was just ready to get the dance over with. Not that I could blame him. Cain's other righthand man, Marty, was eager to do the dirty work. While I certainly wouldn't mind handling Bart's punishment myself, I preferred watching.

I'd remained silent, doing nothing more than studying Bart. I'd rifled through his office, finding a single email tying him to the situation at hand.

Poor Bart was being blackmailed. It would seem I'd underestimated him completely. While he looked like a meek accountant type, complete with wire rim glasses, he had a penchant for dark kink that rivaled even what I enjoyed.

He also had a monster size cock that he didn't mind shoving into the mayor's daughter. I wondered how Bart's wife felt about him fucking a seventeen-year-old?

The stupid bastard was also keeping trophies of his own in a safe in his office that I'd easily cracked. The collection he'd amassed of child porn and other fucked up things would make most people sick to their stomachs.

"What do you want from me?" Bart asked nervously.

I took my time answering. "The truth."

"What?" He was already exasperated, likely realizing he'd be lucky to get out of this alive. Little did he know it was his lucky day. Tomorrow might be a different story, but his blood wouldn't be on my hands at that point.

"Who is blackmailing you?"

For a man who didn't appear to be able to hide behind a façade, he surprised me again, the quizzical look on his face almost believable. "Are you out of your mind? There's nothing to blackmail me over."

I took a deep breath, removing one of the pictures that he'd been stupid enough to keep as a trophy. "Then I guess you won't mind if I email this to the illustrious mayor of your lovely city."

Instead of pleading or denying, screaming to the hills the photograph could be doctored, he grinned like the pervert he was. God, I hated men who vilified women.

"She's of age."

"Not when this picture was taken."

Bart shifted in the seat, and I glanced at Marty. He walked over, taking the sewing needle from my hand. Both Cristiano and Cain had been fascinated when I'd provided instructions on what to do.

"So what? I can easily explain it. That doesn't even look like me."

I leaned forward and cocked my head. "Oh, I assure you that there is more where that came from, Bart." I pulled out two of the photographs I found most disturbing from his collection. At least he'd started to sweat even more. "Now, I need to know who the fuck is blackmailing you and what they know about me and my astute colleagues here."

"I have no clue what you're talking about."

Exhaling, I was already weary of his denial. I nodded at Marty, who immediately moved beside him, grabbing one of Bart's hands. Then Marty showed him what he held in his other hand.

I steepled my fingers, my elbows resting on the thick leather arms as I studied him. "My father was a quiet man, very reserved. He almost never showed his frustration or anger. However, when he was forced to do so, anyone facing his wrath knew to be terrified. He had his share of enemies, like any wealthy businessman. When I learned how he kept them under control, I gave all my respect to him, even though we weren't particularly close. I was proud and happy that he took the time to show me how he managed to build such a powerful empire."

As Marty slipped the needle under Bart's index finger, it took only two seconds before the man reacted.

I waved the soldier off, giving Bart an opportunity to recover and reconsider. After the man howled for a full ten seconds, he glared at me, panting like a dog. "What... do you... want?"

"It's often the little things in life that cause so much pleasure. And pain. A name, Bart. I want to know who is determined to make my life and that of my friends a living hell."

"I can't fucking tell you."

"Why not?"

"Because I'll die." Bart finally started struggling, his face turning red. There was no doubt he was afraid of what the man would do.

"I assure you, Bart, that if you don't tell me what I want to do, you'll wish you were dead."

He twisted his mouth but it didn't seem as if he was going to say anything. I motioned to Marty again and he returned to a task I could tell he enjoyed. Sighing, I rubbed my eyes as Bart expressed his displeasure.

"Enough," I said after a full minute. "You have one last opportunity to tell me what I want to know. Who is the man determined to bring us down?"

Tears were running out of his eyes, his shirt soaked from sweat. I'd forgotten just how effective the method could be. Suddenly, I needed a shower from the stench in the room.

"Listen," he finally managed to say. "Not... Not..."

This was getting ridiculous. "Not what, Bart?" I nodded to Marty and all he needed to do was hold the needle up to Bart's face.

"It's not a man. It's a woman."

As he was yelling the words, a text came through, and I pulled my phone into my hand, reading the message.

Then I lifted my head towards Cain, then to Cristiano, both grabbing their phones.

She's alive...

CHAPTER 21

Rose

There was no such thing as too much information. It was the lack of details that created nightmares. I should know, since the demons I was fighting were clawing the earth beneath my feet in a desperate attempt to free themselves.

I felt as if I was locked inside a vacuum, and it was slowly sucking the life out of me. I had no idea how I'd gotten through the performance, not that I remembered much about it. My hands were shaking as I tried to slide the card into the key slot, dropping it once before managing success.

Before I walked inside, I tipped my head over my shoulder. One of Cain's men had stood watching over me in the auditorium, ready to attack anyone who bothered me. I'd had to push him off a dumb and very drunk guy who'd jumped on stage to paw me. He was lucky Brock hadn't tossed him against the wall.

"You don't need to stay," I told him.

"I follow orders, ma'am. I'm not leaving."

"Okay." I walked inside, taking a deep breath before closing and locking the door. I had no idea when the three men would be back, but I wanted to find out everything I could about what had happened to me and who they were before they did. I'd never felt so anxious in my life, as if I was standing on a precipice of a mountain, staring down into a murky bottomless abyss.

I also had the feeling my life was spiraling out of control.

After pouring a glass of wine, I grabbed my laptop, yanking it into my hands and placing it on the coffee table next to the wilted roses from the first night. As I waited for the computer to boot up, I picked at the petals, pulling a few off one at a time and placing them on the table. They were still soft as well as fragrant, which surprised me.

Red petals.

I closed my eyes and could see a room. A nightstand. And a single petal. What the hell? Then I heard voices inside my head.

"I think someone has been in our suite more than once." I was standing in front of a nightstand speaking. There was someone with me.

The girl was beautiful, staring at me intently. Who the hell was she? *"Why would you think that?"*

"There was a rose petal on my nightstand just like the one I found a few weeks ago. And a pair of my panties has gone missing."

The girl rolled her eyes. It was obvious we were friends. *"Oh, come on. Why would anyone come into a dorm room?"*

"Kelly," I said out loud. I was certain that was her name.

A dorm room. Crandall University? Maybe. I took a gulp of wine and stared at the petals one last time before turning my attention to the computer. I found the news article again, then decided I needed to write down some notes. I grabbed the same pad where I'd written the story several nights before, remembering something else. I used to write stories exactly like the one I'd penned the other night. It was something else I was certain of.

This was crazy. It was like I'd lived an entirely different life. What had happened that was so terrible that my parents had done everything in their power to shield me from whatever it was?

I plopped down on the sofa, making a timeline of what I remembered, adding as many details as possible. Then I read the article again, jotting down a couple notes. A revelation hit me. Ten years had passed. Okay.

"As a member of an elite group, the men who graduated from the austere college were handed more than just a diploma," I read out loud. "They were also provided with a key to wealth and utter success in every avenue of business as determined by their powerful families."

I sat back, thinking about what the reporter was saying. Apparently, Crandall University was also called the City of Hope.

As I googled the name, the first picture that came up reminded me of a cathedral, the ancient stone building appearing as if it had been built centuries before. Kentucky? Hmm... I scrolled through their programs. Then something caught my eye. Music. The university had one of the most esteemed music programs in the country.

My skin began to crawl.

The article also alluded to debauchery and criminal acts, but of course the reporter was smart enough not to name any names in direct connection to the apparent lewd acts. However, the year was mentioned. Ten years ago. Apparently, the Elite had been permanently disbanded, several young men expelled. Where had the reporter gotten such detailed information?

I scrolled for another thirty minutes, unable to corroborate the reporter's findings in a single article or mention anywhere on the internet. Of course the parents had enough power and influence to sweep everything under the rug. I tried a different tactic.

It only took a few minutes to ascertain that all three of my men had been seniors the same year as mentioned in the article. The reporter had also alluded to the fact that there'd been a storm that night. Why did that matter?

Storm.

I clenched my eyes shut, the same vision from months before of running through the forest rushing into the forefront of my mind and played out. Only this time, there was something different. Lights. Headlights. The startling realization kept me on edge, but I was excited that additional pieces of my memory were starting to come back.

What else were my passionate lovers hiding?

After another sip of wine, I allowed my fingers to keep searching through the various pages. All three men had glowing articles and snippets from events attended as well as disparaging ones. Cristiano was even suspected of killing his own father. Wow.

Another forty-five minutes had passed, maybe longer. I'd yet to find anything that intertwined my life with the debauchery the reporter had mentioned. Not one thing. Maybe I was wrong. Maybe my memories were conjured up stories partially from what I'd written. An overactive imagination. Or maybe I needed the mystery of what had happened to me to be a bigger deal than it was. My parents had told me it was a swimming accident. I should just leave it alone and move on with my life.

Did I even know a Kelly? Not that I remembered. I laughed and folded my legs, resting the laptop on my knees. I continued to scroll through the pages, although the stories were starting to drift to other people entirely. The ache in my head remained and there was a nagging that refused to go away.

"I need to surrender to them no matter what they want me to do."

"Whoa. Hold on. That's crazy. Why?"

The girl from my dorm room was sitting right beside me. We were in a vehicle. There was a storm. I was certain of it.

"Because my parents want me to be chosen." The girl was insistent. She'd made the statement as if it was the best thing to ever happen to her.

"Chosen for what?"

"To hopefully marry one of the bastards one day."

While her words had been said with disdain in her voice, I'd seen the glimmer in her eyes. She was excited. Wait a minute. She'd brought me to a… party. That's right.

I took a deep breath, closing my eyes for a few seconds to rest them. When I opened then again, my pupils fixated on a blue tag in the screen. *The Damned Strike Again. Tragedy.*

I hadn't seen this article before. Why?

My fingers were shaking as I read the article. By the time I was finished, I was sick to my stomach. Then on a hunch, I returned to Cain's name, adding the word 'brother' into the search bar. It didn't take long to find a carefully crafted article from twenty years before.

Dayton Cross had been slaughtered in his own home by an unknown assailant who'd never been found. His twelve-year-old brother, Cain Cross, had found the body. "Oh, God."

Revenge. Cain wanted revenge. If what I suspected was true, there was no coincidence to the fact that the four of us had been brought back together. Had Cain orchestrated it?

My thoughts drifted back to the vision that I now knew was a memory. My father had been responsible for Dayton's death. I knew it as certain as I was standing in a room inside a hotel owned by the man who'd likely vowed revenge. My God. I'd been living a lie my complete life, not just because of an accident I still couldn't remember.

All the times my father had traveled. The tight security. The absence of family and friends. My mother not wanting me to come to Chicago. It all fit together in a nice, bloody package of lies and secrets.

As a chill coursed through my body ever so slowly, the ache in my head suddenly disappeared.

I held my arms as I climbed off the couch, grabbing my phone from the bedroom. Then I dialed my parents' number.

When I reached my mother's voicemail, I ended the call and tried my father's. Then a smile crossed my face as I knew what I needed to do. One more call to make. Only then would I find the answers. "Yes, I'd like to book a flight to San Diego."

* * *

Cain

I stared at the text for the fifth time before heading toward the exit from the building. She was alive. Sage. The woman who'd haunted my dreams for years. The beautiful girl I would have given everything I owned to see just one more time. The stunning creature who'd awakened my black soul. Alive.

Only she had a new identity, her face similar but different enough I hadn't recognized her. But now, I realized there was no doubt. None.

Everything made sense now. The way Rose felt in my arms. The intense connection. The electricity that I'd only felt once in my life with a girl who'd died because of my sins. Our sins. Our entitlement.

She was alive.

And she belonged to us.

One thought burned into the back of my mind. Was she behind the nasty game? Had it been invented to satisfy a taste of revenge herself? I wouldn't put it past her. As much as I wanted to keep her as our pet, spending days and nights embroiled in passion, if we found out she had anything to do with our planned demise, she would face my wrath.

The three of us said nothing as we made our way into the night, leaving the asshole Bart to face a demise of a different level. I was certain whoever had used him would clean up their messes. That's the way it worked. The players in the game were vicious. It was obvious they'd underestimated us.

Perhaps I should feel guilty for leaving Bart to the wolves, but he meant nothing to me. I sensed Hunter no longer gave a damn about the lost revenue or the ploy used to get him to Chicago in the first place. It had been a well-orchestrated game, Rose learning much from her father. I wondered if the fuck was even still alive. I'd find out one way or the other, even if I had to go to Fiji personally.

"You don't honestly believe Rose is Sage." There was no emotion in Cristiano's voice, but between the three of us, the current ebbing and flowing could light up an entire city block.

"What do you think?" I asked, cursing under my breath. Marty headed towards the SUV while we stood back under the dim light of the building's entrance.

"Rose is not the same person." Hunter was defiant in his statement, but I heard the question in his voice.

"You know there are too many similarities." I paced the parking lot, needing to crush something between my fingers to try and abate the anger. "The fucking nightmares. The connection we share. The singing. She was a fucking music major. Remember?"

"She doesn't look anything like Sage." Hunter's insistence surprised me. Did he not see what was staring him smack in the face? She'd coordinated the attacks. She'd led the charge in seeking revenge because of the accident. I was certain of it.

I was also certain I was maddeningly, shockingly in love with the woman. I hadn't been able to get her out of my mind for more than a few seconds at a time. I scrubbed my jaw and tried to figure out how to handle this. I couldn't allow her to destroy everything I worked so hard to achieve.

"It's her, Hunter. You fucking know it," Cristiano said. Hunter had his hand wrapped around Cristiano's throat in a split second, issuing a hard punch to his gut before slamming him against the brick façade.

"You motherfucker!"

"You know I'm right. There's nothing we can do about it," Cristiano threw out.

Hunter refused to believe, pulling back then slamming his fist into the man's jaw.

"That's it. Stop it, both of you. This isn't solving anything. We need to think this through. If Sage is a part of this ruse, which I'm not ready to believe, she's not working alone. There are too many working pieces, including being able to successfully handle an extortion scheme. I'm beginning to believe you were right, Cris, in that this isn't her father's doing either. We need to be smart about this. We're acting like idiots, which is exactly what the perpetrator wants." Shit. At this point, I had no idea what to think.

"It's not her," Hunter insisted.

"We can't rule anything out."

"Fuck you!" Hunter crossed into my space, preparing to give me a beat down just like he'd done with Cristiano. Like hell I was going to allow that to happen.

I shoved him hard and he threw himself at me, ready to tear me a new one. At this point, I wouldn't mind getting bloody to ease the tension.

Neither one of us had the chance, the roar of an engine and the pepper of gunfire taking precedence.

"Fuck!" Marty snarled. I caught a glimpse of him, a bullet slamming into his shoulder. Bullets pinged against one of the parked cars, only inches away from both Hunter and myself.

I dropped and rolled, reaching for my weapon, noticing Cristiano had bolted toward them.

"Go. Go. Go!" he was yelling at Marty as he fired off an entire magazine of ammunition. He was always ready for a fight, his father's tutelage superior even to mine.

Another round of gunfire forced me to my knees. I reacted without hesitation, firing off several shots across the street. The fuckers had been lying in wait. They'd known we were headed to meet with Bart. Nothing was coincidental.

"What the hell?" Hunter slammed his body against another SUV, jerking his head around the front fender. He carefully got off a couple rounds, but at this point none of the assailants were in view, the offending vehicle roaring off into the darkness.

But they'd be back.

They'd come here to do a job, and they wouldn't leave until it was finished, or they were lying in a pool of blood. I chose the latter. I had far too much to live for.

Including finishing the revenge started twenty years before. "That's what we need to find out. We're going to end this Goddamn charade once and for all." I could tell the driver was turning around, ready to make another pass.

Hunter laughed. "You remember what we did with that asshole back in Kentucky?"

"Hell, yeah." I peered over the vehicle, realizing both Marty and Cristiano had taken out whoever had been in position on land. With no other shots fired from other locations, perhaps the remaining assassins were in the unknown vehicle. We'd surrounded one jerk who'd been determined to take us down, stealing vital information from the Elite's Estate. We'd hunted him. Cornered him. Flushed him out. Then we'd had our fun deep in the woods. Unfortunately, we didn't have time to skin a cat, but we could corner the sons of bitches.

It would seem Cristiano knew what we had in mind, directing Marty to the middle of the street. Hunter and I raced towards it as well, all four of us with our guns directed at the road. The assassins likely figured out what we were doing, slowing down as they approached. This would be dicey at best, but it was the only way to try and figure out who they were working for.

I sensed the moment the driver pressed down on the accelerator, lifting my weapon even higher, using both hands. Cristiano took his time slapping another magazine into his Glock. A quick glance in his direction and the gas station sign highlighted his evil grin. The man lived for danger and bloodshed.

Some people say near death moments go by in slow motion, allowing the participants to view everything that occurs frame by frame. Maybe I never gave a shit about anything but the outcome because in the matter of a few seconds, a barrage of gunfire ensued from both sides, glass shattering and brakes squealing before the vehicle suddenly veered off course, crashing into the side of a building.

There was no time to waste, the stench of gasoline and the sight of black smoke rolling from the crushed hood a clear indication a fire would start at any time. We raced in the direction, hoping to obtain anything leading us to the instigator of the attempted assassination.

I headed to one side, prepared to throw open a door.

"Get down!" Hunter's voice rang over the creaks and hisses. I did so without hesitation, the single shot followed by one of the enemies falling on his face on the pavement.

I threw him a look of thanks, then grabbed the fallen man, dragging him away from the SUV. After patting him down, the only thing I found was his license. At least I had identification, although that might not help at all. Cristiano checked the others.

"Nothing," Cristiano barked a few seconds later. "They knew we'd check for ID."

I held up what I had and shook my head, all of us coughing. What a shitshow.

The smoke was acrid, burning my eyes. Then a flame licked up from under the hood. The four men were dead.

"Let's get out of here," I told them.

"Boss. Do you want me to get a cleanup crew?" Marty asked, wincing in pain.

"No time. I have a feeling the cops will be all over this." While I didn't like it messy, most of the police force was in my pocket, so there wouldn't be any pushback. Still, it was obvious I was off my game.

"Come on. We need to get back to the resort. We have some things to deal with." There was a faraway look in Hunter's eyes as he made the recommendation. I knew the moment I saw him with Rose that he'd been pulled into her sweet lair.

I still found it difficult to believe she was Sage.

A part of me wanted to shove her in a cage, force her to tell us the truth, then kill her. The other wanted to wrap her in my arms. Fuck. This whole thing was a mess.

That we'd created years before. If only we'd kept our dicks inside our jeans.

We jogged to the other side of the road just as the fire reached the gas tank. Flames rushed towards the heavens.

I shook my head, then climbed inside. "You okay, Marty?"

"Just a scratch, sir."

"Get it checked out back at the resort." I rubbed my eyes before dialing Brock.

"Boss," he answered.

"We had an incident. Make certain you get a couple other men on Ms. Sadler, and have others walk the resort inside and out."

"Uh, boss. We have an issue."

"What do you mean an issue?"

"It's Ms. Sadler."

I sucked in my breath. "What about her?"

"Well, she's gone. I've looked everywhere. She's nowhere to be found."

CHAPTER 22

Cristiano

Betrayal was something I was used to. I'd grown up around it, first from childhood friends, then seeing traitors punished by my brutal father. Everyone had a price, a reason or a dollar amount that would allow them to shift from the right side of the law to the other. Or to betray a confidence or even the location of a friend or colleague.

Or lover.

Money and power were excellent motivators, but often the greatest influence on whether someone selected a different moral code was centered around the need for revenge.

Both Hunter and I had seen it in Cain. We'd watched him hone his evil ways until he was certain of what he'd wanted, which was blood for blood given the murder of his brother.

He'd suffered and still was suffering, never able to get over the horror. Unfortunately, he'd allowed it to consume his life, shaping his decisions, warping them until he'd become a stalker.

Then everything had changed the moment he'd seen Sage years before. She'd performed magic, her goodness conquering a portion of the demons inside of him. There was no difference in the way he looked at Rose. For a man like Cain, it was as close to love as he could possibly get. She was the kind of woman who could be our salvation.

Or she was our curse.

Whether or not they were the same person was the question that would eat at the three of us until the truth was discovered.

However, if she was, the ugliness around the truth would eat us alive.

A single question nagged at the back of my mind and would until I looked her in the eyes again. Could a sweet, beautiful girl turn into a calculating monster, determined to destroy the three men who'd dared tempt her dark desires? I forced myself to think about the night from years ago. All three of us had pushed so hard to drive it from our minds, believing that we could let it go. We also were certain the incident would never come back to bite us.

Sage had witnessed us handling Theodore, all three of us enraged that he'd dared attack her, attempt to rape her. We'd done so violently, our rage knowing no bounds. We'd been intent on killing him. That was in our nature. Even Hunter hadn't shied away from hungering to take his life.

Maybe the act had been the final nail in the coffin, our lives spent in private prisons after watching her broken body on the pavement, her mouth trying to form words from a broken jaw before slipping away into unconsciousness. Then we'd gone off the deep end.

Our actions had been what nightmares were made of.

What we hadn't been certain given the tragedy was whether she'd seen Cain pulling out his knife. Even if she had, she'd fled prior to Theo managing to jerk out a gun, shooting Cain before Hunter wrestled it away.

I'd been the one to pick up the fallen knife, finishing what Cain had started. I would rot in Hell for all eternity because of that and dozens of other atrocities I'd committed, but even then, I would have given my life to protect Sage's.

Just like I would now. Fuck. How had things gotten so far out of hand?

I'd played over the horrific event in my mind so many times I could recite it, but as with all things, in time, certain aspects of what happened had begun to fade. There's been so many people, the driver trying to flee the scene. Cain had almost beaten the guy to death.

Then the police.

The estate where we'd lived had been shut down, several of the Elite students expelled. The scandal had rocked the university, but with dozens of lawyers intervening, the fifteen minutes of malevolent fame had eventually faded. Even with everything that had gone on, including a criminal investigation into Theo's disappearance, we'd been protected. The truth was that we'd been treated as the gods we'd believed we were, not facing one minute of punishment for what we'd started.

Our vicious intentions.

Was I the kind of man who could have remorse or guilt? I'd convinced myself a long time ago that I had no conscience. Hell, my father had nearly beaten it out of me, forcing me to handle aspects of punishment just to dull my senses. It had worked.

Except for when I was with Sage.

She'd been the light to my darkness, the reason I wanted to make changes in my life. It was ridiculous since I didn't really know her, but that's how strongly I'd felt. So had Hunter and Cain.

Now, Rose.

A beautiful, intelligent miracle with the voice of an angel.

Who could be behind the acts of revenge. I found it impossible to believe and would argue it to my grave had my mother not betrayed my father long ago, leaving her only child in the hands of a bastard who could care less if I existed. A bitter laugh erupted in my throat.

Hunter and I followed Cain as he stormed down the hallway towards her suite, his anger increasing. When he reached Brock, who stood by her door, I was certain Cain was going to kill the man. He issued two hard jabs to the man's throat before pushing him up against the wall. "How the fuck were you stupid enough to allow her to get away?"

Brock didn't push back, didn't struggle. He knew what would happen if he did.

"I'm sorry, boss. There was a call about a fire on the floor. Management got everyone out. She managed to leave with the crowd. I tried to stop her, but she ran from me."

Shit. She'd planned it. What was she trying to do?

Cain hissed. "She was responsible for calling it in. I don't need to check. I feel it in my bones."

"Why? Where the fuck could she go?" Hunter demanded.

"Maybe to meet with the people working with her. What else?" Cain remained adamant, but I heard his voice crack. He didn't want to believe it any more than I did.

"Get your head out of your ass, Cain. We don't know anything for certain. I refuse to allow you to condemn Rose, who could be an innocent player in all of this. If you keep doing that, you'll need to come through me. Got it?" Hunter's upper lip curled as he fisted one hand and I took a step closer, daring him to try.

"Fine. But we will determine if she's involved."

"And if she is?" Hunter threw out.

At this point I doubted we had a clue what to say. She'd already managed to crawl under our skin.

"Search her room," Cain stated as he pulled his hand away from Brock. "I'm going to hunt down her assistant. Maybe I'll get some decent answers. I'm also going to have a chat with the detective."

"I find it interesting that this detective you talked to hasn't called me," I told him.

"Me neither." Hunter laughed. "Maybe the man you talked to isn't a detective after all."

"Fuck," Cain snarled, obviously realizing we were right. "This ends today. Period."

Mr. Omnipotent was at it again. He'd yet to learn there were some things and people he couldn't control with violence.

The lovely woman or women was a case in point.

Damn it, my cock twitched just thinking about touching her. An ache had formed in between my eyes.

The game had been well played. And planned. The three of us looked at each other for a few seconds, the tension palpable. We'd been big and bad wolves for years. To think it was possible that we'd almost been taken down by a beautiful woman was disturbing.

Even worse was the fact that the three of us cared for her more than we wanted to admit.

Cain narrowed his eyes as he looked at Brock. "I will deal with you later." He moved towards her door, sliding his keycard into the lock.

He didn't bother going inside, his face remaining twisted as he headed for the elevators.

Hunter shook his head. "He's got it bad for her."

"Just like we do."

I was the first one in, taking a deep breath. Her perfume lingered in the air, the delicate yet exotic scent floating into my nostrils. I could bury my face in her neck for hours, enjoying the closeness and nothing else.

"If she left, her computer wasn't important enough to take with her," Hunter said in passing.

He moved past me, quickly looking in other rooms while I moved towards the laptop that remained on the coffee table.

As I sat down, I noticed she'd written notes on a piece of paper meant for writing songs. As I pulled it into my hands, a knot formed in my stomach. I didn't need to try and break her code for her computer. It was obvious she was searching about the night of the tragedy and anything else she could find on us, including about the university.

Parties? Was I at a party?

Black clothes. They wore them all the time. Like Cristiano?

Kelly. Was she my roommate?

Prince Albert piercing. I've experienced one before. Or have I?

Did someone die?

Is my father an assassin? Cain's brother.

"Shit." Where had she been given the idea that her father was a killer? She'd obviously spent a significant amount of time researching every scrap of information she'd managed to find. It sounded as if it was a recent revelation, not something she'd carried with her for months or years.

And there was one line even more troubling and telling.

Is it true what the anonymous person said, that they are killers?

I'd bet everything I owned on the fact that she'd been played just like we had. That meant someone else suspected who she was.

It was obvious she had more questions than answers. There was no structured path in the information she'd found, the notes random. There had to be at least twenty more of them. That didn't seem like the activity of a criminal mastermind, but a girl fearful that she didn't know what she'd dropped in the middle of.

Hunter returned to the room. I noticed his expression had become grimmer than before. "She didn't take a suitcase, but it's obvious she left in a hurry."

I inhaled, wanting to process what I'd read before mentioning it to him. "She knows about Cain's brother."

"Fuck. If Rose is Sage, then she has to be terrified of us already."

"Do you blame her?"

"No. Goddamn Cain and his bullshit."

"This is what the perpetrator wants to happen. They're leaving breadcrumbs for her to find."

"So she can expose what happened. They won't need to finish the deed," Hunter snarled, fisting his hand.

"We can't sit around waiting for that to happen. Check her drawers, the closet, everywhere she could be hiding something else." She was desperate for answers, although at this point, she didn't seem to be worried if we found out what she'd learned.

"Do you think she's really Sage?"

"The jury is still out but I'm beginning to believe it's possible. It's also possible she was caught up in a horrible game. We need to make certain one way or the other. But the nightmares she mentioned. With people experiencing head trauma, sometimes it takes years for memories to return, if ever."

"Which means her parents had the opportunity to insert a new life in replacement of the old."

"Yeah."

Hunter exhaled. "This is some fucked up shit. You know Cain is likely not to care even if we can find proof of her innocence."

"What makes you think I give a shit about what Cain thinks?" My tone was full of anger, although not directed towards either one of my buddies. I was finished with being jerked around like some goddamn puppet.

He opened his eyes wide, then grinned. "At least you and I are on the same page. I don't plan on letting Rose get away. She's the only reason I've fucking smiled for years."

He was serious. I couldn't blame him. I wanted her with me. Fuck. I loved the girl. Admitting it to myself was a surprise. Admitting it to the other two wasn't necessarily something I wanted to do.

"From what I can tell, Rose managed to find an article on what happened that night. She wrote a few notes down."

Hunter walked closer. "If my memory serves me about the events, her parents were adamant that her name remain out of the paper. I think they used a false name to try and keep reporters from finding out exactly what happened."

I sat back against the couch, folding my arms behind my head. "That's right. I'd forgotten about that. We were definitely not allowed to see her." I thought about what he'd just said and took a deep breath, holding it for a few seconds before letting it out. "Perfect. Her parents had the perfect opportunity to disappear permanently. Let everyone believe she'd died."

"Brilliant."

"Assassins do it all the time. Because they had a daughter, which was unexpected, The Iceman couldn't operate under his usual methods. Her accident was the chance to be able to do so. They just disappeared, selling the fake business. It was done so quickly I was shocked. Did you go to her funeral?"

"No, did you?" He seemed surprised.

I allowed my memories to return to a place I never wanted to visit. "Yeah. I stood on the hill far enough away they didn't see me. I watched them bury her body. Then I turned my back and tried to pretend it didn't happen." I was off everyone's radar then, returning to South America at my father's request.

"Fascinating. What if she's following in her father's footsteps?"

I laughed. "She's a rockstar. I doubt she's sidelining as a hired killer."

"That's not what I mean. What if all this is about revenge? What if she believes we were the ones who tried to hurt her? These nightmares might be providing some details, yet warping the events."

"We did try and hurt her, although not like Theodore."

He sighed. "Not like the bastard. He was out to get to us through her. We talked big back then, Cris. We weren't monsters."

"Weren't we?"

"Maybe you're right. Maybe this is karma's way of forcing us to atone for the part we played in destroying her life."

"She just discovered the additional pieces. She was lured here just like we were. I'm positive of it."

"Then she's scared blind and can't trust us."

If Rose was Sage, then at least she'd managed to enjoy a life similar to what she'd wanted. The signs were all there that Sage was alive, but none of us would have known if she was lying about it instead of not remembering her former life.

"One thing we do know is that Theo's father had something to do with the recent article."

Hunter shook his head. "No, we don't. Remember the reporter refused to reveal his source. Let me make some calls and see if I can find anything. If Xavier Winters changed his life again, there won't be an obvious trail."

A thought entered my mind. There was one place she could find all the answers she was seeking. "Maybe check with the airport and see if she took a flight."

Hunter blinked, then a look of understanding crossed his face. "To see her parents. Good idea."

"As far as Xavier, if Rose is Sage, then you know his current last name. However, if I had to guess, if she confronts them, her parents will disappear again."

"And take her with them?"

"Maybe." We couldn't allow that to happen. I couldn't lose her again.

"We'll get her back."

"Let's hope to hell we do."

As Hunter pulled out his phone, I glanced at the notes again. With what she'd found and if her dreams had provided false information, if Rose had no idea who she was, she'd be convinced she should hate us.

And I couldn't blame her in the least.

I moved around the suite, even checking in the small kitchenette. There was no smoking gun. There was also no evidence that she carried a weapon, and she certainly didn't have a little black book full of names. I laughed to myself for even thinking she could have anything to do with the plan of attack.

Unless she was being used.

Just like she'd been ten years before.

I headed into the bedroom, eyeing the nightstand. As I walked towards it, Hunter ended a call.

"She flew out to San Diego."

I'd been right. "To see her parents. Goddamn it."

"Should we follow her?"

"If we're right, Hunter, we're the reason she has no accurate memory. She deserves the truth about her identity, which she should only hear from her parents. However, learning what happened that night should only come from us."

"If she'll listen."

We stared at each other for a few seconds. Then I opened the nightstand. There were several folded pieces of paper similar to the ones I'd found near her laptop. As I pulled them into my hand, we both heard Cain returning.

I read through page one. Then the second one. Then the third. My cock ached, my balls tightening. I could feel my blood pressure rising, the need for her as all-consuming as it had been ten years before. Maybe more. We were kids then.

"What is it?" Hunter asked.

After I handed him the pages I'd read, a cold chill drifted down my spine. "A dark story that sounds very familiar."

"Ah, shit," Hunter said as he lifted his head. "There is no doubt any longer. Rose Sadler is Sage Winters."

"Yes." I barely got the word out before Cain came in the room, pushing Halo's manager.

"Her assistant, Jillian, is gone. Checked out of the hotel," Cain snarled. "What the hell do you know about this, Brett?"

"Even if I knew, I wouldn't tell you, and get your filthy hands off me." Brett tried to jerk away, but Cain had a firm hold on the man's shoulder.

I walked closer, glaring Brett in the eyes. "What do you know? It will go much easier on you if you tell us everything you even think you know."

"You can't threaten me."

"Brett. I think you know who I am and realize that all the stories about me are true," Cain said quietly, more so than I would have expected.

Brett wiped his mouth, then nodded. "What do you want from me? First, I get some weird call from Rose demanding I tell her exactly why this resort was chosen."

"What did you tell her?" Hunter asked. He nodded to Cain, handing off the story. Then he moved behind and in front of the bedroom door.

Brett craned his neck and shrugged. "That I wasn't the one pushing. Jillian was. She discovered the opportunity and thought it was perfect. I couldn't argue. For the money we were being paid, it was a no brainer."

I took a deep breath. The shit was starting to come together. Unfortunately, the three of us had been played like a fiddle. "What else did Rose tell you? Think carefully."

Obviously exasperated, Brett started to sweat. "It wasn't a long phone call. She acted very strange. She said she was being used. I thought she meant by the other band members. They don't always get along."

"Anything else?" Hunter growled.

"No. Okay? What is this about?"

Cain lifted his head from reading the story, his face expressionless. "Mr. Rollins. You're going to need to cancel the next few shows."

"Wait. We have a contract. I'll see your ass in court if you try and pull us now," Brett snarled. "The crowds love us. The press loves us."

"Shut up!" I snarled.

"I assure you that I have every intention of honoring the contract. In fact. I'll double the terms. Just handle it," Cain told him.

"What is going on? Is Rose in danger?" Brett demanded.

"Yes," I told him. "She is."

"Jesus Christ. This has to do with the weird note she received. Right?"

The three of us looked at each other, then back to Brett. "What weird note?" I growled.

"She barely mentioned it. She just said it was a warning. I didn't think much of it because in this business, there are stalkers and other freaks."

Cain gave me a look. Then he reached into his pocket, pulling out a folded piece of paper and handing it to me.

You don't know who you're sleeping with. They are murderers.

"I found it in her dressing room. There was also a note left in red lipstick on her mirror," he continued.

"Jesus. That's creepy," Brett said.

The man had no idea.

Exhaling, I rubbed my jaw. "We'll take care of it."

"What do I tell people?" Brett whined.

Cain glanced from one of us to the other. "That your star is taking a desperately needed respite to become reacquainted with some friends from her past."

The look on Cain's face forced both Hunter and I to tense. "What did the one on the mirror say?"

"Time to die."

CHAPTER 23

Rose

Death.

It was inevitable that the end would come. Sometimes it loomed over people, those who were sick or had been told they didn't have long to live. Sometimes it was a welcome relief for someone fighting pain or misery. But for many, death was a devastating ghost to be feared, some believing they had the grim reaper following them throughout life.

My situation was entirely different. I felt as if I'd been born again, leaving behind a life that I wasn't certain I missed. Or maybe I did. There was only one way of finding out the truth. I couldn't rely on my memory to provide what I craved desperately.

The truth.

It meant more to me than anything.

Sage.

I was certain that was my name, not Rose. The visions had become more frequent, one assaulting my mind after the other. Mostly random. All disturbing. I was thankful I'd taken a cab from the resort to the airport, the images disruptive. The puzzle pieces were trying to come together. Sadly, it was like trying to drive a square peg into a round hole. It was more frustrating than ever.

I'd also received two texts since leaving Chicago.

One was from Hunter. He'd been the one designated to find out what had happened to me. The simple question shouldn't have meant anything, but I felt an angst unlike anything I'd felt before.

At least that I could remember.

Are you okay?

Then a second one.

We need to talk. Please, baby.

I'd been tempted to text him back. In fact, I'd almost done so three times. He'd known I'd read it, which meant he also knew I was ignoring him on purpose. We both carried iPhones. I couldn't talk to any of them until I found out everything I could. Even then, I wasn't entirely certain what I was going to say. The ache continued, my stomach in knots. Nothing seemed real any longer, yet I felt danger. I felt sadness. Most of all I felt loneliness.

I missed them. All three of them.

During the flight, I'd shove aside the unwanted memories, replacing them with images of their faces and the times we'd shared. Laughter. Passion. What it had made me realize was that I'd felt it before. With all three of them. I was certain of it. The chemistry was too intense. Even now, electricity coursed through every vein and muscle.

The third text was... terrifying.

We're coming...

As in more than one person.

I fingered my phone even now, anxiety creating a breathless feeling. Were they watching me, us? What kind of sick game were they playing?

Perhaps I'd been impetuous taking the first flight out of Chicago. At least it had been nonstop, but four hours had been too long to sit and think about everything I'd read. Even though I'd tried to shove aside the fleeting memories, they'd come pouring in. I wasn't just thinking they were the reason that I'd been targeted not once but twice. I was certain of it.

In finding out from my useless manager that Jillian had instigated the trip to Chicago, I wasn't entirely certain who I could trust any longer. It certainly wasn't my memory. The worst feeling of all was questioning whether or not I trust the men I'd fallen in love with.

I was sick inside, my heart aching. I'd wanted to run to their arms for safety, but in the back of my mind, I couldn't get away from the thought that one or all three had killed someone. It was crazy. Muddled. Even now, I could barely breathe.

I was home in a place I wasn't certain I even knew. There were no pictures, no vivid images of celebrations or holidays. I'd never really thought about it before now.

The light inside the expansive room had cast a beautiful glow on the artistic pieces my mother had selected. I loved this house, although I knew they were considering selling and moving elsewhere. The location I'd yet to be told. With dad retiring, maybe they wanted a fresh start. I'd miss the gorgeous pool that I never spent any time in, the bright sun that San Diego always seemed to have, and the ocean. That was laughable. I couldn't remember the last time I'd gone to the beach in any state.

I was always working.

That's what I loved.

Then the three men had come along, and I'd realized how much of life I'd been missing.

I heard my mother return to the room, and when I pulled away from the window, I was certain what I'd find in her hands. Refreshments. She'd gone to find my father after getting over her initial shock of seeing me standing on her doorstep. I'd been here almost twenty minutes, and he hadn't shown his face.

They had to know why I was here, or at least suspect.

"I thought you'd like some lemonade," she said as she proceeded to pour a large glass from a stunning pitcher that seemed more like an art piece.

"What I want is the truth."

She kept a smile plastered on her face, acting as if this was a typical visit. I'd planned a tight trip and would need to leave within thirty minutes to make my flight. I would return to Chicago where the storytelling would continue. But in doing so, I'd need to control my heart. I couldn't allow Cain, Hunter, and Cristiano to weasel their way back into my system. If I did, I'd never learn the details.

"Sit down, honey."

I shook my head, realizing I wasn't going to get anywhere with her alone. After easing onto the chair, she pushed one of the glasses across the table. I noticed her hand was shaking.

"Who am I, Mother?"

"What do you mean? You're our daughter. You're a beautiful girl. You're famous."

I heard my father's footsteps and took a chance. "Is my name Sage?"

My father stopped in the doorway, remaining silent. I lifted my head, almost taken aback by his haggard appearance. I hadn't seen them in almost a full year. In that time, he'd aged significantly, although he would still be considered a virile man by anyone's standards. He'd kept himself in shape, working out with a vengeance. If it was true and he was an assassin, then of course he'd need to be big and strong.

I was ready to burst into laughter, chastising myself for being ridiculous, except the signs had been there. The strange phone calls. The late-night flights out of the blue. The less than up front answers to questions when I'd bothered to ask. The security. The threats, although I'd never been privy to one. The money I knew they had in several bank accounts.

I'd chosen to ignore every sign, pretending my father was a regular guy.

In his hand was an oversized envelope. As he walked closer, my mother poured him a glass of lemonade. His usually hard expression softened as he sat down.

"Yes."

The simple word was like a sledgehammer. "Go on."

"Your name is Sage Winters. You are our biological daughter. Our only child."

His voice was so quiet, I had to strain to hear him. "Okay. The accident. Was it the truth?"

"Yes," my mother said quickly. "We didn't lie to you. You were severely injured, but not in a swimming accident."

"You didn't lie to me? You mean other than about my name, my heritage, what happened, and why I have memory loss?" I heard the anger in my voice. Was it misguided? At this point, there was no way of knowing.

"Do not be angry with your mother! I forbid her to tell you. We were trying to protect you." He was angrier than I'd seen him in years, but I also sensed fear. The man had been backed into a corner.

"By lying to me? Someone is determined I learn the truth one way or the other. I'd rather hear it from both of you. Please. Do you know what it's like to go through life realizing a huge part of you is missing? Or to have nightmares every time I close my eyes?"

"We didn't want that for you. We made certain the best doctors in the world looked at you." My father sighed. "We need to tell her the truth, Connie."

The two of them looked at each other lovingly. I knew how much they adored each other. It had been easy to see through the years.

"You weren't supposed to be born," my mother said quietly. "The doctor told us that we couldn't have children. In a way, it was a relief given what your father did. I loved him and still do with all my heart. He tried to get me to fall in love with another boy, but we were drawn to each other from the beginning."

Just like I felt around the three men. It was as if I'd always belonged to them.

"When I found out I was pregnant, I was certain your father was going to be furious, but I'd never seen him so happy." She laughed as if remembering the exact moment when she'd told him.

"Because of your job," I said, hating the bitter sound in my voice.

"Yes. Having anyone in my life is dangerous, Sage. I warned your mother that our lives would never be easy or safe. However, we wanted to have you more than anything. You were our miracle, our special little girl."

"Then why no pictures? Was there really a fire as you told me, or was that just another lie?"

A single tear slipped past my mother's face. "No. We put them away. We were afraid you'd remember what happened the night of the accident."

"Do you even know?"

They shared another silent communication. "Only part of what happened that night. We were left to pick up the pieces."

Part of what happened. "So, you're an assassin, Dad."

He seemed shocked that I'd figured it out. "I've had a job to do that I'm very good at. However, I never wanted to put either you or your mother in harm's way."

"That didn't answer the question."

"How did you find out?" my mother asked.

"As I said, someone is doing their best to ensure that I learn the truth. They've sent me threatening text messages. Warnings. About you. About three men I care about. Everything is ready to explode in the open. Whatever happened the night I was injured is the reason."

They exchanged another glance, and I sensed they both realized they'd been defeated.

"That's why we didn't want you in Chicago," my mom said under her breath. She looked petrified.

I shook my head. "I'm fine. Very protected. However, I'm curious. Did you hire Jillian to follow me around?"

The look they shared was one of genuine surprise. "Who is Jillian?" Dad asked.

"My assistant." So what Brett told me was true. Jillian had established the contact with the resort and arranged for the residency. No wonder she'd disappeared. She'd lied to me. Who was she working for? All the personal things I'd told her over the years. Had they gone directly to some unseen enemy?

"You need to leave Chicago and never return," Dad added.

"While I know you want the best for me, that's not going to happen. I need the truth. I can't sleep at night because of the nightmares. I can't breathe any longer because I feel like I'm living a lie. What happened to me ten years ago?" They shared another look, and I did what I could to be patient.

"You were hit by a speeding car. You almost died. You were in a coma for over two weeks. The doctors were worried you'd have brain damage. After brain activity was detected, you had several surgeries, including reconstructive surgery on your face. They were still uncertain how much damage had been done. You were a fighter, refusing to die. You had to relearn how to talk, walk, and almost everything else except for singing. Music pulled you through."

No wonder the three men hadn't recognized me.

I took a deep breath and studied my father. It was obvious the secret had worn him down over the years. "So you faked my death."

Mother dropped her head into her hands. I could tell how upset she was.

My father nodded and took her hand into his, pulling her fingers to his lips. The gentle action was endearing, but I wasn't in the mood for niceties.

"Was it a hit and run on purpose, or truly an accident?"

"An accident. It was dark and there was a significant storm. The police did a thorough investigation. The boy who hit you was sick about it. From what he told police, you ran out in front of him. Unfortunately, he was going too fast. The impact should have killed you."

It had.

"Was the boy's name Cain Cross, Hunter Augustine, or Cristiano Moreno?"

The names struck a nerve with both of them even though they knew who owned the resort.

"No, but he was another member of a group called the Elite at the university that you attended," Daddy continued.

"Crandall University where I studied music. The Elite are very special men who go on to Fortune 100 careers. That's why I was there. Because of your job. It was secure and meant for people with fathers like mine."

His eyes opened wide. "Yes. I could afford to send you to a facility I hoped would keep you safe."

"Except you didn't anticipate that one of your jobs would come back to haunt you. Did you?"

He blinked several times.

"You see, Daddy, my memory is starting to come back because I've been spending time with the three men I mentioned. For some crazy reason, we were all brought together again. Call it fate. Call it karma. I'm not certain. However, I'm performing in Cain's resort, but you already knew that. Didn't you, Mother? You did try and keep me from accepting the contract. If only you'd been up front with me then. Suddenly, Hunter and Cain showed up, supposedly for business, but there's foul play going on."

My mom finally had the nerve to look me in the eye. There was so much pain in her gaze that I couldn't be angry. They'd done their best to protect me. "I'm sorry, baby girl. I wanted to tell you."

"As I said, I wouldn't allow her to. There was too much danger. You need to leave them. They're dangerous."

"You didn't want to tell me because you knew Cain wanted revenge for the murder of his brother. Were you planning on killing him too? Is that why you were traveling again?" I was putting two and two together without the need for warped memories and ugly visions.

I could tell by the expression on his face that he'd thought about it. I was sick inside.

"I was there. In Chicago," he said. "I didn't want them touching you. You don't know the men you seem enamored with."

"Oh yes, I do. You didn't raise me to be a stupid woman, Dad. I know what line of work they're in. Do you honestly think what you've done for a living is any different?"

The sudden tension was disheartening. "I care about you, baby girl. It's different when you have a child."

"Maybe I'll agree with you one day. They're good man underneath the dangerous façade, just like you are daddy. I love them. I think I did all those years ago. I may never get my entire memory back, and that's fine. I know enough to be able to let go of the past. That's what I intend on doing."

"At some point, they will hurt you. That's their nature." my mother said, although I could tell in her eyes she was resigned to my choice.

"No, Mama. It's not. They want to protect me. They have protected me. They allow me to feel alive again. I love them. Maybe it's crazy, but I know what I want." I could see their faces. They'd come to my defense on a dark night in another lifetime. I touched my lips, remembering the way each one of them had kissed me. "Some other boy hurt me that night. Something terrible happened that forced me to run into the road. I know it. Did anyone mention that I was attacked?"

While I couldn't tell if anyone had by the way they were looking at each other, my instinct told me I was right. What I wasn't certain of was whether it was one of the three men I'd thought about spending the rest of my life with.

"No, nothing like that. Sage, we did the best we could do at the time. I still have several enemies, not just Cain Cross. We've had to be very careful."

"You thought it was a hit based on your work."

He nodded. "What else could we think?"

"Because of killing Cain's brother." There was no doubt I'd been invited to the party because the three men knew who my father was. I glanced at his hand. "How did you get that scar?"

I'd asked him about it one time and he'd told me he'd been burned by scalding water. I'd bought it. Of course I was ten or eleven at the time.

He lifted and rubbed his hand. "During one of my assignments."

"That's how Cain made the connection."

My dad seemed even more exhausted, ready for retirement. "That's what I believe."

"Promise me that you won't touch the men I've fallen in love with."

When neither one said anything, my patience was shot.

"Promise me!"

"As I said. I'm retiring once and for all. I understand Cain's pain. I was a different man back then. When you see your child suffering, you begin to realize that playing God will eventually catch up with you. They won't be touched unless they hurt you."

What was he trying to tell me?

I watched as my father's grip on the envelope tightened before he slid it across the table. "You'll find almost everything you need to regain the identity you were born with inside this envelope. At this point, your mother and I are going to disappear. I knew this day would come for both of us, Sage. It's very hard, but necessary. You'll also find information on two bank accounts that have been established in your name. Plus, there's the name of an attorney you can trust. He'll know where we are, but no one else. It's too dangerous."

"You're leaving now?" I was sick to my stomach. I'd thought I had more time.

"For now. There's too much danger, and at this point, the only way you're going to have a normal life is if we disappear. It's best that you not know where we end up. I'd ask you to come with us, but that's not fair to you."

"You won't tell me because your enemies will use me to get to you."

"Yes," he said. "It's past time for the assassin to retire permanently. If what you're saying is true, then there's a focus on hunting me down."

"Because you killed Cain Cross's brother."

He took a deep breath. "It was business. I was hired to do a job."

"Who hired you?"

"As I said. Almost every answer you're seeking is inside the envelope. However, what we didn't learn was why you were at a party at the Elite's estate that night."

"Who is Kelly?"

"You are remembering." My mother allowed herself to smile. "She was your dormmate. She worried about you quite a bit. She even called my old number a few years ago. Of course, I just listened to her message."

"What did she say?"

"That she wished she could talk to you, and that she was sorry."

Sorry. The girl lured me to the party. I was certain of it. I took the envelope and wasn't ready to rip into it. I needed time to say goodbye to my parents. I needed time to adjust to whatever was inside, to the fact that my name wasn't what I'd thought it was.

And I needed a lot of time to reflect on how I felt about the three men. Did they know who I was? No. I didn't think so, but at this point, nothing made any sense. I felt like I was on a merry-go-round that I might never be able to stop.

But running wasn't an option. I'd lost too much time already.

Besides, I'd fallen hopelessly, deliriously in love with them.

CHAPTER 24

Sage

When do you know you're in love?

I remembered I'd asked my mother that one day when I thought the first crush I'd had was going to be 'the one'. Her answer had come easily, the love in her eyes for my father shining like a beacon of light.

She'd said when you'd rather die than spend a single day on Earth without the person.

I'd realized quickly after that the kid I'd been certain would be my happily ever after was more like a frog who'd never turn into a prince.

As I mulled over the memory, the realization that I couldn't live without the three men who'd blasted into my life not once but twice was life-altering.

I loved them.

All three. They were flawed and dangerous, romantic and powerful.

But was love enough?

Evidently, I believed so since I was flying back to Chicago. If they wanted to talk, we were going to have a long conversation. There would be no additional secrets or lies. Not one. They'd tell me everything they knew about who I once was and what they had planned that night so long ago.

Then whoever was sending the threats wouldn't have the needed ammunition any longer. Who was warning me? Why?

Sage.

I repeated my name several times, even twice out loud while in the bathroom at the airport in San Diego. I liked it. It had character, much like the name Rose. However, I wasn't certain I would use it at this point. If I did, my stage name would stay the same. I was reminded that after everything I'd learned, the heartache and fear, the nightmares that had plagued me, I'd managed to carve out a life that I treasured more than I realized.

If what my mother had said was true, my love of music had kept me from remaining in the darkness forever. Even seeing the *People Magazine* article online while waiting to board had been another reminder and one that I'd needed. I couldn't abandon who I thought I was so I could bring the ghost of my former self into the light. I remembered my childhood and after the accident, and that was all I really needed.

Even if there was still a nagging question about what had happened that night. I stared out the window, keeping my phone in my hand. I'd typed out a message to all three men, still unable to hit send. I just wasn't certain how to move forward without looking back.

Or over my shoulder.

Sighing, I pulled the envelope from my purse, fingering the flap. The information inside had obviously been prepared long before my surprise visit. There were letters from my parents, bank statements for the money they'd maintained for me as well as other financial information. There were even a few pictures that had been taken weeks prior to the accident. Some that I'd sent from school. I didn't recognize the face, although my eyes were the same.

Nothing they'd provided was troubling.

Except for the letter from my father to Cain.

It was the one thing that would possibly destroy the last tether we had. It wasn't mine to keep, but as the provider of the horrific statement, including with proof, it was my responsibility to ensure that it got to the person the letter was addressed to.

Only that scared me more than learning the last details about the tragic night of so long ago.

I closed my eyes, feeling the pull of the engines as the pilot began to slow for descent. My stomach was in knots, my mind still in a haze. I didn't know if I'd ever see my parents again. It was crazy to think he'd been an assassin.

As the announcement was made for the approach to the airport, I had one last chance to send the text. I grabbed my phone, sliding my finger across the screen, a single tear slipping down my cheek. What if they believed I had something to do with the horrible game being played?

In admitting to myself that I loved them, it had opened up my heart completely, allowing me to feel the sting of the vacuum we'd pulled ourselves into. We'd been drawn to each other, forced to return to the very edge of darkness that had brought us together in the first place. Maybe a small part of me had sensed I'd known them before.

A tickling sensation pushed into the back of my mind, heat vibrating through every cell as I thought about the three men who'd crashed into my life, awakening not only dark desires that I'd obviously had years before, but also a longing for a family. That was crazy. Yet as I pictured them in my mind, a series of sweeping images of our passion brought a smile to my face and a flurry of butterflies replacing the knots in my stomach.

What we shared was real.

They were all I needed and everything I craved.

I stared at my phone, biting my lower lip.

Then I hit send.

* * *

Cain

Love.

I'd grown up accepting the fact that love wasn't a possibility for a monster like me. At first, I'd told myself the reason was because the woman would be considered a weakness, which still held some merit. Then I'd been certain there wasn't a woman who could tolerate my needs. That no longer remained true. Sage had been... perfect.

My cock twitched just thinking about how passionate we'd been, her needs paralleling mine.

The final reasoning would remain locked in my mind.

I didn't deserve to have joy and happiness, love and passion because of who and what I was. A killer. An evil man. That much she'd known, even accepting who and what all three of us were.

The simple truth was that I wanted Sage in my life so badly I would do anything to keep her happy. Hell, I would lock her in a cage, protecting her against the evils of this world.

Including me.

Including the two other men who wanted her heart.

And I would hunt down the people responsible for hurting her.

I glanced at Hunter and Cristiano as they studied the arrival board for at least the third time. I'd thought about taking my jet to San Diego, but she'd gotten on the plane returning to Chicago, or so I'd been told. She was coming back.

But in what capacity?

As a woman determined to destroy the three men who had a part in the tragedy that had altered her life, or as the girl we'd fallen in love with years before?

I'd seen the notes she'd written down and had been able to feel her anger and anxiety in every word scribbled on the pieces of paper. Then there was the story, one so breathtaking that I hadn't been able to breathe. Now, I paced the floor of the airport, hoping I'd get a third chance to make it right.

Which I didn't deserve.

Hunter turned to face me, the look on his face the exact one on Cristiano's, and if I looked in the mirror, I suspected the same version would be reflected.

She'd managed to get so far under our skin that we had difficulty functioning.

Hunter swaggered towards me, his eyes boring into mine. "We will protect her. We will care for her. She belongs to us."

He made the statement as if I'd argue with him. I couldn't blame him for that.

"I have the jet standing by if she didn't get on that plane. We will find her."

Cristiano overheard and returned. "She's on the plane. She's as connected to us as we are to her."

The tension between us was almost laughable. The few times we'd made incredulous plans of finding the right girl, settling down together had made us laugh. We'd tried to tell ourselves it had been the alcohol talking, but the seed had been planted, watered the night we'd gotten a taste of Sage.

When I tried to look away, Hunter got in my face. "Admit it. You're in love with her."

I lifted a single eyebrow and exhaled. "Yeah, man, I am. That doesn't mean shit if she doesn't want to be with us."

Cristiano studied the runways outside the oversized window. Her flight was due in fifteen minutes.

"Your men are in place around the airport. Right?" he asked.

"No one is getting to her here. In addition, I have Brogan finding out everything he can about Watkins' activities over the last few days and his current location. We're going to pay a visit to the man."

"That'll add gasoline to the fire," Hunter threw in.

"Maybe so, but we're going to start ruling out candidates one by one. Besides, it's time we address the fact that he made our lives a living hell for years."

"I'm down with that," Cristiano threw in.

"Who else could be behind this bullshit?" Hunter was as exasperated as I was.

"We're going to make a list and check them off one by one."

Cristiano nodded. "Do you think Sage's father admitted he killed your brother?"

I raked my hand through my hair. "I don't know." All the years I'd wanted to hunt the man down, taking my time to torture before killing him remained in my mind. However, if I followed through with acting on my revenge, I'd lose Sage forever. "The truth is that I'm not certain I care."

Hunter opened his eyes wide, then offered a nod of respect. "But it might matter to her."

He had a good point.

"Did she answer your text?" I asked him.

"No. She read it."

There was nothing to say to that.

"Whoever is behind this will try and take Sage away from us." Hunter's voice was haunted.

"They won't be able to touch her. But I hope they try."

As a grin shifted across Cristiano's face, I sensed he knew what I was thinking. "You want to call them out in the open."

"You bet I do."

"That's dangerous," Hunter threw in.

Danger.

The word had been one of the first ones I'd spoken as a kid. I'd grown up on adjectives and verbs that most mothers would attempt to keep stricken from a child's vocabulary for as long as possible. I'd valued their meanings because that's what was expected of me.

I'd also learned that danger fed adrenaline. If controlled properly, the rush could be used to generate boosted strength and agility. However, once anyone fell into the darkness that danger often provided, there was no chance of using its core value.

Given I'd never allowed it to happen, I hadn't been prepared for the anger and trepidation that had already spread throughout my system.

There was no doubt in my mind that whoever was behind the charade would make good on their threat. My bets were on William Watkins, although a strange nagging remained in the back of my mind. There were too many cryptic pieces, oddities that seemed amateurish but in truth, were brilliant crumbs dropped in hopes that we'd spend time going down a wrong path.

The driver's license found on the assassin inside the SUV had turned out to be just another part of the game. While the picture had been of the dead man, the reality was that the social security number and name had been stolen from someone who'd died several years before.

While we were completely aware whoever was doing this wanted the three of us, it was also obvious they didn't mind creating collateral damage.

That included the ultimate revenge, taking her life for real. Nothing else could be worse.

If that was the case, then whoever was behind the game knew how much we cared about her. Watkins wasn't the obvious choice. Not for this. But the person responsible had hoped that's what I'd think.

I'd grieved Sage's death more than I'd let on to anyone. I'd thought of her so often at times it had felt as if she were standing in the same room.

It wasn't about ghosts. My reaction has been caused by the desire that had never truly been fulfilled even once.

Did I feel guilt for what had happened to her? Without a doubt. But I didn't feel any remorse for ending Theo's life. He'd deserved what he'd gotten.

We stood in the airport near the terminal where her flight was due in any minute. It was entirely possible once she'd spoken with her parents that she wouldn't return. Why should she? Did that mean I wouldn't hunt then down in San Diego? No.

The sound of my phone drew Hunter and Cristiano's attention.

"Brock. You found something."

"You're not going to like it," he said.

I took a stab in the dark. "William Watkins is dead."

"How the fuck did you know?"

"Call it luck."

Hunter snorted. "What the hell?"

"How?"

"He was shot leaving a restaurant in New York."

"Interesting. See what else you can find."

"Already on it."

Just as I ended the call, all three of our phones made noise.

I took a deep breath before shifting to the correct screen.

A long time ago I met three men who I fell in love with. They were rugged and dangerous, requiring my surrender. They thought me to be innocent, a budding flower. However, in their arms, the woman inside was awakened, the passion we shared undeniable. Until tragedy brought the budding romance to an end. Yet fate had other things in mind. Together again.

Sage...

CHAPTER 25

Sage

"Who was Kelly? My roommate?" I asked as Cain handed me a glass of wine.

Hunter turned around, his eyes opening wide. "She was. She was also a groupie of the Elite, for the lack of a better word."

I thought about the bits and pieces of my memory. "A chosen one."

"Yes," Cain said quietly. "Part of our large flock of women who would do anything we asked."

"Including luring me to the party." I had no anger in my voice. There was no need. We were different people now, the experience altering all our lives significantly. I'd seen the pain in their faces when I'd left the gangway, the desire roaring through them as well as twisted anticipation.

"If you're thinking she had something to do with this, think again. She's currently married to a senator. She had three kids and they own four homes," Hunter said casually.

I'd clung to the three of them as they'd surrounded me inside the airport, realizing that we'd made a spectacle of ourselves. I'd learned soldiers had surrounded the airport and that I was in danger from the person or persons responsible for sending the threats.

"She knew she'd get married to someone who could provide her with a wealthy life."

"You remember more than you let on," Cristiano said as he sat back against the couch.

A whiteboard had been set up, the men determined to work through the mystery methodically. I'd learned someone had attempted to kill the three of them while I was jetting off to San Diego. I'd also heard stories of attempts made on their lives before.

No wonder they were dead set on finding out what was going on.

And it was no wonder they initially suspected I might be behind what they called a game being played. I called it a recipe for disaster.

"I remember enough. Theo hated you. Kelly was in love with one or all of you. Did you know that?"

Cristiano lifted his eyebrows. "Kelly hoped to be selected that night, promised to one of the Elite."

"But that was never allowed again after what occurred."

Hunter shook his head, studying me as he'd done continuously. "It was the last straw for the administration. I can't tell you how many people were angry that the house was shut down. A lot of kids were tossed out, the ripple effect derailing many careers. She obviously did okay."

"A reason for revenge. Maybe not Kelly, but you can't put it past the ones who didn't land on their feet." I said the words in passing, and Cain was the first to react, his chuckle leaving a vibrating hum across my already heated skin.

I dragged my tongue around the rim of the glass, my legs curled under me. I felt more protected than I had my entire life, the three men keeping their weapons close.

There were also at least six of Cain's soldiers protecting the perimeter. They were nervous that the game was escalating. In truth, so was I. The last words written on my dressing room mirror remained in the forefront of my mind.

They'd confessed everything, although Hunter and Cristiano had done most of the talking while Cain had kept his dark eyes pinned on me. He'd tossed back at least three glasses of expensive Macallan scotch while they'd answered my questions, and I'd provided what limited information I had in return.

What none of them had asked about was my father. But it was on Cain's mind. I could feel the intense hum of his anger just below the surface. He wanted to rip my father's head off.

I understood why, but I wouldn't allow the man who'd raised me to be killed because of…

The truth wouldn't set him free. In fact, I suspected it would destroy him more than I originally thought.

To learn my father had been called the Iceman because he showed no remorse was strange, yet almost freeing. He'd killed dozens of people, on call with several crime syndicate families. For as horrid as my father had been, once home, he'd been a doting father and loving husband.

Maybe that's why I could imagine a life spent with three dangerous, deadly men.

"Our little pet has a good point. Perhaps we should broaden our list," Hunter said.

I eased to my feet, moving towards the set of open French doors. I'd removed my shoes, the warm summer late afternoon begging for my attention. It seemed like forever since I'd walked in my bare feet on pristine grass.

Once outside, I took a deep breath, holding the fresh air until my lungs were filled.

It'd hoped it would calm my nerves. But it didn't.

I walked down the steps, keeping my eyes locked on the large body of water as a light breeze drifted through my hair.

Romance.

I'd mastered the art of singing my heart out, writing love songs masquerading as hard rock. My fans had eaten it up. I'd made a lot of money feeding off the energy of sexual tension. The electricity was the thing fantasies were made of. What I'd realized the moment I'd stepped foot off the plane was that every song I'd written, every ballad crooned out to a massive audience, had been about the three men I hadn't been able to remember.

Yet their aura and the erotic magic we'd shared together had never left the back of my mind. I wondered if they had any idea how many top ten songs they'd inspired over the years. Now that I knew the source of my muse, I wondered if it would change my music.

I'd learned from Cristiano that when enrolled in Crandall U, I'd gone on late night adventures, singing my heart out while performing in costumes. He'd been there protecting me.

They'd admitted they'd stalked me, including Cain placing rose petals on my nightstands, and cameras and listening devices in the rooms.

And they'd read my stories, ones similar to what I'd penned in the middle of the night little more than a week before.

Some people would say I was crazy to continue caring about them, but the heart refused to be denied. Was it something I might regret later? I doubted it. I had a new lease on life, a need to explore the joys we shared.

Yet at that moment my heart was still heavy.

Now, I stood staring out at Lake Michigan, the water only a stone's throw away. Cain's estate was incredible, one of the prettiest I'd ever seen. His backyard was perfectly green, the grass rolling towards the water's edge and dock where two boats were moored. There was even a section of beach, a gorgeous gazebo a few feet away.

I'd expected his house to be modern or gothic, but the charming gingerbread detail on the palatial estate added to the charm of the Victorian setting. So many things had surprised me about all three men, but certainly not their possessiveness. I pulled the wine glass to my lips, feeling a presence behind me.

A smile curled across my face, my mind still whirling from the upload of information they'd provided. From what I could tell, they hadn't left out a single thing that had occurred that awful night. I was grateful the pieces had been filled in. However, the weight of having the letter meant for Cain still in my possession was strangling me. It was past time to provide what he needed to be able to heal.

If that was possible.

He was an angry man, his hatred and rage ebbing and flowing like the electricity we shared. As he closed the distance, I was immediately thrown by his exotic scent. It wrapped around me like a warm blanket, soft yet demanding at the same time.

When he brushed his fingers down the length of my arm at a lazy pace, a single tremor drifted down my spine.

"Cain," I whispered, for no other reason than I enjoyed saying his name.

"Beautiful little Sage."

"I'm not so little any longer."

He chuckled. "You're exactly as you should be. Perfect."

"I'm far from it."

"And I'm a cold-blooded killer."

"With a heart."

His sigh was heavy, as if he also felt the weight of the world much like I did.

I couldn't just blurt it out. He needed to read what my father had written. If he could believe him.

"I'm not a good man, Sage. Neither are Hunter and Cristiano. When this is finished, you're free to return to your life."

For the first time, I heard what sounded like remorse. "No one will ever be able to take the music away from me, but I want more. I want all three of you. I know it's crazy. I know people will think badly of us, but I don't care."

He fisted my hair, yanking my head back until I was forced to rest it on his shoulder. "Don't worry about what other people think. Just worry about what you need."

"Then that's easy. All three of you."

"You're certain?" There was a strange sound to his voice, hopeful.

"Very much so."

"Mmm…" he growled. "Then if that's what you want, you do realize there will be rules to follow."

He wasn't asking a question, merely making a statement of what would be. He spun me around and pulled me even closer, narrowing his eyes.

A tiny thrill coursed through me. "Rules. Huh? What happens if I don't follow them?"

"Then you'll be punished." He cracked his hand against my backside and I yelped, which allowed the first real smile to cross his face since I'd returned.

"I'm a good girl."

"That remains to be seen."

There was such heartache in his tone, his voice barely recognizable. I ached inside, wanting to be his everything, but the demons were eating him alive.

"It's so beautiful here. I love it."

He squeezed my waist, pulling me closer. "It's peaceful. Sometimes I come here by myself."

"Without your soldiers?" I teased.

"It's the only place I can reflect and be myself."

"That's so sad, Cain."

"That's what life has been. Without you."

"If you're trying to win points, it's working."

His chuckle was deep, but I sensed he had a great deal on his mind. No matter the lists or the searches into the lives of those Cain and the others had known before, I sensed he didn't feel as if they were any closer to discovering the person responsible.

"I'm sorry about your parents, Sage."

"Don't be sorry. At least I know the truth. It's hard to think of my father as a hitman, but at least now all the pieces are starting to fit. Are you still close to your parents?"

He stiffened. "My mother is dead."

The statement sounded hollow, but I sensed another tragedy. "I'm sorry."

"Don't be. She's out of her misery."

"Families don't need to be weird or contentious. Maybe if we have kids, we can provide an entirely different home."

His breath caught, and I was certain he would tell me in no uncertain terms there would be no children. That made what he said just another beautiful surprise. "I'd like that. No more talking. I need to fuck you. Come inside." When he leaned over, pressing his lips against mine, I couldn't stop tingling. He tangled his fingers in my hair as he captured my mouth.

His hold was more possessive than before, his needs entirely different. All of us discovering the truth had taken us to a different level, our needs heightened. The hum of electricity surrounded us like a protective cocoon, but I knew it would be short lived. Still, as he dominated my tongue, I rolled one hand over his shoulders. His cock was throbbing, pushing into my stomach and as happened around him every time we touched, my core ignited.

My heart was skipping several beats, desire clawing its way to the surface. However, I pressed my hand against his chest, breaking the kiss.

"There's something I need you to know."

He allowed his gaze to fall to my lips then shook his head. "I'm finished with talking."

"This is important."

"So is what I need."

"No. You need to read something. Please."

He took a step back when I pulled the envelope from my pocket. "What is it?"

"My father gave me an envelope of things about my past as well as well as this letter addressed to you."

The afternoon sun illuminated his face in such a way that it was as if his eyes were glowing. I expected anger, but there was only a quiet reverence, as if a small part of him was eager to find out what was inside. He took it from my hand, fingering it for a few seconds. Then he slipped it into his pocket.

"You need to read it."

"I will. Not now. I have more important things on my mind, including fulfilling my needs."

Without hesitation, he hoisted me over his shoulder, taking long strides towards the house, I almost dropped my wine. There was no arguing with him. Once inside, he handed off my glass to Hunter, no words spoken as the hum of electricity increased.

While danger lurked in the shadows, there was no denying what the three men hungered for. I'd seen it in their eyes before. Now, I felt it in the electricity in the room. Cain didn't stop, immediately heading for the stairs, the other two following.

He took them two at a time, moving into one of the bedrooms. As soon as he eased me down, he ripped off my shirt, tossing it aside. His hunger knew no bounds. He cupped my breasts, issuing a deep growl. Then he lowered his head, flicking his tongue across my already taut nipple.

I felt a presence behind me, Hunter sliding his arms around my waist, deftly unfastening my shorts. It was obvious they were in a hurry. He yanked them down, forcing me to step out of them. Then he crawled his fingers around my leg, sliding his hand between them.

"You're so wet, little lamb." His hot breath skipped across my skin seconds before he nipped my shoulder.

I was already euphoric, the longing to be in their arms intense. I slipped my fingers around Cain's thick bulge, stroking him up and down.

He growled in response, shifting his mouth to my other breast, pulling the tender bud between his lips and sucking.

Hunter wrapped his hand around my hair, yanking me back until he was able to kiss my mouth, darting his tongue past my lips.

I shuddered from the touch of the two men, lights flashing in front of my eyes. As he let go of my hair, I noticed Cristiano had already undressed. The sight of his long, thick cock created another flurry of butterflies swarming my stomach.

When Hunter slipped his fingers past my swollen folds, a moan instantly escaped my mouth. I was wet and hot, more so than ever before. Before I knew it, I was pulled from the two men, Cristiano forcing my legs around his hips. He never blinked as he carried me to the bed, but he carried a wicked smile as if he would do nefarious things to me.

He lowered his head, nuzzling into my ear. "The things I'm going to do to you."

The way his hot breath felt was incredible, so much so that a single whimper escaped my lips.

Then he tossed me onto the bed, immediately wrapping one hand around my ankle and yanking me to the edge. I half laughed from shock, prepared to fight him just to see what he'd do. When I almost managed to jump off the bed, he laughed in a low, deep rumble.

"Our girl is feisty tonight."

"Then show her what happens to bad girls who don't obey."

To hear Hunter's dark baritone sent a thrill through me. Both he and Cain had quickly undressed, and I was rewarded with the sight of two additional, delicious cocks. Now, my mouth was watering, my vision slightly blurry.

"Gladly." Cristiano grabbed my ankles with one hand, yanking my legs straight up in the air. Then he brought his hand down across my backside six times in rapid succession.

"Ouch. You're mean!" I tried to smack his hands away but almost instantly Hunter had moved to the other side of the bed, snagging my arms and jerking them over my head.

"I think she needs to have something to fill her mouth." He pressed the tip of his cock against my lips. "Suck it, baby."

I darted out my tongue, whimpering when Cristiano cracked his hand from one side to the other. Even the sound was sexier than it had been before. Perhaps I could get used to this.

Who was I kidding? They had full control over me and would ensure that I obeyed them at all times.

"Wider, little pet," Hunter growled.

I licked around his cockhead but only once before he drove several inches inside. As I wrapped my lips around the thick invasion, the spanking continued. The shock of pain as well as pleasure was as electrifying as their touches.

Cristiano issued a few more before lowering and spreading my legs wide open. Within seconds, I felt the weight on the bed change. The first swipe of his tongue around my clit sent another electric shock through me. A second swipe and I moaned around Hunter's cock. When he sucked on my clit, I was certain I would go mad.

Hunter released his hold on my arms, allowing me to roll his balls between my fingers. As he started fucking my mouth in earnest, the tip hitting the back of my throat, I squeezed my jaw muscles.

"Jesus. Your mouth is so fucking hot."

I sucked with vigor but was distracted by the magical way Cristiano was licking me. He held some kind of evocative power, his mouth and tongue driving me to the point of an orgasm within seconds, then pulling back. Hunter made certain I didn't forget about him, pumping his shaft deep into my throat. I instantly tingled when he tweaked my nipples, pinching them between two fingers.

The combination of extreme pleasure with the hint of anguish was enough to drive me crazy. I struggled in their hold, my body twisting from the ecstasy. Cristiano widened my legs even more, licking up and down in a lazy fashion.

The sound of their heavy breathing was infused with Cain's throaty growls.

"Do you want to come, baby?" he asked as he moved onto the bed. Taking one of my hands into his, he wrapped my fingers around his cock.

I moaned my response as I stroked up and down, twisting my hand to create friction.

"And you promise to be a good girl?"

He was tormenting me on purpose. Goosebumps popped along my arms and legs, my anguished whimper the only answer I could provide.

Cristiano pressed his lips against one inner thigh, then the other. "She's been good enough." He drove several fingers into my tight channel as he sucked on my clit. That was all I could take, an orgasm sweeping through me like a wildfire.

I jerked up from the bed, only to be pushed back down. The ecstasy was intense, and my body was shaking. When I started to ease down from the incredible wave, all three men pulled away.

"No!" The single word popped from my mouth. Almost immediately I noticed the looks on their faces seconds before I was jerked onto all fours, another hard crack issued against my aching backside. The men were perfect in their methods of orchestration, Cain immediately lying on his back, forcing me to straddle his hips, Hunter fisting my hair and lifting my head.

Then I felt Cristiano squeeze my bottom.

"Now, we're going to fill you, baby girl. Just like we will every. Single. Night."

Cain's voice sent another thrill through every muscle and tendon. When he lifted my hips, I wrapped my hand around his cock, pressing the tip against my pussy.

Hunter tapped my cheek, his eyes darkening as his hunger intensified. "Now, you finish what you started." I took his cock into my mouth, swirling my tongue back and forth. Every sound he made fueled the fire shared between the four of us.

As Cain brought me down onto his shaft, my muscles stretching to accommodate the thick girth, my body trembled, every muscle spasming. The feeling of being sandwiched between the three gorgeous hunks kept me lightheaded.

Then as Cristiano pressed his cockhead against my dark hole, my breath hitched. There was nothing like being filled with their cocks. I sucked on Hunter's shaft, dragging my tongue back and forth as Cain flicked his fingers back and forth across my nipples.

"So tight. God, I adore fucking you in your ass," Cristiano muttered. There was nothing gentle about their actions, their desires too intense. As he pushed his cockhead against the tight ring, I shuddered audibly.

Cain pulled me forward, lifting my bottom into the air. "Get ready, baby. Get ready to take your fill."

His dark words only fueled the fire raging deep inside. As Cristiano thrust the remainder of his cock inside my asshole, I closed my eyes, the pleasure driving me straight into a moment of bliss.

Then the three men took full control, driving their cocks deep inside. A rush of adrenaline mixed with an incredible series of vibrations tore through me, my pulse skyrocketing.

There was nothing better than their glorious growls and animalistic sounds, the men completely primal in their needs. Everything about the moment was special, the rhythm as if we were meant to be together. I remained basking in the feeling of euphoria as the men fucked me.

Fleeting images continued to roll through my mind, adding colorful details, some images startling while others were sensual.

They rode me long and hard, doing their best to keep control, but only minutes later, I sensed they were close to coming.

My pussy spasmed, another climax rushing into my system. As the three men filled me with their seed, I finally felt a sense of peace.

This was exactly where I was supposed to be.

CHAPTER 26

Cain

"I wish we could live like this forever," Sage murmured. Her eyes were closed, her breathing easy. She seemed serene while I felt like a raging tiger ready to pounce on my prey. What I'd come to realize after our lengthy discussion was that various indicators pointed to the fact that I had a mole in my organization. That was the only way someone could have known about our whereabouts and other private details. I told few about my comings and goings within my company, my two capos then filtering down necessary information.

The other aspect of the damning situation I knew to be true was that whoever was perpetrating the game had known for years that Sage was alive and living under an assumed identity. Why had the ruse festered for so long?

My answer?

Something had prevented the person seeking revenge from acting on their plan for years. In my mind, that could mean only one of two possibilities.

Health issues or prison.

I'd widened the search overnight, asking Brock to coordinate with my main hacker to narrow down possibilities. I'd included every Elite member from our graduating class. I hadn't kept up with their whereabouts. I could care less about the elitist clique we'd turned into a killing field. My life hadn't been centered around college.

But others had felt differently.

"Why can't we?" Hunter asked, lazily running his fingers down her arm.

She purred, opening her eyes, then nuzzled against his chest. "Here or somewhere else?"

"I think we should purchase two other houses around Lake Michigan. Then we can move from one location to the other," Cristiano suggested, glancing in my direction, his smile bordering on mischievous.

"I'm thinking more tropical," I added. I found it interesting that we all wanted the same thing. Professionally, it would be interesting. While there were still several uncertainties, we'd made one aspect of our kinky relationship very clear to the beautiful woman.

She was going nowhere, at least not permanently.

That allowed me to smile.

"Then we'll buy six houses. You pick the locations, Sage," Hunter murmured.

"That's very dangerous. My tastes are… elitist." She grinned after using the word, and I swatted her on the bottom.

"Uh, no."

She laughed and I realized I'd never felt so comfortable.

"And the three of you can be my bodyguards when I'm on tour."

"Who said we're going to allow you to continued singing?" Hunter teased.

Jerking up, Sage grabbed a pillow, smacking him in the head. "Oh, no you don't. I will continue to be a career woman. I am a star, you know." She held her head up, pressing her hand against her heart in a show of entitlement.

"Uh-huh," I told her. "You'll be wearing a collar, and one of us will have control of the leash."

"You're so mean," she purred.

"You got that right." I grinned, twisting her nipple until she moaned. I could ravage the girl's body for hours and still never get enough.

The moment of passion was short-lived, the sound of Hunter's phone drawing our attention away from the beautiful woman curled at our sides.

He eased off the bed, grabbing his jeans.

"You were expecting a call?" Cristiano asked as he rolled over, kissing Sage on the lips.

"Yeah, one of my employees has a unique ability to find out any information, even if it's been well hidden."

Cristiano grinned. "And you thought our boy was too vanilla."

I had a massive computer system at my disposal, the hackers I employed able to slide by every fire wall from the FBI to the CIA without being detected. It was only a matter of time before connections were made.

Hunter gave him his middle finger before answering the call. "Jarvis. What did you find out?" He paced the floor while Jarvis mentioned whatever he'd found.

I tossed back the covers, dragging my tongue across her nipple before jumping out of bed. "I'll be right back." I'd pushed off opening the envelope for long enough. I yanked it from my trousers, walking to the door leading to the balcony. There was just enough light coming from inside the room that I should be able to read whatever notification Sage's father had dared send.

The old anger jetted to the surface, but I tamped it back. I'd already made the decision the man wouldn't be touched. There would be more harm done than a benefit added.

I was the kind of man who never allowed anything to surprise me. That's because I'd grown up learning to expect the worst. To have my stomach in knots while I pulled out multiple pages was odd, and I debated bagging the read. But something compelled me to find out what was important enough for a man known as the Iceman because of his lack of remorse and his creativity in methods of extermination to dare send me anything.

After taking a deep breath, I read the information.

Then my thoughts drifted to Sage. Everything about the woman had surprised me, including her tenacity and resolve. She was one of the strongest people I'd ever met, her love of her family unwavering. She trusted me enough to be able to share the truth, carrying a burden that shouldn't have been placed on her shoulders.

The three of us had been drawn to each other ten years before, just as we'd been once again, not knowing the truth. In her, we'd found something perfectly unexpected, something as dark and broken as the rest of us. But in the shattered pieces, she'd offered something even more precious.

Hope.

And love.

I adored the woman with everything I had and would honor her until the day I died.

I lifted my head, studying the twilight sky, stars already peeking through the thin clouds from before. There were methods of betrayal that I was accustomed to in the business I was in.

Then there were those that could steal your breath.

Cristiano walked outside, narrowing his eyes. I handed him the letter and accompanying proof, then gripped the railing. As the seconds passed, I concentrated on the sound of my thudding heart as the scent of her continued to linger in my nostrils. Light to darkness. Good to evil.

I didn't deserve a second chance, but I would take it.

Only after righting the wrongs that should have been handled long ago.

"Shit," he said quietly.

"Yeah."

"What are you going to do?" I heard the concern in Cristiano's voice. He'd heard the gory stories, had experienced my battles with what a school psychologist had called PTSD.

I knew a part of me was dangerous as well as unhinged. You couldn't put a child through a minefield and not expect him to come out a little crazy. But this was…

The ache in my gut about my brother swept through me as painfully as it had done all those years ago. "I'm not sure."

Hunter moved outside, shaking his head.

"I appreciate the call." He slipped his phone into his pocket before turning around to face us. "We have some of the answers. I don't know whether to believe what I just heard or not."

Cristiano snorted. "It couldn't be any worse than what we just learned. Read this."

After a few seconds, Hunter issued a low growl. "Fuck me. I don't know what to say."

"No need," I said quietly.

"At least we can be assured what Jarvis learned is factual. And at least we know the truth."

Truth.

Was there such a thing? As an ugly memory surfaced in the front of my mind, I held my breath.

"Get off her!" I roared as I threw myself at him, pummeling his back and neck with brutal punches.

He laughed, tossing me aside with ease.

"Baby! No!" my mother screamed. There was blood, so much blood everywhere. On the carpet and staining the walls. After he'd finished with me, he'd gone after my mother. Goddamn him.

"You're nothing but trash. That's all you'll ever be." He laughed, puffing himself up like he did every time he dealt with one of his men. We were nothing to him. Nothing.

Wham!

The brutal punch cracked against the side of my face. I was pitched backward into the wall. My vision was instantly blurred, the agony blinding. The taste of blood remained in my mouth, the coppery stench filling my nostrils as much as the hatred filled my soul. "I hate you!"

The voice that left my lips I no longer recognize, the syllables garbled.

I crawled forward, my mother's pitiful cries echoing in my ears. When she reached out for me, the glow of the single desk lamp highlighted the horror that my mother had experienced. She couldn't leave him. She'd tried, taking her boys with her. He'd dragged us back, beating her so badly she'd spent two weeks in the hospital.

Tears stained my face. I'd promised myself that I wouldn't cry ever again. I was no longer a boy. This fuck would answer to me.

"Get up, you little punk. Take your punishment like a man," *my father jeered, beckoning me with one of his hands.*

I took in as much air as my lungs would allow, willing my aching legs to work. The beating had lasted longer than normal, the thin razor strap digging into my skin. But the agony was nothing in comparison to the rage brimming the surface. I wanted him dead. Dead!

"Fuck you." *I managed to stumble to my feet, my body swaying. Then I lunged for him, ramming my shoulders into his chest. He tossed me aside, throwing me against the edge of his desk.*

Another bolt of pain exploded in my system, but the anger continued to swell, digging into my muscles and bone.

I heard the single moan my mother issued, and the thought of vengeance kept me going. I pitched my body toward him again, but he was too fast for me, dodging my attempt. Out of the corner of my eye, I noticed him pulling out his weapon. Then he fisted my mother's hair, dragging her to her feet, pressing the barrel of the gun into her mouth. "You want to play hardball, Cain? I have no problem pulling the trigger."

This had to end. The pain. The sufferance. The required silence.

There would be no rescue, no sirens in the distance with help just moments away. My father was too powerful, too influential. He owned the police. He owned just about everybody. And no one would ever dare lift a finger to the monster or fear facing his wrath.

We were alone.

My mother's pleading eyes pulled me to a quiet resolve, and I backed down to save her life.

But I made a promise that no one would ever hurt us again.

I kept my gaze towards the sky as the memory faded. We had to protect her, the woman we loved. The real monster was coming, and he would do everything he could to take away the single happiness in my life.

Just like he'd taken my mother and my brother.

"What now?" Cristiano asked.

My brother's face slowly slipped into my mind as well as the words he'd issued only minutes before he'd been murdered.

He'd planned on handling the situation, exacting revenge before another drop of blood was shed.

He'd been too late.

And I'd been too stupid to see the writing on the wall. I'd allowed the fucker to take control and keep it, using me as his little puppet for twenty fucking years.

"Now, we go hunting. Just like we used to."

* * *

Sage

. . .

A vicious game.

That's what the years of a charade had been about, a need to condemn the rich and powerful boys who'd made it out of the tragic situation unharmed in any way. I'd learned so much in the last forty-eight hours, the families requiring them to attend Crandall University. It hadn't been their choice or for that matter something they enjoyed. It was as much a prison as the private schools, some overseas, the boys had attended. Many of the girls as well.

They had a network, which my father hadn't been a part of. Instead, he'd been hired by one or another syndicate or corporate mogul to trim the fat so a golden path could be provided for their children. It was fascinating, although I'd seen pain in Cain's eyes in particular as he'd spoken of his family. Whatever he'd endured as a child had been horrific.

I'd seen it before, kids who were abused never able to get over the trauma completely. His father had pushed him hard into becoming the head of the Cross Empire. I sensed it hadn't been what Cain had wanted.

Cain had read the letter, and I sensed my father's words had changed him. At least one of the men I loved more than anything had the same answers that I'd been seeking.

They weren't pretty, the ugliness surrounding the reasons why something that would likely never be answered to anyone's satisfaction. But they were the truths that might be able to set him free.

He was darker than before, not allowing me to know what he had planned. What the three of them had planned.

They'd removed the whiteboard, had stopped bothering to check the computer or make any phone calls, but their not-so-subtle meetings held in privacy had allowed me to feel the urgency of ending the charade as soon as possible.

Today was the day.

We'd shared in our passion and need, growing even closer. Sadly, it felt like we'd been living on borrowed time. I was sick inside, more so than I'd been during the entire time since learning my real identity. I missed my parents, but at least I knew they were safe. Would I ever feel safe again?

I stood pacing the floor in the living room of the gorgeous estate where we'd spent so many incredible hours, barely able to look out the window.

There were six guards watching out for me, walking the grounds. I'd seen them from the doors and windows, their weapons in plain sight. It terrified me.

My thoughts turned to the brother who'd been the reason for the destruction of so many lives. It was almost surreal that the plan had been many years in the making.

The pain of losing both his brother and his mother had been horrible enough. While my father, the Iceman, had been paid to end Dayton's life, he hadn't initiated the assassination. I couldn't imagine what Cain was going through.

My thoughts returned to the three men. While we'd teased about forever, buying several houses and even having a huge family together, I had no idea what would happen once this was over. I wasn't unlike every other girl who either believed they were princesses and one day their prince would arrive or who fell hopelessly in love with a rogue of sorts. A man who held life in the palm of his hand.

Maybe I could buy into the concept of true love. At least my mother had set an excellent example. Unconventional? Absolutely, but that I didn't mind. What worried me was that I wouldn't be enough.

"Stop being silly." Saying the words out loud didn't make me feel any better.

A rumble of thunder drew my attention to the French doors. I could see a bolt of lightning in the distance, a storm approaching. I realized now why I hated storms with such a passion. But as the gray clouds turned darker, ominous shadows playing tricks with the light on the water, I was pulled into a horrific vacuum of fear. There was no reason why. I was safer than almost anyone I knew with so many guards prepared to lay down their lives for me.

What I feared the most was never seeing the men who loved me again. I knew they'd also protect me at the cost of their lives if necessary. A slow-burning agony continued to drive through my system, every muscle aching from extreme tension.

I had my phone in one hand, holding it close just in case, even if I didn't expect them to call. It was a lifeline, a safety mechanism.

So, I continued pacing, trying to calm my breathing. I heard a slight knock on the door and jumped, a yelp escaping my throat.

"Whoa, Ms. Sadler. I didn't mean to scare you."

I glanced at the man who'd entered, realizing I didn't remember him. Maybe I hadn't been paying close enough attention to those ordered to protect me.

"It's okay. The storm is making me jumpy."

"Yeah, I can understand. I just wanted to check to see if you needed anything."

"I'm sorry. What's your name?"

"Marty. I'm one of Cain's men."

"Oh, okay. No, I'm fine. I think I'm going to make a drink. Would you like one?"

He didn't answer right away, allowing what appeared to be a heated gaze to fall to my feet. I was instantly uncomfortable, but I chastised myself for being ridiculous.

"I'm on duty. Maybe I'll take one later after this is finished."

This. Even the way he said the single word seemed odd. I moved towards the bar, rolling my finger across the screen on my phone, noticing I'd accidentally scrolled to the text Hunter had sent me when I'd left for San Diego. Just reading the words again offered some comfort.

As I pulled down a glass, I realized he was standing in the same spot staring at me. For some reason it annoyed the hell out of me. I poured a glass of wine, then tipped my head towards him, keeping my rockstar practiced smile on my face. "Did you need anything else, Marty?"

I backed away from the bar, moving towards the set of French doors. Another rumble of thunder sounded closer. I quickly looked outside, unable to see any of the guards.

"No. Not right now. Soon."

Another tremor of fear drifted into my system. The wind was getting stronger, the sense of foreboding worse. As another flash of lightning powered closer to the estate, the sky took on an eerie blue color. Then I noticed something odd. I opened the door and within seconds, Marty was directly behind me.

"You don't want to do that, Sage."

Sage.

He'd called me Sage. I immediately moved outside and tossed the glass in his face. But he was too quick, grabbing my arm and yanking me backward into the house.

But not before I noticed one of the guards. He'd been shot.

After being pitched over the back of the couch, I struggled to stand, shocked the phone was still in my hand. Without hesitation, I typed in four letters.

Help

Then I heard a deep, ominous voice. "Hello, Sage. I thought it about time that we met."

CHAPTER 27

Cain

Anger.

How long had I suffered with its effects, the damning emotion biting into me every chance it had. I'd remained enraged my entire life, forfeiting so much of what others would call happiness because of my hatred. Sadly, I'd used the energy on the wrong people.

The thought of betrayal entered my mind once again. I'd killed men for less without blinking. I'd stood over them as the last seconds of their lives had played out, limbs torn apart, some gutted by my knife.

Yet not one of the kills had provided me with satisfaction or peace.

The sky looked like it was going to open up at any moment, bolts of lightning crisscrossing the sky. The ugly weather was fitting.

Especially for my sour mood.

"I love her." My sudden exclamation brought pointed eyes. "We can't lose her."

"I don't plan on it," Hunter said. "I never did."

"I thought that was apparent." Cristiano shifted in his seat.

"It had to be said. She belongs to us. Period."

"The big he-man makes a proclamation." There was anger in Hunter's voice.

Sighing as my father's estate came into view, for the first time in my life, I felt remorse. "We will do everything in our power to make her happy."

"Yes, we will." Hunter's words were said in reverence.

As Brock pulled in through the gates, a feeling of recoil settled in my stomach. I'd spent the last day preparing myself mentally. I wasn't entirely certain that was possible.

"Are you certain about this?" Cristiano asked.

"Yes. It needs to be done."

"He has loyal soldiers."

I stared out the window, wondering where they all were. "Then we kill every one of them."

"Whew," Hunter said from the passenger seat.

"If you don't want to be a part of this, then stay in the fucking vehicle."

Hunter tipped his head over his shoulder. "Fuck no, asshole. Your father put us through shit as well. Hiring another hitman to track us down. Hell, what did that bastard do, hold the guy's hand down and stick a hot poker against the top of his hand?"

Cristiano snorted. "Your father is a sick man."

"Yeah, well now you see where I get it from," I threw out.

"Then that wasn't good enough," Hunter continued. "Then the bastard had to hire a woman to keep tabs on Sage. What the hell did he think he was going to do?"

"Keep her as his own," I told them. "What better way than to have his cake and eat it to."

"I'll repeat it. Your father is a freaking psychopath," Cristiano huffed.

Brock pulled the vehicle to the front of house, killing the engine. This wasn't a planned visit, although I'd had Marty check to ensure that my father was at home. With the man's car in the driveway, it appeared the information was correct.

"Did you put a hold on the man responsible for working with my father?" I asked him before I climbed out.

"Fuck yeah, boss. He keeps insisting he has no clue what we're talking about," Brock said.

"They all say that shit," Hunter reminded him.

"Yeah, I know, but Harry is a good guy. I know him pretty well. Just shocks the fuck out of me. Sorry, boss. I meant no disrespect."

"Don't worry, Brock. My father won't mind sharing the details, including who worked with him." I moved onto the aggregate driveway, taking a glaring look at the home I'd grown up in. I hadn't returned since college. Any time that I'd met with my father had been in a separate location. Maybe the fucker continued to hold resentment that I'd forced him to retire at gunpoint. What did it matter? He had my brother murdered in front of me on purpose.

Because my brother had dared try and stop the horror that I'd grown up in.

I yanked my Glock into my hand, glaring at the windows on the third floor. My father had often remained staring out, knowing the second when I came home. That's when the beatings began.

Why he hated me so much I wasn't certain, but that also no longer mattered. I was my father's son. Blood for blood. It was his time to die.

The other soldiers we'd brought with us remained closer. I wasn't intending on making much of a surprise entrance. That was impossible given his tight security. However, I doubted he'd be expecting that I'd put a bullet between his eyes so soon.

He'd played the game well, a master manipulator. With the clues he'd left, it appeared that one of the Elite members that I'd gone to school with had been behind the charade.

Jonas. I hadn't talked with the guy since he'd been kicked out of school.

Finding out he'd landed in prison after his father had squandered the family's wealth was unexpected. Sadly, additional fodder for my father's vicious intentions.

The front door was unlocked, and I stormed inside, instantly noticing the quiet inside the house. As the soldiers piled in, I took a deep breath. What I found was nothing but bad memories.

And silence.

Then I knew something was terribly wrong.

"Brock. Go check the grounds. I need to know how many soldiers are on the premises. And make contact with Marty. Make certain the house is locked down tight."

"Of course, boss."

We moved through the lower level. There was no sign of my father. I took the stairs two at a time, bounding into one room after the other.

Then the third floor, heading into the master suite that I swore I'd never enter again.

What the fuck?

"What the hell is going on?" Cristiano barked as he found me coming down the stairs.

"He's not here."

Hunter rushed toward us, holding out his phone. "The fucker knew we were coming."

The single word would forever remain etched in my mind.

Help

*　*　*

Pop! Pop!

I dropped and rolled, firing off another two shots towards the guard who'd taken position on one of the balconies. As if in slow motion, his body pitched forward, tumbling over the wooden railing. Cristiano had taken out a second man at the entrance.

The wind was whipping through the trees, the storm turning violent. There'd been tornado warnings, the lake churning to the point flooding had begun from the torrential downpour. And the fucking lightning refused to give up, the air full of electricity.

"This is getting bad," Hunter said as he crouched beside me.

"The storm or the round of sabotage?"

"Both. Like that night."

He didn't need to remind me of the storm in Kentucky.

Hissing, I glared at one of my fallen soldiers, the close shot nearly ripping off his face. Goddamn it. How had I allowed this to happen?

The one lesson that my father had tried to teach me was that when emotion was involved, mistakes were made. He'd known my entire life how emotional I was. No matter how many times he'd tried to beat it out of me, it had always returned.

He'd counted on the fact, knowing my lust for vengeance would cloud my judgment. Now, I risked losing the only thing that mattered to me.

Not business. Not money. No building could ever matter.

Only the single woman I'd been in love with my entire adult life.

"Are we going in?" he asked.

"Is there any other choice? Whatever happens, Sage comes out of this alive."

Hunter yanked out another magazine, replacing the one in his Beretta. "I'll protect her with my life."

I heard another round of gunfire, but I continued heading to the front door. My father didn't want me killed. He wanted me to suffer first. The three of us wanted it over.

Still, I held the weapon in both hands, knowing what I'd find in the living room.

Cristiano and Hunter moved beside me as we entered the room, both men pointing their weapons at my father.

As anticipated, he sat in one of the leather chairs with Sage in his lap, the barrel of his weapon pointed at her throat.

I casually glanced around the room, noticing Marty was leaning against the set of French doors, a smug look on his face. He'd incriminated his fellow soldier. I would enjoy keeping him on ice for a lengthy period of time, cutting off one extremity at a time until he bled out.

There was nothing worse than traitors in your own midst.

When I returned my full attention to my father, the same angst that I'd always felt crowded my system.

"You had Dayton killed." I said the words in a matter-of-fact way, devoid of all emotion. I could tell I'd surprised him.

"He was a bad seed, although not nearly as much as you are. White trash."

He was only trying to rile me. "I guess that doesn't matter any longer. Does it?"

As he stroked Sage's hair, she kept her eyes locked on mine. "You know. I was curious as to why you found this little bitch so tempting, enough to derail your life, but now I understand."

She jerked her head away and he wrapped his other hand around her throat, squeezing just like he used to do with my mother. He'd almost strangled the life out of her several times.

I tensed, then felt Cristiano's hand on my shoulder. If I didn't control my emotions and my anger now, Sage would be the first victim in the room.

"This is between you and me," I told him, although I knew that would only make him laugh.

He grinned, acting as if my house and everything inside belonged to him. "Did your mother ever tell you the truth?"

"That you were a pig?"

His laughter was the same as I remembered. He'd grown older, his white hair thinning, but he was still a powerful man. Yes, a true psychopath. "That you were a bastard child."

The words were tossed out, but I sensed truth in them. "Is that so?"

"She had an affair with a fucking guard. A stupid fucking soldier. She didn't think I knew. I tolerated you because that's what she begged me to do. Then my real son tried to have me killed. Imagine that. My own flesh and blood wanting me dead while I was required to care for a worthless bastard."

I sensed Hunter shifting, moving to the side a few inches at a time. My father wasn't paying any attention. He was enjoying being in a position to gloat. I couldn't wait to carve out his heart before putting a bullet in his head. Maybe he thought I'd be upset by the news. Instead, it was a welcome relief.

My child wouldn't be subject to the bad blood I thought I'd been born into. I caught the look in Sage's eyes and growled. She was terrified.

"This worthless bastard is going to enjoy redefining my legacy and this beautiful woman is going to help me do it. She will bear my children, my heirs."

"Fuck you," she managed.

"That's exactly what we're going to do, bitch."

There was a moment where I was able to see into my father's mind and knew exactly what he had planned. In a split second, he aimed his weapon at my chest just as Sage thrust her elbow into his chest.

Pop!

As the bullet slammed into my shoulder, I was pitched backward. Marty reacted instantly, but Hunter was too quick, unloading several shots into the man.

Sage screamed, trying to get away from my father's tight hold.

Seconds later, the house went dark, another series of lightning bolts flashing across the sky.

I lunged forward, trying to get her into my arms, but my father's hold remained. Scrambling closer, I threw myself on top of her, fighting my father's hold on the weapon. He still had his hand wrapped around her throat. Anger unlike anything I'd ever experienced rushed into me. I grabbed my father's arm and without hesitation, snapped his wrist. The cracking sound as bones were broken was followed by his angry howl.

"Take her!" I yelled as Cristiano appeared at my side.

He gathered her into his arms, dragging her away.

"No. No!" Her cries of anguish weren't lost on me.

I punched my father several times. Then we pitched and rolled, both fighting for control. I bashed the weapon against his face, but he held on, our bodies twisting and turning.

Then…

Pop!

* * *

Five months later

Sage

"How exciting. It looks like Rose Sandler is exiting the limousine. Let me make certain. Yes, it's Rose from Halo!"

I heard the reporter's voice as Hunter wrapped his fingers around mine, pulling me onto the red carpet leading to the auditorium. The number of photographers snapping pictures was overwhelming. In all the years of attending awards ceremonies, the reception this year was even more glamorous. I'd been coined the 'It' girl of the Grammys, Halo the band to beat for the major awards. We were up for seven of them, which continued to shock me.

I waved at the crowd, taking it all in as both Cristiano and Cain took their positions beside me. They'd become celebrities as well, *People Magazine* calling our unusual relationship 'Caustic Evocative Evolution'.

My hunks had rolled their eyes reading the article while I'd sipped champagne, dancing around our house in Key West in a bikini. They'd stayed true to their word, allowing me to pick out the various houses we owned.

As the crowd swarmed around us, Cain took my other arm. Always the most protective, his dark eyes sweeping the crowd as if anticipating his father would come back to life.

We'd been lucky, his shoulder injury healing within a few weeks.

But the house had never felt the same, getting sold weeks later.

They'd saved my life as they'd promised to do, but I think I managed to save their souls. They were entirely different than they'd been before, the huge weight of the past finally releasing its claws.

While Cain had yet to find out the identity of his real father, it didn't seem to bother him. He was content in the fact that if we were lucky enough to have children, then his blood wouldn't taint the child.

"Rose. Can I ask you a few questions?" The reporter was one I knew, adamant that he speak with me.

When Cristiano started to step in, I pressed my hand against his chest, rising onto my tiptoes and kissing him on the lips. The gesture was caught by at least fifteen photographers. Not to be outdone, Hunter grabbed me for a passionate embrace, driving his tongue inside my mouth while every woman swooned.

They looked delicious in their tuxes, good enough to eat. Which I planned on doing later.

Or perhaps they'd devour me.

The thought sent a thrill all the way to my overheated core.

Cain pulled me away, doing nothing more than drinking in my perfume, rolling his knuckles down my cheek in a sign of possession. As always, I trembled from his touch. His dark eyes bore into mine, but there was a look of mischief that I wasn't used to seeing.

"This is your night until we're on the jet." His words were whispered.

Heat crested across my jaw, and I was happy that the lights likely hadn't caught my flustered look.

"Hi, Steve. I'd be happy to answer a few questions." I waved to the crowd again, smiling from the cheers.

"How does it feel to be expected to win every major award tonight?"

"It feels fantastic, but I couldn't have done it without my band. They are the best in the world. Aren't they?" I jazzed the crowd until the cheers drowned out every other noise.

Steve shook his head, waiting as the virulent applause and loud catcalls died down. "There's a sense that your music has taken a new path. Even Rolling Stone mentioned there's a significant increase in passion to your words and to the sound itself. What would you attribute that to?"

I took a deep breath. "To the three men I've fallen madly in love with."

The crowd went wild.

* * *

"Did you see that metal band's reaction when Halo won for Album of the Year?" Hunter asked as he refilled my champagne glass. I was sitting on Cristiano's lap, bouncing to the music, still holding one of my awards. His cock was already throbbing, and I couldn't help but shift back and forth, teasing him relentlessly.

"I thought they were going to storm the stage," Cristiano said, laughing.

"I almost beat the crap out of the lead singer." Cain grinned after making the statement, but I knew he would have given the chance.

Hunter rolled his eyes and flopped down in one of the seats. The evening had been everything I'd ever wanted, a dream come true. Mostly because I'd been able to share it with the three men who'd stolen my heart.

However, Cain had been moody for the past two days, as if he had something on his mind. He'd pulled away more than once, needing time alone. I was certain he was going to leave our foursome, which would break my heart.

When he suddenly jerked up out of his chair, walking towards the bar, I quickly gave Hunter a look. He shrugged, but I could tell he knew what was going on.

I eased off Cristiano's lap, placing my champagne glass on the table and walking towards Cain. When I placed my hand on his shoulder, he tensed. "What's wrong?"

He took several deep breaths, remaining quiet. "I can't do this any longer, Sage. I'm sorry, but I can't."

Instantly, tears drifted into my eyes. "I don't know what to say. You don't love me any longer, or you just can't handle sharing?"

He shrugged and didn't give me a response.

"Look, the only thing I asked out of this relationship was that you tell me the truth at all times. What is going on?"

The brooding man continued to remain silent. Now, I was getting angry.

"I demand you tell me what is happening. Is there another woman? You waited until this night to tell me this? What is wrong with you?"

Cain finally spun around, barely able to keep the look of amusement off his face. He thought this was funny? I reacted without thinking, returning to my champagne and tossing the entire glass in his face. Then I gasped when I saw his expression. He was truly shocked.

When the other two started laughing, I realized I'd misread what he was doing.

"Oops," I said quietly, backing away from Cain and directly against the two beefy hunks I shared a bed with.

As Cain dragged his tongue across his lips, I chewed on my lower one, uncertain what his reaction would be.

"It seems our little pet needs another lesson in not jumping to conclusions," Cristiano said from behind me.

They were as dominating as I thought they'd be, keeping me in line with rules and delicious punishments. They'd also introduced me to their darker cravings, aspects of BDSM that left me breathless.

"Yes, it does," Hunter said before smacking my bottom once.

"Ouch!"

"There's more where that came from."

Cain held up his index finger, shaking his head. Champagne glistened on his chin, and I wanted to lick off every drop. "Our beautiful lamb will get her punishment after I'm finished."

I folded my arms, waiting to see what he'd have to say. When he dropped to one knee, I couldn't have been more shocked. After pulling a small box from his pocket and opening it to allow me to see the stunning ring inside, he lifted his gaze. I could swear there were tears in his eyes.

"As I said before. I can't do it any longer, not unless you become our wife."

I turned around towards the others, gasping for air as I fanned my face. Tears were definitely in my eyes, the joy of realizing that after everything we'd been through, we were very much in love overwhelming.

I'd been scarred from an event that I'd had no control over. Maybe I should have tried to shove them out of my life, but the thought hadn't entered my mind.

Fleeting visions of the past, the stormy night over ten years before floated into the forefront of my mind. Unlike before, this time I was able to shut them down, putting them in their padlocked place. The past couldn't hold me prisoner any longer. There was only the future in a house full of love and laughter.

"Yes." The word came easily, my heart skipping several beats as Cain slipped the ring on my finger. As they wrapped their arms around me, I'd never felt so much love.

That was good since I had a little secret they wouldn't hear until the right time. It didn't matter who was the biological father. There would never be any tests, no challenge in court. As far as I was concerned, he or she had three daddies.

And I had the loves of my life.

All because fate had intervened, allowing our hearts and souls to heal.

"Now, about that spanking," Cain said as he lifted his head, winking at the others.

"I'm a good girl!"

"That's what we keep hearing," Hunter growled.

As Cristiano sat down, yanking me over his lap, all I could do was smile.

Who knew a girl would find not just one but three perfect Prince Charmings?

Now, onto the happily ever after.

The End

AFTERWORD

Stormy Night Publications would like to thank you for your interest in our books.

If you liked this book (or even if you didn't), we would really appreciate you leaving a review on the site where you purchased it. Reviews provide useful feedback for us and our authors, and this feedback (both positive comments and constructive criticism) allows us to work even harder to make sure we provide the content our customers want to read.

If you would like to check out more books from Stormy Night Publications, if you want to learn more about our company, or if you would like to join our mailing list, please visit our website at:

http://www.stormynightpublications.com

BOOKS OF THE TAINTED REGIME SERIES

Cruelest Vow

D'Artagnan Conti was born into poverty, raised to be a soldier in my father's savage regime. I grew up in luxury, longing to escape my family's cruel machinations, and the young man with sapphire eyes and the voice of an angel became not just my forbidden crush but my everything.

Then he was taken from me, killed in a brutal attack by our enemies. Or so I was led to believe...

For twenty years I did my best to forget him, until a devilishly handsome stranger awakened my desire in a way that I hadn't thought possible, baring my body and soul and setting them both ablaze with passion so intense it burns hotter than the lash of leather across my naked backside.

Every taste of his lips, every whisper in my ear, and every quivering climax pulled me deeper into this dark, twisted rapture, and only when I was already under his spell did I learn the truth.

The man I thought I'd lost is the one who has made me his.

Twisted Embrace

Enzo Lazaro is my best friend's brother, yet the fact that it was taboo only left me even more desperate for him to undress me with those piercing eyes and then strip me bare and ravage me.

But until he found out a secret I hadn't even known myself, I never thought I'd be screaming his name in bed with my belted ass still burning because he decided I needed a lesson in obedience.

...or that he'd be claiming me as his bride.

It turns out I'm the daughter of a Russian mobster, and even though my adopted parents never told me, that means I have dangerous enemies. He says he's making me his wife to protect me.

But we both know he would have taken what he wanted eventually anyway.

BOOKS OF THE RUTHLESS EMPIRE SERIES

The Don

Maxwell Powers swept into my life after my father was gunned down, but the moment those piercing blue eyes caught mine I knew he would be doing more than just avenging his old friend.

I haven't seen him since I was a little girl, but that won't keep him from bending me over and belting my bare backside… or from making me scream his name as he claims my virgin body.

He's twice my age, and he's my godfather.

But I know I'll be soaking wet and ready for him tonight…

The Consigliere

As consigliere of New York's most ruthless crime syndicate, Daniel Briggs rules with an iron fist. But here in Los Angeles, he's just my big brother's best friend, forbidden in every way.

This stunningly handsome billionaire may be the most eligible bachelor on the West Coast, but to him I'm still just a little girl in need of protection from men who would ravage her brutally.

Men like him.

But he'll soon realize I'm all grown up, and then it won't be long before my teenage crush finally shows me the side of him he's kept hidden from me—the savage side that will blister my bare ass for talking back and then take what has always been his with my hair gripped in his fist.

I don't know what comes after that. I just know everything he does to me will be utterly sinful…

BOOKS OF THE CARNAL SINS SERIES

Required Surrender

My first mistake was agreeing to participate in a charity auction. My second was believing I could walk away from the commanding billionaire with a brogue accent and dazzling green eyes.

It was supposed to be one date, but a man like Lachlan McKenzie plays by his own set of rules.

As the owner of Carnal Sins, DC's exclusive kink club, his reputation is as dark and demanding as his desires, and before I knew it I ended up his to enjoy not for just one night but a full week.

I fought his control, but I knew I wouldn't win… and in my heart I don't think I even wanted to. Not after he called me his good girl, stripped me bare and spanked me with his belt, and then made me blush and beg and come so hard I forgot all about being his only for a few more days.

That didn't matter anyway. We both know he's keeping me forever.

Demanded Submission

When he came to my aid after a head-on collision that seemed not to have been an accident, Jameson Stark offered me a ride, help with my car, and a job at the most exclusive club in town.

He also bared me, spanked me until I knew better than to argue with him again, and then showed me what it means to be in the debt of a billionaire who isn't afraid to take everything he's owed.

But as the owner of the Miami branch of Carnal Sins, it isn't just Jameson's wealth and good looks that draw attention, and I knew a man like him must have enemies. I just didn't care.

Not when his every smoldering glance all but demanded my submission…

BOOKS OF THE KINGS OF
CORRUPTION SERIES

King of Wrath

After a car wreck on an icy winter morning, I had no idea the man who saved my life would turn out to be the heir to a powerful mafia family… let alone that I'd be forced into marrying him.

When this mysterious stranger sought to seduce me, I should have ignored the dark passion he ignited. Instead, I begged him to claim me as he stripped me bare and whipped me with his belt.

He was as savage as I was innocent, but it was only after he made me his that I learned the truth.

He's the head of the New York Cosa Nostra, and I belong to him now…

King of Cruelty

Constantine Thorn has been after me since I saw him kill a man nine years ago, and when he finally caught me he made me an offer I couldn't refuse. Marry him and he will protect me.

Only then did I learn that the man who made me his bride was the same monster I'd feared.

He's a brutal, heartless mafia boss and I wanted to hate the bastard, but with every stinging lash of his belt and every moment of helplessly intense passion, I fell deeper into the dark abyss.

He's the king of cruelty, and now I'm his queen.

King of Pain

Diego Santos may be wealthy, powerful, and sinfully gorgeous, but his slick veneer doesn't fool me. I know his true nature, and I had planned to end this arranged marriage before it even began.

But it wasn't Diego waiting for me at the altar.

By all appearances the man who laid claim to me was the mafia heir to whom I'd been promised, but I sensed an entirely different personality, one so electrifying I was swept up by his passion.

A part of me still wanted to escape, but then he took me in his arms and over his knee, laying my deepest, darkest needs bare and then fulfilling them in the most shameful ways imaginable.

Now I'm not just his bride. I'm his completely.

King of Depravity

When Brogan Callahan swept me off my feet, I didn't know he was heir to a powerful Irish mafia family. I didn't find that out until after he'd taken me in his arms… and over his knee.

By the time I learned the truth, I was already his.

I went on the run to escape my father's plans to marry me off, but it turns out the ruthless mob boss he had in mind is the same sinfully sexy bastard who just stripped me bare and claimed me savagely.

He demands my absolute obedience, and yet with each brutal kiss and stinging lash of his belt I feel myself falling ever deeper into the dark abyss of shameful need he's created within me.

At first I wondered if there were bounds to his depravity. Now I hope there aren't…

King of Savagery

I knew Maxim Nikitin was a man to be reckoned with when I went undercover to help the FBI bring him down, but nothing could have prepared me for his raw power… or his icy blue eyes.

He caught me, and now he's determined not just to punish me, but to tame me completely.

Every kiss is brutal, every touch possessive, every fiery lash of his belt more intense than the last, yet with every cry of pain and every scream of climax the truth becomes more obvious.

He doesn't need to break me. I belong to him already.

King of Malice

When I met Phoenix Diamonds, I didn't know anything about him except that he had a body carved from stone and a voice that left me hoping he'd order me to strip just so I could obey.

By the time I learned he's the head of a Greek crime syndicate intent on making me pay for the sins of my father, he'd already mastered me with his touch alone, belted my bare ass for daring to come without permission, and ravaged me thoroughly both that night and the next morning.

All I can do is try to pretend he isn't everything I've always fantasized about…

But I think he knows already.

BOOKS OF THE SINNERS AND SAINTS SERIES

Beautiful Villain

When I knocked on Kirill Sabatin's door, I didn't know he was the Kozlov Bratva's most feared enforcer. I didn't expect him to be the most terrifyingly sexy man I've ever laid eyes on either...

I told him off for making so much noise in the middle of the night, but if the crack of his palm against my bare bottom didn't wake everyone in the building my screams of climax certainly did.

I shouldn't have let him spank me, let alone seduce me. He's a dangerous man and I could easily end up in way over my head. But the moment I set eyes on those rippling, sweat-slicked muscles I knew I needed that beautiful villain to take me long and hard and savagely right then and there.

And he did.

Now I just have to hope him claiming me doesn't start a mob war...

Beautiful Sinner

When I first screamed his name in shameful surrender, Sevastian Kozlov was the enemy, the heir of a rival family who had just finished spanking me into submission after I dared to defy him.

Though he'd already claimed my body by the time he claimed me as his bride, no matter how desperately I long for his touch I vowed this beautiful sinner would never conquer my heart.

But it wasn't up to me...

Beautiful Seduction

In my late-night hunt for the perfect pastry, I never expected to be the victim of a brutal attack… or for a brooding, blue-eyed stranger to become my savior, tending to my wounds while easing my fears. The electricity exploded between us, turning into a night of incredible passion.

Only later did I learn that Valentin Vincheti is the heir to the New York Italian mafia empire.

Then he came to take me, and this time he wasn't gentle. I shouldn't have surrendered, but with each savage kiss and stinging stroke of his belt his beautiful seduction became more difficult to resist. But when one of his enemies sets his sights on me, will my secrets put our lives at risk?

Beautiful Obsession

After I was left at the altar, I turned what was meant to be the reception into an epic party. But when a handsome stranger asked me to dance, I wasn't prepared for the passion he ignited.

He told me he was a very bad man, but that only made my heart race faster as I lay bare and bound, my dress discarded and my bottom sore from a spanking, waiting for him to ravage me.

It was supposed to be just one night. No strings. Nothing to entangle me in his dangerous world.

But that was before I became his beautiful obsession…

Beautiful Devil

Kostya Baranov is an infamous assassin, a man capable of incredible savagery, but when I witnessed a mafia hit he didn't silence me with a bullet. He decided to make me his instead.

Taken prisoner and forced to obey or feel the sting of his belt, shameful lust for my captor soon wars with fury at what he has done to me… and what he keeps doing to me with every touch.

But though he may be a beautiful devil, it is my own family's secret which may damn us both.

BOOKS OF THE BENEDETTI EMPIRE SERIES

Cruel Prince

Catherine's father conspired to have my father killed, and that debt to the Benedetti family must be settled. Just as he took something from me, I will take something from him.

His daughter.

She will be mine to punish and ravage, but when she suffers it will not be for his sins.

It will be for my pleasure.

She will beg, but it will be for me to claim her in the most shameful ways imaginable.

She will scream, but it will be because she doesn't think she can bear another climax.

But when she surrenders at last, it will not be to her captor.

It will be to her husband.

Ruthless Prince

Alexandra is a senator's daughter, used to mingling in the company of the rich and powerful, but tonight she will learn that there are men who play by different rules.

Men like me.

I could romance her. I could seduce her and then carry her gently to my bed.

But that can wait. Tonight I'm going to wring one ruthless climax after another from her quivering body with her bottom burning from my belt and her throat sore from screaming.

She will know she is mine before she even knows she is my bride.

Savage Prince

Gillian's father may be a powerful Irish mob boss, but he owes a blood debt to my family, and when I came to collect I didn't ask permission before taking his daughter as payment.

It was not up to him… or to her.

I will make her my bride, but I am not the kind of man who will wait until our wedding night to bare her and claim what belongs to me. She will walk down the aisle wet, well-used, and sore.

Her dress will hide the marks from my belt that taught her the consequences of disobeying her husband, but nothing will hide her blushes as her arousal drips down her thighs with each step.

By the time she says her vows she will already be mine.

BOOKS OF THE MERCILESS KINGS SERIES

King's Captive

Emily Porter saw me kill a man who betrayed my family and she helped put me behind bars. But someone with my connections doesn't stay in prison long, and she is about to learn the hard way that there is a price to pay for crossing the boss of the King dynasty. A very, very painful price...

She's going to cry for me as I blister that beautiful bottom, then she's going to scream for me as I ravage her over and over again, taking her in the most shameful ways she can imagine. But leaving her well-punished and well-used is just the beginning of what I have in store for Emily.

I'm going to make her my bride, and then I'm going to make her mine completely.

King's Hostage

When my life was threatened, Michael King didn't just take matters into his own hands.

He took me.

When he carried me off it was partly to protect me, but mostly it was because he wanted me.

I didn't choose to go with him, but it wasn't up to me. That's why I'm naked, wet, and sore in an opulent Swiss chalet with my bottom still burning from the belt of the infuriatingly sexy mafia boss who brought me here, punished me when I fought him, and then savagely made me his.

We'll return when things are safe in New Orleans, but I won't be going back to my old home.

I belong to him now, and he plans to keep me.

King's Possession

Her father had to be taught what happens when you cross a King, but that isn't why Genevieve Rossi is sore, well-used, and waiting for me to claim her in the only way I haven't already.

She's sore because she thought she could embarrass me in public without being punished.

She's well-used because after I spanked her I wanted more, and I take what I want.

She's waiting for me in my bed because she's my bride, and tonight is our wedding night.

I'm not going to be gentle with her, but when she wakes up tomorrow morning wet and blushing her cheeks won't be crimson because of the shameful things I did to her naked, quivering body.

It will be because she begged for all of them.

King's Toy

Vincenzo King thought I knew something about a man who betrayed him, but that isn't why I'm on my way to New Orleans well-used and sore with my backside still burning from his belt.

When he bared and punished me maybe it was just business, but what came after was not.

It was savage, it was shameful, and it was very, very personal.

I'm his toy now, and not the kind you keep in its box on the shelf.

He's going to play rough with me.

He's going to get me all wet and dirty.

Then he's going to do it all again tomorrow.

King's Demands

Julieta Morales hoped to escape an unwanted marriage, but the moment she got into my car her fate was sealed. She will have a husband, but it won't be the cartel boss her father chose for her.

It will be me.

But I'm not the kind of man who takes his bride gently amid rose petals on her wedding night. She'll learn to satisfy her King's demands with her bottom burning and her hair held in my fist.

She'll promise obedience when she speaks her vows, but she'll be mastered long before then.

King's Temptation

I didn't think I needed Dimitri Kristoff's protection, but it wasn't up to me. With a kingpin from a rival family coming after me, he took charge, took off his belt, and then took what he wanted.

He knows I'm not used to doing as I'm told. He just doesn't care.

The stripes seared across my bare bottom left me sore and sorry, but it was what came after that truly left me shaken. The princess of the King family shouldn't be on her knees for anyone, let alone this Bratva brute who has decided to claim for himself what he was meant to safeguard.

Nobody gave me to him, but I'm his anyway.

Now he's going to make sure I know it.

BOOKS OF THE MAFIA MASTERS SERIES

His as Payment

Caroline Hargrove thinks she is mine because her father owed me a debt, but that isn't why she is sitting in my car beside me with her bottom sore inside and out. She's wet, well-used, and coming with me whether she likes it or not because I decided I want her, and I take what I want.

As a senator's daughter, she probably thought no man would dare lay a hand on her, let alone spank her thoroughly and then claim her beautiful body in the most shameful ways possible.

She was wrong. Very, very wrong. She's going to be mastered, and I won't be gentle about it.

Taken as Collateral

Francesca Alessandro was just meant to be collateral, held captive as a warning to her father, but then she tried to fight me. She ended up sore and soaked as I taught her a lesson with my belt and then screaming with every savage climax as I taught her to obey in a much more shameful way.

She's mine now. Mine to keep. Mine to protect. Mine to use as hard and as often as I please.

Forced to Cooperate

Willow Church is not the first person who tried to put a bullet in me. She's just the first I let live. Now she will pay the price in the most shameful way imaginable. The stripes from my belt will teach her to obey, but what happens to her sore, red bottom after that will teach the real lesson.

She will be used mercilessly, over and over, and every brutal climax will remind her of the humiliating truth: she never even had a chance against me. Her body always knew its master.

Claimed as Revenge

Valencia Rivera became mine the moment her father broke the agreement he made with me. She thought she had a say in the matter, but my belt across her beautiful bottom taught her otherwise and a night spent screaming her surrender into the sheets left her in no doubt she belongs to me.

Using her hard and often will not be all it takes to tame her properly, but it will be a good start…

Made to Beg

Sierra Fox showed up at my door to ask for my protection, and I gave it to her… for a price. She belongs to me now, and I'm going to use her beautiful body as thoroughly as I please. The only thing for her to decide is how sore her cute little bottom will be when I'm through claiming her.

She came to me begging for help, but as her moans and screams grow louder with every brutal climax, we both know it won't be long before she begs me for something far more shameful.

BOOKS OF THE EDGE OF DARKNESS SERIES

Dark Stranger

On a dark, rainy night, I received a phone call. I shouldn't have answered it… but I did.

The things he says he'll do to me are far from sweet, this man I know only by his voice.

They're so filthy I blush crimson just hearing them… and yet still I answer, my panties always soaked the moment the phone rings. But this isn't going to end when I decide it's gone too far…

I can tell him to leave me alone, but I know it won't keep him away. He's coming for me, and when he does he's going to make me his in all the rough, shameful ways he promised he would.

And I'll be wet and ready for him… whether I want to be or not.

Dark Predator

She thinks I'm seducing her, but this isn't romance. It's something much more shameful.

Eden tried to leave the mafia behind, but someone far more dangerous has set his sights on her.

Me.

She was meant to be my revenge against an old enemy, but I decided to make her mine instead.

She'll moan as my belt lashes her quivering bottom and writhe as I claim her in the filthiest of ways, but that's just the beginning. When I'm done, it won't be just her body that belongs to me.

I'll own her heart and soul too.

BOOKS OF THE DARK OVERTURE SERIES

Indecent Invitation

I shouldn't be here.

My clothes shouldn't be scattered around the room, my bottom shouldn't be sore, and I certainly shouldn't be screaming into the sheets as a ruthless tycoon takes everything he wants from me.

I shouldn't even know Houston Powers at all, but I was in a bad spot and I was made an offer.

A shameful, indecent offer I couldn't refuse.

I was desperate, I needed the money, and I didn't have a choice. Not a real one, anyway.

I'm here because I signed a contract, but I'm his because he made me his.

Illicit Proposition

I should have known better.

His proposition was shameful. So shameful I threw my drink in his face when I heard it.

Then I saw the look in his eyes, and I knew I'd made a mistake.

I fought as he bared me and begged as he spanked me, but it didn't matter. All I could do was moan, scream, and climax helplessly for him as he took everything he wanted from me.

By the time I signed the contract, I was already his.

Unseemly Entanglement

I was warned about Frederick Duvall. I was told he was dangerous. But I never suspected that meeting the billionaire advertising mogul to discuss a business proposition would end with me bent over a table with my dress up and my panties down for a shameful lesson in obedience.

That should have been it. I should have told him what he could do with his offer and his money.

But I didn't.

I could say it was because two million dollars is a lot of cash, but as I stand before him naked, bound, and awaiting the sting of his cane for daring to displease him, I know that's not the truth.

I'm not here because he pays me. I'm here because he owns me.

BOOKS OF THE CLUB DARKNESS SERIES

Bent to His Will

Even the most powerful men in the world know better than to cross me, but Autumn Sutherland thought she could spy on me in my own club and get away with it. Now she must be punished.

She tried to expose me, so she will be exposed. Bare, bound, and helplessly on display, she'll beg for mercy as my strap lashes her quivering bottom and my crop leaves its burning welts on her most intimate spots. Then she'll scream my name as she takes every inch of me, long and hard.

When I am done with her, she won't just be sore and shamefully broken. She will be mine.

Broken by His Hand

Sophia Russo tried to keep away from me, but just thinking about what I would do to her left her panties drenched. She tried to hide it, but I didn't let her. I tore those soaked panties off, spanked her bare little bottom until she had no doubt who owns her, and then took her long and hard.

She begged and screamed as she came for me over and over, but she didn't learn her lesson...

She didn't just come back for more. She thought she could disobey me and get away with it.

This time I'm not just going to punish her. I'm going to break her.

Bound by His Command

Willow danced for the rich and powerful at the world's most exclusive club... until tonight.

Tonight I told her she belongs to me now, and no other man will touch her again.

Tonight I ripped her soaked panties from her beautiful body and taught her to obey with my belt.

Tonight I took her as mine, and I won't be giving her up.

MORE MAFIA AND BILLIONAIRE ROMANCES BY PIPER STONE

Caught

If you're forced to come to an arrangement with someone as dangerous as Jagger Calduchi, it means he's about to take what he wants, and you'll give it to him… even if it's your body.

I got caught snooping where I didn't belong, and Jagger made me an offer I couldn't refuse. A week with him where his rules are the only rules, or his bought and paid for cops take me to jail.

He's going to punish me, train me, and master me completely. When he's used me so shamefully I blush just to think about it, maybe he'll let me go home… or maybe he'll decide to keep me.

Ruthless

Treating a mobster shot by a rival's goons isn't really my forte, but when a man is powerful enough to have a whole wing of a hospital cleared out for his protection, you do as you're told.

To make matters worse, this isn't first time I've met Giovanni Calduchi. It turns out my newest patient is the stern, sexy brute who all but dragged me back to his hotel room a couple of nights ago so he could use my body as he pleased, then showed up at my house the next day, stripped me bare, and spanked me until I was begging him to take me even more roughly and shamefully.

Now, with his enemies likely to be coming after me in order to get to him, all I can do is hope he's as good at keeping me safe as he is at keeping me blushing, sore, and thoroughly satisfied.

Dangerous

I knew Erik Chenault was dangerous the moment I saw him. Everything about him should have warned me away, from the scar on his face to the fact that mobsters call him Blade. But I was drawn like a moth to a flame, and I ended up burnt... and blushing, sore, and thoroughly used.

Now he's taken it upon himself to protect me from men like the ones we both tried to leave in our past. He's going to make me his whether I like it or not... but I think I'm going to like it.

Prey

Within moments of setting eyes on Sophia Waters, I was certain of two things. She was going to learn what happens to bad girls who cheat at cards, and I was going to be the one to teach her.

But there was one thing I didn't know as I reddened that cute little bottom and then took her long and hard and oh so shamefully: I wasn't the only one who didn't come here for a game of cards.

I came to kill a man. It turns out she came to protect him.

Nobody keeps me from my target, but I'm in no rush. Not when I'm enjoying this game of cat and mouse so much. I'll even let her catch me one day, and as she screams my name with each brutal climax she'll finally realize the truth. She was never the hunter. She was always the prey.

Given

Stephanie Michaelson was given to me, and she is mine. The sooner she learns that, the less often her cute little bottom will end up well-punished and sore as she is reminded of her place.

But even as she promises obedience with tears running down her cheeks, I know it isn't the sting of my belt that will truly tame her. It is what comes next that will leave her in no doubt she belongs to me. That part will be long, hard, and shameful... and I will make her beg for all of it.

Dangerous Stranger

I came to Spain hoping to start a new life away from dangerous men, but then I met Rafael Santiago. Now I'm not just caught up in the affairs of a mafia boss, I'm being forced into his car.

When I saw something I shouldn't have, Rafael took me captive, stripped me bare, and punished me until he felt certain I'd told him everything I knew about his organization... which was nothing at all. Then he offered me his protection in return for the right to use me as he pleases.

Now that I belong to him, his plans for me are more shameful than I could have ever imagined.

Indebted

After her father stole from me, I could have left Alessandra Toro in jail for a crime she didn't commit. But I have plans for her. A deal with the judge—the kind only a man like me can arrange—made her my captive, and she will pay her father's debt with her beautiful body.

She will try to run, of course, but it won't be the law that comes after her. It will be me.

The sting of my belt across her quivering bare bottom will teach Alessandra the price of defiance, but it is the far more shameful penance that follows which will truly tame her.

Taken

When Winter O'Brien was given to me, she thought she had a say in the matter. She was wrong.

She is my bride. Mine to claim, mine to punish, and mine to use as shamefully as I please. The sting of my belt on her bare bottom will teach her to obey, but obedience is just the beginning.

I will demand so much more.

Bratva's Captive

I told Chloe Kingstrom that getting close to me would be dangerous, and she should keep her distance. The moment she disobeyed and followed me into that bar, she became mine.

Now my enemies are after her, but it's not what they would do to her she should worry about.

It's what I'm going to do to her.

My belt across her bare backside will teach her obedience, but what comes after will be different.

She's going to blush, beg, and scream with every climax as she's ravaged more thoroughly than she can imagine. Then I'm going to flip her over and claim her in an even more shameful way.

If she's a good girl, I might even let her enjoy it.

Hunted

Hope Gracen was just another target to be tracked down… until I caught her.

When I discovered I'd been lied to, I carried her off.

She'll tell me the truth with her bottom still burning from my belt, but that isn't why she's here.

I took her to protect her. I'm keeping her because she's mine.

Theirs as Payment

Until mere moments ago, I was a doctor heading home after my shift at the hospital. But that was before I was forced into the back seat of an SUV, then bared and spanked for trying to escape.

Now I'm just leverage for the Cabello brothers to use against my father, but it isn't the thought of being held hostage by these brutes that has my heart racing and my whole body quivering.

It is the way they're looking at me…

Like they're about to tear my clothes off and take turns mounting me like wild beasts.

Like they're going to share me, using me in ways more shameful than I can even imagine.

Like they own me.

Ruthless Acquisition

I knew the shameful stakes when I bet against these bastards. I just didn't expect to lose.

Now they've come to collect their winnings.

But they aren't just planning to take a belt to my bare bottom for trying to run and then claim everything they're owed from my naked, helpless body as I blush, beg, and scream for them.

They've acquired me, and they plan to keep me.

Bound by Contract

I knew I was in trouble the moment Gregory Steele called me into his office, but I wasn't expecting to end up stripped bare and bent over his desk for a painful lesson from his belt.

Taking a little bit of money here and there might have gone unnoticed in another organization, but stealing from one of the most powerful mafia bosses on the West Coast has consequences.

It doesn't matter why I did it. The only thing that matters now is what he's going to do to me.

I have no doubt he will use me shamefully, but he didn't make me sign that contract just to show me off with my cheeks blushing and my bottom sore under the scandalous outfit he chose for me.

Now that I'm his, he plans to keep me.

Dangerous Addiction

I went looking for a man working with my enemies. When I found only her instead, I should have just left her alone… or maybe taken what I wanted from her and then left… but I didn't.

I couldn't.

So I carried her off to keep for myself.

She didn't make it easy for me, and that earned her a lesson in obedience. A shameful one.

But as her bare bottom reddens under my punishing hand I can see her arousal dripping down her quivering thighs, and no matter how much she squirms and sobs and begs we both know exactly what she needs, and we both know as soon as this spanking is over I'm going to give it to her.

Hard.

Auction House

When I went undercover to investigate a series of murders with links to Steele Franklin's auction house operation, I expected to be sold for the humiliating use of one of his fellow billionaires.

But he wanted me for himself.

No contract. No agreed upon terms. No say in the matter at all except whether to surrender to his shameful demands without a fight or make him strip me bare and spank me into submission first.

I chose the second option, but as one devastating climax after another is forced from my naked, quivering body, what scares me isn't the thought of him keeping me locked up in a cage forever.

It's knowing he won't need to.

Interrogated

As Liam McGinty's belt lashes my bare backside, it isn't the burning sting or the humiliating awareness that my body's surrender is on full display for this ruthless mobster that shocks me.

It's the fact that this isn't a scene from one of my books.

I almost can't process the fact that I'm really riding in the back of a luxury SUV belonging to the most powerful Irish mafia boss in New York—the man I've written so much about—with my cheeks blushing, my bottom sore inside and out, and my arousal soaking the seat beneath me.

But whether I can process it or not, I'm his captive now.

Maybe he'll let me go when he's gotten the answers he needs and he's used me as he pleases.

Or maybe he'll keep me...

Vow of Seduction

Alexander Durante, Brogan Lancaster, and Daniel Norwood are powerful, dangerous men, but that won't keep them safe from me. Not after they let my brother take the fall for their crimes.

I spent years preparing for my chance at revenge. But things didn't go as planned...

Now I'm naked, bound, and helpless, waiting to be used and punished as these brutes see fit, and yet what's on my mind isn't how to escape all of the shameful things they're going to do to me.

It's whether I even want to...

Brutal Heir

When I went to an author convention, I didn't expect to find myself enjoying a rooftop meal with the sexiest cover model in the business, let alone screaming his name in bed later that night.

I didn't plan to be targeted by assassins, rushed to a helicopter under cover of armed men, and then spirited away to his home country with my bottom still burning from a spanking either, but it turns out there are some really important things I didn't know about Diavolo Montoya...

Like the fact that he's the heir to a notorious crime syndicate.

I should hate him, but even as his prisoner our connection is too intense to ignore, and I'm beginning to realize that what began as a moment of passion is going to end with me as his.

Forever.

Bed of Thorns

Hardened by years spent in prison for a crime he didn't commit, Edmond Montego is no longer the gentle man I remember. When he came for me, he didn't just take me for the very first time.

He claimed my virgin body with a savagery that left me screaming… and he made me beg for it.

I should have run when I had the chance, but with every lash of his belt, every passionate kiss, and every brutal climax, I fell more and more under his spell.

But he has a dark secret, and if we're not careful, we'll lose everything… including our lives.

Morally Gray

Saxon Thornburg is known to the world as a reputable businessman, but I knew his true nature even before he kidnapped me, bared, bound, and punished me, and then shamefully ravaged me.

He is not just the billionaire boss of a powerful crime family. He is the Patriarch.

Women drop to their knees on command for him, but he chose me because I didn't surrender.

Until he took off his belt…

BOOKS OF THE MISSOULA BAD BOYS SERIES

Phoenix

As a single dad, a battle-scarred Marine, and a smokejumper, my life was complicated enough. Then Wren Tillman showed up in town, full of sass and all but begging for my belt, and what began as a passionate night after I rescued her from a snowstorm quickly became much more.

Her father plans to marry her off for his own gain, but I've claimed her, and I plan to keep her.

She can fight it if she wants, but in her heart she knows she's already mine.

Snake

I left Missoula to serve my country and came back a bitter, broken man. But when Chastity Garrington made my recovery her personal crusade, I decided I had a mission of my own.

Mastering her.

Her task won't be easy, and the fire in her eyes tells me mine won't either. Yet the spark between us is instant, and we both know she'll be wet, sore, and screaming my name soon enough.

But I want more than that.

By the time my body has healed, I plan to have claimed her heart.

Maverick

When I found her trapped in a ravine, I thought Lily Sanborn was just another lost tourist. Then she tried to steal my truck, and I realized she was on the run… and in need of a dose of my belt.

Holed up in my cabin with her bottom burning and a snowstorm raging outside, there's no denying the spark between us, and we both know she'll soon be screaming my name as I take her in the most shameful of ways.

But when her past catches up to her, the men who come after her will learn a hard lesson.

She's mine now, and I protect what's mine.

BOOKS OF THE MONTANA BAD BOYS SERIES

Hawk

He's a big, angry Marine, and I'm going to be sore when he's done with me.

Hawk Travers is not a man to be trifled with. I learned that lesson in the hardest way possible, first with a painful, humiliating public spanking and then much more shamefully in private.

She came looking for trouble. She got a taste of my belt instead.

Bryce Myers pushed me too far and she ended up with her bottom welted. But as satisfying as it is to hear this feisty little reporter scream my name as I put her in her place, I get the feeling she isn't going to stop snooping around no matter how well-used and sore I leave her cute backside.

She's gotten herself in way over her head, but she's mine now, and I protect what's mine.

Scorpion

He didn't ask if I like it rough. It wasn't up to me.

I thought I could get away with pissing off a big, tough Marine. I ended up with my face planted in the sheets, my burning bottom raised high, and my hair held tightly in his fist as he took me long and hard and taught me the kind of shameful lesson only a man like Scorpion could teach.

She was begging for a taste of my belt. She got much more than that.

Getting so tipsy she thought she could be sassy with me in my own bar earned Caroline a spanking, but it was trying to make off with my truck that sealed the deal. She'll feel my belt across her bare backside, then she'll scream my name as she takes every single inch of me.

This naughty girl needs to be put in her place, and I'm going to enjoy every moment of it.

Mustang

I tried to tell him how to run his ranch. Then he took off his belt.

When I heard a rumor about his ranch, I confronted Mustang about it. I thought I could go toe to toe with the big, tough former Marine, but I ended up blushing, sore, and very thoroughly used.

I told her it was going to hurt. I meant it.

Danni Brexton is a hot little number with a sharp tongue and a chip on her shoulder. She's the kind of trouble that needs to be ridden hard and put away wet, but only after a taste of my belt.

It will take more than just a firm hand and a burning bottom to tame this sassy spitfire, but I plan to keep her safe, sound, and screaming my name in bed whether she likes it or not. By the time I'm through with her, there won't be a shadow of a doubt in her mind that she belongs to me.

Nash

When he caught me on his property, he didn't call the police. He just took off his belt.

Nash caught me breaking into his shed while on the run from the mob, and when he demanded answers and obedience I gave him neither. Then he took off his belt and taught me in the most shameful way possible what happens to naughty girls who play games with a big, rough Marine.

She's mine to protect. That doesn't mean I'm going to be gentle with her.

Michelle doesn't just need a place to hide out. She needs a man who will bare her bottom and spank her until she is sore and sobbing whenever she puts herself at risk with reckless defiance, then shove her face into the sheets and make her scream his name with every savage climax.

She'll get all of that from me, and much, much more.

Austin

I offered this brute a ride. I ended up the one being ridden.

The first time I saw Austin, he was hitchhiking. I stopped to give him a lift, but I didn't end up taking this big, rough former Marine wherever he was heading. He was far too busy taking me.

She thought she was in charge. Then I took off my belt.

When Francesca Montgomery pulled up beside me, I didn't know who she was, but I knew what she needed and I gave it to her. Long, hard, and thoroughly, until she was screaming my name as she climaxed over and over with her quivering bare bottom still sporting the marks from my belt.

But someone wants to hurt her, and when someone tries to hurt what's mine, I take it personally.

BOOKS OF THE EAGLE FORCE SERIES

Debt of Honor

Isabella Adams is a brilliant scientist, but her latest discovery has made her a target of Russian assassins. I've been assigned to protect her, and when her reckless behavior puts her in danger she'll learn in the most shameful of ways what it means to be under the command of a Marine.

She can beg and plead as my belt lashes her bare backside, but the only mercy she'll receive is the chance to scream as she climaxes over and over with her well-spanked bottom still burning.

As my past returns to haunt me, it'll take every skill I've mastered to keep her alive.

She may be a national treasure, but she belongs to me now.

Debt of Loyalty

After she was kidnapped in broad daylight, I was hired to bring Willow Cavanaugh home, but as the daughter of a wealthy family she's used to getting what she wants rather than taking orders.

Too bad.

She'll do as she's told or she'll earn herself a stern, shameful reminder of who is in charge, but it will take more than just a well-spanked bare bottom to truly tame this feisty little rich girl.

She'll learn her place over my knee, but it's in my bed that I'll make her mine.

Debt of Sacrifice

When she witnessed a murder, it put Greer McDuff on a brutal cartel's radar... and on mine.

As a former Navy SEAL now serving with the elite Eagle Force, my assignment is to protect her by any means necessary. If that requires a stern reminder of who is in charge with her bottom bare over my knee and then an even more shameful lesson in my bed, then that's what she'll get.

There's just one problem.

The only place I know I can keep her safe is the ranch I left behind and vowed never to return.

BOOKS OF THE DANGEROUS BUSINESS SERIES

Persuasion

Her father stole something from the mob and they hired me to get it back, but that's not the real reason Giliana Worthington is locked naked in a cage with her bottom well-used and sore.

I brought her here so I could take my time punishing her, mastering her, and ravaging her helpless, quivering body over and over again as she screams and moans and begs for more.

I didn't take her as a hostage. I took her because she is mine.

Bad Men

I thought I could run away from the marriage the mafia arranged for me, but I ended up held prisoner in a foreign country by someone far more dangerous than the man I tried to escape.

Then Jack and Diego came for me.

They didn't ask if I wanted to be theirs. They just took me.

I ran, but they caught me, stripped me bare, and punished me in the most shameful way possible.

Now they're going to share me, and they're not going to be gentle about it.

BOOKS OF THE ALPHA DYNASTY SERIES

Unchained Beast

As the firstborn of the Dupree family, I have spent my life building the wealth and power of our mafia empire while keeping our dark secret hidden and my savage hunger at bay. But the beast within me cannot be chained forever, and I must claim a mate before I lose control completely...

That is why Coraline LeBlanc is mine.

When I mount and ravage her, it won't be because I want her. It will be because I need her.

But that doesn't mean I won't enjoy stripping her bare and spanking her until she surrenders, then making her beg and scream with every desperate climax as I take what belongs to me.

The beast will claim her, but I will keep her.

Savage Brute

It wasn't his mafia birthright that made Dax Dupree a monster. Years behind bars and a brutal war with a rival organization made him hard as steel, but the beast he can barely control was always there, and without a mate to mark and claim it would soon take hold of him completely.

I didn't know that when he showed up at my bar after closing and spanked me until I was wet and shamefully ready for him to mount and ravage me, or even when I woke the next morning with my throat sore from screaming and his seed still drying on my thighs. But I know it now.

Because I'm his mate.

Ruthless Monster

When Esme Rawlings looks at me, she sees many things. A ruthless mob boss. A key witness to the latest murder in an ongoing turf war. A guardian angel who saved her from a hitman's bullet.

But when I look at her, I see just one thing.

My mate.

She can investigate me as thoroughly as she feels necessary, prying into every aspect of my family's vast mafia empire, but the only truth she really needs to know about me she will learn tonight with her bare bottom burning and her protests drowned out by her screams of climax.

I take what belongs to me.

Ravenous Predator

Suzette Barker thought she could steal from the most powerful mafia boss in Philadelphia. My belt across her naked backside taught her otherwise, but as tears run down her cheeks and her arousal glistens on her bare thighs, there is something more important she will understand soon.

Kneeling at my feet and demonstrating her remorseful surrender in the most shameful way possible won't bring an end to this, nor will her screams of climax as I take her long and hard. She'll be coming with me and I'll be mounting and savagely rutting her as often as I please.

Not just because she owes me.

Because she's my mate.

Merciless Savage

Christoff Dupree doesn't strike me as the kind of man who woos a woman gently, so when I saw the flowers on my kitchen table I knew it wasn't just a gesture of appreciation for saving his life.

This ruthless mafia boss wasn't seducing me. Those roses mean that I belong to him now.

That I'm his to spank into shameful submission before he mounts me and claims me savagely.

That I'm his mate.

BOOKS OF THE ALPHA BEASTS SERIES

King's Mate

Her scent drew me to her, but something deeper and more powerful told me she was mine. Something that would not be denied. Something that demanded I claim her then and there.

I took her the way a beast takes his mate. Roughly. Savagely. Without mercy or remorse.

She will run, and when she does she will be punished, but it is not me that she fears. Every quivering, desperate climax reminds her that her body knows its master, and that terrifies her.

She knows I am not a gentle king, and she will scream for me as she learns her place.

Beast's Claim

Raven is not one of my kind, but the moment I caught her scent I knew she belonged to me.

She is my mate, and when I claim her it will not be gentle. She can fight me, but her pleas for mercy as she is punished will soon give way to screams of climax as she is mounted and rutted.

By the time I am finished with her, the evidence of her body's surrender will be mingled with my seed as it drips down her bare thighs. But she will be more than just sore and utterly spent.

She will be mine.

Alpha's Mate

I didn't ask Nicolina to be my mate. It was not up to her. An alpha takes what belongs to him.

She will plead for mercy as she is bared and punished for daring to run from me, but her screams as she is claimed and rutted will be those of helpless climax as her body surrenders to its master.

She is mine, and I'm going to make sure she knows it.

MORE STORMY NIGHT BOOKS BY PIPER STONE

Claimed by the Beasts

Though she has done her best to run from it, Scarlet Dumane cannot escape what is in store for her. She has known for years that she is destined to belong not just to one savage beast, but to three, and now the time has come for her to be claimed. Soon her mates will own every inch of her beautiful body, and she will be shared and used as roughly and as often as they please.

Scarlet hid from the disturbing truth about herself, her family, and her town for as long as she could, but now her grandmother's death has finally brought her back home to the bayous of Louisiana and at last she must face her fate, no matter how shameful and terrifying.

She will be a queen, but her mates will be her masters, and defiance will be thoroughly punished. Yet even when she is stripped bare and spanked until she is sobbing, her need for them only grows, and every blush, moan, and quivering climax binds her to them more tightly. But with enemies lurking in the shadows, can she trust her mates to protect her from both man and beast?

Millionaire Daddy

Dominick Asbury is not just a handsome millionaire whose deep voice makes Jenna's tummy flutter whenever they are together, nor is he merely the first man bold enough to strip her bare and spank her hard and thoroughly whenever she has been naughty. He is much more than that.

He is her daddy.

He is the one who punishes her when she's been a bad girl, and he is the one who takes her in his arms afterwards and brings her to one climax after another until she is utterly spent and satisfied.

But something shady is going on behind the scenes at Dominick's company, and when Jenna draws the wrong conclusion from a poorly written article about him and creates an embarrassing public scene, will she end up not only costing them both their jobs but losing her daddy as well?

Conquering Their Mate

For years the Cenzans have cast a menacing eye on Earth, but it still came as a shock to be captured, stripped bare, and claimed as a mate by their leader and his most trusted warriors.

It infuriates me to be punished for the slightest defiance and forced to submit to these alien brutes, but as I'm led naked through the corridors of their ship, my well-punished bare bottom and my helpless arousal both fully on display, I cannot help wondering how long it will be until I'm kneeling at the feet of my mates and begging them take me as shamefully as they please.

Captured and Kept

Since her career was knocked off track in retaliation for her efforts to expose a sinister plot by high-ranking government officials, reporter Danielle Carver has been stuck writing puff pieces in a small town in Oregon. Desperate for a serious story, she sets out to investigate the rumors she's been hearing about mysterious men living in the mountains nearby. But when she secretly follows them back to their remote cabin, the ruggedly handsome beasts don't take kindly to her snooping around, and Dani soon finds herself stripped bare for a painful, humiliating spanking.

Their rough dominance arouses her deeply, and before long she is blushing crimson as they take turns using her beautiful body as thoroughly and shamefully as they please. But when Dani uncovers the true reason for their presence in the area, will more than just her career be at risk?

Taming His Brat

It's been years since Cooper Dawson left her small Texas hometown, but after her stubborn defiance gets her fired from two jobs in a row, she knows something definitely needs to change. What she doesn't expect, however, is for her sharp tongue and arrogant attitude to land her over the knee of a stern, ruggedly sexy cowboy for a painful, embarrassing, and very public spanking.

Rex Sullivan cannot deny being smitten by Cooper, and the fact that she is in desperate need of his belt across her bare backside only makes the war-hardened ex-Marine more determined to tame the beautiful, fiery redhead. It isn't long before she's screaming his name as he shows her just how hard and roughly a cowboy can ride a headstrong filly. But Rex and Cooper both have secrets, and when the demons of their past rear their ugly heads, will their romance be torn apart?

Capturing Their Mate

I thought the Cenzan invaders could never find me here, but I was wrong. Three of the alien brutes came to take me, and before I ever set foot aboard their ship I had already been stripped bare, spanked thoroughly, and claimed more shamefully then I would have ever thought possible.

They have decided that a public example must be made of me, and I will be punished and used in the most humiliating ways imaginable as a warning to anyone who might dare to defy them. But I am no ordinary breeder, and the secrets hidden in my past could change their world… or end it.

Rogue

Tracking down cyborgs is my job, but this time I'm the one being hunted. This rogue machine has spent most of his life locked up, and now that he's on the loose he has plans for me…

He isn't just going to strip me, punish me, and use me. He will take me longer and harder than any human ever could, claiming me so thoroughly that I will be left in no doubt who owns me.

No matter how shamefully I beg and plead, my body will be ravaged again and again with pleasure so intense it terrifies me to even imagine, because that is what he was built to do.

Roughneck

When I took a job on an oil rig to escape my scheming stepfather's efforts to set me up with one of his business cronies, I knew I'd be working with rugged men. What I didn't expect is to find myself bent over a desk, my cheeks soaked with tears and my bare thighs wet for a very different reason, as my well-punished bottom is thoroughly used by a stern, infuriatingly sexy roughneck.

Even though I should have known better than to get sassy with a firm-handed cowboy, let alone a tough-as-nails former Marine, there's no denying that learning the hard way was every bit as hot as it was shameful. But a sore, welted backside is just the start of his plans for me, and no matter how much I blush to admit it, I know I'm going to take everything he gives me and beg for more.

Hunting Their Mate

As far as I'm concerned, the Cenzans will always be the enemy, and there can be no peace while they remain on our planet. I planned to make them pay for invading our world, but I was hunted down and captured by two of their warriors with the help of a battle-hardened former Marine. Now I'm the one who is going to pay, as the three of them punish me, shame me, and share me.

Though the thought of a fellow human taking the side of these alien brutes enrages me, that is far from the worst of it. With every searing stroke of the strap that lands across my bare bottom, with every savage thrust as I am claimed over and over, and with every screaming climax, it is made more clear that it is my own quivering, thoroughly used body which has truly betrayed me.

Primitive

I was sent to this world to help build a new Earth, but I was shocked by what I found here. The men of this planet are not just primitive savages. They are predators, and I am now their prey...

The government lied to all of us. Not all of the creatures who hunted and captured me are aliens. Some of them were human once, specimens transformed in labs into little more than feral beasts.

I fought, but I was thrown over a shoulder and carried off. I ran, but I was caught and punished. Now they are going to claim me, share me, and use me so roughly that when the last screaming climax has been wrung from my naked, helpless body, I wonder if I'll still know my own name.

Harvest

The Centurions conquered Earth long before I was born, but they did not come for our land or our resources. They came for mates, women deemed suitable for breeding. Women like me.

Three of the alien brutes decided to claim me, and when I defied them, they made a public example of me, punishing me so thoroughly and shamefully I might never stop blushing.

But now, as my virgin body is used in every way possible, I'm not sure I want them to stop...

Torched

I work alongside firefighters, so I know how to handle musclebound roughnecks, but Blaise Tompkins is in a league of his own. The night we met, I threw a glass of wine in his face, then ended up shoved against the wall with my panties on the floor and my arousal dripping down my thighs, screaming out climax after shameful climax with my well-punished bottom still burning.

I've got a series of arsons to get to the bottom of, and finding out that the infuriatingly sexy brute who spanked me like a naughty little girl will be helping me with the investigation seemed like the last thing I needed, until somebody hurled a rock through my window in an effort to scare me away from the case. Now having a big, strong man around doesn't seem like such a bad idea…

Fertile

The men who hunt me were always brutes, but now lust makes them barely more than beasts.

When they catch me, I know what comes next.

I will fight, but my need to be bred is just as strong as theirs is to breed. When they strip me, punish me, and use me the way I'm meant to be used, my screams will be the screams of climax.

Hostage

I knew going after one of the most powerful mafia bosses in the world would be dangerous, but I didn't anticipate being dragged from my apartment already sore, sorry, and shamefully used.

My captors don't just plan to teach me a lesson and then let me go. They plan to share me, punish me, and claim me so ruthlessly I'll be screaming my submission into the sheets long before they're through with me. They took me as a hostage, but they'll keep me as theirs.

Defiled

I was born to rule, but for her sake I am banished, forced to wander the Earth among mortals. Her virgin body will pay the price for my protection, and it will be a shameful price indeed.

Stripped, punished, and ravaged over and over, she will scream with every savage climax.

She will be defiled, but before I am done with her she will beg to be mine.

Kept

On the run from corrupt men determined to silence me, I sought refuge in his cabin. I ate his food, drank his whiskey, and slept in his bed. But then the big bad bear came home and I learned the hard way that sometimes Goldilocks ends up with her cute little bottom well-used and sore.

He stripped me, spanked me, and ravaged me in the most shameful way possible, but then this rugged brute did something no one else ever has before. He made it clear he plans to keep me…

Auctioned

Twenty years ago the Malzeons saved us when we were at the brink of self-annihilation, but there was a price for their intervention. They demanded humans as servants… and as pets.

Only criminals were supposed to be offered to the aliens for their use, but when I defied Earth's government, asking questions that no one else would dare to ask, I was sold to them at auction.

I was bought by two of their most powerful commanders, rivals who nonetheless plan to share me. I am their property now, and they intend to tame me, train me, and enjoy me thoroughly.

But I have information they need, a secret guarded so zealously that discovering it cost me my freedom, and if they do not act quickly enough both of our worlds will soon be in grave danger.

Hard Ride

When I snuck into Montana Cobalt's house, I was looking for help learning to ride like him, but what I got was his belt across my bare backside. Then with tears still running down my cheeks and arousal dripping onto my thighs, the big brute taught me a much more shameful lesson.

Montana has agreed to train me, but not just for the rodeo. He's going to break me in and put me through my paces, and then he's going to show me what it means to be ridden rough and dirty.

Carnal

For centuries my kind have hidden our feral nature, our brute strength, and our carnal instincts. But this human female is my mate, and nothing will keep me from claiming and ravaging her.

She is mine to tame and protect, and if my belt doesn't teach her to obey then she'll learn in a much more shameful fashion. Either way, her surrender will be as complete as it is inevitable.

Bounty

After I went undercover to take down a mob boss and ended up betrayed, framed, and on the run, Harper Rollins tried to bring me in. But instead of collecting a bounty, she earned herself a hard spanking and then an even rougher lesson that left her cute bottom sore in a very different way.

She's not one to give up without a fight, but that's fine by me. It just means I'll have plenty more chances to welt her beautiful backside and then make her scream her surrender into the sheets.

Beast

Primitive, irresistible need compelled him to claim me, but it was more than mere instinct that drove this alien beast to punish me for my defiance and then ravage me thoroughly and savagely. Every screaming climax was a brand marking me as his, ensuring I never forget who I belong to.

He's strong enough to take what he wants from me, but that's not why I surrendered so easily as he stripped me bare, pushed me up against the wall, and made me his so roughly and shamefully.

It wasn't fear that forced me to submit. It was need.

Gladiator

Xander didn't just win me in the arena. The alien brute claimed me there too, with my punished bottom still burning and my screams of climax almost drowned out by the roar of the crowd.

Almost…

Victory earned him freedom and the right to take me as his mate, but making me truly his will mean more than just spanking me into shameful surrender and then rutting me like a wild beast. Before he carries me off as his prize, the dark truth that brought me here must be exposed at last.

Big Rig

Alexis Harding is used to telling men exactly what she thinks, but she's never had a roughneck like me as a boss before. On my rig, I make the rules and sassy little girls get stripped bare, bent over my desk, and taught their place, first with my belt and then in a much more shameful way.

She'll be sore and sorry long before I'm done with her, but the arousal glistening on her thighs reveals the truth she would rather keep hidden. She needs it rough, and that's how she'll get it.

Warriors

I knew this was a primitive planet when I landed, but nothing could have prepared me for the rough beasts who inhabit it. The sting of their prince's firm hand on my bare bottom taught me my place in his world, but it was what came after that truly demonstrated his mastery over me.

This alien brute has granted me his protection and his help with my mission, but the price was my total submission to both his shameful demands and those of his second in command as well.

But it isn't the savage way they make use of my quivering body that terrifies me the most. What leaves me trembling is the thought that I may never leave this place… because I won't want to.

Owned

With a ruthless, corrupt billionaire after me, Crockett, Dylan, and Wade are just the men I need. Rough men who know how to keep a woman safe… and how to make her scream their names.

But the Hell's Fury MC doesn't do charity work, and their help will come at a price.

A shameful price…

They aren't just going to bare me, punish me, and then do whatever they want with me.

They're going to make me beg for it.

Seized

Delaney Archer got herself mixed up with someone who crossed us, and now she's going to find out just how roughly and shamefully three bad men like us can make use of her beautiful body.

She can plead for mercy, but it won't stop us from stripping her bare and spanking her until she's sore, sobbing, and soaking wet. Our feisty little captive is going to take everything we give her, and she'll be screaming our names with every savage climax long before we're done with her.

Cruel Masters

I thought I understood the risks of going undercover to report on billionaires flaunting their power, but these men didn't send lawyers after me. They're going to deal with me themselves.

Now I'm naked aboard their private plane, my backside already burning from one of their belts, and these three infuriatingly sexy bastards have only just gotten started teaching me my place.

I'm not just going to be punished, shamed, and shared. I'm going to be mastered.

Hard Men

My father's will left his company to me, but the three roughnecks who ran it for him have other ideas. They're owed a debt and they mean to collect on it, but it's not money these brutes want.

It's me.

In return for protection from my father's enemies, I will be theirs to share. But these are hard men, and they don't just intend to punish my defiance and use me as shamefully as they please.

They plan to master me completely.

Rough Ride

As I hear the leather slide through the loops of his pants, I know what comes next. Jake Travers is going to blister my backside. Then he's going to ride me the way only a rodeo champion can.

Plenty of men who thought they could put me in my place have learned the hard way that I was more than they could handle, and when Jake showed up I was sure he would be no different.

I was wrong.

When I pushed him, he bared and spanked me in front of a bar full of people.

I should have let it go at that, but I couldn't.

That's why he's taking off his belt…

Primal Instinct

Ruger Jameson can buy anything he wants, but that's not the reason I'm his to use as he pleases.

He's a former Army Ranger accustomed to having his orders followed, but that's not why I obey him.

He saved my life after our plane crashed, but I'm not on my knees just to thank him properly.

I'm his because my body knows its master.

I do as I'm told because he blisters my bare backside every time I dare to do otherwise.

I'm at his feet because I belong to him and I plan to show it in the most shameful way possible.

Captor

I was supposed to be safe from the lottery. Set apart for a man who would treat me with dignity.

But as I'm probed and examined in the most intimate, shameful ways imaginable while the hulking alien king who just spanked me looks on approvingly, I know one thing for certain.

This brute didn't end up with me by chance. He wanted me, so he found a way to take me.

He'll savor every blush as I stand bare and on display for him, every plea for mercy as he punishes my defiance, and every quivering climax as he slowly masters my virgin body.

I'll be his before he even claims me.

Rough and Dirty

Wrecking my cheating ex's truck with a bat might have made me feel better... if the one I went after had actually belonged to him, instead of to the burly roughneck currently taking off his belt.

Now I'm bent over in a parking lot with my bottom burning as this ruggedly sexy bastard and his two equally brutish friends take turns reddening my ass, and I can tell they're just getting started.

That thought shouldn't excite me, and I certainly shouldn't be imagining all the shameful things these men might do to me. But what I should or shouldn't be thinking doesn't matter anyway.

They can see the arousal glistening on my thighs, and they know I need it rough and dirty…

His to Take

When Zadok Vakan caught me trying to escape his planet with priceless stolen technology, he didn't have me sent to the mines. He made sure I was stripped bare and sold at auction instead.

Then he bought me for himself.

Even as he punishes me for the slightest hint of defiance and then claims me like a beast, indulging every filthy desire his savage nature can conceive, I swear I'll never surrender.

But it doesn't matter.

I'm already his, and we both know it.

Tyrant

When I accepted a lucrative marketing position at his vineyard, Montgomery Wolfe made the terms of my employment clear right from the start. Follow his rules or face the consequences.

That's why I'm bent over his desk, doing my best to hate him as his belt lashes my bare bottom.

I shouldn't give in to this tyrant. I shouldn't yield to his shameful demands.

Yet I can't resist the passion he sets ablaze with every word, every touch, and every brutally possessive kiss, and I know before long my body will surrender to even his darkest needs…

Filthy Rogue

Losing my job to a woman who slept her way to the top was bad enough, and that was before my car broke down as I drove cross country to start over. Having to be rescued by an infuriatingly sexy biker who promptly bared and spanked me for sassing him was just icing on the cake.

After sharing a passionate night, I might have made a teensy mistake in taking cash from his wallet in order to pay the auto mechanic, but I hadn't thought I'd ever see him again...

Then on the first day at my new job, guess who swaggered in with payback on his mind?

He's living proof that the universe really is out to get me... and he's my new boss.

ABOUT PIPER STONE

Amazon Top 150 Internationally Best-Selling Author, Kindle Unlimited All Star Piper Stone writes in several genres. From her worlds of dark mafia, cowboys, and marines to contemporary reverse harem, shifter romance, and science fiction, she attempts to delight readers with a foray into darkness, sensuality, suspense, and always a romantic HEA. When she's not writing, you can find her sipping merlot while she enjoys spending time with her three Golden Retrievers (Indiana Jones, Magnum PI, and Remington Steele) and a husband who relishes creating fabulous food.

Dangerous is Delicious.

* * *

You can find her at:

Website: https://piperstonebooks.com/

Newsletter: https://piperstonebooks.com/newsletter/

Facebook: https://www.facebook.com/authorpiperstone/

Twitter: http://twitter.com/piperstone01

Instagram: http://www.instagram.com/authorpiperstone/

Amazon: http://amazon.com/author/piperstone

BookBub: http://bookbub.com/authors/piper-stone

TikTok: https://www.tiktok.com/@piperstoneauthor

Email: piperstonecreations@gmail.com

Printed in Great Britain
by Amazon